ICA CITY

Chris Beckett is a former university lecturer and social worker living in Cambridge. He is the winner of the Edge Hill Short Fiction Award, 2009, for *The Turing Test*, the prestigious Arthur C. Clarke Award, 2013, for *Dark Eden* and was shortlisted for the British Science Fiction Association Novel of the Year Award, for *Mother of Eden* in 2015 and for *Daughter of Eden* in 2016.

Also by Chris Beckett

AMERICA CITY

Chris Beckett

First published in Great Britain in 2017 by Corvus, an imprint of Atlantic Books Ltd. This edition published in 2018 by Corvus.

The quotation from Seamus Heaney's translation of *Beowulf* is included by kind permission of the estate of Seamus Heaney, and Faber & Faber Ltd.

10 9 8 7 6 5 4 3 2 1

A CIP catalogue record for this book is available from the British Library.

Paperback ISBN: 978 1 78649 154 1

E-book ISBN: 978 1 78649 153 4

Printed and bound by CPI Group (UK) Ltd, Croydon, CR0 4YY

Corvus
An imprint of Atlantic Books Ltd
Ormond House
26–27 Boswell Street
London
WC1N 3JZ

www.corvus-books.co.uk

There was Shield Sheafson, scourge of many tribes,
A wrecker of mead-benches, rampaging among foes.
This terror of the hall-troops had come far.
A foundling to start with, he would flourish later on
As his powers waxed and his worth was proved.
In the end each clan on the outlying coasts
Beyond the whale-road had to yield to him
And begin to pay tribute. That was one good king.

Beowulf, translated by Seamus Heaney

For my dear son Dom

PART 1

CHAPTER 1

Two hundred miles south of the Azores, warm moist air is rising rapidly. It forms a kind of gigantic cylinder, a hollow tree trunk made of moving air. The tree has roots that are also air: warm, humid air rushing over the balmy waves toward that central trunk. The air cools as it rises. Eleven miles up, it spills over sideways like spreading branches. In the roots below, air still flows inwards over warm sea.

The planet, meanwhile, is spinning beneath its loose skin of air. At that latitude it spins faster than a jet plane flies, and it wraps those inward-flowing winds around one another to form a counter-clockwise spiral of warm wet air. It's huge, that spiral, twice the size of Texas, but it's simply air made turbulent by heat, as water in a pan is made turbulent by the hot plate beneath it.

According to the United States Weather Bureau this spinning patch of turbulence is one of the largest ever recorded. It's going to strike shore somewhere on the coast of Delaware, which is toward the northern end, at this particular point in history, of what has become known as the Storm Coast. The government gives out instructions on the news hubs and through the whisperstream: Superstorm Simon is a seriously big storm. It will disrupt the whole of Delaware and parts of New Jersey and Maryland as well. You should board up windows and secure your house (more guidance here). You should stay home! You should not, repeat *not*, try to leave your home, unless you happen to live in one of the nineteen low-lying coastal communities within the affected area designated as being at VERY HIGH risk of flooding (full list here), in which case you will be personally contacted by federal agencies who will arrange your evacuation in good time before the storm surge comes over the levees. Otherwise, dear citizens of Delaware and neighboring states, do the safest thing and *stay home*.

Four hundred thousand people choose to ignore this. Everyone knows that when a superstorm strikes, people die. What the government is asking of them is that they draw a ticket in a lottery and hope that their number doesn't come up. Those four hundred thousand don't feel like taking that chance. They pile trucks and cars with refrigerators, broadscreens, dogs, settees, babies, washing machines, and head inland, thus causing the total gridlock that will be the single largest cause of death. For it means that, when the hurricane strikes, four hundred thousand people who could have been inside houses with walls and roofs reinforced with steel cages anchored in concrete (as per federal regulations under the Hurricane Defenses Act), are sitting in fragile metal boxes on a gridlocked highway, unable to move anywhere at all.

And here he comes now. Here's Simon. Here's the superstorm. He's sweeping in. He's reached the land. He's come ashore, spinning like a giant circular saw at 170 miles an hour. He doesn't care where the people are. He doesn't care if they're babies or 105 years old. He doesn't care about the government guidance. SMASH, he hits the coastal towns. CRASH, he throws down trees. SPLASH, he flings the ocean over the flood defenses and tosses boats onto the land. And when he reaches those gridlocked cars, he sucks out their windscreens, he throws them down embankments, he opens them like tin cans to the screaming air, snatching settees, teddy bears, reading lamps from overloaded roof racks and flinging them out over the fields, and into the floodwaters, and onto the snapped-off branches of broken trees.

Those who have followed the government's advice are lying inside houses with boarded-up windows, hoping that someone else's ticket will come up. Many have built shelters inside their houses made of doors and tables and sandbags, as instructed by government videos. Hiding like children in these playhouses, they hear huge loutish lumps of air striding about outside in hollow streets that once were theirs. They hear those giant louts banging and roaring, flinging stuff around, shoving at roofs and walls. Even steel cages, they know, have sometimes been known to snap.

They can't see what's happening, of course, but who in America hasn't watched these scenes many times over? Houses straining and bulging until they burst, cars doing cartwheels end to end, truck cabins crushed by fallen trees. Some people's houses will blow down, they know. And some people's bodies, now completely whole, will be crushed, or impaled, or filled up with water, or cut wide open by flying glass.

One woman somehow gets dropped onto the weathervane on a church. All of America sees her body hanging there with her butt turning purple and her dress over her face. She's like Superstorm Simon's flag.

CHAPTER 2

olly and Richard had spent a lazy evening in their spacious home, twenty miles out of Seattle. Their painter friend Ruby, who they'd known since New York, had messaged earlier to tell them that finally, after several years' wait and many frustrating hours dealing with bureaucracy, she and her partner Ossia had been awarded the much-prized 'red pass' from the Canadian immigration authorities. They could live and work there as permanent residents now, rather than having to renew visas every year, and were on a path that led, more or less automatically, to full citizenship. This was quite an achievement in those days, after Canada had introduced its super-strict 'population cap'. Holly and Richard had decided to celebrate their friends' success. They'd ordered in some food and opened a bottle of bubbly Canadian wine. Now, they called Ruby and Ossia to give their congratulations.

'We still can't get our heads round it,' said Ruby. 'And would you believe, we've found a house too? An amazing house with a beautiful studio. You must come and see it!'

And then there were just the two of them again, Holly and Richard on their new cream-colored sofa, with Holly's legs draped over Richard's, his hand resting on her knee.

'Lucky them,' Richard said, 'a new country, a new home, a new chapter of their lives ahead of them.'

'Well, what should *we* do,' Holly asked, 'to start a new chapter ourselves?'

They discussed whether they should move to Canada too – those green vineyards, that civilized political system – but somehow, it didn't appeal to either of them. Then Richard asked Holly if there was even a little part of her that wanted to return to England, but she dismissed that idea with an incredulous laugh. Of course not! Her parents still lived there, which was not a plus, and Fortress Britain these days was a nasty, desperate place.

Not so much a fortress, really, Richard observed, but more a sinking ship, a sinking pirate ship, in a sea full of the victims of pirates, many of them still stubbornly swimming toward it, in spite of the musket fire from the decks. And America was a pirate ship too, of course, but at least for a moment it was pretty much afloat.

They talked about having kids. They asked themselves, as they'd done before, whether it was even fair bringing a child into a world like this. And as before, they concluded that their parents could have asked themselves the same question, but they were kind of glad they existed in spite of everything. Just two kids at most, they agreed: there were more than enough human beings on the planet. Rick would be the main carer; Holly earnt more than he did, and anyway, he had *much* more patience. They'd have a boy called Saul and a girl called Penny. Just naming them seemed to have brought them close to existence, as if they were people already, who just happened to be very far away.

They opened another bottle of wine and kissed lingeringly. They were *definitely* going to make a start that night on the whole making-kids routine. Or a symbolic start anyway: Holly would have to see the doctor to have her IUD taken out, and they'd need to make a decision on the timing of that, which was probably a job for when they weren't both half-drunk. They kissed again. Warm summer air wafted in through the window from the gentle night outside. Should they take the wine upstairs right now? But they decided they'd catch the news first. This was still the aftermath of Superstorm Simon and it seemed disrespectful not to keep up to date with what was going on over there.

Drones and drigs were peering down from the sky all over Delaware. 'America's worst storm…People were prepared for storms but not for this…A continuous line of vehicles across four states… Scenes we've gotten used to seeing in the south, but now right up to New Jersey.'

Some of the drigs descended to earth and reporters climbed out to speak to the cops and to the storm people on the gridlocked highways, and to various kind folk who were helping out in heart-warming ways, inviting the storm people in, or walking across fields with sandwiches and flasks of coffee. A woman in Wisconsin had offered her entire house. A town in Pennsylvania had raised half a million dollars. Three men and a woman from upstate New York had hired four trucks, loaded them with tents and sleeping bags, and were heading south.

But not everyone was feeling so kind. The drigs came down outside a town that had been cut off from the rest of America by that glacier of cars and trucks. Four men and two women stood by a barricade. 'Everyone cries about these storm people,' said one of the women, cradling a rifle in her arms. 'But what about us? We can't go to work, we can't go to the stores, we can't even get our kids into school.' Behind them was a hand-painted sign. 'Keep out,' it read. 'No shelter or food here. Stick to the highway.'

Holly rested her hand on Richard's leg, and stroked the inside of his thigh. Richard gently caressed her hand with his. All of this was bad, they knew, but for them it was just a particularly severe instance of something that had happened at least once every year, somewhere on the Storm Coast, all of their adult lives.

'Horrible people,' Holly said.

'Yeah, but I heard a couple of women talking just like that up at the store earlier today. One of them said something about "those poor folk down there" and I thought at first she was talking about the storm people, but it turned out that what she meant was the ones on the barricades. The other said the storm people had only got themselves to blame. They'd chosen to stay there in the storm country so what did they expect? And now they were causing problems for everyone. I asked them what *they*'d do, if they'd invested everything in their home and it became completely unsaleable.'

Holly grimaced. 'And?'

'They just glared at me.'

'Yeah, and after you'd gone I bet they told each other you were a typical well-to-do delicado, living with your nice things in your nice expensive house, and telling everyone else off for not being more generous-spirited.'

On the broadscreen the governors of Alaska, Idaho and Montana were giving a joint statement. There were only so many storm people their states could take in. They were already struggling to cope with the migrants from the Dust Country in the southwest that had been streaming in all through the summer. The governors were looking at the possibility of their states putting border controls in place to suspend inward migration from the rest of the

USA. Some said this would be unconstitutional, but they disagreed, and were willing to defend their position in court.

There was brief footage of a demonstration in Billings, Montana. 'Enough is enough', 'Montana is full', 'YOUR lack of planning is not MY problem'...

But then a US senator came on, Senator Slaymaker, familiar to both of them because he represented Richard and Holly's own state of Washington, though neither of them had voted for him. 'They are fellow Americans,' he said. He was a big, handsome man, who'd been something of a war hero and had then set up a hauling business which had become one of the biggest in the country. He'd flown to Delaware himself to see what was going on. Slaymaker fixed the camera with his very bright and penetrating eyes. 'We need to remember that. These people are our fellow Americans.'

In the warm darkness outside, branches sighed and rustled, were silent for a while, then sighed again. Richard stroked Holly's knee. Troubling as the news might be, they were still intending to go upstairs directly after this item, and give themselves over to the pleasures of skin and breath and touch.

'I know it's hard for folk in the northern states,' said Senator Slaymaker, 'seeing all these people coming in from the south, but we need to fix things so they can settle down properly, and earn a living for themselves and their families, and don't have to keep having their lives trashed by these storms. It's the same with the people from the Dust Country. No point any more in helping them rebuild where they are,' he said. 'The federal government needs to build more homes up north. And I mean proper homes, not these government camps.'

'Weird,' said Richard. 'He's spent his whole political life battling against big government. And yet now he's calling for a level of government intervention which no Unity Party government would even dare to suggest! I mean, what *is* his game?'

Holly frowned. Her eyes were still on the broadscreen, but the news had already moved, via trouble in the disputed territories between Russia and China, to a massacre that had happened earlier in the day in the Spanish enclave of Ceuta in North Africa. Thousands of refugees outside the border fence, it seemed, had taken it into their heads to simply force their way through, though Holly barely registered this news.

'Why do we always assume that people who don't agree with us have some sort of dishonorable motive?' she said. 'How do we know *we're* not the ones playing a game?'

'Because he's not being consistent with what he's said before. Remember his comment about the famine in Mexico?' Richard imitated the senator's soft, firm, Seattle accent: '"Mexicans have got to look after themselves. We didn't *ask* them to live in Mexico. We didn't ask them to have more kids than they knew how ta feed." Staggeringly callous!'

Then they told the screen to shut down and were alone in their living room again. They began to put things away for the night, ready for bed.

'Maybe Senator Slaymaker's selective in his sympathies,' Holly said as she carried their glasses to the dishwasher. 'We all *are* really, aren't we? The way we delicados talk, you'd think we took personal responsibility for all the problems of the world. But we don't really *act* that way, do we? I mean, what did you and I actually *do* about the famine in Mexico, apart from clucking our tongues at dinner parties and maybe shelling out fifty dollars to some appeal?'

Richard laughed. 'That, I'm afraid, is a fair point.'

'Slaymaker's a self-made man. He had a hard start in life.

A teenage mum on a trailer park, wasn't it? With a drink problem, I think. Or maybe drugs. He had to look after himself from the beginning, so naturally self-reliance is what he believes in. I guess these storm people have touched some chord in him.'

And right at that moment, Holly's cristal bleeped.

It was her boss Janet. She worked at that time for a Seattle-based public relations consultancy. She helped businesses with damage limitation when they got themselves into trouble, and she helped them manage public opposition when they wanted to do something controversial. The main account she was working on right then was a local hydro company which was seeking to build new dams in spots that were inevitably someone's favorite bit of wilderness.

'Sorry to call so late, Holly.' Janet's voice was shaky. 'I've got a bit of a crisis going on here. Jack's had to go into hospital. Nothing too terrible, I don't think, but I'd kind of like to be there for him. I was wondering if you could help me out by covering something for me tomorrow. I was going to meet a potential client for lunch, a rather important potential client. Could you take my place?'

Holly said 'yes, of course, absolutely, no trouble at all...' et cetera, and, while she went over in her mind the diary commitments she'd have to reschedule, she asked about Janet's husband and how he was getting on (it was heart trouble) and then about the client.

'Well, it's *very* confidential at this stage, Holly, but if we play our cards right, it could become one of our most important accounts.'

'Wow! Exciting! But you know me, Janet, I'd always—'

'I know, Holly. But this is kind of extra delicate, that's all. You see, the client is Senator Slaymaker. He wants to talk over some aspects of his current project. I don't know if you know he's launching a campaign for a big resettlement program in the northern states.'

'Rick and I were just talking about it.'

'I did a little bit of work for him once, back when he was heading up the Haulers Federation. We were going to meet at Le Lac for lunch tomorrow, and, seeing as he's already flown up from DC, I said I'd see if you could meet him instead. I told him you were way smarter than me.'

'Wow!' said Richard as Holly hung up. 'Working for Slaymaker? He's a big figure these days. Some people are saying he'll run for president. But—'

'Well, it's not a presidential campaign we're going to help with, I assure you. It's just this campaign of his for more federal help for the storm refugees.'

'Well, good luck with that. As far as I can see, fewer and fewer people are willing to pay out tax dollars to help out for—'

He broke off because he could see Holly wasn't listening any more.

'Listen, Rick, I'm so, so sorry, but I'm meeting him tomorrow, and that means I'm going to have to set aside the rest of this nice evening and put in a couple of hours of preparation.'

Richard walked over to the window to close it for the night. 'Sure. Of course. Shall I make you some coffee? To clear your head a bit?'

She kissed him. She was already mentally compiling a list of topics that she needed to research. 'That would be great. But don't wait up for me after that. I'm not sure how long I'll be.'

CHAPTER 3

Richard stared up at the ceiling in the light of his reading lamp.

He'd grown used to Holly acting for clients he didn't approve of. How she explained it was that she was like an attorney in a court of law: her job was to represent people whether she agreed with them or not. And he kind of got that. He was also a little in awe of her for being out there in the world of affairs, and not just the world of ideas that he inhabited. In fact, he loved that about her. Picturing her in her study now, for instance, he smiled to himself. She'd already be *deep* into this new job, those alert, bright eyes darting about as she muttered instructions to her jeenee, had it conjure up data for her onto the multiple screens that she like to array around herself.

And when it was just some hydro company or something, well, there wasn't that much of a downside. Big hydro fought pretty rough, it was true, and upset some of Holly and Richard's friends, but what was the alternative, Richard had always privately thought? America needed power from somewhere to keep the lights on, and the cars on the roads.

Slaymaker, though...

The trees outside began to move again, building up to a level of agitation that was almost a gale, and then falling silent once more.

Slaymaker of all people, that ferocious American nationalist, that bloodstained warrior from America's wars in the African Copper Belt, that self-made man who thought that just because he'd been able to claw his way up from nothing, then everyone else could too. As if being exceptionally smart had nothing to do with it, and exceptionally driven, and exceptionally ruthless.

Again the wind built up, all the trees sighing and hissing together as their branches bent and strained, creaked and groaned, like this time something was going to happen, like this time they were going to really see it through.

But no, the pulse passed, and the night fell still.

There was a side of Holly, he knew, that was drawn to people like Slaymaker: these big, tough, vivid people whose imaginations expressed themselves not in ideas but in tons of concrete, in gigawatts of power. She liked them and she got on very well with them. This was mysterious to him. He knew he'd feel uncomfortable with such people. He knew he'd feel simultaneously disapproving and inadequate. But she was completely at ease with them. It was one of the things that made it impossible for him to resolve Holly into something he could fully understand.

Yes, he dreamily thought, but that was a good thing. He needed her to be different, otherwise the two of them would just be – he pictured this rather than thought it in words, for words were slipping away from him: he was in the factory where words are made – otherwise the two of them would just be a single blob of sameness and they would be alone all over again, looking for something else to reach out to, something else to desire, out there in the world beyond...

The air slithered round the world outside, like soft, loose layers of silky skin, sliding over one another, and under, brushing the cooling surface of the shadowy world.

When Holly finally came into the bedroom, Richard was deeply asleep. She'd worked for three hours by then, searching for information, organizing it, memorizing it: facts about Slaymaker's life and his place in American politics, information about America's internal refugee problem, data about public attitudes. At her company's expense, she'd even conducted a couple of small instant polls, throwing out questions into the Pollcloud – there were always people awake from every demographic who were willing to answer a few questions – and having AI statisticians analyze the answers.

She laid her cristal on her bedstand and turned out the light. Even now, she hadn't finished working. She spoke soundlessly to the jeenee inside her cristal and asked it to give her a taste of what people were saying out there on the whisperstream, right now, about the storm people. So, as she settled herself down, she was hearing conversation after conversation through the tiny implant that she wore in her right ear. It was like opening a chink into a huge dark room, buried beneath America, full of voices – some showing off, some complaining, some trying to be original, some loudly proclaiming their orthodoxy. All were telling stories about themselves and the world, their own particular stance in relation to the world, the way they and the world connected together.

The torrent of voices continued until the jeenee could tell from her brain rhythms that its mistress was asleep. And then, like a gentle grown-up pulling up the bedcovers and tiptoeing from the room, it slid the volume very slowly down until there was no sound left but Richard's breathing and the wind outside.

CHAPTER 4

Rosine Dubois

I guess we were lucky none of us were hurt. We'd done what the government asked, just stayed there under the table in our kitchen, watching the walls bulging and bending around us, and suddenly, SMASH, a car came through our roof, right through the metal cage and everything. It must have been blown off the flyover, though God knows what that kid was doing, driving a car in a hurricane. But whatever the reason, there he was, or there was his body anyway, his broken body, dangling through the windscreen upside down, right there in our kitchen, with the wind screaming and howling over the hole he'd made.

'Okay,' Herb said, when the storm had finally passed over us. 'You take the boys round to Charlene's and I'll try and figure out how to get that poor kid out of the car.'

Debris lay strewn all around us: pieces of tin roof, torn-off branches, the striped awning from some store. Below us in the lower town, folk were huddled up on the ridges of their roofs, while big choppy waves rolled through the streets.

'The walls are still standing anyway,' Herb said, 'and most of our stuff is okay as well. Tricky part is going to be getting the car out of there without doing more damage, but we'll figure out something.'

But I told him no. This was it. I was done with the Storm Coast. I'd lived here all my life – my ma and pa too – but I was done with it.

'We should've got out of here years ago, when the house was still worth something,' I told him.

We both knew I'd suggested this way back, and that Herb had firmly said no.

'Okay, Rosine,' he said, 'if you want me to say you were right I'll admit it now. You *were* right, and I'm sorry. But it's kind of late for moving now. No one will give us a penny for this place, so how are we going to get somewhere else to live? And how are we going to feed the kids? There's going to be thousands of people heading away from the coast after this, hundreds of thousands most likely, and they'll all be looking for jobs and homes, along with all those Californians and desert people. At least we've both got work here, and the land and the house.'

'We're not staying, Herb. You got to think ahead. Things aren't going to stay the same, are they? That's not how it works these days. If we don't leave now, we'll be wishing we did in two years' time, the same as we wish now we'd left two years ago.'

Neighbors were outside as well by now, under the darkening sky, looking round at the damage.

People started to come over to ask if we wanted beds for the night. Our friend Charlene took our boys in, fed them ice cream, and let them play with a couple of new broadscreen-games that she'd put aside for her own kids for Christmas, and then me and Herb, Charlene and two or three others levered open the door of the upside-down car, wrapped a sheet round that dead kid, and pulled him out, laying him down at the back of the yard where we wouldn't have to keep looking at him. He was awful broken-up.

Charlene's husband Luther fetched some rags to wipe up the blood that had dripped out onto the kitchen floor, and after that, we went and inspected our truck. It was okay. The storm-proof door on our garage had held out, and the main battery and the spare had both been fully charged up before Simon brought down the power lines. We lifted the spare battery into the flatbed, and then loaded up everything else we could fit in that was of any value: the broadscreen, the washing machine, the best bed.

'Sure you want to leave right now?' Charlene asked. 'Hubs say the traffic's backed up twenty miles out of town north, south and west.'

'Sooner we get into the line, the sooner we'll reach the end of it,' I said.

'Where you going to go?' Luther asked.

'North and west, I guess,' Herb said. 'Out of the storm country as fast as we can.'

'We may not be far behind you,' Charlene said. 'Make sure you tell us where you all end up, you hear?'

She glanced over at the dead body lying against the yard fence.

Beyond, over the lower town, a couple of police drigs were moving slowly over the rooftops – not picking anyone up, as far as I could see, though folks were waving and yelling for them to come down, just sweeping search lights back and forth. Looking for looters, I guess. Looking for someone they could shoot.

CHAPTER 5

The Le Lac restaurant was at the top of a slender tree-like tower on the shore of Lake Washington. Holly's company often used the place. The food was stylish, the view was spectacular, the tables sufficiently separated from one another that you could talk without being overheard, and the kind of people who could afford to eat there weren't overly interested by the presence of a national celebrity such as Stephen N. Slaymaker.

The senator arrived about ten minutes after her: that thick gray hair, those blue, penetrating eyes, those austere cheekbones, which (as she'd found out in her researches) he liked to say he'd inherited from his Cherokee great-grandmother. Often famous people from the TV seemed smaller than she'd expected them to be when she met them in real life, but he was, if anything, bigger: a very tall, very fit man in his mid-fifties, wearing an expensive but not particularly fashionable blue suit and a pale blue shirt open at the collar to show the strong lean sinews of his neck.

'Senator Slaymaker! I'm Holly!'

'Hey!' he said as he shook her hand. 'Nice to hear someone speaking English for a change.'

He was being nice. He meant British English. In spite of great efforts on her part, Holly had never managed to shake off the accent.

'Or the obscure European offshoot thereof, at any rate,' she said as they sat down at the table that Janet's jeenee had reserved for them. 'My husband tells me that back in Shakespeare's time the English all spoke like Americans.'

It was the best she could manage in that benign, yet very penetrating gaze.

'Is that a fact?'

Slaymaker had never seen a Shakespeare play, was Holly's guess. He just wasn't the kind to invest his time in something that was made-up, or from the far-off past. But he was visibly pleased all the same by what Holly had told him. He was always pleased to hear things that placed America at the centre of things.

'Okay, Holly. Can I call you that? Well, to get straight down to it, I guess you know about my campaign?'

'Certainly. You're calling for large-scale, federally funded resettlement for folk from threatened areas on the east coast and in the southwest.'

'Correct. Resettlement in the northwestern states, including Alaska. Did you know that Juneau, Alaska, is now the second fastest-growing city in the union after Seattle, and Anchorage the third?'

'The whole country's moving northwest.'

'It is. It has been for some time. But so far, that's just the result of folks individually making those tough calls to cut their losses down on the Storm Coast, or the Dust Country, and moving north to start again. Which is great, and it's what America's all about. But it's happening too slowly and leaving too many people behind.'

'I think it's good of you to try to help those people. A lot of folk don't want to know.'

'Well, thank you. But this isn't just about helping those folks. It's about America itself. We're not distributed properly any more. Folk aren't in the places where they can be productive.'

'When they could be really prospering somewhere else?'

'Exactly. And they're soaking up tax money. I'll show you the figures. I've had people look this stuff up for me. The Storm Coast is a drain on our country's resources. So is the Dust Country. So are all those towns on coasts and rivers where they have to keep building the levees higher all the time. Basically, the government needs to shift most of the US population inland and to the north. And then get off people's backs again and let them get on.'

'Most of the US population? That's an incredibly ambitious plan, Senator.'

'We've done it before. Go back a few hundred years and there was no America at all. Just Indian tribes and a lot of empty space.'

'I guess so.'

'It's doable. I don't care what anybody says. But to make it happen I need to sell the idea to the American people. Your Janet has done some solid work for me in the past so I thought I'd ask her for some advice. Then her guy went into hospital and of course she had to prioritize. She spoke very highly of you.'

'I'll try to live up to it.'

'I'm sure you will, Holly.' Again, that very intense and focused gaze. 'I have every confidence in you already.'

A waiter arrived and they gave their orders. Slaymaker wanted a steak. Holly chose a fancy concoction of lobster meat and clams. Neither of them went for wine.

'Tell me something about your general approach to these kinds of problems, Holly.'

'Well, we usually work with a kind of triage model. We look at the audience we're addressing and we divide it into three. There are the core supporters who are already on board, there are the firm opponents who won't come on board no matter what, and there are the floaters who are open to persuasion. It's the floaters you need to focus on of course but, in doing so, it's really important not to alienate your core supporters by making them feel taken for granted.'

Slaymaker nodded, and was about to say something, but Holly held up her hand.

'Sorry, but I was just going to add that your present campaign is a kind of unusual case which totally messes up that whole model because you're cutting *right* across the normal pattern of allegiances. The demographic groups that your party normally relies on are precisely the ones that are *most* resistant to large-scale federal welfare projects and the most worried about migration from other states into their communities. You're going completely against the instincts of your own people.'

She laid her cristal on the table so he could see the graphics she'd put together in the early hours of that morning.

'The demographic groups that are the *most* enthusiastic about large federal spending projects are unskilled service workers, government employees, first- and second-generation immigrants, and the professions we tend of think of as typically delicado: university people, writers, artists, scientists, computer architects, and so on. And they are precisely the sectors that are *least* likely to vote for you or your party and most likely to vote Unity Party. And even Unity voters aren't that keen on federal spending if it means paying more taxes.'

She touched the cristal to bring up another graphic. 'Never mind party. Northerners of all parties aren't keen on tax dollars going to southerners. I haven't done all the polls yet, but I'm willing to bet they'd be even *less* keen on the idea of paying for the privilege of having millions of barreduras descend on them.'

'Barreduras. I don't like that word. It means dirt, you know? The dirt you sweep up off the floor.'

'I'm afraid that's how a lot of people see the folk from the Storm Coast and the Dust Country, especially people who vote for your party.'

'I know. But I'm not talking about an election here, remember. Not at the moment. I'm talking about building up support for a program. And I'm not talking about a welfare project either. I hate handouts. I hate making people into victims. This is about reconfiguring America, you know? Making America stronger in the face of a threat. If we don't do something, the whole country's going to break up.'

'*Reconfigure.* I like that. It's a strong, businesslike word. So that's the story you were thinking of, is it? Reconfiguring America to keep it together?'

'Never mind the story, Holly,' Slaymaker growled. 'That's how I really *see* it.'

She laughed. 'Yes, I know. But you've got to understand that *my* job isn't about how things actually are, or even about how they ought to be, it's simply about how they would best be presented. I'm a storyteller, basically. I assume that's what I'm here for.'

He smiled. 'Whatever your clients want to say, you make it into a pretty story? Regardless of your own opinion?'

Holly could see that he wouldn't have minded a little digression in which he could tease her a bit about the ethical vacuity of her job but she decided to stick to the matter in hand.

'That's right,' she said matter-of-factly. 'And it seems to me that to maximize your support across the country we're going to need to present your message so that it will work in two quite different ways. Firstly, in that patriotic way you've just demonstrated, in order to try to win over as many as possible of your usual Freedom Party-type supporters, but secondly in a way that's going to appeal to a reasonably large tranche of Unity Party and minor party voters who wouldn't normally see you as someone they relate to. And at the same time as walking that tightrope, we're going to have to deliver your message in a way that works for northerners and southerners. That's a lot of different constituencies, and a lot of nuances to work on and refine and marry up with one another to make sure they don't clash or cancel each other out.'

She dropped her cristal back into her jacket pocket. 'People talk about using the whisperstream to deliver customized messages to each different affinity group, but actually that's something you've got to be very careful about, because affinity groups aren't airtight. One way or another, people get to hear what you're saying to other folk as well as what you're saying to them, and then you end up looking two-faced. One workaround for that, of course, is to make use of feeders. It's very expensive but it can—'

She stopped because the meal had arrived, exquisitely presented on white pentagonal plates. While they ate, Holly talked a bit more about the value bases and psychological drivers of the various groups he'd need to try to get on his side.

'So,' he said, 'to sum up. The people who like me don't agree with me on this, and the people who are most likely to agree with me are the folks who don't like me. Yup. That's my problem in a nutshell. And of course that's why I'm hiring you.'

Holly suddenly realized that she'd spent rather a lot of time telling the senator things that must already have been obvious to him.

This was a man of the world, after all. Before she was even born, he had commanded a battalion in the Copper Wars and built the Slaymaker Corporation up from a single truck to a continent-wide business. She felt a fool. She was on the point of making herself look more foolish by apologizing, but managed just in time to snatch back her customary professional cool.

'Sure,' was all she said. 'If it was easy, you wouldn't need our help. I'm not saying it can't be done. I'm just setting out the challenges we'd have to overcome. By the way, one of the things we need to look at is areas of vulnerability.'

'For instance?'

'Areas that may lay us open to charges of inconsistency or hypocrisy.'

Slaymaker speared a piece of steak, put it into his mouth.

'I reckon I've always been pretty straight.'

'Well, up to now you've been a strong opponent of big government.'

'Still am. If you want to build up this country, get government off people's backs and let them get on with it. But there are exceptions. When the nation's in danger, like in a war, or...'

'Like in a war. Okay. Good. It's a war-type scenario. Because there's a threat to the country itself. We could do with a more tangible enemy, though, than just the changing weather. Who are our opponents? Who are we fighting *against*? The current government, obviously, but it's not like the government is opposed to helping the barreduras. In fact, they're spending an awful lot of money on helping them. *Too* much, according to your own party in Congress.'

'There's no vision there,' said Slaymaker, 'that's the problem. We should be looking at this weather problem as an opportunity. Like, you know, "Go west, young man!" But old Jenny Williams there looks at it more like, "Oh, those poor poor folks down south!" I do *not* want to treat those folks like victims, Holly. More than that, I don't want them to *feel* like victims. And I do *not* want them to feel that they have to *act* like victims in order to get what they need. Nothing worse than going through life like that. And nothing worse for the country. I want them to think of themselves as pioneers.'

Go west! Pioneers. Holly made a note. There was something to work with here, though the language was *way* too old-fashioned.

Slaymaker lay down his fork. 'You're right about my own party. Worst thing is that we've got this group of assholes in the Freedom Party these days – Governor Hendricks in Alaska, for instance – who are raising this question of interstate frontiers. I mean, I'm all in favor of states' rights, but once you put up border posts between states, you've basically given up on the USA.' He laid his napkin next to his fork. 'This campaign is *all* about keeping America together, Holly. Like Lincoln did.'

Note those last sentences, Holly silently told her cristal. It was positive stuff, but it didn't yet differentiate Slaymaker's position sharply enough from that of the president, Jenny Williams, who was also strongly opposed to interstate frontiers. And as to Lincoln, well, without conducting a poll you could never be sure, but she was willing to bet that three out of four Americans wouldn't be able to say who he was.

'Another possible area of vulnerability,' she said, 'is the issue of what caused the weather problems in the first place. Pretty much every scientist on the planet agrees that floods and droughts and so on are the result of human activity, but of course you've got a track record of denying this, particularly back in your days at the Haulers Federation. The president, on the other hand, can honestly claim to have been campaigning about it since her college days. She might well argue that all this sudden concern about hurricanes and droughts is a bit rich coming from you.'

Slaymaker laughed. 'You're damn right. That's exactly what the president *will* argue.' He took a drink of water, laid down his glass and looked straight at her. 'What do you think about this weather business yourself, Holly? What do you *personally* think? Do *you* think it was caused by people?'

Holly had read about the controversy Slaymaker had stirred up during his last-ditch campaign against the shift from hybrids to all-electric trucks. But the whole issue seemed pretty straightforward to her. 'Yes, I'm sure it *was* caused by people,' she told him, then laughed. 'Maybe not the answer you wanted, Senator, but I think we'd have been better off if we'd stopped burning that stuff about thirty years earlier than we actually did.'

Slaymaker smiled. 'What I wanted, Holly, was for you to tell me what you thought. But my feeling is this. We don't make thunder. We don't make the tides. We don't make the day and the night. The Lord does. And if He wants the Earth a little warmer and the weather a little livelier, well then, we've just got to deal with that fact. I guess that seems pretty old-fashioned to you.'

It certainly did – it seemed positively medieval, in fact – but all the same there was something about Slaymaker's position that struck Holly as rather attractive in a way she wouldn't have anticipated. It was so different to the perpetually agonized attitude she'd grown up surrounded by, the attitude of her parents and their friends, with their constant fretting about suffering in faraway places and threats in the future, their disapproval of just about anything that seemed to her like fun. It was so different too from all her friends who clucked their tongues at America's selfish isolationism in a world whose problems it had played such a large part in causing. She liked how the senator had found a place to park all of that and get on with what life threw at him here and now. It connected with the impulse that had brought her to America in the first place. This was a country where people *did* things, that was how she'd seen it. They did things for better or for worse, and, if it didn't work out, they tried something else.

'Not that I'm some kind of religious nut or anything,' Slaymaker added. 'But the way I see it, we may as well leave it to God to look after the things that are just too big for little creatures like us.'

The waiter came for their plates, a young Latino man. Behind him, as he stood at the table, the lake, the mountains, the vault of the sky, with streaks of grayish cloud moving east in a brisk, high-altitude wind.

'Now that was a *steak*,' the senator told the waiter. 'I could have done without the fancy bits and pieces, but that was a steak.'

'Thank you, Senator, I'll pass that on to the chef. Senator, I...' The waiter hesitated. 'I hope you don't mind me telling you, sir, that me and my family are big fans of what you're doing for the people from the droughts and fires in California.'

Slaymaker beamed at him, and reached out and took his hand.

'Why, thank you! Thank you very much. What's your name, my friend?'

'It's Luis, sir, Luis Vargas. We've always voted for the Latino Party in our family till now, but, like my pa says, the Partido's gotten completely obsessed lately with the problems below the border. He says you're the only one who's really taken hold of the problems we have right here in the US, all of us, Anglos and Latinos alike.' The waiter blushed. 'I'm sorry, sir. I shouldn't interrupt your meal.'

The senator was still firmly grasping the waiter's hand, and fixing him with that extraordinarily focused gaze. So much so, in fact, that for a moment, absurdly, Holly felt excluded and a little jealous.

'Not at all, Luis, not at all. As it so happens, myself and Ms Peacock here – don't you just love her British accent? – we were just discussing how we're going to win the support of people who don't normally vote for my party, and I think she'll find what you've just said most helpful.'

Finally, he released the waiter's hand.

'But now if you could bring me a couple of scoops of chocolate ice cream and a cup of strong coffee, that would be just great,' he said. 'And whatever Miss Peacock wants, of course. After all, it's her that's paying for this meal!'

'Just a coffee for me,' Holly said. She'd pulled up a map of North America on her cristal and was looking at the cities that Slaymaker had earlier identified as the growth points of his new America – Seattle, Juneau, Anchorage – stretched out in a long chain along the continent's north-western edge. And she was noticing the slightly untidy fact that, in between Seattle and the other two cities, were several hundred miles of coastline that belonged to another country. This wasn't news to her, of course, but it occurred to her that she had no idea how it had come about. She'd have to ask Rick sometime.

'Well,' she said as Luis Vargas headed back to the kitchen, 'there's a lot here to work on in terms of pulling together a message that will clearly distinguish you both from the government and from the interstate frontiers people in your own party. I'll push some ideas out into the Pollcloud and see what comes back. If you like, we could also commission some more in-depth surveys. It's really a matter of how much you want from us. There's also a question of how much you want to involve us in actually *delivering* your message. We're pretty experienced at running feeder campaigns, for instance, and, like I said before, they can be very useful in a case like this where you're targeting several very different audiences.'

'Those damn AIs. Can't stand the things: feeders, jeenees, the whole damn lot of them. Should have been strangled at birth.'

'Well, the fact is that, expensive as they are, they are very effective, and they end up way cheaper than the human alternatives if you measure by results.'

'Yeah, I know, I know.' Slaymaker smiled. 'I'll tell you what, when you get back to your office, write down what you *want* to do and how much it would cost, and send it to me. I'm pretty certain I'm going to go along with whatever you suggest.'

Luis came back with the ice cream and coffee.

'I like you, Holly,' Slaymaker went on, picking up his spoon but pausing to twinkle across at her. 'I like you a lot. And I can see you're *very* smart. If you're willing, I'd very much like to carry on working with you on this job, even when Janet's back in action, and I want you to know that I'd be very pleased if you'd come and work for me full time, when you and Janet are ready.' He pointed his spoon at her. 'Think it over. Don't decide now. But I could really do with someone like you right at the heart of the project, to help me think these things through.'

He took a mouthful of ice cream, watching her as he savored and swallowed it.

'Oh and don't be afraid to *talk* to people. I know it's quicker doing polls, I know it's cheaper, but there's no substitute for actually talking with folk. Budget some time for it. I'll pay.'

Holly's car drove her home on the expressway. All around her was a forest of dead and dying trees, rotting from the inside out and the outside in at the same time, weakened by weather conditions that they had not evolved for, attacked by the insects and fungi that had come north with the warmer and wetter air. But this was just the world, as far as she was concerned. What was new was that she was twenty-eight years old, and she'd just been offered a top job by one of America's most well-known and popular politicians.

'Hey, jeenee,' she said, 'give me a sample of what people are saying right now about Slaymaker. No affinity filters, just a random sample.'

At once a chain of disembodied voices began to speak to her, while the lichen-choked trees passed by.

'Word is that Slaymaker's going for the presidency next time round.'

'No way will he win, though. No way. That guy's a traitor to the north.'

'Yeah, exactly. Fuck the storm people. *Fuck* them. If they're dumb enough to still live in those places, how is that our problem?'

'Ha ha. Very true. Beggar came up to me the other day with the usual fucking sob story about his farm in Nevada, and all the dirt drying up and blowing away. I fucking laughed in his face.'

Holly held out for about thirty seconds, then told the jeenee to flip to another thread.

'Slaymaker? I love that guy,' someone else was saying. 'Gray Jenny talks the talk, but *he* comes right down to the Storm Coast and tries to figure out what would help.'

'*President* Slaymaker, do you reckon?'

'I'd vote for him, no problem, and I've never voted Freedom Party. Who else is really thinking about people like—'

Holly flipped again.

'He's an amateur, really. He's got this sentimental idea about keeping the country together, but he's basically just a trucker who struck it lucky.'

'*Si, si*. And he seems nice, but he'd turn nasty soon enough when things turned out not to be as easy to fix as he thought.'

The car's battery was running low and it shifted itself over into the dodgem lane to top itself up. A shower of blue and white sparks burst harmlessly round her like a little firework display as her slightly worn connectors settled into place against the overhead lines.

Pale wisps of cirrus were moving across the upper sky. There wasn't much wind at ground level, but up there the air was moving fast.

CHAPTER 6

Rosine Dubois

I don't know how many times me and Herb had to get out and drag branches and stuff out of our way, or how many times we went down a road and found it blocked with debris or flooded up and had to go back and find another way. All around us the wind was tossing around leaves and bits of paper, sometimes whistling softly, sometimes making things rattle. It was like some huge animal that was resting up after eating its fill. And we were its prey, tiptoeing past it while it slept.

We took all night just getting out as far as the interstate. And then we sat on that road all the next day, sometimes not moving an inch for two hours at a time. It was awful. It was a real hot sticky day, and we were surrounded by scared people and screaming kids in cars with their trunks bulging open and tied up with string. Some of the people were hungry and thirsty too, and a few had lost members of their families. There was one woman, maybe ten cars back, who kept up a constant sobbing and wailing and howling, on and on. And for five hours or so we were next to the wrecks of four cars that Simon had flung off the highway when he came ashore. Someone had cut open one of them and got the people out, but it didn't look like anyone had done anything with the others, which were so badly crushed that there couldn't possibly have been anyone left alive inside them.

The police were there, and the National Guard too, going up and down the line just above us in military drigs, and sometimes coming down beside the highway. We thought at first they were there to help, but if we asked them questions like 'How long is this line?' or 'What's being done to help us folks who've lost their homes?' – natural enough questions, you'd have thought, for folk in our position to ask of a public official – they'd act like it was too much trouble to answer, like it was kind of rude and disrespectful of us even to ask. They asked *us* plenty of questions, though. Where were we going? What ID did we have? How come we were leaving the city? Did we own this truck and what had we got in back? It was like we were criminals. It was like having your house mashed up by a car was some kind of criminal offense.

'It's like we're not Americans any more,' was how Herb put it. 'It's like we're Mexicans or Haitians or something.'

But that was Superstorm Simon. We came from his country now. We *weren't* Americans, we were just storm people. We were outsiders trying to get in.

The only time that whole day that anyone made us feel like we might be welcomed anywhere was when Senator Slaymaker came down. He was walking down the line of cars and trucks, talking to the people. He shook hands with me and Herb – we were sitting on a barrier by the roadside, swapping stories with some of the other folk – and he asked how we were doing and what our plans were. And then he walked over to our truck, and leant in to say hi to Carl and Copeland. You felt like he'd really seen you, you know? You felt like he'd really listened.

But then he was gone and it was back to waiting, and listening to that woman wail. Apparently she lost a kid to the storm.

CHAPTER 7

'I guess you can't be picking and choosing all the time, Holly,' said Holly and Richard's journalist friend Mariana, 'but I mean *Senator Slaymaker*! Are you really sure you feel comfortable working for a guy like that?'

Holly was seated next to Richard on one of the long sides of an oval table of pale polished wood. Opposite her sat her artist friend Ruby, and Ossia, the ballet dancer who was Ruby's partner: the two of them on a trip south from Canada. At each end of the table were their hosts, Sergio and Mariana. The room around them was smooth, clean, pale, softly lit. They'd all just finished eating. The picture wall was unfolding a complex and semi-abstract work by a fashionable video artist.

'I feel totally comfortable,' Holly said, laying her napkin down as she looked straight at Mariana with bright, fierce, dangerously friendly eyes. She was not going to flinch. She was not going to allow anyone to imagine, even for one second, that she was not completely at ease with her own conscience. '*Totally* comfortable. I mean, we were talking earlier on about Governor Hendricks' proposal to close off the Alaska border to the storm people. Well, Slaymaker's taking a stand against that.'

'So is the president, Holly,' Sergio pointed out. He was an

electronics engineer who specialized in the arrays of synthetic neurons that housed the new generation of AIs. 'The president all of us here voted for. So why doesn't Slaymaker support her, instead of undermining her every times he gets the chance?'

Holly turned her brilliant gaze to him. 'He doesn't agree with her approach. He thinks it's short-sighted. That it isn't a—'

'It's a real shame,' interrupted Ossia the dancer, 'that Slaymaker has never shown the same concern about truly desperate people from *outside* of America as he suddenly seems to feel about the storm people.'

'Yeah,' said Mariana. 'And after all, it's the people outside of America who need the help most. I mean, I know it's really terrible for our storm people, but at least there's some kind of safety net for them. At least they aren't going to starve.'

'What was that awful thing Slaymaker said about the famine in Mexico?' asked Ruby.

Holly's eyes darted from one to the other of them. She hadn't known Ossia for very long, but the others were old friends. Big, loose-limbed Ruby in particular she thought of as someone she really loved. She'd known her since her New York days and considered her the first real friend she'd made in America. But right now, for reasons that she didn't entirely understand, Holly felt a sour contempt for them all.

'Believe me, it's not just Slaymaker who hasn't got much time for people outside our borders,' she said. 'It's America. *America* isn't in the mood for helping foreigners. America thinks it's got enough problems of its own. And right now, even—'

'I'm sorry, Holly, but how do *you* know what "America" is in the mood for?' demanded Ossia.

I really don't like you, Ossia, Holly thought. She'd never really understood why warm, relaxed Ruby was drawn to these bottled-up types. The elegance and gracefulness of Ossia's movements, which everyone said were so lovely to watch, had always struck her as showy and artificial, as if a poet were never to stoop to ordinary conversation, but insisted on speaking continually in flawless verse.

'I know what America's in the mood for, Ossia, because I've been doing large-scale nationwide cloud polls on this for the whole of last week, along with focus groups and interviews, at Slaymaker's expense. The overwhelming feeling in this country is that we have enough problems of our own without helping anyone outside, or letting anyone else in. And, like we were discussing earlier, it's not just foreigners now that people don't want to help. It's the barreduras, too. Our own people. What Slaymaker sees is that, if we're not careful, America will end up breaking into pieces, like India did, and Europe, and China, and Russia.'

Ossia shrugged. 'Well, I don't think we've got any right to give up on the rest of the world. Have you seen what's been happening in North Africa lately? Or Bangladesh? Or Nicaragua?'

Richard had been poised to mediate between Holly and their friends. 'We already *have* given up on the rest of the world, Ossia, I think that's Holly's point. We've been isolationists going right back to the Tyranny. The only reason America is still a relatively prosperous country is that we keep our population fairly stable, and have enough land and resources to be able to produce most of what we need within our own borders—'

'Barring the minerals we get from our warlord clients in exchange for arms,' muttered Sergio.

'But we should fight that parochialism,' said Ossia. 'I don't consider myself a citizen of America. I'm a—'

'Well, you *aren't* really a citizen of America, honey,' her partner reminded her, laughing. 'Or you won't be much longer, anyway. You're well on the way to being a citizen of Canada.'

Ossia pursed her lips. What *did* Ruby see in her? Holly wondered. 'I'm not a citizen of *any* country, that's my point. I'm a citizen of Earth.'

'I'm not saying you're wrong, Holly,' began Mariana. She was someone Holly normally *did* like, but tonight she was being irritatingly prissy. 'But if it was me, I'm not sure I could bring myself to work for a man like—'

'What do you actually mean, Ossia,' Holly interrupted, ignoring Mariana, and turning back to the dancer, 'when you say you're a citizen of Earth?'

'I mean that borders are just meaningless lines and have nothing to do with our responsibilities as human beings.'

'None more meaningless than the Forty-ninth Parallel,' Ruby chuckled, referring to the border that the two of them had crossed earlier that day, and rather obviously trying to move the conversation on to something more cheerful and less intense. 'The good old Medicine Line. Literally a straight line drawn across a map.'

'Okay,' said Holly, still addressing Ossia, 'well, we haven't visited your new place yet, but I know you and Ruby have bought a large and lovely house, which you'll fill with lots of lovely expensive things, just like Sergio and Mariana, and just like me and—'

'What in hell has that got to do with it?'

'I mean that, in practice, we all do look after ourselves first: ourselves and those we know and care about.'

Ruby looked troubled. 'We're not perfect, it's true. We fall short of what we'd ideally like to—'

'But maybe that's the wrong way to look at it, Ruby. That's the difference between someone like Slaymaker and delicado types like us. We all look after ourselves first, him and us both, but he's comfortable with that, he sees that as entirely natural and the way things should be, while we feel guilty about it. Not guilty enough to do anything much about it, mind you, but guilty enough to take the position that we think things should be different, and to find fault with those who disagree.'

'I don't feel guilty,' Sergio said, 'I don't feel guilty in the slightest.'

'You're speaking for other people again,' Ossia said. 'How do you know what I feel guilty about?'

But Holly's focus had shifted to Ruby. 'I love you the way you are, Ruby. I don't want you to feel badly about your good fortune. That's the problem with people like us. We value empathy, we value sensitivity of any kind, and we're afraid to own our toughness, our setting of limits, our willingness to go so far but no further. We *are* tough, we *do* set limits, we *do* look after ourselves, just like everyone else does, but for us it's a dirty secret we don't talk about. For someone like Slaymaker it's as natural as breathing. He has limits to what he's prepared to take responsibility for, and most of them extend no further than the borders.'

'But that makes no sense, ethically!' Mariana protested. 'If you think like that—'

'Listen,' said Holly, and suddenly she was really riled, 'empathy's important, yeah, but so are limits to empathy.' She could sense Richard watching her anxiously, but that just made her angry with him as well. 'Otherwise no one in the world would ever, ever be happy. Believe me. I grew up in a home where I was expected to empathize deeply with every human being and every living creature on the whole fucking planet. And I tell you, I used to think, Fuck the planet, fuck the people dying in the Copper Wars, fuck the dead whales, how about a little empathy right *here*? How about a little warmth and happiness for *us* before we die ourselves?'

They were all watching her with concerned faces. *Oh God, how embarrassing.* She'd become upset, she'd allowed one of her demons to get its hands on the controls, and everyone could see it. Richard was squeezing her hand under the table.

She laughed. 'Yeah, okay, I'm sorry. My personal history peeking out there. Enough of me. Let's talk about something else.'

'I do get what you're saying, though, Holly,' Ruby said. 'You've got me thinking, actually. The reason we moved to Canada is there's more space, less poverty and nicer politics. But the reason it's so is that it has fewer weather problems and a *way* smaller population. And I guess that's a lot to do with the fact that Canada's frontier is every bit as strict as America's. Ossia and I might complain about those strict borders – we've signed petitions, we even went on a demonstration once about letting more people in – but...'

Holly leant across the table, pulling her hand away from Richard so she could reach out to Ruby instead. 'I'm *not* trying to give you things to feel guilty about, Ruby,' she said. 'Just the opposite. What I'm saying is, enjoy it! Don't beat yourself up about it. We're not going to fix everything. We're not even going to try. We may as well enjoy what we have.'

Two hours later, Holly and Richard emerged under a starry sky, to walk the two miles home across the prosperous commuter village of Schofield. Soft streetlight, not much brighter than moonlight. Lamps still glowing here and there behind closed curtains. Two tiny figures walking between little toy houses with miles of atmosphere above them. The air around them soft, mild, scented.

'I made a bit of a fool of myself over Slaymaker there,' Holly said, slipping her arm through Richard's. 'Hope I didn't embarrass you too much.'

'I wouldn't say you made a fool of yourself. Mariana *was* fairly accusatory. I reckon you had a right to defend yourself.'

'Thanks.'

'And it's true what you said about us as a class. The US and Canada are kind of an island of privilege and wealth in this world but you're quite right, within that island, the delicado class is an island of privilege itself. It *is* a bit rich us lecturing other Americans about global justice, or claiming to care more than they do about the wider world.'

Holly nodded but didn't answer. They walked for a while in silence through the balmy air. Hard to believe that this same mild, invisible stuff had driven thousands of people out of their homes a matter of days ago.

'I guess what Americans are starting to wake up to,' Richard said, 'is our relative good fortune beginning to unravel. We've got all this space, all these resources. But slowly, slowly we're becoming more like the rest of the world. And yeah, I completely get your point. Whatever we might say, whatever some abstract notion of social justice might dictate, the issue isn't really whether America opens its gates voluntarily to the entire world, because that's not going to happen, period, any more than you and I are suddenly going to invite a bunch of poor folk off the street to share our nice home. The issue is whether America hangs together or falls apart.'

They passed a racoon under a lamp-post on the opposite side of the street, gnawing at a bone it had retrieved from someone's trash, and stopped for a moment to watch it until it sloped off.

'You okay now?' Richard asked as they continued. 'About your mom and dad? The old wound was aching a bit there, I could see.'

'I'm fine.'

It's NOT a wound, she privately thought. *I am NOT wounded. It's just something from the past that makes me cross.* But Richard was trying to be supportive and she didn't feel like arguing.

'Not all delicados are like your ma and pa, you know, Holly.'

'I know.'

A little two-person car swished by, its occupants cuddled up together with their backs to the street in front of them, leaning close in to each other, gazing intently into each other's faces as the car's AI took them home.

'I'll tell you what, though,' Holly said suddenly. 'Never mind his politics, I would have loved to have someone like Slaymaker for a dad.'

Richard laughed. 'More fun than your real dad for sure. Come to think of it, I don't recall ever hearing anything about Slaymaker's kids.'

'He hasn't got any.'

'Ah well, that explains it.'

Richard glanced down at her. 'I love you, Holly. You do know that, don't you? There's no doubt in my mind that in all the world, you're the one I care most about.'

Holly squeezed his arm, pressed herself against him. She knew he was doing his best, the best that anyone could do, to fill up the hunger inside her and it wasn't his fault that she still felt hungry.

CHAPTER 8

Johnson Fleet

I lived in Idaho back then with my wife Karla and our daughter Jade, but we were both from Brooklyn originally. We moved over to the northwest when Jade was two because we didn't like the way things were going, with the crime and the floods and everything, and all those new people coming in from all over. New York wasn't a good place to raise a family any more.

We lost a lot of money on that decision. Property prices were falling through the floor, and what we got for our house was $370,000 less than the mortgage still left to pay. Negative equity: *not* good. I sold my garage business for less than I'd have liked as well, and I mean a whole *lot* less. But we took the hit and we moved. We'd put in a lot of work finding a new garage up in the northwest, and a house up there we could afford. Ended up in this little town called Dickensville in the Rockies. It was a smaller business than the one in Brooklyn, and a much smaller house, but we just about managed, figuring that if we both worked hard, and Karla established herself again as a hairdresser like she'd done in Brooklyn, we could maybe upgrade to something bigger later. And the crime rate was way lower up there, and the air cleaner, and there were no hurricanes or droughts to worry about.

And here's the thing. We didn't ask the federal government for *anything*, and we didn't *expect* anything from the federal government. Government isn't there to hold people's hands and wipe their asses, that's how we saw it.

So we moved, and we worked hard and we saved, and we built ourselves another life. We made new friends, we got to know our neighbors, we found a decent school for Jade, we built up our two businesses.

About the time we finally started to feel settled was when you started hearing a lot more on the hubs about these storm people down south losing their homes to hurricanes. And pretty much the same time, you started to hear about dusties down in states like California and Arizona: farmers who'd had to leave their farms because of drought, people in towns with no more water...all of that.

These things weren't new, though. They'd been happening for years. They'd been happening since before Karla and me were born. But for some reason, about that time, they became big news all of a sudden. Yeah, I know the problem was getting worse, but my point is it didn't exactly come out of the blue. Yet you wouldn't know that from watching the broadscreen. 'We've got to help these poor guys,' was what we kept hearing. 'They're desperate. They don't know what to do.'

And of course old Gray Jenny Williams was always very generous with other people's money. Now she was spending billions on those people, helping them rebuild houses, providing insurance that no sane insurance business would normally have been willing to sell, and setting up these trailer parks for people who claimed not to have anywhere to go. There was one just near our town, up in Idaho.

Well, you kind of expected that from Gray Jenny. She's Unity Party, which basically meant the party for losers. But then Senator Slaymaker started off, too. Karla and I had always voted for the Freedom Party, and we both liked Slaymaker a lot, but now he'd got the bug too. In fact, he was talking about spending ten times more than Gray Jenny, building whole new towns and cities in the north and the northwest, and making towns like ours into cities, just so all those people from the east coast and down in the south-west could move up here whenever they wanted.

I couldn't think what or who had gotten into him. A guy I followed on the whisperstream – Cynical Sam – said that Senator Slaymaker was getting a whole lot of money from the construction industry for his election fund. 'Just a coincidence, I guess!' he said innocently. Old Cynical Sam could be pretty funny, but he talked sense, as far as I was concerned.

Anyway, Karla and me had no time for any of that: not for Gray Jenny's program, and certainly not for Slaymaker's. If we could move up here without asking for government money, why in hell should we work ourselves to the bone to help other people do the exact same thing as we did? I mean, we lost a whole lot of money on our move, and now we were being asked to lose even more money on theirs. Where was the justice in that? It wasn't like they didn't get fair warning down there. These problems had been building up for more than two whole generations! How much warning did you need?

Anyway, like I say, one of those government camps was right outside our town, and you could see the impact on our property values from the day it was first planned, and that was before we had barreduras hanging out all over town. Cynical Sam got hold of the figures: *real* figures, I mean, not the massaged government ones. Half of those people had never paid tax in their lives, he said, and you could see that was true just by looking at them. They were the sort of people that just sit there and expect the government to provide for them.

Yeah, and a lot of them were Mexicans too, or Cubans or Dominicans or whatever, Latinos of one sort or another. I met some of them that could barely speak English. These people came over the border, they got US citizenship handed to them on a golden platter, they got federal welfare money and those goddam Spanish schools so they never even had to bother to learn our national language, and now they got help with moving too, when they didn't like the prices at their local water company! Cynical Sam said that at times he wondered if we might do better just to hand the border states over to Mexico and build a new wall further north. He was kidding, I guess, but it actually made a lot of sense. It wasn't really America down there any more. Crap's sake, those Mexicans had even gotten themselves their own separate party in Congress.

And now they expected me and Karla to pay for houses and towns to be built for them, with the government paying half the rent for pretty much ever. *Really?* We didn't think so.

It wasn't like we didn't have weather problems of our own up in Idaho. Our town sat on the banks of a river at the bottom of a steep valley, with three or four streams running down into it on either side. One of those streams came down right next to my garage, as a matter of fact. (When I had a quiet moment with no motor or power tools running, I could hear the little waterfalls. It was kind of nice, I guess.) But things were shifting up in the mountains – ice melting, more rain and less snow – and sometimes a huge pile of dirt got pushed away and the water came rushing down the river in a great muddy torrent. So we had to pay a lot of extra money in our taxes for flood defenses, which had never been needed before: storm drains, levees, and all of that. And we paid willingly, of course we did. No one likes taxes, but you do *need* taxes for some things, and that's one of them. But here's the thing, they were *local* taxes. We didn't expect a handout from the federal government, and we didn't get one either. So we didn't see why we should pay with our federal taxes for other people's defenses, or to help them out when they hadn't bothered to protect themselves.

That's the way I saw it, and Karla was just the same. And I doubt you could have found anyone in the whole damn town that would have said anything different. It was just common sense.

CHAPTER 9

On the morning after the dinner party, Richard woke up in an empty bed. Holly had already been out for a three-mile run, and was hard at work in her office. When he went up to say good morning, her cristal was laid in front of her, her various screens ranged round her, bright with charts and text, and her jeenee, that tireless servant, was girdling and regirdling the earth on her behalf, as it unearthed nuggets of data, solved logistical problems and enlisted the services of other equally non-corporeal beings.

Holly and Richard lived at a time of famine, poverty, war and disease, an epoch when historic nations were falling apart in bloody civil wars, million-year-old forests were dying, and vast and ancient ocean reefs, full of life and color within the memory of their own grandparents, had turned to crumbling white skeletons of stone. Yet oddly it was also a time of unprecedented technological power. No one talked about the Turing Test. The jeenee inside Holly's cristal was quite capable of talking for hours without revealing that it wasn't human.

'So what are you working on?' he asked.

'The usual thing. Trying to get a feel for how people think, and trying to find chinks in their armor, you know? Places where they are open to influence.'

She leant forward as Richard left her, and murmured a new question to her jeenee. She could get an answer to any question within minutes from several thousands out of the tens of millions who were signed up to the Pollcloud. And, in those few minutes, the AIs that ran the Cloud would have processed the raw responses, broken them down not only by age, ethnic affiliation, income, level of education, gender and geographical location, but also by personality type, interests, musical tastes. They would also have taken account of heart rate, brainwave activity and facial expression, all routinely gathered by the jeenees that came with even the cheapest cristals, to provide a measure of the mood of participants when asked the question, and the degree to which it engaged them. And in the few seconds they took to weigh all of this, they would also have factored in each Pollcloud member's previous responses so that those whose preferences had been shown by subsequent events, such as elections or sales figures, to be currently typical of any one particular demographic category would receive more weight than those whose responses had been proving less predictive.

Holly experimented by preceding questions with human stories: 'Susan is a mother of two with her own one-woman design business, working from home in a small town in southeast California. Her husband is an AI center supervisor. They live in an average-sized house which, like most people, they bought with a mortgage. They both work hard and things were going well for them until a few years ago when the price of water started going up. Now, what with massive water bills and failing businesses – the town is shrinking and half the homes in their street are empty – they aren't making enough to keep afloat, but they can't sell the house either. The price hasn't just gone down. It's literally worth nothing at all. And yet they still have $900,000 of that mortgage to pay off.'

The AIs made their calculations. Sympathy for the barreduras did increase among those who had read the story, but it was a short-term response. Even just separating the scenario and the question by twenty minutes was enough to wipe out the effect.

She tried preceding questions with short lectures on the shared interest of every American in a thriving economy: 'Every farmer who goes bankrupt is someone who could have been contributing value to our economy for the last ten years, but in fact has been contributing next to nothing. All of America is poorer if these farmers aren't helped to start again.'

The AIs found that a small increase in support followed, an increase that was less closely associated with short-term emotional response, and somewhat more durable than the effect that had followed the personal stories, but it was still small, and still very easily canceled out.

Holly drummed her fingers on her desk for a moment, then sent her jeenee out again into its invisible universe of ones and zeros.

According to the Pollcloud's calculations, she learnt, as many as 19 percent of Americans thought there was 'some truth' in the belief of the Tribulationist Church that droughts and storms were sent to punish wicked communities, while nearly 63 percent generally agreed with the statement, 'I wouldn't expect the government to help me, so why should I help others?'

Richard brought in a cup of coffee, kissing the top of Holly's head and looking bemusedly at the animated graphs and diagrams on her screens.

'People insist that the barreduras are to blame for their own problems,' said Holly, 'that's what we're up against. It's weird, that, isn't it? It really doesn't take much imagination to see that they aren't.'

'I guess it doesn't take much imagination to see that an abattoir is a horrible place, but—'

'But we choose *not* to imagine it, so we can eat the meat on our plate. That's it, I guess.'

As he left her again, she had her jeenee engage the services of so-called silvertongue AIs, which specialized in lateral thinking, metaphor and the rhetorical use of language, to see if she could improve on the messages she was testing on the Pollcloud.

An hour later, frustrated by her lack of progress, she set that task aside and asked her jeenee to begin compiling a list of individuals she could interview herself from all the various key demographics.

Slaymaker didn't wait for Holly's conclusions, though. That very day, he went right ahead and made a speech to a conference of freight executives in Washington, DC, in which he mocked the president's program of building hugely costly carbon dioxide extractors.

'Are we going to blow even more federal money on the president's billion-dollar Christmas trees that achieve nothing and fall down in a puff of wind, or on those so-called storm-proofed roofs that turn out not to be storm-proof after all? Or are we going to spend it on doing what America has always done before, moving our population round this great continent to make the best of new opportunities?'

The businessmen clapped politely. Outside the conference

center, fierce gales were lashing the capital with summer hail, and making the trees in the parks rock and sway like crazed dancers. Even in the calm interior of the storm-proofed building, they could hear it out there, that huge invisible mass flinging itself against the triple-glazed windows and the concrete walls. Slaymaker tried to play this to his advantage.

'Listen to that sound, Mrs President! I guess you can hear it from the White House too? It's a wake-up call from nature. It is nature telling America that the time's come to get out those old bullock wagons again, and start 'em rolling!'

Again the assembled businessmen clapped, but, watching the video link, Holly wasn't so pleased. All her instincts told her that this wasn't going to work.

Sure enough, President Williams was on all the main news channels before nightfall with a stinging comeback:

'Senator Slaymaker might want us to run away from the weather, but I happen to think it's better to stand our ground and face what we're dealing with. After all, as the senator himself points out, the bad weather is moving north. So what's he going to do when it catches up with those bullock wagons of his? What's he going to do when we reach the Forty-ninth Parallel and there's no more north to go to?'

Holly had to admire whatever combination of human speechwriters and silvertongues had worked with Jenny Williams on that one. It was a nice touch to turn Slaymaker into the one who was running away, and the president into the warrior standing her ground.

'As to my so-called Christmas trees, yes, I admit it, they look kind of weird. And yes, I admit it, they won't solve this problem for us on their own. There's a long way to go. But those Christmas trees took nearly a billion tons of CO_2 out of the atmosphere last year. Remember CO_2? Remember the stuff that everyone has known for the last century and a half is trapping in the heat? And remember how Senator Slaymaker has spent his life denying that $CO2$ has got anything to do with it? Because that's another thing that Senator Slaymaker likes to run away from, isn't it? He likes to run away from the truth!'

Her delivery as ever was rather flat. She came over a bit too like a high-school teacher – Principal Williams, she was often called in the whisperstream – but on this occasion her authentic anger came through very well, and all the polls showed that, in this particular dogfight, she'd come out on top.

Holly called Slaymaker that evening.

'You should have talked to me first, Senator. You can't afford to just wing it. You've got to think about how she might come back at you.'

She was surprised by her own boldness in speaking to him like that. But the senator responded with playful yet seemingly genuine remorse.

'Yeah, you're right, Holly. What's the point of hiring you to help me with these things, and then me just shooting my mouth off? Listen, I'm kind of stuck here in DC for a while. Any chance you could get down here so we can go over all this together and figure out where we go from here?'

CHAPTER 10

She set off late that night. Although the car could have brought itself home, Richard went with her to the airport. She was kind of touched that he insisted on this, and yet secretly she would have preferred the time in the car alone to begin to gather her thoughts. In fact, when he kissed her goodbye, she almost forgot to kiss him back, so keen was she to settle herself inside the drig and get to work with her jeenee on the data and ideas that were buzzing and fizzing inside her head.

As it turned out, it would have been better to take the train. The wind was bad. The drig's departure was delayed for several hours and then it had to divert to Philadelphia. She took a hire car from there, and finally arrived early the following evening, nearly twenty hours after leaving her home in Schofield. Slaymaker met her in his office in the senate building on Constitution Avenue. He had an assistant order in food, and then they settled into the large leather armchairs he favored for informal conversations. The wind was still blowing hard outside, periodically flinging hail against the warm, triple-glazed window.

'No major demographic group in the northern states is keen on welcoming any more southerners,' Holly told him, 'whether from the east or the west. They're not keen on it period, and Anglo northerners are *especially* resistant to taking Latinos.'

'That's the result of our leaky border. Most people figure the more Latinos you help settle, the more will sneak over from Mexico and South America.'

Holly wasn't sure about that. What he was calling a leaky border consisted of a twenty-foot-high wall from coast to coast, a twenty-foot-high fence running parallel to it topped with razorwire, and a minefield in the no man's land between the two. Pretty much every president in the last century had garnered votes by making that barrier even more fearsome.

'You weren't completely wrong to target the president's Christmas trees, because there's a lot of skepticism about addressing our problems by doing something about the composition of the air. Most people know that carbon dioxide caused this weather problem but the majority are pretty fatalistic when it comes to trying to reverse it. Which actually is consistent with expert opinion. An awful lot of the science these days suggests we missed the boat and it may be too late to put the genie back in the bottle.'

She pulled a graph up onto her cristal. 'But here's the thing. People may not be much interested in the president's efforts to reverse what's happened to the atmosphere, but if you present northerners with a straight question: would they prefer money to go (a) on Christmas trees or (b) on building new neighborhoods and towns near them so that barreduras can move into their states, suddenly they become keener on Christmas trees. You've really got a *long* way to go there, Senator. And the distance is even further today than it was yesterday, now you've given the president a chance to come back at you. She really hit the spot when she made this an issue about standing firm or running away. You could see her approval rate jumping up right there on the real-time polls, and it still hasn't come back down. She's made those Christmas trees seem suddenly sexier, and you helped her to do it.'

Slaymaker nodded. 'She's done well this time, I'll give the old schoolmarm that. She was on form.' He sipped at a glass of water. Holly had never seen him touch alcohol of any kind. 'By the way, Holly, feel free to call me Steve.'

'Uh...okay – Steve – I will.'

Holly wasn't sure she liked the idea of calling him that. You don't necessarily want your favorite uncle asking you to stop calling him Uncle Jim, or your dad telling you to call him Eric.

'You've done a lot of work in a short time, Holly.'

'Well, it's not so hard these days, when you can just push scenarios out into the Pollcloud.'

'Goddam AIs,' Slaymaker grumbled. 'We're selling our souls to those things.'

The assistant came and took their plates and Slaymaker requested coffee for them both and ice cream for himself.

'Anyways, where do we go from here? Maybe I should ease back on those darned Christmas trees if people like them? I mean, I'm not a scientist. I dropped out of school in the ninth grade. If folk think those things might really help stop the storms and all, I don't want to stand in their way.'

For a moment Holly froze. How *could* he say that so calmly and casually after spending so many millions of dollars, in his Haulers Federation days, on a last-ditch effort to rubbish the notion that CO_2 was a major factor in the climate? He'd stubbornly resisted more than a century's worth of scientific consensus and now he was willing to change his mind in response to a couple of opinion polls – and the inconsistency didn't seem to bother him at all.

But she knew there was really nothing here to be surprised about. Her whole profession rested on the fact that people's views were subjective, mutable. People chose the story that worked for them, made them feel good, justified the way they wanted to behave in any case.

'As for that bullock-wagon image of yours,' Holly went on, 'Jesus! I know you were thinking of the Old West, but that was a long time ago, and a lot of people these days have barely heard of it. Meanwhile, we've had a whole century of images of people on wagons of one kind or another trying to escape from impoverished foreign countries and into countries that looked more like ours. When you talk about bullock wagons, *that's* what comes to people's minds: not fellow Americans striking out into new lands, but foreigners fleeing from famine. You know? Queues of ramshackle vehicles on the far side of the Mexican border. Or all those millions who try to cross into India from Bangladesh after each new flood.'

A distant look had come into Slaymaker's eyes, as if Holly had lost him by referring to events outside America, but he nodded to acknowledge that he'd heard and understood her.

'*Si*,' Holly added, 'and, in the days of the Wild West, as I understand it, there were sparsely populated territories out there beyond the edge of America waiting to be settled and civilized. It's not *like* that any more. Your bullock wagons will be rolling into land where Americans already live. In fact, they'll be rolling into the backyards of the kinds of folk who vote for you. Damn it, your core supporters, the people you rely on, are *not* the pioneers in the wagon trains rolling into new lands. They're the Indians who are already there, dreading their arrival.'

Slaymaker laughed. 'I guess so. So how do we sell it to them?'

'Not as some kind of exodus, that's for sure. Something more on the lines of what you said before – reconfiguring America, building a new nation that will be stronger for everyone. I'm still working on that, and I'm not there yet, but that *has* to be the way to go.'

She was doing her best but, even as she spoke, trying to sound confident and in control, she knew there was something missing. All of this was way too abstract.

'I'll be truthful, we haven't nailed this yet. You've got a story to tell but there are potent rival stories that have far more immediate appeal. Like this new state border thing, for instance. Erecting walls has *always* been a popular idea: a big high wall to shut out all your worries and fears. We need to find something as simple and powerful as that.'

Slaymaker twinkled at her. 'Well, I trust you, Holly. I trust you to come up with something good. Did you think about my offer?'

'I did. And, yes, I'd be pleased to join your team, just so long as you know I can't actually do magic.'

'All I ask is that you do your best.'

'Thanks. Well, okay then, just let me sort it out with my boss.'

He beamed with pleasure. 'That's great news, Holly. You've made my day. Welcome aboard.' Then he leant forward confidentially, though the two of them were alone in his office. 'I'd probably better let you know at this point that I'm planning to run for president.'

CHAPTER 11

Quite unexpectedly, a sharp, clinging sadness had gripped Richard's chest as he watched Holly disappear into the departure area. Why, he wasn't sure. This wasn't exactly a bereavement, after all. It was hardly even a parting. She was just going away for a couple of nights. But he'd always felt there was something precarious about Holly's attachment to him, always secretly doubted his ability to compete with her other enthusiasms.

The car drove him home past the new thousand-acre Boeing weapons complex. High walls and fences. Cameras and gun turrets. Cold white lights. Not a single human being in sight in that icy castle. Later he passed a group of foreign contract workers in yellow jumpsuits, repairing some barriers along the road under a floodlight, their overseer leaning on a tree as he watched them, his hand resting on his gun.

At home Richard stayed up, skipping between news hubs and channels on the broadscreen and his cristal. Another storm was coming in, Superstorm Thomas. It would slice into the North Carolina coast. More refugees, more floods and roofless houses. The size of these storms was unprecedented, and so was the speed with which they followed one another. The pot had been bubbling for some time, everyone kept saying, but now it felt like it was really beginning to boil. But being unprecedented was not itself unprecedented. Records were always being broken. Previously unknown scenarios were regularly becoming part of everyday experience. And even a rapid rate of change can become routine. He let the news wash over him and waited for more interesting stories to come along.

He saw some pictures of Ceuta – smashed fences, corpses, burnt-out shopping malls – and got to thinking about what it was that those people were running away from so desperately that they were willing to risk being crushed to death. He found a piece about Southern Africa and a phenomenon emerging down there which someone had named the Memetic Hordes. Gangs of deserters from armies whose governments could no longer afford to pay them had grown into large stateless armies in their own right with names like the Lions of God, the Children of Zion...

They were the next stage on from warlords, so it was said. Warlords controlled specific territories, and maintained a level of economic activity. But the hordes simply wandered back and forth across a swathe of drought-ridden nations, raping, plundering what they could – once they'd slaughtered elephants for ivory, but of course there were no elephants left – and killing whoever opposed them, often in deliberately spectacular ways. They maintained their numbers by press-ganging children into service, and funded themselves by selling plundered goods and taking protection money. The stolen kids grew up in the hordes and became part of them. The current leaders of the various hordes had all themselves started out as abducted children. Growing up without love, their only security lying in service to the horde, the ones who rose to the top were those who were the purest in their savagery.

They wore gold rings on their fingers and mirror shades, had cold skull-like smiles and actively encouraged atrocities among their lower ranks – rape, public torture, cannibalism – knowing from their own experience that complicity, even more than fear, would bind their followers to them.

Richard laid down his cristal and went to stand at the back door looking out into the warm darkness. A gentle wind stroked his face. The air was like some fierce beast at rest, a lion curled up for a nap after devouring a wildebeest.

Of course there were no lions these days, either. Or wildebeests. Any land in Africa that could support large animals had long since been given over to farms.

He felt strangely detached and calm. Perhaps those hordes were really a cleansing force, he thought. They could hardly be described as alive. They were more like glaciers or lava flows, methodically scouring the land, so it could revert to the pristine, mineral, peaceful desert it once had been before those peculiar self-replicating molecules started to coagulate in the primeval oceans, bringing fear and craving into the world.

And then there would just be rock and earth and water and air, spinning quietly through space. Storms could rage, droughts could desiccate whole continents, but they would have no more consequence than the fall of a single drop of rain, or a single grain of sand.

CHAPTER 12

Margot Jeffries

I used to live in a beautiful little town in Arizona called Santa Jordania, just fifty miles north of the Mexican border. The sky was bluer than you'd believe possible and the air so clear that the mountains twenty-five miles away across the desert looked like you could reach them in fifteen minutes.

Tourists came in the dry, intense heat of summer, to take pictures of our Spanish church and our pretty painted houses. I made pots and sold them in my little craft shop. And when I wasn't potting, or drawing, or reading in my backyard under the shade of my orange tree, I'd get together with some friends and sing. There were downsides, like there are anywhere, but even at the time I knew how lucky I was and wondered how long it would last.

There turned out to be an answer to that. It was twelve years. The wells the town relied on began to dry up. We got by on rationing for a while, and then we got a new kind of water recycling plant so the same water could be used over and over again. At one point the mayor looked into laying a pipeline hundreds of miles across the desert. But it turned out to be too costly to be viable. If I was going to pay the higher bills that would have involved, I'd have had to charge twice as much for my pots and still sell just as many.

Same for the hotels, same for the restaurants. And that just wasn't going to happen.

The hardest part was that our houses and businesses were now worth nothing at all. No one was going to move into a town with no water, so pretty much all of the money we had invested there was gone for good. And for me, and for a lot of others too, that meant ending up with *less* than nothing, because I still owed money on my house and my kiln.

We'd kind of seen it coming for several years, though – the same thing was happening all over the south-west – and we made up our minds as a community to have one last big party under the stars, sell whatever movable stuff we could, and then go our separate ways.

I had no savings, but I guess I could have rented a one-room apartment somewhere, and maybe taken up teaching again, but for some reason I chose to become a proper barredura and see what it was like. I moved to Federal Resettlement Camp 134 in central Illinois. It was a bare grid of nine hundred identical aluminum trailers, right next to a little prairie town about the same size as the town I'd left behind down in Arizona.

The local people didn't like us being there. There were only about four thousand of them, they were all related, all Lutherans, and most of them were descended from Swedes who'd settled that part of Illinois the better part of three hundred years previously. They were proud of their neat little town with its tidy white church, where everyone knew everyone, and no one even had to lock the doors.

There were about three thousand of us in the trailer park. We came from California, Arizona, Nevada and New Mexico, and were a pretty mixed bunch: some of us were Anglos like me, but most were Mexican Americans and Native Americans, including a big group of Navajos. The town news hub carried gloomy articles about how the new arrivals were driving down their property values and committing crimes, and when it came to the elections to the town council, the mayor actually went to court to try and get us barreduras off the voters' roll. We were only temporary residents, was his argument. We should vote in elections back where we came from.

That was a joke. Where I came from wasn't there any more! The houses, the church, the stores, the fire station: they were just a bunch of empty shells with the wind blowing through them and the sand building up against the walls.

There was this new group in the Midwest back then, calling itself the Norsemen. Vigilantes, basically, who wore Viking-style helmets with facemasks. They posted signs: 'Town elections. Dust trash not invited.' And then one evening some of them came through the camp with guns, shouting abuse and flinging red paint about. A woman called Patricia had become a kind of leader in the camp. An imposing half-Navajo woman, six foot tall, she'd spoken out publicly in a town meeting for our right to vote. The Norsemen tossed a firebomb through the window of her trailer and then stood and jeered at her and her wife June when they came running out in their nightclothes.

'Go home, redskins!' they yelled. 'Go back to the desert, lesbian scum!'

Redskins. Lesbian scum. You heard more and more of that. I even got to wondering whether there was – I don't know – some kind of genetic thing inside us that switches on when things get hard, and makes us notice distinctions that we wouldn't previously have bothered about. I mean, defining groups of people as 'them' and not 'us' sort of reduces the number of folk we have to feel obligations to, doesn't it?

Anyway, the firetruck and the sheriff didn't arrive for an hour, by which time Patricia's trailer was completely burnt out, and the Norsemen had long since gone. Which was kind of suspicious, when you remembered that the fire station and the sheriff's office were both only three miles away, and that there weren't any other fires to put out that night, or any reports of crimes. Well, hadn't they been telling us that? That this was a peaceful place without any crime? And one of my neighbors swore that one of the firemen had red paint on his hands.

Afterwards, people gathered together around Patricia. Some talked about fighting and revenge, others about lawyers and letters to congressmen. One woman said they ought to talk to Senator Slaymaker: 'He's the only one of the lot of them that gives a shit about people like us!'

I don't like shouting and indignation soon tires me. I could tell that this scared, angry litany could easily go on all night, so I went to bed.

I lay awake for hours, thinking, thinking, thinking. It was such a strange situation I found myself in: a refugee in my own country. But I'd always lived on my own, and that did make things easier when it came to adapting to change. I had no one to worry about but myself. I was troubled, of course, but I wasn't really scared.

And, unlike some of the people here, I'd kind of chosen this life. Once, when I was in the town, a woman in the drugstore asked me why I stayed in the camp. 'You're not like the rest of them,' she said to me, meaning I guess that I had an educated voice, and my ancestors came from northern Europe. 'We wouldn't mind if they were all like you.'

I remembered that now. And as I lay there listening to those indignant voices rising and falling outside, I found myself thinking about the Mexican border. It had only been about fifty miles south of our little town, but I'd very seldom given it any thought. The only time it really came home to me what that border meant was when a tunnel caved in down near Naco and about fifty people inside it were crushed to death. A few months previously, there'd been a noisy demonstration on the Mexican side going on for many weeks, and it turned out all that noise had basically been cover to allow the tunnellers to do their work without being detected by acoustic sensors. The tunnel itself was a horrible narrow hole, no more than four foot high. Illegal migrants had been coming in through it all that time.

Now, as I lay in my trailer in Illinois, I remembered feeling sad about that, sad that some people were so desperate to get out of their own country that they'd take that kind of risk. And I remembered feeling angry that *my* country had put up that ugly wall. I'd signed some kind of petition about it, I seemed to recall, though I couldn't now say what it said (to be honest I probably hadn't even read it through). And once I'd gone down to Naco with a bunch of people in the town and taken part in a small demonstration. But that was it, and within a few weeks, I'd forgotten all about it.

Thinking about it now, it struck me how much my whole way of life down there had depended on that wall. I hadn't wanted to admit it to myself at the time – I'd wanted it to be the responsibility of someone else – but really I'd known quite well that it was the wall that made possible our pretty little town in the desert, where the tourists came to buy my pottery. It was like a dam, holding back all that desperation and need, and allowing us to continue to enjoy beauty, peace and prosperity, just fifty miles north of it. Without it, we'd quickly have become a crowded, poverty-stricken Mexican town, like a hundred others to the south of the border.

At least that drugstore woman was honest, I thought. At least she came out and said who she wanted in her town and who she didn't. We wouldn't have wanted migrants from Mexico in Santa Jordania – shacks spoiling our view, beggars making us feel bad, hawkers undercutting our prices. I wouldn't have flung red paint at them, of course, or called them names, or tried to scare them into leaving, but I would have moved away myself. We were living in a pretty little pastiche of Mexican life, and the real thing would have completely spoiled it. So we let others build the wall and guard it, and pretended it was nothing to do with us.

As I lay there thinking about this, rain began to fall, a few big drops at first, but pretty soon a proper downpour, which finally broke up that little gathering of scared indignant folk outside. I lay and listened to it, the steady hiss and patter of rain falling on the roof of my trailer, and the little gurgles and splashes, and sometimes in the distance the crack and boom of enormous clumps of air colliding in the darkness, thousands of feet above the prairie.

CHAPTER 13

'**O**kay,' Holly said in that big comfortable office on Constitution Avenue. 'Well, that changes everything. If you're going for the presidency, there's no sense at all in carrying on with this resettlement campaign as a separate project. Every single thing you say from now on is going to be a part of your election campaign. And I can't pretend I know the slightest thing about elections.'

Slaymaker leant forward. 'This isn't you quitting, is it?'

'It's me saying I don't think I've got anything to offer.'

He laughed. 'Hey! I'll be the judge of that! But maybe you don't want to get involved in a political campaign, is that it? I've kind of got you down as someone who doesn't normally vote for the Freedom Party?'

'You're right. I've voted Unity ever since I became a US citizen.'

'But you were happy to help me with my resettlement campaign?'

Holly's party affiliation didn't seem either to bother Slaymaker or to strike him as a particular difficulty.

'*Por cierto*. And not only because I'm a professional. I actually agree with it.'

Slaymaker nodded. 'Well, it's going to be the centerpiece of my campaign, Holly, reconfiguring our country to stop it from falling apart.'

'I wouldn't make it the centerpiece if I were you. You should go with...I don't know, some part of your program that's easier to sell, like...maybe...tax cuts, or a foreign war or something. Or building this starship people talk about.'

'I want to make it the centerpiece. This is the thing I most care about, and, if I'm going to drive it through, seems to me I need a proper mandate from the American people. And I'd be really pleased if you'd carry on helping me figure out how to get that message over. I've got other people to help me with taxes and defense and all the rest.'

'I need to think about it,' she said.

'Okay, well, let me at least introduce you to some of my team!'

They met Sue Cortez, who was to be Slaymaker's campaign director, in one of the dull, expensive restaurants he favored. She was a tough, compactly built African American woman in her fifties who'd been a sidekick of his for many years: a professional troubleshooter with sour, coolly appraising eyes. It was obvious she didn't welcome this British, delicado, Unity-voting upstart. She and Holly circled each other, obliged to be nice with Slaymaker there.

'Welcome aboard, Holly,' Sue said in a tone that was as flat and indifferent as it was possible to be without actually being openly rude. 'We've been hearing a *lot* from Stephen about your communication skills.'

Slaymaker watched the two of them, beaming benignly like he just *knew* they were going to get along. Did he not notice the hostility, or was he just untroubled by it?

A thin, tall, small-faced woman with long bony legs was picking her way toward them, in black pants and a white blouse; her eyes narrowed as she appraised Holly across the restaurant. Her name was Ann Sellick, and she was to be the communications lead in Slaymaker's team. She was well known in Holly's industry as a formidable dogfighter: a publicist whose expertise lay in discrediting individual opponents.

'You'll need to work closely with Ann,' said Sue, 'to make sure that your input on Stephen's – uh – special project, dovetails with the rest of what we're trying to get over.'

'Yeah, this isn't some little hydro scheme in Oregon,' Ann said as she took Holly's hand limply for a moment and let it go again. 'Half a billion people are going to be watching every single thing we do. You can't afford to fuck this one up.'

Holly's eyes narrowed. 'I won't fuck up if you don't fuck me around. Deal?'

Slaymaker laughed. 'Well, that's you told, Ann.'

Ann's brightly painted lips puckered into a sour little smile as she settled into her seat. Slaymaker was already greeting the next and last arrival across the room.

Jed Bulinski was one of those super-bright, super-confident Ivy League types who populated the think tanks and consultancies of DC, clustering round power like exotic life forms round undersea vents. He was a strikingly good-looking man in an immaculate dark suit, with thick brown hair, a rather full, cruel mouth, and a quick mocking smile.

'This guy has the morals of a rattlesnake,' Slaymaker warned Holly as Jed seated himself, 'but that's why I hired him. He notices things that most folk are just too nice to think about.'

'Why thank you, Senator,' said Jed bowing his head in modest acknowledgment. 'You say the sweetest things.'

The two older women glanced at each other, eyebrows just perceptibly raised. It occurred to Holly that, to them, Jed was another upstart like her, which made him (not a welcome thought) a potential ally, if she decided to join this team. And she realized too that of *course* Slaymaker was aware of the undercurrents of jealousy and hostility. He was an instinctive leader. He rewarded the loyalty of his old lieutenants, but he knew their limitations. He needed fresh perspectives, new ideas, new energy from outside, and he needed competition to keep things sharp.

The unimaginative, unnecessarily bulky food arrived. Holly listened to Ann and Sue as they surveyed the political scene. What they said was often ugly. They didn't attempt to conceal their contempt for the alliance which the Unity Party represented: the delicados with their exquisite and expensive tastes and their ever-bleeding hearts, the unskilled and semi-skilled workforce, and the desperately poor in the bottom 20 percent of American society. This last group's fecklessness was the particular focus of their contempt (though, in deference to Slaymaker, they avoided mentioning that the barreduras from east and west were now the largest constituent of this group). In Sue and Ann's world the people who *really* mattered were the top 10 percent – the 'creators of wealth', as they called them.

Slaymaker was in the very unusual position of having traveled all the way from the bottom to the top, and his views on what they were saying were hard to fathom because he said very little, watching the conversation in that attentive, respectful, amused way that he had, almost as if politics weren't really his thing, and he was an interested outsider. Jed did join in, but Holly noticed he was more even-handed in his scorn than Ann or Sue. His was an equal-opportunities contempt, it seemed. Rich or poor, Freedom Party or Unity Party, Partido Latino or Christian Party, no one escaped it.

Holly thought of her friends – Richard, Mariana, Ruby, Sergio – and wondered how she'd managed to find herself among these cold harsh people. What was she even doing here?

Finally, when Slaymaker had finished his customary ice cream, he turned the conversation back to his favorite project.

'First and foremost, we've got to move people north. There are literally tens of millions up and down the Storm Coast and over in New Mexico, Arizona and California, and sitting behind flood defenses up and down America, who should be up in Alaska by now, or Washington or Idaho, in decent homes and in proper jobs that will help our nation to prosper.'

Ann and Sue glanced at each other. They were old-school Freedom Party people, instinctively opposed to any sort of big government program. They had no real sympathy for Slaymaker's pet project, a fact that encapsulated what was difficult about his position. How could he expect to sell it to Freedom Party voters, if he couldn't even sell it to his own lieutenants?

That, of course, was a good reason for bringing in an outsider like Holly. But did she *really* want to work with people she didn't like on a project they'd prefer to bury?

'I'm not saying it can't be done,' Jed observed, 'but that is one hard sell. Northerners basically do not give a flying fuck about homeless barreduras.'

CHAPTER 14

As she settled in the drig, Holly was still torn. She was excited and flattered by the scale of the responsibility that Slaymaker was offering her, but she was aware that, if she took on this job, it would no longer be about helping a politician with a personal project. It could no longer, even at a stretch, be seen as just another PR account. It would mean abandoning her own…she searched for the right word…it would mean abandoning her own *tribe* and going over to help another. A terrifying prospect.

Yet in some ways, the very transgressiveness was precisely the aspect that appealed to her.

The drig was still on the ground but all around her on its middle deck, passengers were playing with their cristals. A few were using them to watch movies or listen to music or read books but Holly could tell, from the movement of their jaws, that most of them were in the whisperstream. Eleven people, just in her row of sixteen seats, were already deep in there, muttering soundlessly with almost closed mouths, their attention turned away from those who were physically with them to companions they might never have met.

Holly knew that every one of those eleven people would have affinity filters running. They might well not know it – some of them might not even know such things existed – but each one of them was being silently corralled into his or her own individual stream, its content hand-picked by AIs to ensure optimal congruence with that individual's views, interests, demographic characteristics, consumer habits, tolerance of difference (as indicated by their decisions in the past), and emotional responses to previous messages.

Of course Holly also used affinity filters when she wasn't at work. Not doing so would be like deliberately hanging out with people you didn't like. But, while most folk were fooled by affinity filters to some extent into imagining they were part of a much wider consensus than really existed, Holly knew this to be an illusion. She'd first begun to notice this kind of self-deception, in fact, when she was still a child. Her father and mother would come back elated from some demo in London. Hundreds of thousands had attended, they would tell her excitedly. The streets had been packed with protestors, mile after mile after mile. How could the government ignore any more the voice of the people? But she knew that in school the next day – the tough, working-class school they'd sent her to – she'd have a job finding even one single child who agreed with whatever it was that her parents had been marching for.

Cristals allowed people to carry around with them in their pockets the same comforting illusion that her parents had experienced on those marches, without the inconvenience. But Holly knew that to shatter that feeling, all you had to do was step aside for a moment from your own stream and pick up on some other stream that intersected with it. In a matter of seconds you'd find yourself in another conceptual universe, where another entire set of people were busily reassuring each other that *they* were the clear-eyed ones, *they* were the true majority, *they* were the people who knew what was really going on.

People were resistant to this truth. Holly had found that if she suggested to her friends that their views were not very widely shared, they'd first of all hotly deny it and then, if presented with evidence, they'd shrug and say that other people were simply wrong. Those people were stupid, or blinded by prejudice, her friends would say. If they were underprivileged, they'd been deceived. If they were privileged, they were either being manipulative or had deceived themselves, their beliefs nothing more than a rationalization of their own self-interest. Didn't slave-owners once persuade themselves that slaves were happy? Didn't people a hundred years ago persuade themselves that the composition of the air was less important than their own comfort? Her friends alone, apparently, were immune to such self-deception.

Holly wished in a way that she could be more like her friends, could dismiss the evidence, as they did, that her own tribe was no different from any other, for then she could truly feel part of the group she lived among. But she was a professional storyteller. Every day she crafted narratives that made self-interest feel like virtue. And she couldn't see how the delicados, among all the tribes of America, could be sure that they alone were in possession of truths untainted by any calculation of self-interest. Most of them led comfortable lives, after all. They were smart, educated, comfortably-off people from smart, educated, comfortably-off families. They were the people with skills that AIs and robots still couldn't match. They designed things, taught things, ran things, discovered things, made things into stories. Their niche in society was secure, and they were very well rewarded by comparison with the great majority of Americans, whose skills were no greater than those of machines, and had to make a living in the little cracks and crannies where it was still cheaper to use humans, or where human labor was protected by politics like some kind of endangered animal.

'But now I'm constructing a story for *myself*,' she said to herself, smiling, in the same silent closed-mouth whisper that other people around her were using to talk to their jeenees (for even the cheapest models could read language from facial muscle movements). 'I'm constructing a story to make me feel okay about turning my back on my own people.'

Was this really what she wanted? Did she want to place herself in opposition to the values of her friends? 'If I was stuck on a desert island,' she said to herself, 'wouldn't I rather be with the likes of Ruby or Mariana, who believe in kindness, than with people like Sue or Ann or Jed?'

Yes she would, but what if she could be with Slaymaker on that desert island? That would be a different thing. The two of them would build a house in no time, work out how to make weapons and clothes from skins, spend days on the beach experimenting with designs for boats. And—

'Okay,' she interrupted herself impatiently. 'I get it. Slaymaker fascinates me. But why?'

Did she find him sexy, was that it? Was this some kind of schoolgirl crush? Was all this admiration, this need to please him, really just sublimated lust? Was there some deep, wired-in instinct kicking in, some ancient Cro-Magnon imperative, carried on the X chromosome, to desire the leader, the alpha male, and his genes for strength and leadership?

Holly examined this possibility. She was no prude about sex. She had no difficulty in admitting to herself that sometimes she felt desire for men other than Richard, and even occasionally women. It wasn't unknown for her to meet a man – or, once in a while, a woman – and think to herself quite openly and unabashedly, *I wouldn't mind fucking you.* But as a matter of fact, this wasn't a thought that had come to her when she was with Slaymaker. Even now, when she challenged herself to think it, it just didn't seem to work. He was an attractive man, certainly, and she enjoyed his physical presence, but it wasn't quite lust that drew her to him.

'Never mind all this,' she said to herself, in that silent whisper. She disliked excessive introspection. 'I need to decide one way or the other.'

The drig jolted slightly as it was released from its moorings. As its own buoyancy lifted it, Holly asked her jeenee to make her a map of the USA with each state shaded according to the percentage of homes unoccupied as a result of being abandoned by their owners. States that had the highest percentage to be shaded in dark red, states with the lowest percentage left white. It took the jeenee about three seconds to assemble the necessary information from federal and state statistics. The map showed a clear line across the middle of America, with red or dark pink states below it, and white or pale pink states above. Mexico and Canada were both just colored gray, but Holly guessed that if they'd been shaded in too, most of Mexico would have been solid red, and most of Canada would have been white or pale pink. There was a new frontier across North America that didn't coincide with a political border. Instead, it lay right there in the middle of the United States, half-way between the continent's national boundaries.

Holly hadn't expected the map to make up her mind for her.

And yet now, seeing it there in front of her, she knew that she was going to work for Slaymaker. He was the only one who was really trying to deal with this stark new reality, she thought, the only one trying to rebalance America before this rift became too wide to heal, and the northern half of the country simply cast the southern half adrift. Jenny Williams was spending a lot of federal money on strengthening homes in the stressed parts of the country, on improving water supplies and moving people inland, but wasn't that really equivalent to the aid that prosperous countries in the northern hemisphere had once used to send to poor countries in the southern half of the world? That had never been anything like enough to bridge the gulf between the two halves, and, when things got tough, and the south needed help more than ever, the aid had dried up anyway, and the northern countries had simply erected walls and built up their armies. What Slaymaker was really doing was trying to prevent a similar scenario *within* the United States. Okay, his horizons were limited, but anyone could have broad horizons if they weren't really going to *do* anything. He at least was going to make something happen.

It would be difficult to explain to Richard, she knew, but he would come round. Her friends, too, she thought – her real friends, anyway – once they understood her thinking. After all, if there was one thing delicados believed in, it was tolerance.

Pleased with her conclusion, buoyed up by it, Holly suddenly decided to write to her mother.

She'd been more or less estranged from her father before he became ill. There'd been no formal rift, but she just couldn't bear to talk to him for any length of time, and he never tried to talk to her.

These days he was confined to a wheelchair and his contribution to a conversation consisted of him going round a cycle of four or five statements, over and over, each one followed by a bark of bitter laughter:

'Of course when *we* were young, we used to *protest* about things. Your generation seems to have forgotten that. You get what you settle for, you know. *Ha!* You get what you settle for! It may be too late now, of course. We don't live in a democracy any more. This is a plutocracy. We've sleepwalked into it. Some of us tried to warn people, but no one wanted to listen. Same with these climate problems. We spent half our youth trying to get something done about it, but of course nobody listened to that either. All they're interested in is short-term profit, I'm afraid. They don't give a damn about ordinary people. *Ha!* They don't give a damn!'

God, he was tedious! And it wasn't just his dementia. He'd always been tedious.

She didn't feel close to her mother either, who was a humorless, gray, little creature with the strange ability to suck the joy out of her surroundings. Whatever you might be feeling pleased or cheerful about, she was sure to find a reason why you should really be feeling guilty or sad or disapproving.

But Holly did feel sorry for her, partly because she could see it wasn't much fun *being* her mother, and partly because she had to put up with Holly's father. Holly only went back to England once every couple of years – resentfully aware that her parents had never visited her – and she could seldom bring herself actually to talk to her mother, but she tried to maintain at least some sort of contact by cristal mail, hoping to reassure the repressed and joyless woman who'd given birth to her that she hadn't completely abandoned her.

It wasn't going to be easy, telling her mother that she'd decided to join the staff of a Freedom Party politician.

'Hi, Mum,' she murmured soundlessly. 'Sorry I haven't been in touch for a while. Are you and Dad okay? Hope Dad's new medication is making things a bit easier for you. Just wanted to let you know I've got a new job. You aren't going to approve, but hear me out. I'm going to join the staff of Senator Slaymaker. I know! I said you wouldn't like it. But I really do think he's doing more than any other politician right now to stop America being divided between a wealthy north and an impoverished south, which is surely a good thing.

'Richard's okay. Still teaching one day a week, and working on his latest book the rest of the time. Or so he says, anyway! Ha ha.

'Say hello to Dad from me.

'Love Holly.'

So that was done. The thought of writing just a few lines like that always felt like a colossal task, which she'd often put off for days or even weeks. But now she could return to her work. She told her jeenee to play her some of the interviews she'd commissioned: people from key demographics talking about how they saw the world. Slaymaker was quite right: polls were no substitute for this, because what they generated was data, and what people told were stories. Data was nothing without stories to animate it.

'Hi, I'm Henry McKenzie...' said a middle-aged voice through Holly's implants.

Outside of her window, the whole of Washington was laid out beneath her. There was the tiny, perfect Capitol, the miniature Lincoln Memorial, the Washington Monument thrusting upwards like a matchstick. There was the Reflecting Pool glinting in a shaft of sunlight like a slither of mirrored glass.

And above it all there were clouds. They were piled up in layers, white and gray, puffy cumulus clouds and streaky cirrus wisps, continents of cloud, continents and islands and shoals, one above another, and all of them made of nothing but water and air. It was as if the whole city, tiny and fragile, lay at the foot of a gigantic well.

CHAPTER 15

'Hi, I'm Henry McKenzie. I'm sixty-six. I live in Spokane, Washington, home of Father's Day. I've done all kinds of jobs. Used to drive a delivery vehicle before they all went driverless. Then I worked as a security guy in a supermarket. Did building work for a time, too, until my arthritis wouldn't let me. These days I'm a truck supervisor. I work for a hauling company. I check over the robot trucks when they come back to the depot for a service. Not the motor or the tyres or anything, obviously – the AIs do that – but I make sure the paintwork's okay, that kind of thing, and I sign off the work that the service machines do: it's kind of a legal formality. I'm also responsible for the depot itself. I organize the contractors to keep it clean, and about once a week something comes up on a service that requires the hands of a human being to fix it, and it's my job to arrange that. We don't have a mechanic on-site, but there are contractors you can hire and of course I get to know the guys pretty well.

'I've been doing this for a couple of years, but I'm always looking around for the next job. Kelly's, the other big trucking company with a depot in Spokane, has gone fully automated now. They have machines to check the paintwork and everything, and they have a contract with a delegated-authority service, which means that a machine can even sign off the paperwork and call in human mechanics when they're needed. So no one's there at all most of the time. A regional manager comes in once a month to look around and contractors still bring in yellow-coats every couple of weeks to wash the floors, same as they do in our place. Otherwise it's just robots.

'My wife and I rent a two-bedroom apartment four miles out of town, where we live with our daughter and her guy. It's kind of cramped, but it's the best we can do on our pay. We've never tried to buy a place. Too hard to raise the deposit, plus the mortgage companies make you pay insurance these days in case some AI takes over from you and you can't afford to keep up the repayments. It can put the cost up by nearly 50 percent for a guy like me.

'What do I do for fun? Watch the broadscreen mainly, like most people. Go to a ball game a couple of times a year.

'No, I've never been outside of the US, except once to Canada, and that was just a day trip, which my son bought me and my wife for an anniversary present. Can't afford foreign travel and who'd want to go out there anyway? Canada's alright, I guess, but from what I've heard, most other places are basically hell on Earth. Life's not easy here but at least we've got laws and cops. Thank Christ for that wall!

'No, I've got no medical insurance. Can't afford that either. A case of keeping my fingers crossed and hoping for a healthy life and a quick death.

'I like Senator Slaymaker. He's worked his way up from the bottom, done jobs like mine and worse. Plus he owns the company I work for. But I don't know if I can vote for him, all the same. I don't want this town filling up with Californians or storm trash or whatever. They say they won't take our jobs, but that's what they say about the yellow-coats and I've never figured out how having some Venezuelan guy with a tracker cuff on his wrist coming in and sweeping our floors isn't taking a job from an American. Okay, an American wouldn't sweep floors for the shit money they pay those suckers but if there were no yellow-coats, maybe companies would have to pay out something resembling a decent wage.

'And it's the same with the barreduras, I figure. Slaymaker says they'll create new jobs, but who's to say that's true? And anyway, I like this town the way it is. I don't want folk from the south coming in here with their funny accents and their spicy food changing it and making me feel like I don't belong.'

'Hi, I'm Danielle Schutz, I'm a checkout oversight operative for the Great Lakes Mall in Buffalo, New York. What does that even mean, right? Believe me, I get asked that a lot! Basically, we remotely monitor the checkouts of all the stores in the mall. The checkouts are all automated, of course – they just read the contents of customers' bags and bill them when they leave a store – but once in a while there's a problem. We send in security guards if need be, though the store AIs have usually done that before we get to hear about it, and if a customer needs to talk to someone we link to them by videophone...'

'Hey there, my name's Dave Brooks. I'm a so-called "forestry site supervisor", working out of Portland, Oregon. My company gets paid to take out trees that are going to die. There are *lots* of those in Oregon. What do I actually do? Well, if you want the truth I spend most of my time sitting around doing nothing, while robot loggers cut down trees, saw off their branches and load them onto robot trucks. Basically, we're there because state health and safety regulations require a human supervisor be present in case of difficulty. There's no real need for us at all. Just one of those rules they make to create jobs for saps like me. But I'm not going to argue. It just about pays my rent and buys the groceries. The logging companies are trying to get the law changed, but I'm kind of hoping this will see me out because I'm seventy-six years old...'

'Hi there, I'm Peter Curie from North Dakota. I've done several jobs but I'm a manufacturing maintenance engineer these days. My old job was in a canning factory, but we got phased out when the factory upgraded its systems and I got a grant from the state to retrain for this job. Course lasts three days. At the end you have to answer some questions on a screen, and then you get a certificate printed out and you're done. Basically we go out to production systems in factories where a fault has been identified. The factory AI tells us the unit that needs replacing, and then we lift it out and drop a new one in. It's not that hard, all the units are color-coded, and the AIs give you precise instructions, right down to how many turns to give to a bolt. But it can be dangerous because some of those units are pretty damn big, and there are a couple of guys in my team who've lost fingers trying to get a job done in too much of a hurry. You get a set allowance of time per job, you see, and if you go over it, well, that's your own time and you have to make it up...'

·

They were Americans, like Holly's friends, but they weren't Americans that Holly's friends would encounter socially, or read about in the novels they read, or see in the movies they watched on their broadscreens. Holly's friends led interesting and elaborate lives that lent themselves to such stories. These people's jobs were dull and precarious and poorly paid, their educational level low, their horizons limited and, unless they came from areas affected by drought or floods or storms, their sense of responsibility for those affected by such disasters was almost always practically zero.

PART 2

PART 2

CHAPTER 16

In the winter, moist air from the Pacific Ocean streams inland from the Californian coast. It flows over the Coast Ranges, down into the Central Valley and up again onto the Sierra Nevada. As it's pushed upwards by the mountains, it cools. The moisture condenses and falls on the peaks below, sometimes as snow and sometimes rain.

The air is a few degrees warmer now than it would have been a few decades ago and that means more rain and less snow. The snow used to settle up there, many meters deep in places, and it would form drifts and glaciers whose meltwaters flowed all summer long down into the Central Valley and into the states to the east. Some was so deep that it lasted years. But now what snow still falls will all melt off in the spring, stripping bare the rocky peaks before summer has even reached its height. And rain just runs straight off, evaporating all the while back into the air.

It's no big deal as far as the planet is concerned. The mountains themselves are still the same huge shapes against the sky. Earth still follows the same old track round the sun. But living things depend on small contingencies. On the slopes of the Sierra Nevada, and down in the valleys, there are plants and animals that depend on streams flowing for such-and-such a time, farmers who depend on meltwater to irrigate their crops, towns that depend on water tables being replenished every year. There has only been a small change in the air, and only a small change in the way that water comes down the mountains, but an entire web of consequences are flowing out from it.

Trees die. Animals starve, or climb higher up the mountains, or wander north. And in the human world, farmers dig deeper wells, invest in costly water-saving devices, experiment with expensively engineered low-water crops, until a time comes when they can no longer borrow the money or no longer service their debts. And then they abandon everything and follow the animals north, becoming another stream, a human stream that branches and divides across America, a river of people with no money and no home, leaving crumbling buildings and rusting machinery and empty fields.

People in the north watch their arrival with suspicion and hostility. It's dangerous to feel sorry for them, for that might mean acknowledging an obligation to help them, to give up some part of the comfort blanket that folk wrap around themselves against the frightening world. And isn't that blanket always threadbare? Doesn't it always feel too thin? And anyway, if you were to look those new arrivals in the face and really acknowledge them for what they are, wouldn't you also have to face the thing that follows behind them, the thing that has driven them north, the thing that everyone knows is moving north itself, coming closer and closer with every year? Who in their right mind would want to do that?

CHAPTER 17

The key was to tell a story that would connect in the right way with people's hopes and fears. You had to make them think, *If this guy wins, these fears that press in on me all the time will be eased, at least just a little bit, and the things I value, the things I rely on for comfort, will be at least just a little bit safer.* It wasn't about dispassionate analysis of the facts, it wasn't about philosophical debate about ethical principles. It was much more visceral than that. It was about the calculus of dread and comfort that every living creature engages in, from a swallow soaring across the sky, to a mole in the darkness underground. Which way should I go? Which way offers, if only fractionally, the higher level of security, the lower level of threat?

The calculus of dread and comfort: Holly had an instinct for it, and it was that instinct that won the presidency for Stephen Slaymaker. She even knew exactly when it happened, the precise moment when he stopped being just another contender and became instead the future occupant of the White House.

•

The campaign team was in the living room of Slaymaker's ranch in the Cascades. In the huge medieval-style fireplace that Slaymaker himself had built with chunks of rough-hewn stone, a log fire was crackling on an enormous grate. It was February, and the primary season was a month away. In December and January, Slaymaker had been out in front in the race for the Freedom Party nomination, but now he'd fallen behind. He was third in the polls behind Lucy Montello and Soames Frinton, and there was some evidence that even his apparent initial surge had been in part the result of foul play, someone manipulating the polls to mislead him and send him down the wrong path.

They were ranged in a big semicircle round the fire, with Slaymaker himself presiding in the middle. Over to the left of him there was Sue Cortez, the campaign director, the squat tough black woman Holly had first met in that dull but showy restaurant in DC. Next to her sat Jennifer Anka, director of fundraising, immaculately groomed, with a bright smile and cold, relentless eyes. After that was Ann Sellick, the communications lead, Sue's close ally, who Holly had also first met in that DC restaurant, with the same little splash of red lipstick in the middle of her spidery face. And then there was Eve Slaymaker, the senator's beautiful film-star wife, whose donor liaison role was about looking after the campaign's billionaire backers. On Slaymaker's right, there was Pete Fukayama, who led the nationwide force of volunteers; Zara Gluck, another British exile like Holly, who led on technology, and Phyllis Kotkov, the events coordinator. And then, at the very right-hand end, sat the three youngest members of the team: Jed Bulinski, who'd been given the title of strategy consultant; Quentin Fox, Slaymaker's affable head speechwriter, and finally Holly herself, the youngest of them all. Her job title was special communications adviser, and she was paid four times more than she'd ever been paid before.

Jed was speaking, in that smooth, super-confident way he had that always verged on boredom, as if he was being forced by the stupidity of others to repeat something that ought to be too obvious to need to be said.

'I'm sorry, Senator, but our only option now is to figure out a way of radically changing track. You've given it your best shot, but we're basically trying to sell a flagship policy whose appeal is mainly southern, to a party whose support and whose national convention delegates are mainly northern. Chrissakes, down along the border there we're the fourth party. Most Latinos vote for the Partido, most black people vote Unity, and at least 50 percent of white folk vote for the Christian Party. Our heartland is here in the northwest, and yet it's the people up here we're asking to make sacrifices. There was a moment there, I admit, when I thought that war-footing language you worked on with Holly was going to fix that, but I'm afraid it's obvious now we were clutching at straws. We need to find a way of ditching the policies that are turning off northern voters, and beginning to prioritize their concerns. It's going to be tricky to do without looking like we're waverers,' he flashed a grin at Holly, 'but you've got Ann here to help you, and I'm sure Holly can work her magic and make everything alright.'

'So what you're saying, Jed,' Slaymaker growled, 'if I've understood you correctly, is that to become president, I've got to give up on the single goal that was the reason for my running in the first place?'

Behind him, on the far wall, hung a large old-fashioned map of America such as might have hung in some high-school classroom a century ago. For no particular reason, Holly noticed that it wasn't the Peters projection map that her parents had always favored – the one that distorted the shape of countries so as to fairly represent their size – nor any of the newer projections, but the old Mercator kind: the one that preserved the shape of countries, but made them look bigger and bigger the further north you went.

Jed shrugged. He didn't believe that people like Slaymaker were motivated by anything other than the desire for power. He thought finer motives were just window-dressing, branding, or, if they weren't actually the product of cynical calculation, self-deception at least. 'Well, that's your choice entirely, Senator. But we can all see that this whole Reconfigure America message is just not cutting it any more with Freedom Party supporters in the north, no matter how carefully we refine it, or how many billions of dollars we spend on feeders and so forth to get it over. If anyone was going to sell it, you were certainly the guy to do it, with your northern credentials and all, but people are just not buying it, even from you.'

Holly suddenly had an idea. It was so wonderfully simple, she was amazed she hadn't come up with it before. She raised her hand. Several other people were trying to come in – Ann, Pete, Sue, Eve – but, whether because he was already looking in her direction, or because she was his favorite, or because she represented the last hope for his precious plan, it was her that caught the senator's eye.

'Holly. What do you reckon? Can you rescue me from this guy's rattlesnake logic?'

'I think I can,' she said. 'I think we've been missing something. I think there's a really simple solution here that's been staring us in the face.'

CHAPTER 18

Back in October, when Holly was in that drig on the way back from DC, Richard had been busy at the school where he taught drama for a few hours every week. He and a colleague called Alice were putting on a production of *Doctor Faustus*, and they were meeting to finalize the substantial cuts they were going to make to Marlowe's rambling play. When Holly messaged him to say she was on her way, Richard and Alice were sitting side by side in the sunshine, with cups of coffee and sheets of script weighed down by pebbles, spread out on a table. Ahead of them were the school playing field and then some trees, live trees, tinged with autumn gold, blowing around a little in the wind. Richard's cristal pinged, he touched it and heard Holly through his implants:

'Hey, Rick, I'll be landing in an hour. Okay if I send for the car?'

'Sure. I won't need it for a while,' he mouthed. 'Welcome back.'

He felt uneasy, some sort of premonition, some sense of news being held back.

'You alright, Rick?' Alice asked him. He looked round at her. She had very black hair and very blue eyes, an unusual combination that reminded him of the heroine of some old Celtic legend.

'Yeah, fine, just Holly saying she'll be back later.' He turned back to the text. 'Yeah, let's cut out this whole scene.'

'Must be strange thinking of her down in DC with Senator Slaymaker.'

'Very strange. It's her job and I completely respect that, but I must admit I'll be glad when this particular piece of work is over.'

It was as if some force that he couldn't see was there in the background all the time, like a leaking pipe in a basement.

Holly was oddly reserved when they met again at the house. Richard had made a chicken casserole for them, and as they ate, he tried to find out how her meeting had gone down in DC.

'Did you persuade him not to shoot his mouth off?'

'I certainly hope so.'

'I mean, how does that work? How do you tell a US senator to check with you before he makes a speech?'

'Well, you know, I just tell him he's not doing himself any favors. It's up to him whether he wants to take that on board.'

Richard watched her hopefully, waiting for a story or two to bring this alive for him. Holly looked up at him, saw this hope, turned her attention quickly down to her food. And then abruptly she looked up again.

'This is confidential, Rick, okay, really confidential, but he's going to stand for president and he invited me to join his election team.'

'You...? I'm sorry, Holly, I'm confused. I thought you were just helping him with this campaign to settle more people in the north?'

'It's still what I'd be working on – in fact, I'd be leading on it – but he wants it to be the central plank of his whole presidential bid.'

What he felt was dread. Like a creature safe in its warm burrow that suddenly feels the soil falling away behind him and cold bright sunlight shining in.

'But Holly, if he gets the nomination, he'll be the Freedom Party candidate. The party that says everyone has got to look after themselves. We've always voted against them, remember?'

'He's going to help the barreduras, and he's going to keep the country together.'

'Jenny Williams is trying to keep it together too. She's not doing as much as we might like but that's because no one wants to pay. But she's doing her best and, unlike him, she also recognizes the humanity of people outside this country.'

'I'm sorry, Rick. I know this is hard. I'm finding it hard myself. I don't like the people he's got around him, and I don't like his party, but I like him and what he's trying to do. I really want to work with him.'

'So when have you got to decide by?'

'I decided on the drig. I said yes.'

Richard looked down at his plate, poking a piece of chicken about as he tried to take this in. 'So…So a job like this…Well, it won't be nine to five, exactly, will it, and it'll be all over the country. We'll be apart a lot and—'

'Yeah, we will, but it'll only be for a—'

'You could have waited to talk to me, Holly. This is going to be hard for me. It's not just that we'll be apart a lot. It's that when you're not here, I'm going to have to think of you working for a party I've disliked pretty much all my life, and voted against in every election, the party that rose out of the ashes of the Tyranny.'

'Yeah, but Rick, does the party label really matter? Does the history matter? All parties change. I remember you telling me that the party that abolished segregation was the very same party that used to defend slavery. Like I said, I think—'

'Have you thought about what our friends will say?'

Holly's face darkened. 'If they're real friends, they'll respect my choice. I'm going to do something that will make a difference, which is more than most of them can say.'

'You're trying to expunge your parents, Holly. That's what you're really doing. You're trying to prove to yourself that you're the exact opposite of them. Their hearts bled for everyone in the world except for you, and now you're getting a kick out of trashing the things they believed in. Can't you see that? It's understandable, of course, totally understandable, but at the same time isn't it just a little bit infantile?'

Holly regarded him steadily for several seconds, her eyes bright. 'It seems to me,' she finally said, 'that you're allowed to have your own opinions, but I'm not. *My* opinions are simply symptoms. I don't think that's fair. It's true I grew up seeing the drawbacks of my parents' worldview, but that's not some kind of pathology on my part. Yeah, and when it comes to being infantile, look at our friends. What are they actually doing? Sergio works on putting even smarter jeenees in our cristals. Ruby makes giant messy pictures that people with a lot of money and very big houses can buy to hang on their walls, which is *really* going to help some poor bastard from Delaware or California whose life savings have been turned to matchwood. And you, Richard—'

'Okay, Holly, okay. I just feel I'm losing you, that's what it boils down to. I feel you're going to a place where I won't be able to follow. And I don't want that to happen. I'm worried we'll end up—'

'We'll end up falling apart? *Jesucristo*, Richard, is that really what you think?'

Now it was Holly that felt dread, a deep dread welling up inside her. She didn't quite *belong* anywhere, that was the thing. She lived among Americans but she came from another country, her friends were delicados but she wasn't quite a delicado herself. She was working for Slaymaker but she wasn't one of his kind either. Without Richard, so it felt to her in that moment, without this little nation of two that he and she made up, she really would be alone.

'I don't want that, Rick. I do understand it's difficult for you. If it had been you that suddenly said you were going to work for some Freedom Party politician, I would have found it difficult too. But I think we should learn to see past these labels. They're just…I don't know…tribal markings. There are good guys and bad guys in most tribes, and believe me, Slaymaker is a good guy. You'd agree with me if you met him yourself. And when you hear what he wants to do for the barreduras, I'm sure you'll agree on that too. Okay, there are going to be lots of things he doesn't do that you'd like him to do, but be honest, isn't that true of Jenny Williams? Isn't it going to be true of anyone?'

She stood up, she came round the table, she stood behind Richard and put her arms round him.

'You must meet him,' she said. 'You'll like him a lot, I promise. But please don't stop me from doing this, Rick. Please don't make it a choice between doing this and being with you.'

They went for a walk through the village. The sky was fiery red over the darkening ridge, smeared with rough brush strokes of black cloud.

'One thing,' said Holly. 'If I work for Slaymaker he'll pay me a ton of money. I can definitely afford to buy us a drink.'

There were just two men sitting at the bar, half-watching the broadscreen, on which a squadron of bombers somewhere were attacking a flooded town. The sound was turned off and in its place rocket music was playing softly through the bar's speakers: a largely AI-generated genre with human singers, that took nostalgia for the far-off golden days of the mid-twentieth century, very gently sent up that nostalgia, and then layered more nostalgia on top. Holly bought Richard his favorite whiskey, and gin for herself. They settled in their usual sagging sofa. The music segued into a song called 'Moonshot', the sound moving between different speakers round the room to create a sense of movement through space.

As she took off her coat Holly found something in her pocket, an old-fashioned booklet printed on paper.

NOWHERE LEFT TO RUN! it read.

NO TO MIGRATION.

She wondered for a moment if it came from the Unity Party, or maybe one of those state frontiers people in the Freedom Party, but then she read on:

NO TO TRADE. NO TO INDUSTRY.

CANCEL THE STARSHIP PROJECT.

REWARD CHILDLESS ADULTS.

NO MORE SLASH AND BURN.

'Looks like you've got yourself an illegal document there,' Richard said, pointing to the initials at the bottom of the page. *WSS*, Holly read: *World Salvationist Society*. 'The whisperstream AIs are getting so good at weeding out their stuff, they're having to resort to paper. Where did you pick that up?'

'Someone must have stuck it in my pocket at the airport.' Holly had turned the page and was looking at a long list of extinct animals, printed in a text box: polar bears, giraffes, blue whales, tigers, rhinoceroses, dolphins...

'*No to migration*,' she said. 'Well, *they* won't support Slaymaker, that's for sure!'

'Hardly. You might want to put that away, Holly, before someone sees it. There's some pretty strong feelings around about the Salvies, since they blew up those freight trains last year.'

She studied the booklet for a few more seconds then dropped it back into her pocket. '*Just stop doing stuff*,' she concluded. 'That seems to be what they're basically saying, though they could do with some help with presentation.'

'Yeah, I think that's about it. The great doers we admire in history, they just see as the diggers of the hole we're in. Agriculture, medical science, you name it. In the end they just made things worse.'

'I don't think they'd like me.'

Richard laughed. 'Probably not.'

'And they *really* wouldn't like Slaymaker.'

'Ha! *Definitely* not. Nor Williams either, actually. Listen, are you *really* sure you want to help that guy get elected president?'

'I want to see through the job I've already taken on. Helping get his message over about moving people north.'

'But *why*? Why's it so important to you?'

'Because it's a big challenge, I guess. The biggest I'll ever have. And, you know, just because that's how I earn my living, that's what suits me, that's my niche in the ecosystem: doing this stuff and doing it as well as I can. Yeah and, as a bonus, I think his plan might be a good idea. Dammit, Rick, it's not like I'd help him if he was planning a war or something.'

'But—'

'Hang on, Rick, why don't you answer the same question? Why do you write books on history?'

'Hmm. Because...I guess...Well, I guess it's like a Venn diagram. One circle is the stuff you really like doing, the other is the stuff people would pay you to do. I've found a place where the fun circle and the job circle overlap. And...well, I hope my books make people think a bit, reflect a bit more deeply about how societies work, and...' Richard tailed off.

'Thinking and reflecting. That's such a delicado value, isn't it? We place so much store by the subtlety of our thought, the *exquisite* refinement of our self-awareness. But—'

'*Jesucristo*, Holly, you're obsessed with this delicado thing at the—'

'I'm just noticing it, Rick. I'm just noticing it. Like you notice your hometown when you've spent time away from it, you know? Things look different from outside. I saw something on the broadscreen the other week about some woman who's worked for years to be able to cycle round a track 0.05 of a second faster than anyone else. I thought to myself, So fucking what? What a waste of energy, what an incredibly tedious and pointless way of filling up your time. But for her that goal just seemed self-evidently worth striving for.'

'What are you saying? That reflection and self-awareness are no more important than that?'

'They're important to the people who find them important. Not to everyone. That's one of the things that's interesting about being with Slaymaker. He's smart, obviously, and he thinks about things, but he's really not reflective in that kind of way. He sees something he wants to make happen and then he goes after it.'

'Which, I guess, is exactly the attitude the Salvies are against.

The desire to make things happen, no matter what.'

'But what do they think people should do with their lives? Tend their vegetable patch? I'd die of boredom. People are *meant* to do things.'

Baby, sang the languid human vocalist from the bar's sound system, accompanied by faux-analogue electronic effects, *come and ride with me in my car / We'll watch the moonshot, we'll watch the moonshot. / And then we'll drive and look up at the stars...*

'You're fascinated by Slaymaker, aren't you?'

'Yeah, I am. Hey, don't look at me like that! I mean, suppose I'd asked you about your drama classes and why you do them, one of the things on the list would be that you like hanging out with your pretty friend Alice.'

'Well, yes, I guess. But come on, Holly, you *know* that's as far as it goes.'

'And the same for me. Exactly the same for me.'

'Okay.'

He laid down his drink. He reached for her hand. They kissed. Somehow it had been accepted by both of them that Holly really would be part of Slaymaker's presidential bid.

We'll watch the moonshot, we'll watch the moonshot / and then we'll dream, we'll dream of our trip to Mars...

'After all,' Holly said, 'it's only until next November, and that's assuming he gets the party nomination.'

All that was left of the red sky was a faint smoldering glow.

CHAPTER 19

Slaymaker announced his candidacy for the Freedom Party nomination in November in front of a giant sign that read, *Building a New America*. Jenny Williams and her predecessors, he said, had allowed America to become soft and weak. It was time to stop the decline and reverse it, laying the foundations for a new golden age whose powerhouse would be in the northern states.

The crafting of this message had been worked on in the main by Holly, Ann Sellick, Jed Bulinski, and the speechwriter Quentin Fox. Sue Cortez had insisted on close oversight, and Slaymaker himself had reviewed the various options and made the final choice, but weeks of work had gone into an announcement that took five minutes to make, and Holly had done the largest part of it.

This mustn't be about welfare, that had been clear from the beginning. Holly's polls had established that it didn't matter how many smashed houses and abandoned farms you showed them, most people had long since learnt to shut off fellow-feeling when they saw those kinds of pictures or heard those kinds of stories. Pity could be evoked in the very short term, but would then be typically replaced not just by indifference but by a sullen, resentful anger: *We're always being told these sob stories about them, but no one ever talks about us.* For most people in America, the future was scary, threats were pressing in, their way of life was precariously balanced over an abyss. To ask them to pity others was to ask them to abandon any hope that they themselves might be worthy of pity.

When it came to understanding the limits of empathy, the others in the team were way ahead of her. Ann, Sue and Jed all started off from a point where welfare was self-evidently bad, handouts a sign of weakness, and compassion and pity dangerous emotions to be held in check. Humanity took different forms, Holly was discovering. Human hardware could run many different applications. And difficult as this was to confront, it was helpful too. All her cloud polls showed that the way most Americans thought about the world was much closer to her colleagues' way of thinking than it was to the worldview of her friends.

With Quentin and the other speechwriters, she had worked and reworked the language of the Reconfigure America program, employing silvertongues from time to time to assist – they had no human intuition, but they didn't get into human ruts either – and running every permutation out into the Pollcloud to test how it went down with the key demographics whose support Slaymaker needed. She had ruthlessly squeezed out the smallest suggestion that Reconfigure America was a program of assistance. She had marshaled metaphors of strength and safety: building fortresses, underpinning foundations, shoring up walls. Wherever they lived, people needed to feel they were being given something, and not just being asked to give to others.

'So yeah, it's true, this will cost trillions,' Slaymaker said in his short declaration, 'trillions to build new towns and cities in the safe places, and trillions to fund the loans that would allow people to settle there. But this is an investment in our future as a nation, as a strong, united country, a fortress of peace and prosperity in a ravaged world, a shining city where our children can grow up with a secure future. The price of doing it, believe me, is a real bargain compared with the price of leaving things as they are.'

Holly had road-tested every one of those words, right down to whether he should say 'yeah' or 'yes'.

CHAPTER 20

Rosine Dubois

We were just over the state line of Montana. We'd been noti-fied about fours day back that a place had been found for us in a government trailer park up there, and there were maybe two hundred miles to go.

Me and Herb were too tired to carry on driving so we'd pulled up by the roadside one last time. We were all asleep, and it was maybe four or five in the morning, when we were woken by three cars pulling up. We heard doors being flung open and angry crash music blaring out, and then a bunch of men started yelling and banging on the truck, and shining flashlights under the tarp where me and Herb had been sleeping. The kids were in the truck. Carl began to cry. Half-blinded by the light, me and Herb scrambled out of our makeshift bed.

I've never been so scared.

These guys weren't cops. They were wearing these metal hel-mets, like in some old story, that covered up their faces so you could just see their eyes peering out, and their mouths.

'What's the problem, guys?' asked Herb.

'Stand up against the truck,' one of them said, and they frisked us both for guns. Carl was still crying in the cabin, Copeland look-ing out, his face stiff with fear.

'Where are you people headed?' one of them said, but when Herb told him, he shook his head. 'No, my friends. Your kind don't belong up here. This is Norsemen country. This is where the real Americans live.' He laughed and shone his flashlight over the piled-up stuff in the back of the truck. 'Where are you from, anyway?'

'Delaware,' I told him. Straight away he shone his flashlight right into my face, completely blinding me. I put my hand over my eyes. 'We're not looking for trouble,' I said. 'We lost our home to Superstorm Simon. If you guys don't want us in your neighborhood, just let us get in the truck and we'll go.'

'Sure,' the guy said. 'You get in the truck and drive. But you're heading back the way you came, you understand? There's no place for you in *our* America. If we hear you're still in Montana in twelve hours' time, we won't be so nice as we're being now.'

The men lined up across the road with their guns, barring the way forward, so me and Herb had no choice about it. We had to go back, Herb driving, Copeland sitting beside him and me in back trying to comfort Carl while I searched on my cristal for another way round to where we were going.

We drove something like a hundred miles back south again, a hundred miles east, then north and west again: four hundred extra miles, just to go right round the place we met those guys in the Viking helmets. But of course we didn't know who their friends were. It wasn't so scary when we were still heading back south, because that's what they'd told us to do, but once we'd turned west, we worried all the time that any one of those cold-eyed people out there watching us pass might be a Norseman too. I mean, look at us, our old truck piled up with everything we could cram on it! We stuck out like a goddam turkey in a field of ducks.

Once we had to stop to charge up in a little prairie charge station. A farmer was there as well, leaning on his truck while it powered up, watching us, and from time to time muttering to his cristal.

CHAPTER 21

Slaymaker invited Holly and Richard to have lunch with him and his wife Eve on their ranch. He sent a car, which took them to what was in fact an entire valley, with cattle grazing on lush pastures between forested slopes that climbed on either side up to bare rocky ridges. Everything was immaculate, the fences and gates were brand new, the trees gold and red – if any trees had rotted they must have been speedily removed – and the house with its many beautifully made timber outbuildings sat beside a stream of clear mountain water, surrounded by pristine lawns. There were various discreet servants hovering around, but Eve Slaymaker herself had made the salads, and the senator was outside at the barbecue. It was a mild, bright late autumn day.

Richard was struck immediately by the *size* of Stephen Slaymaker. Physically the senator stood only an inch or so taller than Richard himself but there was something about the way Slaymaker carried himself that made him large. Every single ounce of him was fully present in the world, while Richard's own presence was much more provisional and sometimes little more than an answering machine, minding his calls while he attended to business in some interior realm.

'Great to meet you, Rick!' Predictably, Slaymaker's handshake was firm enough to be painful. 'Gives me a chance to apologize for taking up so much of your beautiful wife's time.'

Eve was also tall, but slightly built – 'willowy' was a word often applied to her – and a combination of her famous bone structure and a certain fragility that seemed to radiate from her made Richard think of fine porcelain. Under the surface, though, he sensed she was every bit as tough as her husband. She'd been a movie actress, and there was something very actorly about her now as she touched his cheek with her own beautifully scented one, and murmured, 'Lovely to see you, Rick. I do sympathize. I never get to see Steve, either.'

'So…er…this is meat from your own herd, is it?' Holly asked.

She felt oddly diffident in this new environment. It seemed she didn't know Slaymaker as well as she'd imagined. In a work meeting, she knew him well enough to tell him off and even tease him, but now she found herself falling back on small talk. She felt as if she'd assembled him up to now from a few lines of dialogue, like a character in a novel or a play.

'That's right. I have a guy come out to kill them when the time comes. I don't like slaughterhouses. We've got a great cook, and he fixes the burgers in batches and freezes them for us.'

They ate at a table on the lawn laid out with a checkered cloth. There was beer, and wine made from the Slaymakers' own grapes. The senator asked Richard where he grew up (a small town in upstate New York) and then came a question Richard had not been looking forward to.

'Holly tells me you teach a bit of school, but your real work is writing books?'

Writing. Surrounded by friends raised to be impressed by

culture, he was proud of his many well-received books. But now, when he thought of the kind of effort involved in accumulating the wealth that was all round him, he wondered how he could describe his days at home, his cups of coffee, his walks in the forest, his breaks for lunch in front of the broadscreen as even being work at all.

'That's right. I enjoy the teaching well enough but yeah, insofar as I've got ambitions to make a mark in the world, they're kind of centered on my writing.'

'What do you write about?'

'Well, various things, but right now I'm working on a chapter about Anglo-Saxon poetry.'

The senator's blue eyes were fixed on his face. It was quite apparent that he had very little idea what Richard was talking about, but it was also clear that he'd persist until he'd understood. As for Richard, he felt as if he just admitted to spending most of his time masturbating.

'Do you mean poetry from Anglo people round the world?' asked Eve. 'Like Australians, and British people?'

'No, no. Actual Anglo-Saxon poetry. Poetry from the beginnings of the English language.'

Stephen Slaymaker nodded. 'I don't believe I've ever seen any of that. I guess it must be kind of hard to read?'

'Oh, *por cierto*. It's another language entirely, but it's the ancestor of the language we speak.'

'Is that so?'

The senator's education, Richard knew, had finished when he was sixteen, and it was obvious that up to now he'd not given any thought to the origins of the English language, any more than Richard had given thought to things he must know about, like the price of tires, the best places to locate distribution centers, the optimum time to replace trucks. And, although Slaymaker's gaze was entirely friendly and interested, Richard felt reproached by it. The real purpose of intelligence was to solve problems and make things happen, it suddenly seemed to him. There really *was* something masturbatory about purely intellectual activity.

'Can you say something in Anglo-Saxon?' asked Eve.

'Sure he can,' Holly said, looking across at Richard with an obvious pride that startled and melted him. 'My husband's a total freak. He's a fluent speaker of a language that's had no native speakers for something like two thousand years.'

'Okay, here goes,' Richard said. He cleared his throat and recited a few lines from *Bēowulf.*

Stephen and Eve Slaymaker clapped when he had done.

'You know what,' the senator said, 'I liked that. I like the sound of it. It sounds *strong.* But it's kind of hard to believe it's English. I don't believe I got a single word.'

'I was telling you about a King called Scyld Scefing. Or Shield Sheafson, as some people translate it. I told you how well he'd done for himself, abandoned by his own parents as a child, but still managing to become a great and powerful leader, who smashed the mead-benches of his rivals, terrified their soldiers and forced them to pay him tribute. "Þæt wæs god cyning," I said at the end, which means: *That was a good king!*'

The two of them laughed and clapped again.

'He sounds like one tough guy,' Slaymaker said.

And just like you, Richard thought, realizing now why he'd chosen that passage. *Exactly like you. I could be sitting in front of King Scyld right now.*

Eve asked Holly about her family. Holly told her that her parents were both librarians who'd lived all their lives in a city called Reading, which wasn't far from London. She knew from experience that librarians in a city that no American had ever heard of were not a very promising start for a conversation, so she threw in something else that might be a little more controversial.

'And they were both passionate socialists,' she said with a smile.

The senator took this in for a second or so, his blue eyes fixed on her face.

'That's kind of an exotic animal,' he said. 'So, they believed…?'

'They were the real deal. They believed that all the means of production should be taken over by the government – factories, farms, banks – and the wealth they produced should be shared out according to people's needs.'

'You see, I've never got that,' Slaymaker said. 'I've heard of it, but I've just never got it at all. I guess I can see how it might look kind of fair on paper, but I've never been able to see how anyone might think it would actually work.'

'Why not?' Richard smiled. The conversation had moved to territory where he felt at home.

'Well, because it means stopping people from doing what people naturally do: looking after themselves and their own people, and it means taking away all the incentives to work hard and figure out better ways of doing things. You'd need so many laws and bureaucrats in a system like that, so many cops snooping around to keep people working for the government and to stop them working for themselves. No disrespect to your mom and dad, Holly, I'm sure they were good people, but it kind of seems obvious to me that something like that must end in tyranny, just like it really did back in the day. And then what would be the point? You'd have all those cops and bureaucrats ordering you about, but you still wouldn't get the fairness that you were hoping for in the first place.' He looked at Richard and Holly in turn. 'Am I missing something? Can either of you guys set me straight?'

'There are some pretty tyrannical capitalist societies too, Steve,' Holly pointed out. 'Our own Tyranny here was capitalist. Those tyrants started out as billionaires.'

'Any system will lead to tyranny, won't it,' Richard said, 'if it concentrates power too much in too few hands?'

The senator leant toward him slightly, giving him once again that exceptionally focused attention which Holly had described to him, the kind of concentration most people can summon up only briefly in an emergency.

'In fact,' Richard said, 'I reckon that every society that's ever existed that might very roughly be described as free, or as a democracy, has run on a mixture of the market principle and the collective principle, each one providing some kind of check on the other.'

Eve Slaymaker laughed. 'You better watch this guy, Steve. Sounds like he lines up with Gray Jenny!'

'I do,' Richard said, 'I vote Unity. I'm not going to lie. But my point is that every more or less democratic government is to some degree socialist. I mean, look at your plans, Senator, the ones Holly's helping you with. You want this demographic shift to happen, but you're not leaving it to the market, are you? I mean, the market *would* do it, given time – a shift northwards has been happening for several generations without being government policy – but you reckon that to leave it to the market would be too slow, and create too many losers, and maybe divide our country so much as to break it in two. So you want the federal government to step in, subsidize housing projects up in the north to create new towns, and provide special assistance to move for people who've lost all their money. All of which is fine. But it's collective action, which is essentially the thing Holly's parents are in favor of.'

Slaymaker laughed. 'So what you're saying is, *I'm* a socialist? Well, that's a new one, I must say.'

After they'd eaten, the Slaymakers took Holly and Richard riding, Eve picking out horses for them from the nine or ten in their stables. They headed up the slope across the stream from the ranch, with five big lurcher dogs bounding around them. Holly loved riding – she would unwind at weekends at a local stable whenever she had the time – and she was very confident on a horse, just like the senator. Richard had ridden enough times to know what he was doing, but was nothing like as confident as her, and Eve too was competent, but not really a natural rider. Pretty soon, Holly and the senator were some way out in front, while Richard and Eve followed after.

They didn't talk much. Eve didn't project herself in the way her husband did, and Richard couldn't quite work out who she was exactly, or what they might have in common. Insofar as he had the measure of her at all, she struck him as the type of person he'd normally have nothing to say to. But at one point, they both stopped on a small ridge to admire the view behind them and see how far they'd climbed. As they were about to set off again, they looked up at the other two ahead of them: the senator half-turning in the saddle to call something out to Holly, Holly shouting something back. And right there, of course, was their natural subject of conversation. That was the thing they had in common.

'It's not just a business relationship for him, you know,' Eve said. 'He really *loves* your Holly.'

She glanced at Richard and burst out laughing at the expression on his face. 'Oh, good Lord, not like that, Rick! That's not Steve at all. But you probably know we couldn't have kids. Steve always refused to adopt a child because he didn't think it would be the same, but he would have loved a son or a daughter to share his business with. And I don't know why, but I reckon there's something about your Holly that hits that spot for him. You should hear how he goes on about her: her British accent, how smart she is, the way she stands up to him, the way she can't be bothered with frills and nonsense, just like him.'

The two up ahead had just realized how far behind them Eve and Richard were, and had pulled up their horses side by side to wait, the dogs milling around them, and both of them beaming down at their slower companions.

'I make do with the dogs,' said Eve, 'but you can see for yourself that, even with the dogs, I have to take second place!'

In the car on the way back, Richard thought about teasing Holly about her daddy-substitute, but it seemed unkind, and he was aware that the jealousy behind this impulse might make his words come out more mean and twisted than he'd intended.

'He loved your *Beowulf* recital,' Holly said.

Richard laughed. 'He would have absolutely *thrived* in Beowulf's world.'

'Really? Why?'

'It was the natural element for a guy like him. It wasn't about fairness back then, it wasn't about rights. It was about honor, and courage, and a narrow, rigid loyalty. A good king was a "ring-giver", a man who was generous to those who fought for him. And if that meant smashing up some other king's drinking halls and forcing him to pay tribute, well, there was no shame in that. In fact, quite the opposite: all the shame would be on the other king for not being strong enough to protect his own.'

They passed a big logging camp with huge robot tree-cutting machines and a gang of foreign workers in yellow overalls who were removing rotting timber to make way for a solar farm. There was a blue sky ahead. Behind, big clouds were forming over the Cascades, seemingly out of nothing, as warm air was forced upwards over the peaks.

'I was just thinking about that phrase "ring-giver",' Richard said. 'I can't think of a single society in history that didn't have an inner circle who got given rings and an outer circle who the rings were taken away from. It's almost as if you pretty well *have* to take things from people whose support you don't need in order to pay off the people who keep you in power.'

'Like, for instance, you can take things from people you know as a fact won't vote for you anyway.'

'Exactly. Or do deals with leaders of other countries. Give them weapons so they can take stuff for you from other people.'

'And of course sometimes you can plunder the future,' Holly said.

'Ha! Now that's the easiest of all. Stealing from people who don't yet exist. Living in comfort at their expense. You don't have to face them and they can't fight back.'

They were passing through completely cleared forest now, solar panels stretching away in every direction.

'I can't help thinking,' said Richard, 'that King Scyld would have told Slaymaker he's got it the wrong way round. He wants to give out rings to the very—'

'Yup. We've spotted that. The answer to it is that he's not really taking rings from the northern people and giving them to southern people. He's building a stronger America for everyone, so there'll be more rings all round.'

Richard pulled a comically unconvinced face. Holly laughed and poked him in the ribs.

'You can cut that out, *compañero*. We are *way* out in front in the polls.'

CHAPTER 22

Rosine Dubois

The trailer park was huge. Rows and rows of identical alumi-num trailers reflecting the big empty sky, with nothing to tell them apart except the numbers. It was the most miserable place I'd ever seen, but we were so relieved to be there that all four of us cried.

We soon found out that even within the park people were divid-ed. Two-thirds or more of the folk there came from the dustbowl, and a third were storm trash like us from the east coast and the south – and I'm saying 'storm trash' because that's what the dust-bowl people called us. A lot of them had been farmers, people with their own land, and they thought of us as lazy bums who'd never done anything at all. 'Why are you guys even up here?' one dustie kid taunted our boys in school. 'Weren't there any more stores left down there for your dad to rob?'

Me and Herb tried to find work. The government people occa-sionally put a few days our way, stacking shelves, maybe, or making beds in a motel, but we spent many hours just sitting in our trailer and watching the broadscreen. Herb would watch it for hours on end. There were trashy shows on there in the daytime that made me almost throw up, I was so bored of them, but he just sat there and watched them anyway.

I tried to make friends among the people round us. All day, you could hear someone somewhere screaming at their kids to give them some peace, so two or three of us decided to start a little crèche that would meet round one of our trailers. The woman from the trailer next to ours got involved. She and her husband were farmers from California, older people in their late sixties, Tracey and Pete Suarez. The two of them had rigged up a little homemade polytunnel next to their trailer, and had planted winter vegetables and flowers in old cans. They'd been pretty frosty with us at first, but Tracey had a kind face and I persevered with her. When she finally figured out we weren't like she imagined storm trash to be, she loosened up and we became friends. I told Herb to work on Pete too.

'I think he's a good man,' I said. 'I know he seems a bit unfriend-ly, but I think he's like you really. He's kind of sad, and he's finding it hard to admit to himself that a trailer park in Montana is where he's ended up.'

But Herb just shrugged and carried on watching some show about fat guys racing giant trucks.

A bunch of bored kids cut the polytunnel to shreds with knives while Pete and Tracey were having a nap. They upended the cans and chucked the dirt at the sides of the trailers all around. Pete came out with a gun and roared at them but when the kids had run off laughing, he kind of slumped down into a camping chair that he'd put out there to watch his plants grow, covered his face with his hands and wept.

'We had a beautiful farm, Rosine,' Tracey told me. She'd tried to comfort her husband but he'd shaken her away angrily. 'We worked hard. We grew potatoes and peppers and tomatoes and corn. We raised our own chickens and pigs. We even had a guy working for us for a while. We were proud, and our families were proud of us, because we were the first generation, on his side or mine, to own our land.'

Hearing Pete shouting, Herb had come out too, tearing himself away from some hub show where he'd parked his brain, about plastic surgery gone wrong, or the world's ugliest women.

'What happened with your farm?' he asked Pete.

'Water prices,' Pete said. 'Our wells dried up. Me and Tracey spent tens of thousands of bucks buying this damn thing and that damn thing to cut down our consumption, but in the end we just couldn't make it work.'

'We'd built it all ourselves,' Tracey said. 'Our fences, our tunnels, our barn, our house even.'

'The bank took it,' said Pete. 'Not that it'll do them any good. There are people giving up their farms every day in that part of California. The land's worth nothing at all.'

There wasn't much to say to that. You could look around all you liked at the rows of identical trailers under that great lonely prairie sky and you wouldn't find any source of comfort.

'One thing I'm hoping for,' Herb said, 'and that's that Senator Slaymaker gets in. He's the only one that's really trying to help folk like us.'

CHAPTER 23

Holly met Mariana in Seattle to do some Christmas shopping. They had lunch together, they found some nice things to buy, and managed quite successfully to edge around Holly's job without getting into a fight. Now, chatting and laughing, they were walking back through the pretty colored lights to where they'd left the car, and avoiding eye contact, without even thinking about it, with the dozens of barreduras who were begging insistently in the busy streets. You screened them out just as you screened out your own painful memories. There would otherwise be no happiness at all.

Next to the car park at the edge of the pedestrian area, a little Victorian church squatted incongruously between two tall office blocks and outside it was a nativity scene set on a dais: a little stable lit up from inside, and plaster figurines the size of human fingers.

'You'd think we'd have given up those fairy tales in the twenty-second century, wouldn't you?' said Mariana.

Holly shook her head and laughed as she stopped to look. 'No chance, Mariana. No chance. Stories are what we live by!'

It was actually rather a fine nativity, it seemed to her, cleverly lit so as to draw the eye inwards to the baby at the center of it all, with the little people and animals ranged around him.

'Very pretty,' acknowledged Mariana. 'If only we weren't expected to believe it was real. That just feels, I don't know, *embarrassing* at this point in history.'

Holly squatted down so the tableau was at head height, and tried to imagine that she was there herself inside the miniature stable.

'Well, what do people like us believe in?' she said, standing up again, but still facing the tableau.

'Uh…reason, I guess. And fairness.'

'I'd say so too. And we believe that we're reasonable and fair, don't we? We believe that if only the world would come to its senses and become as reasonable and fair as us, then everything would be okay.'

Mariana considered this for a couple of seconds. 'I think I do believe that, yes. Don't you?'

'That belief of ours looks a bit threadbare now, don't you think? We're running out of time, and the world's as bad as it ever was.'

'Well, maybe,' she laughed. 'But what's that got to do with this nativity?'

'It just struck me: suppose our belief is just as unreal as all the others. Suppose humans *can't* really get any better? I mean, we're the product of millions of years of evolution, yes? The ones who weren't so good at looking after themselves were winnowed out, the ones who were best at it survived. With that kind of lineage, it's asking a lot of us to really care that much about anyone other than ourselves. And yet, we do have reason, and with our reason we are able to form ideas like fairness, and freedom and justice. We can see them, we can see that they're something good, but maybe they're beyond our reach? Like we're two-dimensional beings and they exist out there in 3D space.'

She shrugged and half-smiled, acknowledging that the thought wasn't characteristic of her, and that Mariana shouldn't feel obliged to take it any further. They started to walk again.

'How do you know they're beyond our reach?' asked Mariana.

'Well, I talk to people a lot these days on the whisperstream, not just people like us but people from every demographic across America, and that's how it seems to me. Everyone lays *claim* to virtue. Everyone clothes themselves in ideas like fairness or justice or freedom, but they do so in their own interests, to make themselves feel entitled, or virtuous, or more virtuous than others. It's all on the surface, like painting a cross on your shield before you sack Jerusalem. But underneath, everyone still plays the same old animal game.'

'There's always that element in us, I guess.'

'In fact, even our precious reason is pretty selective about what it chooses to take into account. It always comes out in our favor, doesn't it? It always turns out that we delicados and our needs are really really important, along with whatever oppressed groups we are currently identifying with. It doesn't take much notice of less appealing folk like Henry McKenzie in Spokane, Washington.'

'Who's Henry McKenzie?'

'Exactly! Who is he, and who gives a shit?'

Mariana glanced sideways at Holly. She'd never seen her in quite this mood.

'And truthfully,' Holly said, 'when it comes to the reality of those shining things out there in the third dimension – their real essence, I mean, as opposed to their use as badges of virtue – we can't really do more than glimpse them far off in the distance.'

'Are you...are you having second thoughts about...you know... the work you're doing for...?'

'No, I'm bloody not,' snapped Holly. 'That's not what this is about at all.'

And then she laughed and took Mariana's hand.

'Sorry. Ignore me. I'm not sure what I mean myself. I guess just for a moment it made sense to me, that nativity story, the idea of someone from that other dimension being born into the 2D world, someone capable of forgiving us for our inability to be what we know we ought to be.'

'You're not getting religious on us, are you, Holly? Going over to the Freedom Party is kind of challenging enough.'

'Oh no, not at all. It just struck me what a powerful story that is. How it reaches right in there and addresses a deep core need. And I like powerful stories.'

She gave a hundred-dollar bill to a startled farmer from New Mexico and then they went into a shop to buy shoes.

By that time, the competition for the Freedom Party candidacy had resolved into a three-way race.

Lucy Montello, a former governor of Montana, was a sharp-faced, bitter woman whose core support was among middle-class northerners. She focused a lot of her campaigning on the so-called 'Mexican problem', a tried and tested gambit, though it always carried the risk of alienating the 40 percent of Americans who defined themselves as Latino. Montello maintained that there were as many as thirty million illegal Mexican immigrants in the US and that, in spite of the wall and the fence and the mine-field, illegal migrants from Mexico were still entering the US at the rate of twenty thousand a month. Her solution to the problem of weather-related homelessness in the southern half of the country was to find and remove illegal immigrants, thereby freeing accommodation for the use of American citizens: 'Let's not ask hard-working Americans in the north to make yet more sacrifices for a problem that isn't of their making,' she said. 'And let's not tell hard-working people in the south that they have to move away from their own communities to make room for Mexicans.'

Under her presidency, she said, illegal migrants would face not just deportation but long prison sentences with hard labor, such as were now being used in several European countries. (In Britain, she pointed out, highly profitable prison factories staffed by interned immigrants had become a key component of the economy.) They could replace those indentured workers in their yellow jumpsuits, now brought in by licensed contractors to perform time-limited tasks where there were local labor shortages. And *these* foreign workers wouldn't need to be paid anything at all.

Soames Frinton was a multi-billionaire engineer who'd founded the Electric Highway Corporation, the company that developed and rolled out the so-called dodgem lanes where cars could charge up on the move. He believed that states had the right to control their own frontiers – 'If any state is struggling to deliver to its own citizens,' he said, 'it should be entitled to close the door until better times come round again' – and he was strongly opposed to any federal government support for barreduras wishing to move from their own states. If people wanted to move away from storm- or drought-ravaged areas to states that had the capacity to receive them, then they must do so themselves, just as people had moved back and forth across America over the centuries: 'My own great-grandfather moved with his family from Chicago down to Atlanta, and then Houston, and then LA. My grandfather and grandmother moved from LA up to Portland, Oregon. My father moved from Oregon to New York City. My wife and I started our family in Seattle, spent two years in Boston, and right now we're based in the fine city of Juneau, Alaska. And guess what, people, we made all those moves just fine without any help from the federal government.'

Of course, this approach too carried risks. It might please voters in the north, but many in the south would be angered by its callousness. How could the movements of a wealthy family be compared to an exodus from abandoned homes? But Frinton and Montello both knew that, when it came to the party convention, strong support from northern states could be enough to win the Freedom Party nomination.

'Who's going to pay for these new houses Senator Slaymaker proposes to build?' asked Lucy Montello. 'Who's going to fund his scheme to help southerners move north? Well, what do you know? It's going to be the good old northern taxpayer as usual. The hard-working heroes who slog their guts out for this country, and then find they've got to pay for everything as well.'

'If you want to pay out your own money,' said Soames Frinton, 'to build a housing estate for barreduras next to your home, which will spoil your view, reduce the value of your property, increase the local crime rate and place your job at risk, well then, be my guest, go out and vote for Slaymaker.'

As the New Year began, almost all Holly's time was spent unpicking Montello's and Frinton's stories. Over and over, she and the team pushed out images of strong fortresses, deeply laid foundations, mighty powerhouses. Over and over they told stories about an America regrouped, retooled, rejuvenated so as to be able to face the challenges ahead. Over and over they stamped on any suggestion that the barreduras would be helped out of kindness, or pity, or altruism, insisting that Slaymaker's entire program was about the needs of America as a whole.

And it seemed to be working. Slaymaker, with his folksy charm, was seen as more trustworthy than Montello and Frinton, in spite of his controversial program, and was holding his own in the polls.

'I have to hand it to you, Holly,' Jed admitted, over a working lunch in the kitchen of Slaymaker's Seattle offices. 'I never really thought you'd pull this off.'

'Well, you helped, Jed. Until I met you, I might have made the mistake of appealing to people's kindness. You showed me just how little kindness can be worth.'

Jed laughed easily, showing his long white teeth. He enjoyed digs like these. In fact, Holly had an uneasy feeling that he read them as a form of flirtation. 'You really aren't one of us, are you, Holly? That Native American broach, those comfortable clothes, that bag that cost no more than two thousand dollars. There's an unmistakable delicado glow coming off of you, no matter how you try to hide it.'

It was one thing for Holly to criticize her own tribe, but another for the likes of Jed to do so. 'I looked up "delicado" once,' she said. 'It means subtle, refined, sensitive, polite. I can live with that.'

'It was a term of abuse back in the days of the Tyranny,' Jed said. 'Like "snowflake" or "bleeding heart".'

'I think we delicados should be proud that the tyrants felt the need to abuse us.'

'The tyrants didn't make up the word, though. They just deployed it. They figured out that ordinary folk were sick of being told off for not being generous enough by people who were way better off than themselves. Don't forget, our delicados aren't the first privileged class to flatter themselves that they're kinder and gentler than their social inferiors. Think about the word "gentle-folk" and what it means.'

'You really despise gentleness, don't you? Didn't your mum and dad love you enough, or what?'

'Didn't my mum and dad love me? Wonderful! The classic move of the delicado trying to explain why other people don't see the world as they do!' He grinned at her. This was all play to him, play if not actual flirtation. 'Make other people's views into pathology! That way you can have the satisfaction of being right *and* being magnanimous! I just happen to admire strength and self-reliance, okay? My own impression is that pretty much all so-called kind-ness, if not all, is ultimately self-serving. So I figure if we're going to be self-serving, then why not just be so openly, rather than wrapping it up in sugary fluff.'

She noticed his defensiveness, the shining-eyed defiance, as he spoke words very similar to ones she'd used herself with Richard and her friends.

Later that day, she took some time out to buy a few things, and was making her way down Broad Street back to the office. The sun was bright and low and the air sharp, with long thin strands of cirrus streaking the cold blue above her. She passed some graffiti on a brick wall:

NO MORE SLASH AND BURN

It was the slogan of the World Salvationist Society, the violent faction who wanted to stop human expansionism and restore equilibrium with the rest of nature. But standing right in front of it was the representative of another creed entirely. A Tribulationist preacher with bushy white eyebrows was telling whoever would listen that the floods on the east coast and the droughts in the south-west were God's punishment for the sin of sodomy.

'They can run from their wrecked homes,' he bellowed. 'They run like naughty children from the parent who comes to reprimand them, but they can't hide from the wrath of God.'

Ping! A message arrived in her cristal. 'We're absolutely devastated,' her mother said. 'Me and your father are absolutely devastated. We just can't believe that you're working for a party that both of us, and our parents, and all our friends, have struggled against all our lives. Antonia thinks you must be punishing us for something.'

Holly thought at first it meant nothing to her. She felt oddly indifferent. The reaction was so predictable, after all, that it barely constituted new information. Richard would probably even argue that she'd deliberately provoked it. Of *course* her mother would refuse to accept that Holly could have made a choice that was different to her own. Of *course* she'd have spoken to her psychotherapist friend Antonia.

Holly remembered Antonia well from her teenage years, that slow, quiet presence, those lingering soft brown eyes. Many times Holly had slouched in from somewhere to find her sitting with her mother at the kitchen table. Antonia would always greet her warmly, her smiling eyes searching Holly's surly face with loving concern, and Holly would know, she'd just know, that the two of them had been discussing her moods, her outbursts of temper, her hostility. Her mother had to believe some kind of psychological disturbance was the explanation for Holly disagreeing with her. She always had done.

But why fret about it? That was just the way her mother was. She'd never change and Holly was grown up now, and a long way away.

But then, in spite of what she'd just told herself, anger came welling up. No doubt, if she'd been present, Antonia would have nodded wisely as she saw the rage break from cover. 'Let it out,' she'd have advised, 'let it out, Holly darling.' Tears came pricking into Holly's eyes, right there in the winter sunshine, and she dashed them furiously away. She'd *tried* to explain her decision to her mother. She'd tried to show that she actually *hadn't* discarded everything she and her dad believed in. But they hadn't even tried to understand. They hadn't engaged in any way with what she'd said.

To the north of the pier, there was a sort of park between the city's flood defenses and the sea, which had become a meeting place for jobless barreduras from the desert states (the storm people had their own gathering place in Denny Park). There were scores of them down there, rugged, suntanned men and women, wrapped in coats, scarves and sometimes blankets, standing stamping their feet, or sitting on the benches, filling in time before the next job interview, the next appointment with the welfare department, or perhaps just waiting until the sun went down, and it was time to go back to their trailers, their rented tenements, their crumbling families. Seattle residents, some on bicycles, some on foot, passed through them on a narrow pathway, mostly looking straight ahead so as to avoid meeting the eyes of these troubling fellow Americans. It was as if the fact of their losing their homes had made these people in some way dangerous and unclean.

Holly walked a little way along the path, took a photo, sent it to her mother. Then she turned and headed back the other way, where she'd been going. Damn it, her parents had taken way too much of her life already, way too much of her energy. She was not going to spend any more time on this.

CHAPTER 24

As Richard had feared, Holly was away a lot, in a place that Richard had no feeling for and didn't want her to be. But they still worked hard at staying together. One weekend in February, when Holly had been working even longer hours than usual, the two of them drove north across the border to spend an evening with their friends Ruby and Ossia.

They took the coastal highway, entering Canada at the busy Peace Arch crossing. There was no actual barrier there, but computers logged more than thirty identifiers from the chassis number of their car to the irises of their eyes so as to be able to track them down if they overstayed the thirty days allowed for visa-free visits.

Sergio and Mariana were already there when they arrived at Ruby and Ossia's house: a low long structure of wood and glass at the top of a ridge overlooking the Salish Sea. It was the first time the six of them had come together since Slaymaker announced his presidential bid.

'*Jesucristo*, darling,' Ruby whispered in Holly's ear as she took her in her strong arms. 'You sure know how to challenge us.'

Then she took Holly's hand and led her on a tour of the house, while Richard was drawn into conversation with the other three.

Holly admired the huge master bedroom, the cave-like bathroom, the spacious guest bedrooms where the four visitors would spend the night.

'Oh, I love this little hallway,' Holly said. 'It's almost like you're outside with these windows on either side but it's got that indoor cosiness at the same time.'

Last time the six of them had met together, Holly had spoken about the beautiful houses all six of them lived in, and how these demonstrated the limits of their professed concern for humanity. Neither Holly nor Ruby mentioned that now, but as they walked hand in hand round this, the newest and most luxurious to date of the three couples' homes, both of them remembered it. It hung there between them, unspoken. There could be no doubt that the materials, the land, the labor that went into this house represented a share of the Earth's wealth that the vast majority of North Americans could never hope to possess, never mind people in the rest of the world. The planet simply couldn't provide such luxury for everyone. Holly would have had to have been the worst kind of killjoy to mention this – even her priggish parents wouldn't have done so – but she and Ruby both knew it, and they both knew that the other was aware of it right now. They was even the hint of an unspoken bargain in the air between them: *I won't mention your membership of a wealthy elite, if you don't give me a hard time for working on Slaymaker's presidential campaign.*

'Ah, and this is the best bit,' Ruby announced, letting go of Holly's hand to throw open a pair of doors.

'Your studio! Oh, it's wonderful, Ruby! So much space! And all that glass. It must be absolutely *full* of light in the daytime.'

'It *is* wonderful, Holly. Not just the studio, but the whole house. And just being here in Canada too, being here and knowing we can stay for good, away from all the craziness in the US. It's just kind of...unlocked me, you know? Having a home. Standing in front of a canvas and knowing that I'm exactly where I belong. I'm doing my best work ever just now. Everything just flows.'

'That's lovely, Ruby,' said Holly, hugging her big bear-like friend. 'That's really great.'

Art had redeemed luxury, like Christ washing away the sins of the world. This too Holly noticed, but she sensed that for Ruby there was nothing to *be* noticed. The story worked for her, and that was that, just as Slaymaker's story worked for him, the one about hard work and self-reliance and standing up for America.

And she was truly happy for both of them. Everyone needed those stories and they were hard to find. Often when you looked for meaning it was like grabbing at empty air. Or so it seemed to her. But perhaps that was the price you paid for being a storyteller.

Ossia, beautiful and brittle as glass, had cooked narrow slices of three different kinds of fish in three different ways, and served them with pale blue nasturtium flowers and cirrus-like streaks of pink and yellow sauces. The six of them ate in a dining room with a ceiling the height of a two-storey house. On one side a huge window looked out over the water, the twinkling lights of settlements out on Vancouver Island, the last faint streaks of glowing cloud. On the other hung one of Ruby's enormous paintings: its rich oranges and reds and browns layered so thickly as to be almost sculptural.

The subject of Holly's boss couldn't be avoided any longer and it was raised by Sergio, whose views were delicado, but whose manners were not especially delicate.

'So what in hell are you playing at, Holly? Not just working for Slaymaker but being part of his campaign team. I mean, *Jesucristo*, have you seen what he said yesterday about the death penalty?'

Oddly, Holly hadn't, and that bothered her. She insulated herself to some extent from Slaymaker's pronouncements on topics unconnected with her own brief, but she knew she ought to keep up with them in a general way, so as to make sure everything connected together.

Never mind. That was something to think about later.

'Actually, my job is just the same as it was last time we met,' she told Sergio. 'Slaymaker knows I've always voted Unity. The whole team tease me for being a *delicado*. And all of them know I won't agree with them about the penal system, or taxes, or foreign policy, and probably a whole load of other stuff. But I'm there to get the message out to America about the Reconfigure program, which I happen to believe in myself.'

She took a sip from her glass of white wine, her eyes bright as she looked straight at Sergio. 'You know, there are whole cities down in Arizona and New Mexico that are completely empty – just crumbling back into the desert – because it's not economic to supply them with water. There are coastal towns and neighborhoods up and down the country – about fifteen million homes in all – which have been abandoned to the sea. Walk the streets of Seattle right now and you can see the people from all over America who've lost their homes and their livelihoods as a result of these catastrophes. Mariana and I saw them when we were shopping before Christmas. Gray Jenny throws money at them. Montello blames Mexico. Frinton wants them shut out of the north. But only Slaymaker has a real vision. I'm not ashamed of backing him. You should too.'

She could feel her friends glancing at one another. Sergio opened his mouth to speak, but Holly hadn't finished. 'It's actually an incredibly hard sell we're attempting here,' she said. 'We're basically asking Slaymaker's core supporters to pay more taxes *and* put up with new towns and neighborhoods more or less in their own back yards. Who would have thought we'd pull that off, eh? But we're managing it somehow, with a *lot* of hard work – more work than you'd believe. And I don't mean to be rude, Sergio, I really don't, but what have you been working on lately? What's your contribution to fixing this problem?'

Holly was pleased with herself. Her palms weren't sweating, her pulse rate was steady. She'd managed to keep her tone level and friendly, rather than heated or defensive or self-righteous as it could so easily have become. And Sergio laughed and backed down.

'Touché,' he said, raising both hands in surrender. 'You've got me. Right now I'm working on personality simulation in jeenees. Enough said.'

And they all laughed and moved onto other things.

'It's good for you, isn't it?' Richard said, as they climbed between the smooth sheets in one of Ruby and Ossia's spacious guest rooms. 'This job is really good for you.'

'It is,' Holly said. 'When we arrived, Ruby told me how this beautiful house had set her free, and it was lovely to hear. Really lovely. She can have all the fancy houses she likes as far as I'm concerned, as long as it makes her feel like that. All the fancy houses in the world. And, yes, you're right, what her house has done for her is *exactly* what working for Slaymaker has done for me. I really,

really love it, Rick. So challenging! So many problems! So many irreconcilable things and awkward people that somehow have to be taken into account! It's like this incredible many-layered game. It's wonderful. I really do feel incredibly alive!'

Richard laughed and kissed her.

'I'm grateful to you, Rick,' she said. 'I know this is hard for you on many levels, but I do need to do it, and you've been so great in understanding that.'

They cuddled up together, Richard raising himself on one elbow so he could look down at a face and gently stroke her breasts with his free hand. She pulled his face toward her and kissed him again.

'This was what human brains were made for,' Holly said. 'Or my brain anyway. Not the construction of some…some great flawless static utopia like my parents dreamed of, not the discovery of some final truth, but picking a team – any halfway decent team will do – and then using your wits and your skills, as best you can, to make your team the best.'

'Hmmm. I used to wonder about teams sometimes when I was a kid. The teacher divides the class up into two groups with different color armbands, and the next thing you know you are really desperate for the blue armbands to win and the yellow armbands to be defeated, even though the teacher could just as well have divided you up in another way. I used to wonder how come.'

'Because it's fun, Rick. That's all you needed to know.'

'Maybe you're right. It *was* fun, I agree.'

'Speaking of games, I was watching someone playing a fantasy game on their cristal the other day. You know the ones? Where you have to colonize a planet or something, or build a city? You see people playing them all the time, on their cristals or sometimes in immersion goggles. And it suddenly struck me that those games are a kind of porn. They connect with a real human need – a need to make things happen, a need to impose shape on the world – but they don't really satisfy it, because when the game is over, you know you've changed nothing at all. And I thought to myself, Well, if that's the porn, what I'm doing is the real warm living sex. I was so pleased I almost laughed out loud.'

Richard smiled. 'And then of course there's *actual* sex.'

She pulled him toward her again. 'Ah well, that's another whole story. That feels fantastic too just now. It's like I'm right out at the edge of myself – you know? – right here beneath my skin.'

They'd always been lucky in that way. They'd been able to rely on sex as a healing thing, a kind of alchemy that drew the energy from the anger and hostility that built up between them and used it to bind them together again. It varied over time, of course, but it had never seriously failed them.

And a thing like that, an ancient natural force that has remained stable and reliable for years: you assume it will carrying on working in the same way for ever.

'Any urgent messages?' Holly asked her jeenee wordlessly when she and Richard were finally ready for sleep.

'There is one from Slaymaker,' the jeenee answered in her ear.

It had no emotions in the human sense. Where humans have desire, love, pity, hunger, fear, ambition, all in competition with one another, the jeenee inside her cristal had only one single driver: the imperative to serve its owner. But it could recognize emotions with great accuracy, knew which were desirable and which were not, and was able to anticipate the emotion that any given piece of news was likely to evoke. So now it used the exact tone that is used by human bearers of bad news, as if speaking the words but trying to suck them back at the same time.

'Apparently, we're suddenly crashing in the polls. There's a team meeting at his ranch tomorrow.'

CHAPTER 25

Johnson Fleet

Someone screwed up. They were supposed to have instruments up there measuring the ice and rain and all of that. They'd got satellites and drones and everything. They should have spotted what was building up. In fact, it was a crime they didn't, just like it'd be a crime if I ran over a kid when I was driving on manual and not paying attention. You don't fuck with people's lives like that.

Anyway, whoever's fault it was, we had a flash flood, not down the river where all the flood defenses had been built, but down that little side stream next to my garage. I'd never really thought where that stream came from, but it turned out it was the overflow from a lake up in the mountains, held in place by a kind of natural dam of dirt and stones. And one night the dam broke. It had been raining a lot up there in the spring, raining when in the past there would still have been snow, and the snow and ice on the mountaintops had melted quicker than usual too. We'd had heavy rain all through the night. Me and Karla could hear it beating on the roof as we went to sleep, gurgling down the drains in the street, and dripping and trickling from the trees, and when we woke up we could still hear it just the same, dripping and trickling as strong as ever. We didn't think much of it at first, other than, you know, 'Damn, we are going to get *wet* when we get out of our cars at work,' and Jade going, 'Think you've got problems, Pa! I've gotta wait outside for the bus!' Then we heard the news on the radio: floods in Dickensville, Idaho. Jesus! Our town! But even then we weren't *too* worried because our house was fine, and so were the houses all round us. We knew we were way up above the river. Jade headed out for the bus as usual, Karla drove off to her salon, and I set out to the garage.

But there *was* no garage. That dam of dirt in the mountains had broken, and the entire lake behind it had come down that little stream all at once, carrying trees and tons of mud and boulders the size of cars. There was a great big gash gouged out of the hillside, and everything that had stood there had pretty much gone completely. And that included my garage. The buildings, the robots, the vehicles they'd been working on: it had all been washed down into the river. I could just see the outline of the inspection pit, but it was full of mud and stones, and all that was left of the hydraulic jack was a few stumps of twisted metal.

I guess I was in shock for a while. I just stood there staring as I tried to get it through my head. The rain was still falling, but I didn't notice it. And the stream was still running down the middle of that great gouged-out gash, back to its ordinary size again, like it had nothing to do with what had happened.

Then Karla called.

'Hey, Jon honey, how are you doing? Me and Jade have both had to go home again, because the whole lower town is—'

'There's no garage,' I said.

'What? You mean it's flooded too? I'd have thought—'

'No, I mean it's gone.'

·

I got in my car but I couldn't start it. I literally couldn't figure out what I had to do to make it go. Karla came and fetched me, took me home, made me strip off my drenched clothes and have a shower to get warm again. Then she called the insurance company and waited for thirty minutes in a queue.

'Apparently, there's an exemption for "unprecedented weather events",' she told me eventually, turning from the phone. 'We're not covered for this kind of thing at all.'

I snatched the phone from her. 'What the fuck's the *point* of insurance!' I yelled into it. 'What the fuck's the point if, when the bad thing happens, you're going to say it wasn't fucking included!'

'Honey, there's no—' Karla tried to interrupt, but I wouldn't have it.

'I'm not fucking accepting this. I don't care what it says in the fucking small print. The whole fucking point of insurance is—'

Karla pulled the phone away from me. 'Honey, it's just an AI. There's no point yelling at it. There's nobody there to hear you.'

We went to a lawyer, who told us the insurance company was right and there was nothing we could do. That advice cost us $400. Then we went to the bank to ask about a loan to rebuild the garage from scratch.

'But you're already borrowing up to the max,' the woman told us. 'And your previous loans were based on both of you having your own businesses up and running.'

'My business is fine,' said Karla, 'and you can see for yourself that Johnson has been doing well. Soon as he's got a garage set up again, he'll be able to pick up right where he left off.'

'I'm so sorry, but you were only just managing to pay off your previous loan, and now you're asking to double it. It just won't work. I wish I could help, I really do, but we're a business too, and we can't take that kind of risk. If you want to talk about rescheduling the previous loan, or switching to interest-only for a while, we can certainly talk about it.'

'How are we going to get out of this if I can't start up my business again?' I asked.

'I'm sorry, but this just isn't the kind of thing our bank can take on. I believe the federal government has agencies that can help with things like this.'

One weird thing on that first day, when we were all kind of frozen and didn't know what to do next or where to turn: I was sitting in my armchair with my cristal, flicking through the whisperstream for something to do, when a post came up from Cynical Sam.

'Floods in Idaho, I see! Anyone care to bet how long before we hear the usual whining voices asking for the government to bail them out?'

A few hours later he changed his mind.

'Hey, I'm so sorry about what I said there about Idaho. Seems folk are getting me wrong, and I've upset a lot of good people. I didn't mean that people in Idaho were whiners. I meant I knew they *wouldn't* whine, unlike some of those folks we've grown used to down in the southwest and over on the so-called Storm Coast.'

But that hadn't been what he said, had it? There was no way you could read that first message like that. What the fuck was going on? It came out in the end that so-called Cynical Sam wasn't a real person at all. He was just some kind of AI. All this time, I'd been getting my opinions from some damn machine. I guess it was then that me and Karla started to listen to Senator Slaymaker again, and think about what he was trying to say.

CHAPTER 26

Everyone was talking about it on their cristals as they converged on the Slaymaker ranch. Zara Gluck, the technology lead, thought there was a possibility that there'd been some kind of attack on the integrity of the Pollcloud system to give the Slaymaker team an inflated estimate of the popularity of their flagship policy and lead them down a path they wouldn't be able to go back on, like an army that's been led into an ambush. It had happened before in other countries, Zara pointed out. The American Pollcloud was heavily protected against the risk of AIs pretending to be human participants, but any such protection, however smart, was going to be penetrated sooner or later by an even smarter attack.

Others were skeptical about this scenario. Wasn't it more likely that Reconfigure America had flown for a while on good presentation, but now the bald facts of its huge cost and enormous implications for northern voters were finally becoming uppermost in people's minds? No one pointed the finger at Holly – or no one did in the conversations she had access to – but of course the entire campaign team was well aware that this policy had been Holly's special baby.

'I bet they're crowing over this,' she told Richard as they drove back across the border after a largely sleepless night. 'They're all jealous of me because they know I'm Steve's favorite, and this is their chance finally to get rid of me.'

'But you warned him from the off that this was going to be a hard sell.'

'They need someone to blame, someone other than themselves. And I'm the perfect target.'

'But not Slaymaker, right? I've always had the impression that he—'

'I've let him down, Rick.'

'But if he asked you to do something that was impossible, then surely—'

'I should have been more careful with those polls.'

'You're not the tech person in the team.'

'I let myself get carried away. I should have known it was all too easy.'

She hated to cry and very rarely did, but she was fighting tears.

So then there she was in front of the fire in Slaymaker's ranch. She felt like a character in a fairy tale whose seven-league boots had suddenly been taken away. She was surrounded by the ogres she'd thought she could easily outrun and now they were closing in. They'd never liked her. They knew she wasn't one of them. They were jealous of her closeness to the Mountain King. There were only a few seconds left before they laid their hands on her.

'I think we've been missing something,' she said. 'I think there's a really simple solution here that's been staring us in the face.'

The map on the wall had given her the idea: that long straight border that Ruby called the Medicine Line, though Holly had never got round to asking why. Looking at it reminded her of something Jenny Williams had said after Slaymaker's 'bullock wagon' speech: If everyone moved up north, she'd asked, where were they going to go next? And it made her think about Ruby, who'd spent all those hours trying to persuade immigration AIs that she'd be of benefit to the Canadian economy.

'Canada,' she said.

There was an incredulous silence.

'Invade Canada?' cackled Jed. 'Hey! Good idea, Holly! *Everyone* loves a war!'

They all laughed rather too loudly at that, as embarrassed people do when laughter is offered as a way out.

'No, of course not,' she said shortly. 'But we should demand that Canada take more people in. I've no idea how many they take at the moment, but I do know it's very hard to get an extended visa, let alone one of those red passes.'

'Millions of Americans go there anyway,' Pete Fukayama pointed out. 'It's hardly the same as us and Mexico. It's not like there's a wall or anything.'

'But you can't get a decent job without a visa, or buy a house, or even rent an apartment. And if you overstay, sooner or later the cops track you down, and you end up paying a big fine and being sent back south.'

Ann Sellick rolled her eyes upwards in disbelief. 'Why are we even discussing this? What the *fuck* has this got to do with—'

'Human beings look after themselves first, right?' Holly said. 'They look after themselves and their families. Well, that's basically your party's philosophy, isn't it? People won't really make sacrifices for the country as a whole unless they can see some kind of external threat. We've been trying to get the message over that there *is* a threat to them from the changing weather, because it's endangering the integrity of the country as a whole. That has the advantage of being true, and we've done pretty well with it thus far, but the trouble has always been that it's way too abstract. In the end people's attention has been drawn back to more concrete, immediate things, like having to pay more taxes, or having barreduras with strange accents moving in around them and spoiling their view. What we've always lacked is some tangible external human opponent to bring us together.'

'But Canada?' snorted Quentin Fox. 'Come *on*, Holly. Who hates Canada, for Christ's sake? Who hates Canadians? What is there to hate?'

'Look how big Canada is!' Holly said. That old-fashioned Mercator map made Canada look far bigger than it really was, but there was no need to point that out. 'They have all that land but only – what? – 10 percent of our population. We're having to deal with water shortages and storms and floods that are making many tens of millions of homes uninhabitable, but, apart from some coastal flooding and local challenges, they just aren't having problems on the same scale. In fact, some of their territory is even getting *more* hospitable than it used to be.'

'I'm sorry, Holly,' Slaymaker said, 'I guess I'm being slow, but I'm just not getting how we're going to make use of this.'

'Northerners don't like the idea of being the dumping ground for displaced people from the south. They figure they've already got problems of their own – we get floods right here in Washington, after all, and dying forests, and fires – and they can see things getting worse, and yet we're asking them to be a refuge for the rest of the country. So what I'm suggesting is that we demand Canada take its share of southerners. Like I say, I don't know how many Americans they let in each year these days but—'

Zara, her fellow Brit, had got her jeenee to look it up. 'They give permanent resident status to twenty thousand Americans a year.'

'Well, there you are!' Holly said. 'It's nothing. Yes, we can move people up to the north of the US, but there needs to be somewhere to go after that, and there needs to be some way of sharing the burden more widely. So a major part of your platform, Steve, has to be that some of our barreduras be allowed to settle up there across the border. Not twenty thousand a year but a million a year, or two million, or – I don't know – maybe even a completely open border. You see what I mean? That's something that *all* Americans can get behind. And when you think about those Canadians with all that beautiful space and far fewer weather problems than we've got, well, it's a bunch of people right there we can easily all feel pissed with.'

Sue Cortez snorted. 'Come on, guys, we're just wasting time. I mean, how in hell can we demand they open their border to *our* displaced people when we've built a two-thousand-mile wall *and* a minefield *and* a fence *and* a specially designed fleet of drig gunships, to keep out displaced Mexicans?'

'But can't you see that's not an inconsistency at all?' Holly said. She had her seven-league boots back. Her brain was working at twice the speed of everyone else's. She was bounding along at a hundred miles an hour. 'We don't let homeless Mexicans in for the simple reason that so many of our own people are already homeless. Probably Canada should take in Mexicans, I don't know, but we certainly shouldn't.'

Jed nodded slowly, beginning to smile. 'You know what, Holly? I'm liking this. We used to be a destination country for migration, like northern Europe or Russia or Argentina, but what you're saying here is that now we're a source country, like China or Mexico. We just haven't quite faced that yet.'

'Well, we're *half* a source country and half a destination country. America has become two countries with quite different needs, meaning it's hard to get the support of both. But Canada is another country again, and if both parts of the US can agree that Canada should do more, it will allow us to win support on *both* sides of that line. Frinton and Montello have basically given up on the southern half of the country so as to get as much backing as possible in the north, but if we can offer something that north *and* south can get behind, we're going to beat them easily. After all, the line is moving north all the time, much more quickly lately than the weather scientists predicted even a few years ago. The hurricanes are hitting the coast higher up each year, the desert's spreading northwards at – what's that figure? – fifteen miles a year, and we don't know when, or if, the weather will stabilize again. So northerners feel vulnerable too.'

Slaymaker looked round at the people in the room, a broad smile spreading over his face. 'You see why I hired this woman, guys? She is *smart*. Holly, say some more about how exactly we might play this.'

Holly's head was bursting with ideas now, but she knew she needed space to put them in order. 'We'll have to give it some thought, but off the top of my head, how about we organize some big rallies at border crossings? Demand they open the gates and let us in?'

'But there's no room in the calendar for that!' complained Phyllis Kotkov. 'We've got a whole schedule worked out for the beginning of the primary season.'

'People don't hate Canadians,' Quentin said. 'They're too like us. They've been our allies in pretty much every war we've fought for the last two hundred years. Last time they were our enemies was 1812. Who in hell is going to turn up to your rallies?'

'Jesus, Quentin, that's our *job*! That's my job and your job and Ann's job. *Si, si*, up to now Canadians have been virtually invisible, but that's exactly how they've got away with this for so long. All that lovely space has been hidden in plain sight. Our job is to change that! And you know what? I don't even think it'll be hard to do.'

Slaymaker laughed. He looked round delightedly at the resentful faces of his team. He rubbed his hands together in anticipation of the task ahead. He knew quite well that very few of them were happy about Holly's sudden prominence, but that was all part of the fun for him.

'*Not even hard to do*,' he chuckled. 'Well, how about that, *compañeros*? Let's give it a go, eh? I'm not dropping the Reconfigure program, period. So what have we got to lose?'

'Well, there's one plus, as far as I'm concerned,' said Jed. 'I have *never* liked the Canucks. I mean, what really is the *point* of them? No one outside this continent can even tell the difference between them and us. And they are just *so* fucking smug.'

Canucks. Holly had never heard the word before, and she didn't like it any more than she liked Jed himself, but she couldn't help noticing its usefulness. Canucks. Not a press release word, of course, not a word to put in speeches, but a great word to use in a whisperstream campaign, in much the same way that Frinton and Montello were using words like 'storm trash'.

What did the doctor say to the Canuck who complained she couldn't get pregnant? You've got to let them in...Three Canucks walked into a bar...

Well, obviously, she'd have to work on it, but there were AIs that could pour out half-decent jokes at the rate of ten per second. She'd get them onto it right away. She needed to reinvent Canada. She needed to make it into a 'them' so that Americans could once again be an 'us'.

Jed found her later, working with her jeenee in the leathery room that the Slaymakers liked to call their library, though the books were basically decorative, and many of them weren't even real. She'd poured herself a coffee from the flask that the servants kept constantly replenished, and he fetched a cup for himself and came to join her.

'That was pretty smart, Holly, that Canada idea.'

'Thanks.'

'I actually think it could work, if we really give it everything, and don't give way to squeamishness.'

'How do you mean?'

'It won't work if we start dancing the delicado dance and asking ourselves whether the Canucks really deserve this, are they any different from us, all that shit. We're us and they're them. Period. Like a football game. That's how it's got to be. By the way, personal question, but you're not fucking the senator, by any chance?'

Holly glared at him. 'No I'm bloody not. Why? Is that what people are saying?'

He scrutinized her face, amused by her indignation. 'More of a mutual crush type of thing, huh? The old Slaymaker hands pretend to throw up these days every time they hear your name. Not that that's your problem. Congratulations on becoming the darling of the next president of the United States of America! The next president and one of the last.'

'One of the last?'

'Well, pretty much all of science seems to agree that we've set too many positive feedback loops in motion for the air temperature to stop rising any time in the next century, whatever we do. Billions of tons of methane every day from the melting permafrost, billions from the rotting forests, billions from the dead molluscs on the ocean floor. Or should that be trillions? Or tens of trillions? I've no idea, to be honest, but whatever it is, it's a lot. And each ton heats the air up enough to release a couple of tons more. Time will come when someone strikes a match and the whole atmosphere goes off with a bang.'

He laughed loudly at this, a harsh, barking, jackal's laugh, while Holly regarded him with slightly narrowed eyes. How ugly he could be! But the strange part was that even though Jed came from a wealthy family and had been to the best and most expensive schools, he could walk into a bar and get talking to some average American or other – one of those Henry McKenzies struggling to get by in the precarious niches that robots had left for human beings – and he and his savage views would most likely be much better received than, say, her Richard with his average middle-class background and his concern for everyone. People at the bottom had a harsh view of the world because that was how they experienced it. People at the top had a harsh view because that was how they got there. The delicados sandwiched between them were the odd ones out.

'Don't get me wrong,' said Jed, 'I can see your idea working politically, I really can, but in terms of any sort of long-term solution, well, shifting our population northwards, whether it's to Montana or to Yukon or – I don't know, fucking *Baffin Island* – won't buy us much more than a generation's respite. Where will we go after that? They're supposed to be building this star ship, I know, but how many people is that going to carry? Two? Three?'

'Why are you part of the team, Jed, if you think it's all pointless?'

'I've got to pay for my vices. And, okay, I could probably get paid to campaign for Christmas trees or for spraying sulfur into the stratosphere or whatever, but this looks like being way more fun. Plus I don't give a shit, to tell you the honest truth. Any more than the last four generations on planet Earth have given a shit.'

Holly thought about her parents, their recycling and their bicycles, their little wind generator at the bottom of the garden, their demonstrations. They'd given a shit, hadn't they? Whatever else you could accuse them of, surely you couldn't say they hadn't given a shit? But now, picturing them in her mind, it seemed to her that they didn't really care either. They just needed to think of themselves as caring. That, in fact, was the whole problem she had with them. Their efforts had been a matter of ritual, of placating some kind of god, of preserving their spotless innocence.

'I believe in what Slaymaker's doing,' she said stubbornly.

'So suppose old Gray Jenny had picked up the phone first? Suppose she'd told you she had to have you on her team. Okay, she's not quite so sexy as our Steve, but still, I reckon you'd have gone for it.'

After Jed had gone, Holly thought about Ruby, her warm, kind friend, who'd been so good to her in those early days in New York. Ruby would hate the direction Holly was taking Slaymaker's campaign. And yes, Ruby was naïve in some ways, and, yes, she avoided thinking about things that made her uncomfortable, playing in her studio like a gifted child while others made the deals and the messy compromises that kept the world moving. But still, if you compared Ruby with Jed, who prided himself on facing even the bleakest realities, could you seriously doubt that she was the better human being?

'What am I doing with these people?' she whispered. 'How have I ended up here?'

'Because of all those people who are losing their homes,' her jeenee softly answered her. 'You and Slaymaker are trying to help them.'

She was a little startled. She had mouthed the words without thinking, but hadn't been seeking an answer. Still, she thought, the jeenee was right. The Slaymaker campaign wasn't telling a story about helping the barreduras but only because that wasn't a story their voters were willing to hear. The fact remained that it *was* those people they were working for. So, never mind comparing Jed and Ruby, that wasn't the real question. The question that mattered was: which was more important, (a) avoiding upsetting Ruby, who had a lovely home and no worries about earning a living, or (b) doing something for all those people who didn't have anywhere to live?

CHAPTER 27

It was already growing dark when she climbed from her car the following afternoon. The house was in shadow, only the top of the ridge was still in sunlight, the trees picked out against the sky. Richard came out to meet her. They kissed.

'How did you get on?' he asked as he set a fish lasagne on the table. '*Was* it someone hacking your polls?'

Holly piled food onto her plate. 'Zara went into that with our Pollcloud providers and it seems not. They even sent out drones across the country to physically check on a random selection of their volunteers – they actually have them walk out of the house, would you believe, so the drones can see them standing there when they read their iris patterns – and they were all bona fide humans. But the cloud AIs think there could have been some sort of coordinated intervention by a fairly large number of human volunteers, to vote one way for a while and then suddenly switch.'

'Who would have organized that? Montello? Frinton?'

'The WSS, we think. There are a lot of Salvies out there these days, and of course they're totally opposed to any kind of mass migration – they think people should reduce their numbers, change their behaviour, whatever, but definitely stay where they are – so they've got every reason to dislike Slaymaker and to want to undermine his campaign.'

'So...you're saying that the apparent success of Slaymaker's campaign so far has just been a kind of...well...illusion?'

Holly took a swig of white Canadian wine. Richard felt there was a certain guardedness about her that hadn't been there when she set off for Slaymaker's ranch. She was animated and keen to talk, and yet she wasn't quite talking to *him*.

'It's not mainly about the Salvies,' Holly said. 'We paid for the AIs to do a really deep analysis and it seems there have been several distinct patterns going on out there, which have come together to create this slump. A bunch of people do seem to have made a sudden switch, but the main problem is simply a growing doubt about the whole Reconfigure policy. We managed to sell it for a while, on the back of Slaymaker's popularity, and – you know – by very careful presentation, but that's not quite cutting it any more.'

'Oh, I'm sorry, Holly. And that's your baby, of course.'

'Ah, well. I always knew it was a long shot. How you tell a story is important, but it can't alter the basic facts. This policy *will* cost the taxpayer a lot of dollars, and it will mean a lot of new residents in northern states where people have begun to think of southerners as sort of foreigners.'

'Sadly, we just assume these days that no one wants actual foreigners.'

'I'll tell you what this is like. You know how it is when we go out on Sergio's boat? You don't have to have the wind right behind you, but there's only so close to it you can sail and still keep moving? It's like that. We were trying to sail just a bit too close to the wind.'

'So what happens now? I guess drop the Reconfigure thing and emphasize other aspects?'

Richard tried to expunge any trace of hopefulness from his voice. He assumed that if the Slaymaker campaign dropped Reconfigure America, there'd no longer be a place for Holly.

But Holly laughed. 'Oh *Jesucristo*, no! No *way* am I giving up, Rick! No chance! We've just redesigned it, that's all. We've reworked it so that it'll, you know, catch the prevailing wind a little bit better. The basic problem was that we were asking northern voters to take on the whole burden.'

'Which I thought was pretty reasonable, given that we've got it so much easier here in the—'

'*Si, si,*' Holly interrupted impatiently, 'but it doesn't matter whether a thing's reasonable or not. People are always full of worry, wherever they live, whatever their situation. People fear all the time that the world they're used to will be taken away from them. And no one votes to have their worries increased, however reasonable or fair that might be.'

Richard thought about this for a couple of seconds. 'Okay. I guess that's probably true. So how are you going to get round it?'

Holly hesitated, the guardedness now very apparent. 'What we're proposing to do is ask Canada to take in some of the barreduras, so it doesn't look like the whole burden is going to fall on northern states.'

'*Canada?*' Richard was startled. He had a forkful of food halfway to his mouth, but he laid it back on the plate. 'How on earth is that going to work?'

'In his speeches, Steve will say that Canada ought to help us out more.'

'But Canada will just shrug its shoulders and say no, won't it? And anyway, how—'

'He'll be making a statement later. Let's wait until then.'

●

They sat side by side in front of the broadscreen to watch Slaymaker, side by side but not touching, Holly with her cristal on her lap, muttering silent instructions.

They joined a twenty-four-hour news channel in the middle of a cycle. There was an item about a fight in Philadelphia between crowds of local youths and storm people, another about Spain's sudden, panicky withdrawal from its enclaves in North Africa, another about a ferry from Liverpool to Ireland that had been accidentally sunk by one of the unmanned guns that protected British beaches against refugees. And then finally there was Slaymaker, standing in front of one of those old Mercator maps, demanding that America's huge northern neighbor share the burden of rehoming climate refugees:

'We need Canada's help here. It's richer than America, it's larger, and it has less than one-tenth of the population. We need to ask Canada to take in some of our homeless people. Our northern states will roll up their sleeves and do their part – of course they will, they're Americans, and that's what Americans do – but they can't do it all by themselves. They've got their own problems to deal with, and there's only so much they can give. So, over to you, Canada. We're waiting. We're listening.'

Richard shut down the broadscreen the moment the news moved onto other things. '*Jesucristo*, Holly. You said "ask", but that sounds to me more like "demand". That was really aggressive.'

'Well, he has his own style.'

'I guess.' Richard relaxed slightly. 'So this was a case where Slaymaker wouldn't be guided by you?'

Holly's face had taken on a stubborn expression that he knew very well. 'No, I wrote pretty much every word of that.'

'*You?*'

'*Por cierto.* In fact, I came up with the whole idea.'

Richard stared at her for a couple of seconds, Holly squirming in his gaze. 'It doesn't strike you as a bit of a nerve, when Slaymaker's been saying for years that Mexicans have to sort out their own problems, and we're under no obligation whatever to let them in?'

Holly sighed, like this was an old argument she'd dealt with a long time ago. She answered him as if he'd been a journalist calling out a question at a press conference. 'Not at all. It would be irresponsible for the US to allow inward migration by climate refugees from other countries, when we've got millions of climate refugees of our own.'

'Oh, come on, Holly. That may be the official line but you can't *possibly* believe it! There's just no comparison! Mexico and the countries south of it are *desperate.* There are people starving down there. The Mexican state has all but collapsed. Much of the country is ruled by gangsters. The US may have problems in some areas but it's still one of the rich countries of the world. With the political will, we could easily look after all our own barreduras. Easily. But the Mexicans can't look after theirs. They really can't. They can't even feed them. If anyone has a claim on Canada, it's them not us.'

Holly fiddled with something on her cristal. 'Steve needs to get elected, if he's going to get anything done at all. There's just no point in talking about what we *could* do if only the political will existed, because it *doesn't* exist. You might as well talk about what we could do if we owned a magic wand.'

'The art of the possible.'

'Yeah. Exactly.'

'Even if that means jettisoning—'

'For Christ's sake, Rick, you sound just like my dad.' She began to imitate her father's rather thin and querulous voice: "'If we can't make things perfect then there's no point in doing anything at all." Steve's approach will help several tens of millions of people – desperate people who wouldn't otherwise be helped. It's a shame about folk in Mexico and all those places, I know, but at least we'll be doing something.'

'But you only even thought of Canada because you knew your side was losing the nomination race.'

'Of course. But what's wrong with that? You know all those cristal games we were talking about? Where you're competing to rule the world or something? Everyone's happy to be ruthless when they're playing those games, aren't they? Everyone can see that they've got to play that way or they'll just be wiped out. Well, it turns out that's true to life.'

They sat in silence for a while in front of the blank screen. 'It's not like Slaymaker's threatening Canada or anything,' Holly finally said. 'He's just asking them to—'

'He's asking them to do the very thing that he has always completely refused to countenance, when it comes to our own southern neighbors.'

'Well, I guess,' Holly conceded, 'but I'm afraid that's how these things work. There's a certain number of arguments that can be used to justify our actions, and we pick out the ones that best serve us at the time. I know it's dirty, I know it's inconsistent, but Slaymaker wants to do something that's worth doing, and he can't make it happen unless he can win enough support to put him in power.'

Richard shrugged. 'Well, I understand the point, but maybe you should ask Ruby and Ossia how this is seen in Canada.'

Holly visibly tensed at that. 'Sure. I'll message Ruby. It won't play the same way in Canada, I can see.'

'Okay.' Richard's tone was uncharacteristically cool. 'You do that. In the meantime, I'm going to take this coffee up to my office for half an hour because I promised Alice I'd do a bit a prep for our *Faustus* rehearsal tomorrow.'

Holly fetched her cristal and, sitting at the dining table, drafted a message to Ruby.

'Hey, Ruby. You'll have seen Slaymaker's statement tonight, and I just wanted to say I know it will sound kind of harsh up there. He's trying to find a way of helping us live with these weather problems, though, he really is, and he's got nothing against Canada. I know you had your own frustrations trying to get Canada to let you in, and I remember you telling us at Mariana and Sergio's that you and Ossia had been on demos up there about Canada's immigration policy, so I'm hoping you'll understand. Much love, Holly.'

'You done?' her jeenee asked.

'*Si*. I'm done. Send it off. Oh, and let me know when she replies, even if I'm in bed. I'd kind of like to know what she says.'

They didn't talk much for the rest of the evening, but when they were in bed, Holly reached out to Richard and they had sex again, seeking that old alchemy that always worked so well, as if anger was some kind of hard and angular crystal that formed in the gap between them, and could be crushed to powder if they pushed their bodies together with sufficient force.

It usually worked, and it kind of worked this time too. But as they lay in the darkness afterwards waiting for sleep, each of them was aware that the gap was still there, the crystals already reforming. Richard was thinking how different the two of them were, and how working for Slaymaker was drawing out a side of Holly that he had found interesting and appealing when it was a nuance, an unstated presence, but really would not get on with if it were to become her dominant self. Holly was thinking about an aspect of Richard that she had always carefully thought of as gentle, but could also rather easily be described as weak.

A faint *ping* from her ear implants told her that the reply from Ruby had arrived.

'Thanks, Holly. We were a bit shaken, I admit. Ossia was *really* cross. She said it was funny how Slaymaker made that speech the very day you got back from Canada. I told her not to be paranoid. Yeah, you're right about Canada's immigration policy. It stinks. Not that the US is really in a position to criticize. But never mind. I still love you. Just no tanks along the border, okay?'

Hugely relieved, Holly sent 'Okay, no tanks!' back to Ruby with a little red heart, and then told her jeenee no more messages, no more anything.

Rick took the story too seriously, she thought as she lay in in the darkness. Or too *literally*, rather. (You couldn't take stories too seriously!) He mistook the story for the fact.

All politicians told stories that couldn't be taken literally. They were like the stories told by branded products. Did any man take literally the claim that a fragrance would make him irresistible to women? Of course not, but it still made that stern and angular bottle feel like something it would be nice to own. And without a story what would that fragrance be? A chemical compound. Cold, cold glass.

Bloody Ossia, Holly thought suddenly. And the idea of the dancer, her sharpness and coolness, exposed a pulsing red node of discomfort in her sleepy brain, hidden up to now behind soft black wads of mental padding. Did Ossia have a point? Had Holly suggested Canada because she was resentful in some way of Ruby and Ossia's life together? Sudden anger toward Ruby welled up inside her: big, friendly, cuddly Ruby, with her loud laugh and her sloppy bright colors, as banal and innocent as some goofy cartoon bear. Anger from nowhere, it seemed to Holly, or anger from a place which she had never allowed herself to enter.

But she forced her attention away, like a drig forcing itself downwards against its own buoyancy. Those border rallies would do the trick. They'd bring people round. Slaymaker would be pleased with her. Everyone would tell her how well she'd done.

That felt good. The red pulse was covered over again. The dark warm padding let her sleep.

CHAPTER 28

People sometimes asked Tobin if he had Chinese ancestry, which always annoyed him, because it felt to him like they were suggesting he was some sort of recent arrival (recent to him meaning any time in the last six hundred years). But it was an understandable mistake. His face was broad, his nose quite flat, and his eyes distinctly oriental-looking, even though the hair in his wispy beard was blond and his skin too pale to conceal the violent blushes that seemed to accompany almost every emotion. He was like that all over, big and awkward, blundering through the world, a bull in a china shop, as people sometimes said, a young bull, barely able to contain the strength of his passions.

Now he was standing in the middle of a jangle bar in New York, in jeans and a red-check lumberjack jacket. The gimmick of this particular place was that the music wasn't precomposed but was improvised on the spot by a resident AI. It monitored the activity in the room – the number of people, the amount of movement, the degree of animation in the voices and faces – and adjusted its output accordingly. Now, as the bar was filling up and building toward the busiest time of the evening, the AI was matching that sense of things starting to happen by piling up layer upon layer of sweet ascending arpeggios over a steady, loping beat that seemed all the time to climb upwards, as if this night was going to end in heaven.

'Hey, Tobin!'

He turned toward the woman who had just tapped him on the shoulder. She had a lean, austere face and looked about forty, which would make her ten years old than him.

'Hi. You must be—'

The woman held up a finger to silence him, and laughed. 'First rule, Tobin, if someone is going to identify themselves to you with a code word, you don't tell them the word before they speak!'

Tobin blushed. 'Oh shit. Sorry.'

'But yeah, I'm Oak Tree.'

'Hi. You want to go and find a corner somewhere to talk?'

'No it's best in the middle of the room. Noise from all directions. People in the way of any pesky lip-reading cameras.'

'Sure.'

'So I gather from our mutual friend,' she said, 'that you want to join the WSS?'

'I'm already a member, have been since I was—'

'You're a member of a support group, Tobin. That's not the real organization. That's kind of a nursery where we grow potential members, and pick out the promising ones for the real jobs.'

'Well, I don't want to be part of the support group. I want to be...I don't know what the right word is...I want to be operationally involved.'

'Good. I hear you're smart, and very reliable, and very very motivated. Tell me a bit more about that last bit.'

Tobin blushed again. 'This country has been raped. When it was just our people who lived here, we looked after it. Not perfectly, of course, but forests were forests, plains were plains, oceans were oceans. And then the white settlers came, and covered it with roads and shopping malls and fields of wheat. They told us we were savages and to get out of their way because we didn't know anything. They told us we'd used the land so little that it didn't really belong to us at all. But now look at it. What did they really know?'

'*Your* people?'

'Well, my mother's people.'

Oak Tree frowned. 'We're not fighting some kind of race war here.'

Tobin blushed some more. 'Oh sure, I know, I know. I didn't mean that. This isn't about one race or another. It's about stopping that thing where people just trash one place and then move on and trash another. It's just that—'

'Okay,' she smiled, 'okay. That's fine. Your frustration is understandable. So long as you know your genes don't confer any special virtue. This is *not* about making claims to virtue. We leave that stuff to the delicados. Our position is simple. The human race is at the bottom of a very deep hole and yet, crazily, it's still digging. We need to make that stop, period. We've got no use for anyone who tries to make it anything more fancy than that.'

'I agree. When we hit those freight trains – when the *WSS* hit those freight trains, I should say – everyone was going, *Why did they do that? What point are they trying to make?* And I thought, No, there's no point. Not in that way. It's about stopping freight trains. As simple as that.'

Oak Tree nodded. A new, louder and almost joyful voice, somewhere between a trumpet and a pipe organ, had just joined in with those multiple, overlapping sequences of ascending notes. It began to weave a melody through the dense matrix of harmony and rhythm, strong and positive but tinged with a calm and fatalistic melancholy. It was like some large and beautiful sea creature playing slowly and gracefully among columns of bubbles that were streaming upwards all around it toward the light.

CHAPTER 29

The first of the border rallies took place at Ambassador Bridge, Detroit. Holly watched in her office upstairs in her home, leaning forward on her elbows, her head cupped in her hands, from time to time muttering to her jeenee to make a note of moments she wanted to revisit.

Only three or four hundred people turned out, which was much fewer than she'd hoped for, but all the same, while Slaymaker was speaking, she picked up a steady stream of encouraging responses in the whisperstream. As planned, the senator's tone was friendly, conciliatory even. He said nice things about Canada, called it 'our sister nation', spoke of Canada and the US as being 'two peas in a pod', and reminded his audience that no one in the rest of the world could even tell Canadians and Americans apart. And, though he insisted it was time for that fine country across the bridge to play more of a part in resolving 'the human problems of our shared continent', he did so very gently, as if reminding Canada of something it would have wanted to do anyway but might possibly have temporarily forgotten. Someone like Ruby could not have pointed to a single word that was hostile or negative toward Canada. Holly had insisted on that. It was personally important to her.

But still, it was a pretty unusual thing for a senior US politician to stand on the borders of another country and ask for his people be let in, and this, for certain key audiences, was always going to be more important than the words spoken. Holly was gratified to see, within an hour, an angry reaction from the Canadian government: 'Canada already lets in many thousands of Americans every year... We must protest in the strongest terms about Senator Slaymaker's deliberately provocative demands.'

'Provocative, *me*?' would of course be his innocent response. 'Where, in my whole speech, did I criticize or make demands?'

Holly sent a string of questions out into the Pollcloud straight away. There had been a measurable upturn in support for Slaymaker, but it was a small one, and not the immediate surge she'd secretly been hoping for, and not enough to lift him from third place behind his two rivals. Meanwhile, both Montello and Frinton were putting out sharp, well-targeted and well-crafted reactions.

'I'm starting to worry about the senator's mental health!' Lucy Montello sneered. 'Not only is Canada a sister-nation, with the same language and the same way of life as us, but it's been our stalwart ally in no less than – count them! – twenty-eight different wars, all the way from World War I in the early twentieth century through to the Fourth Copper War less than ten years ago. I thought it was weird enough Slaymaker wanting to move everyone from the south to the north, but it seems that wasn't enough for him. Now he's trying to drag a neighboring country into his crackpot plan.'

'Crackpot' was a good word, Holly had to acknowledge that. And a crackpot is just what he looked like in the image Montello's people put out. It showed Slaymaker at Ambassador Bridge, caught at an unflattering moment, with his eyes oddly half-lidded, his hair thrown all over the place by a gust of wind, and his mouth wide enough open to see his tonsils, all taken from an angle that left almost all of the crowd out of view, apart from a small cluster of confused-looking elderly folk who happened to be at the front.

'You almost feel sorry for the guy,' said Soames Frinton. His team of humans and AIs had also scoured every millisecond of the footage from Ambassador Bridge, and the image *they'd* managed to find showed Slaymaker looking old and tired and defeated, a lame old dog reduced to rummaging in trashcans because it could no longer hope to catch living prey.

'It just shows how desperate he is,' Frinton went on, 'that this is what he falls back on.'

'Desperate' was a good word too, and it had the advantage of actually being true. Slaymaker's team *was* desperate. This Canada plan was its last throw of the dice.

And it was the last throw for Holly as well. She'd always been isolated within the Slaymaker camp, and now she was more so than ever. Apart from Slaymaker himself, only Jed was willing to take her side in any way.

Richard came up with a cup of coffee and a cupcake from a batch he'd baked.

'So? How's it gone? Any sense that it's having an effect?'

She'd just put on immersive goggles that allowed her to receive material in three dimensions, but even with her upper face hidden, he recognized that dangerous brightness that burnt inside Holly when she felt cornered.

'The rally was just raw material,' she said shortly, without removing the goggles or turning toward him. 'It's the story I build on it that's important.'

Richard said nothing, just put down the tray for her, kissed her head, and backed quietly out. He was convinced that Holly's plan would fail. Slaymaker, having belatedly realized that his followers would not be keen on giving rings instead of receiving them, was proposing to mitigate this by asking a neighboring country to provide some rings as well. It seemed obvious to him that this wasn't going to be enough.

Holly herself feared that this might be the case. 'Make demands on Canada!' she could imagine Ann saying to Sue. 'That turned out to be a *great* idea, didn't it?' They were circling her now, with their claws and their hooked beaks, waiting for her to fall.

But she shook off her doubts and peered back down into the whisperstream, not at a single timeline, but at a representation of the American stream in its entirety. As she leant forward on her elbows, looking at 3D charts and graphs, listening to the clamor from within, she had the feeling that she was peering through a crack in the earth into an enormous cave where millions of bats were roosting. She felt the pull of gravity. She heard the din of tiny voices, squabbling, flirting, jockeying for position. She saw the dominant animals that others deferred to. She smelt the stench of centuries of dung.

As had happened for many years, every candidate in the election was making use both of official attributable channels of communication and of unofficial channels that, in a strictly legal sense, they were not connected with. So, for instance, in spite of loud public protestations that she wasn't in any way anti-Latino or anti-Mexican, Montello's people were pumping anti-Mexican material that she could never have said herself, insinuating that the entire problem of homelessness and unemployment in the southern states was due not to the rapid changes in the weather but to illegal Latino immigrants.

> You won't hear it on the news hubs, but there're whole towns down there in the south that have been taken over by Mexican gangs...

> And get this! The federal government won't help homeless Anglos – literally won't even touch them – unless they promise to blame it all on the weather problems...

> Government doesn't want to admit that it's lost control of the border...

And, in spite of public pronouncements about the 'fine people of the south', Montello's team was also putting out insinuations about the refugees from the southern half of the country. Storm trash were feckless, lazy and potential rapists. Dusties were incompetent peasants who blamed their bankruptcies on the weather and then asked the taxpayer to clear their debts.

None of these were officially part of Montello's message, and if she was asked a direct question about them she would of course have shrugged them off as nonsense. But Montello's people ensured all the same that a steady stream of these stories were poured out day and night by thousands of high-quality feeders – so-called 'seasoned' feeders – which had been participating in whisper-stream conversations over a period of months or years, and were assumed by those who interacted with them to be real human beings like themselves.

A well-constructed feeder came over as a friend of a friend, that was the idea, someone that you felt you were connected with in some way but had forgotten exactly how. Holly's profession had been using armies of feeders for several decades to manufacture a consensus by creating the illusion that a consensus already existed. Montello's people were using them now to provide a kind of compost in which Montello's attributable utterances about tighter border controls and punishments for illegal immigrants could put down roots and grow. It didn't matter that there was no factual basis for what they said. Shit is the best fertilizer, as people said in the industry.

Immersed in and surrounded by three-dimensional graphics, Holly watched the stories flickering back and forth across the surface of the whisperstream. Of course, it wasn't really a stream at all. It only seemed that way to the individual subscriber. If you wanted a watery metaphor an ocean would be more accurate, an ocean with tides, waves, dark abysses, sunny shallows and currents that streamed in different directions at different depths. But ocean didn't really capture it either, because the whisperstream in its entirety was constantly transforming itself. It was not inanimate matter but a web of life, a vast chattering matrix of living souls, Holly's cave of bats, with ripples of fear and excitement moving back and forth through a packed mass of warm agitated bodies.

No analogy was really adequate, though. It was a dreaming brain. It was the boiling surface of the sun. It was a sewer. It was bacteria dividing, second by second, on a sheet of agar jelly. In front of Holly's eyes the stories about floods of Mexicans and lazy storm trash and feckless dusties multiplied and mutated many thousands of times in every second. And right there among these endlessly branching lines, she could see the 'crackpot' bacillus, often accompanied by that unflattering image of Slaymaker at Ambassador Bridge, reproducing itself with great vigor:

Apparently, his original idea was to send folk down to Mexico...

Word is that Slaymaker consults an astrologer before every decision...

The news hubs are covering up for him but he's had five kids with some kind of voodoo woman down in Delaware, and she reads his fortune in chicken guts...

Which messages came from humans, which from feeders? Even with the specialist tools at her disposal, Holly couldn't always tell. Each was amplifying the other.

Soames Frinton's regiments of feeders had opened a new line of attack in the last two weeks, putting out rather elaborate stories about how southern states were bribing their own work-shy citizens to move north and live at the expense of northern taxpayers. His team had had fun developing an entire narrative about a fictional family from Mississippi called the Surettes who'd been paid $50,000 to cross the state line and never come back. Countless sightings of them had been claimed by whisperstreamers across America (some of whom at least were probably human) and an entire genre of Surette stories had spread themselves across that dark, agitated cave. Some of the stories were very funny. Professional stream-stars – people like Lucy Sharp and Johnny Truth, each followed by tens of millions of Americans – had been recycling them with great enthusiasm.

It was an 'open secret', according to Frinton's feeders, that Slay-maker was in cahoots with all of this. ('Open secret' was good, Holly knew: it made people feel naïve and out of touch for not being in the know, and therefore *very* much disposed to recycle the supposed secret as often as possible in order to re-establish their credentials.) Never mind Slaymaker's 'nice guy' image, Frinton's feeders were saying, never mind that rugged charm, Slaymaker was a total sleazeball, and very reliable sources had confirmed that he was receiving substantial illegal payments for his campaign from 'at least four' state governors near the Mexican border, all of whom were on record 'whining' about the northern campaign for state frontiers.

Stream-stars were picking up on this stuff as well. Lucy Sharp in particular was whispering steadily on this theme. But again, Frinton himself had never said these things, had never claimed they were true, and would if necessary roundly condemn them as a slur on the fine upstanding people of the American south and southwest, where he had so many relatives and so many dear, dear friends. In fact, a conscientious reporter from one of the news hubs had actually looked into the 'Surette' story recently and proved there was no such family, but there was no comeback on Frinton. He'd laughed the whole thing off as typical whisperstream non-sense, even while the feeders his people had hired were hinting darkly that there'd been a cover-up: the Surettes really *did* exist, and the government just didn't want you to know.

And into this fertile manure Frinton had continued to plant his signature message: if people from southern states were going to move, they needed to move at their own expense, and only to states that were willing to welcome them. As to Slaymaker, he was corrupt, but worse than that, he was a sad desperate old has-been, who had resorted to corruption because he knew no other way to make his mark, and now, when even that had failed, had finally turned to this embarrassing and desperate performance at Ambassador Bridge.

Right now, in front of Holly's eyes, this new refined version of the 'desperate' message was fanning out through the stream, taking on additional material, mutating and frequently hybridizing, in many different ways, with Montello's 'crackpot' narrative.

Alone in her study, Holly removed her goggles and passed her hand over her eyes: a weary soldier in the middle of a battlefield, worn down by unremitting combat.

She was not defeated, though. Slaymaker had his own army of feeders, after all, every bit as powerful as Frinton's or Montello's and many battalions of those feeders were under Holly's direct command. She and Ann had also invested heavily in so-called scoopers, which scoured the stream for useful messages already out there for their feeders to recycle. And it was to her scoopers that Holly turned now, shoving aside the goggles and returning to the multiple screens she preferred to work with: one for each separate strand within her current strategy.

There was some good material coming in, flickering in front of her at a rate of one item a second. For example, she found a cartoon posted by a tiny local news hub in Slope County, North Dakota, which normally got no more than thirty or forty hits a day. The drawing showed Canada as a fat little lapdog lying in a manger, while a half-starved but very dignified American horse stood patiently waiting to be allowed to eat. The scoopers had already passed it on to a selection of feeders, but Holly took the decision to crank this right up. She sent the cartoon to a graphics AI for a bit of tidying up, and then instructed the entire feeder army under her command to get it out there, to be picked up, modified, recycled, imitated and improved upon by human streamers.

On a second screen she was working on Canuck jokes. She'd already put some out in the build-up to Ambassador Bridge, but only a few, because the news needed really to be created on the ground before the jokes could properly find purchase. Now, with Ambassador Bridge behind her, she launched a whole torrent of them into the whisperstream through a thousand feeders – *An American, a Mexican and a Canuck walk into a bar...A Canuck goes to her doctor and...What's the difference between a Canuck and a...?* AIs were brilliant at generating formulaic jokes like these. She instructed her scoopers, meanwhile, to seek out and reward every single freelance effort, however weak, by passing it to her feeder centers for multiple recycling. She even had her feeders create a few dozen quasi-competitions for 'the best Canuck joke', 'the funniest thing about Canadians', 'the ten meanest things that Canucks have done in history'.

She was working at full speed. Having originated the Canada plan, and written the original draft of Slaymaker's Ambassador Bridge speech, what she was doing now was crafting the underbelly of that same message. She and Slaymaker had agreed he should say that Canadians were good people and fellow North Americans, but that was all the more reason why her feeders must say that Canucks were greedy, selfish and even spiteful, refusing access to space that they themselves had no use for. She had her jeenee find images of verdant meadows overgrown from lack of use, and rows of fine houses standing empty behind razorwire fences:

Land going to waste last year in Northern Ontario. And
Canada claims it has no room!

The Canucks say they've got no space, so how come these
houses in Saskatchewan are boarded up?

The pictures didn't necessarily come from Canada, but that
mattered very little. AIs could doctor them in fractions of a second
to replace details like signs in foreign languages, or cars on the
wrong side of the road. And these pictures weren't going to be put
out in Slaymaker's name, in any case. They would enter the stream
from sources that, for all anyone could tell, were simply private
citizens. If anyone found out they weren't genuine, it wouldn't be
Slaymaker's problem. He could rise above the whole thing, con-
demning the slur on a friendly nation, and resuming his courteous
requests for help.

CHAPTER 30

Holly didn't go to bed until three in the morning, but she still ate breakfast with Richard at seven, and headed straight back out to the Slaymaker ranch for a team meeting to discuss the way forward after the rally. Sue and Ann were already there when she arrived, as was Quentin, all drinking coffee in the library with their cristals on their laps.

'Polls are *not* looking good this morning,' said Sue grimly.

'To sum up the general view,' said Ann, pursing her little red mouth, 'Ambassador Bridge just made Steve look random and weird.'

'Of course it did,' Holly snapped. 'Because it's a sudden and unexpected turn and people don't quite get it yet. There's a ton of work we need to do to build on it and get the ground ready for the next rally.'

Sue shook her head sadly. 'You never give up, do you, Holly? *More* rallies will make him look *more* weird. The primary season's beginning, and instead of working the states we need to win, he's canceled prearranged events to wander along the border.'

'Like a demented old man who's forgotten where he is or where he's supposed to be,' added Quentin, 'beating on random doors.'

'And we all know that's not Steve,' said Sue. 'That's not him at all. Come on, Holly, help us out here. He listens to you. Tell him we need to rethink this. It's not too late.'

Slaymaker came in then, in a check shirt and jeans, beaming round at everyone as if he had no sense at all of the tension in the room. 'Hey! So how are all you guys this morning? Thanks for coming. Holly, can I have a word with you first?'

In his large wood-paneled office, he beckoned her to one of the leather armchairs. 'I've asked Jed to join us when he arrives.'

'I'm sorry if I've led you down the wrong path,' Holly said.

He frowned, leant forward. 'Sorry for what? The others been getting at you out there?'

'Well, they've got a point. The polls aren't great after Ambassador Bridge. I did a lot of work overnight, but I'm not really shifting anything. Sue and Ann have always thought the Canada idea was crazy, and I'm starting to think they may be right, because an awful lot of Freedom Party voters seem to feel the same way. Ann and Sue never liked Reconfigure America much, either. I knew it was going to be a hard sell, but I persuaded myself – and maybe persuaded you – that it could be done. I have to admit that perhaps Sue and Ann had a point there, too.'

He settled back into his chair with a comfortable sigh. 'I knew it was a long shot, Holly. I've never thought it could be done for sure. You just persuaded me that you were going to give your best try, and that if anyone *could* do it that person would be you.'

'That's nice of you. I appreciate you having so much trust in me. I'm just saying that this Canada plan may not work. Our opponents are making fun of us and, so far at least, their mud is sticking.'

The senator shrugged. 'Well, I'm sure you're fighting back.'

'Certainly. I'm using every trick I know. Shame we have to resort to these things but—'

'You mean AIs and such? Couldn't agree with you more. Hate the things.'

'I wasn't thinking so much about the AIs. I was thinking more about making up stories.'

Slaymaker's eyes took on that slightly distant look they sometimes had, when you spoke about something outside of America, or outside the sphere that he cared about. 'What can you do about it, though? That's just how it is these days. Everyone does it, and if we don't, we'll be fighting with our hands tied behind our backs while they have both hands free.'

'Anyway, Steve, all I'm saying is, listen to the others as well as me. I've no political experience. I don't even come from this country. They may be right.'

'They may be, but I'm willing to take that risk. Stick to what you're doing. If I lose, I lose. I'm okay with that. It won't kill me.'

A car scrunched on the drive as it parked itself outside, and Jed came in, in a sharp blue jacket and black pants.

'Holly's having doubts,' said Slaymaker. 'Polls aren't great and she's wondering if Sue and Ann have been right all along.'

'Ha. Can't say I blame you for wavering, Holly, what with the constant onslaught from those two, but I still think Canada was pure genius. Obviously it's going to take a while to build up momentum. People aren't used to blaming the Canucks for things, and they need to get the hang of it. But it's pure genius all the same. Oh, and I've seen some of the stuff that our feeders are putting out – your work, I assume, Holly – and I think it's amazing: the Canuck jokes and everything. Only thing I will say is that we need to increase the temperature at the rallies themselves. Bus in a lot more people, whip them up, get a bit of real rage going.'

'Well, I'm not sure about *rage*,' Slaymaker muttered. 'I'm not saying Canada is the bad guy here. Come to that, I'm not planning to ask them to take in all of our barreduras, or even most. I don't even *want* that, for Chrissakes! I don't want to grow Canada. I want to grow *America*.'

'*Por cierto, por cierto*. But there has to be rage for Holly's plan to work. We're not going to gain any traction unless people are really, really resentful of Canada for holding on to all that land. You may not want Canada to take in too many barreduras – that's entirely up to you – but what you really *do* need Canada for is to absorb the anger of the American people about all the uncertainty they're having to live with, the sacrifices they're having to make. Otherwise, Americans are going to turn on one another, and you're going to lose the election.'

Holly nodded. 'We need Canada for storytelling purposes, in other words.'

'*Exactly!*' In his enthusiasm, Jed slapped his hands down on the armrests of his chair. 'What you need in an election is a story with good guys and bad guys, and preferably a story so darn simple a half-witted kid could get the gist of it. And that's the genius of Holly's idea. We need land and they've got loads of it: who could find that hard to follow? And if you're feeling badly about the Canucks, Steve, well don't. They're doing pretty well. They're doing better than we are, better than almost any other country in the world.'

He laughed, and turned to Holly. 'Hey, do you know what the Indians used to call the Forty-ninth Parallel?'

'Yes. The Medicine Line. I've no idea why, but my friend Ruby always calls it that.'

It felt strange to mention Ruby's name here, and she wished she hadn't.

'They called it that because they noticed that, for some magical reason they couldn't understand, US soldiers in pursuit of them would suddenly stop when they reached it. There seemed to be some kind of invisible force field there that had the power to stop Americans. Maybe you could make something of that, Holly? The arbitrariness of—'

'Okay, so we'll hire a load more buses next time,' Slaymaker said. 'That should be easy. Can you get Sue onto it? We can give the poor bastards in the trailer parks a day out. And let's put someone on each bus to get them going: a warm-up guy, kind of thing. There'll be people we can hire for that. Yeah, and we'll give them all free food, free coffee, free beer, while we're about it.'

Holly smiled and nodded a little distractedly. Mentioning Ruby in this context had stirred up painful feelings that she was now having to suppress. 'Jed's right about riling people up,' she said. 'That has to happen for the plan to work. We have to get America angry. And not only that. We need to rile the Canadians, too. The more anger we get from their side, the more material we'll have to work with on ours. Right now we need as much "them and us" as possible.'

Slaymaker rubbed his hands together and laughed, already looking forward to this new game.

'Brilliant!' exclaimed Jed. 'And if we get that right, then Montello and Frinton will be put in the position of having either to belatedly back us against Canada, which will make them look weak, or take the side of a hostile nation against us, which will make them look unpatriotic. *Man*, this woman is good, Steve!'

Slaymaker beamed proudly at Holly.

•

'This Canada thing of yours has unleashed some nasty stuff on the stream,' Richard said when they sat down to eat that evening. 'Really ugly stuff about Canadians.'

'I know,' said Holly, 'but what can you do? There are some very mean people out there.'

It was the first time she'd so deliberately concealed from him the full extent of her complicity in what was going on. He didn't know that, of course, but she felt she could have taken out a ruler and measured the distance as it grew between them.

'It's...It's hard to say it, Rick, but a bit of hostility toward Canada may not be a bad thing. Americans need somewhere to direct their frustrations other than at one another.'

'*Jesucristo*, Holly. Are you suggesting that—'

'What would King Scyld have done?'

Richard didn't hesitate. 'He would have said the Canadians have got something we want so we should beat the shit out of them until they give it to us. But since when has King Scyld been your benchmark?'

'You referred to him yourself not so long ago, Rick. You said we were taking rings from the people we needed to give them to. You were quite right, and we had to find a way round that. Otherwise, Montello or Frinton will win the candidacy, and, given Jenny Williams' slumping ratings, most likely the presidency too.'

'But what about Canada? Ruby says it's been terrible on the Canadian side. Everyone's really shocked by this gale of anti-Canadian feeling that suddenly been blowing toward them.'

Holly shrugged. 'Ruby is shocked every time she catches a glimpse of the machinery of the world, even though it's the same machinery that feeds her and makes her rich.'

'*Jesucristo*, Holly, that's horrible! That's a really horrible thing to say about your friend.'

'I guess. But she can't expect to have the rest of us protect her innocence all the time, like she's some kind of privileged child.'

Richard regarded her in silence for a few seconds. 'You want to be careful, Holly. If we know we're going to hurt someone, we make ourselves get mad at them first, so we can tell ourselves they deserve it. Are you sure that's not what's going on here?'

CHAPTER 31

The second border rally was at Oroville, Washington, on a narrow strip of flat land beside a lake. There were over a thousand Americans there, and Holly saw Slaymaker handle them with great skill, never saying anything explicitly anti-Canadian, but building up a real sense of grievance about this entirely arbitrary line that prevented them from moving any further north across the continent. Coached by the warm-up artists who'd ridden with them in the buses, the American demonstrators soon got an angry chant going: 'Let us in! Let us in! Let us in!'

Holly had planned the rally to ensure that roughly equal numbers of northerners and barreduras had come, and had instructed the campaign's camera people there to shoot a bunch of heart-warming clips of the two groups together.

'We've always wanted to help guys like Jeffrey here,' said a middle-aged farmer from only twenty miles south of the Oroville crossing. He'd just been introduced to a displaced farmer from California of about the same age, and the two were filmed standing side by side, the northerner with a protective arm across the Californian's shoulder. 'Trouble is, with the unpredictable weather we're having ourselves and the flash floods and what-all, we just can't. And that's why it makes sense to ask our Canuck friends over there to help out a little too. I mean, they owe their freedom to us, after all. We've defended their freedom against Germany and Russia and…uh…Britain, and all, and now it's pay-up time, I reckon.'

Canada as *ungrateful*: now that was good, thought Holly as she watched on one of her screens. AIs were all very fine, but you couldn't beat real, ordinary human beings when it came to material like that. The farmer's grasp of history was somewhat shaky but that didn't matter. Calling Canada ungrateful very nicely turned on its head the message coming from across the border that Canada had supported the US loyally over the centuries, and that Americans should be more grateful to *them*. She made a note. She would work on this; she would set the feeders and scoopers on it: Canada wasn't just a dog in a manger, though that was bad enough. Canada was a dog who only even had a manger to lie in thanks to American generosity and support.

By the end of the day of the Oroville rally, it was clear that things were starting to move. Slaymaker was climbing in Holly's polls, and the cave of bats was buzzing with excited gossip about the rallies. Americans – genuine ones as well as AI simulations – were talking about how inspiring these events had been. People anywhere near the border were wanting to know when the next one would be and how they could get there. Canadians – encouraged by a corps of Canadian feeders that Holly had purchased – were getting worked up about the unreasonableness of American demands, something which only served to make wavering Americans more certain that the demands were in fact fair. After all, the Canucks had ten times as much space as America per head of population, so how could it not be fair to ask them to take in a few desperate Americans?

•

Slaymaker pulled back into the lead among Freedom Party supporters right across the country, and he began winning primaries,
even in states which he'd had to neglect almost entirely. Public
demonstrations of support broke out. There were big marches in LA,
Boston and Chicago. And Holly had a bunch of professional demonstrators unfurl a giant banner in front of the Canadian embassy
in Washington, with the famous dog-in-the-manger cartoon, and
the caption: 'YOU'RE NOT USING IT. WE NEED IT.' That big
gray building, bristling defiantly with maple leaf flags, looked like
a hostile fortress with its long row of black slit windows looking
coldly down.

Seeing the way things were going, Frinton and Montello both
tried to claim that they'd always intended to demand a more
generous immigration policy from Canada. But it was too late.
They were already on record saying that leaning on Canada was
a crackpot idea and that Slaymaker had only done it because he
was desperate. And Holly's feeders made sure this wasn't forgotten:

Who's desperate now, eh?

Still think Stephen Slaymaker's a crackpot?

Thousands of feeders repeated these questions in hundreds
of variations, individually tailored for each main demographic
group from college-town delicados to city slum-dwellers to prairie
fundamentalists, so that all over the country people would feel that
the friends of their friends were coming to the same conclusion:

Slaymaker was the one in front, and so he should be, for didn't everyone agree he was the one with the vision?

•

President Williams was also feeling the pressure. All the polls had shown her lagging behind all three Freedom Party front-runners, and now they were showing her with less than half the approval rating of Senator Slaymaker. She asked for urgent talks with the government of Canada about 'their current untenable immigration policy' and the Canadians, equally keen to head off Slaymaker, hastily agreed. But of course the voting public could see perfectly well that it was Slaymaker who'd started this, and Williams who was following his lead. Holly made sure of that. She even commissioned a little ten-second animation – rather an old-fashioned tool, but still very effective if used sparingly – that showed Slaymaker driving a train that was leaving a station. Montello and Frinton were hauling themselves, sweating and panting, into the caboose, while Williams, who was famously overweight, was still desperately waddling along the platform. The clip ended with a close-up of her shining, gasping face.

Holly's stock rose within the campaign team. Even Ann Sellick admitted that 'this stupid Canada stunt may just have saved us'. And Sue Cortez suddenly started being nice.

'I want you to come along and meet some of our donors, Holly. Steve and Eve keep telling them about you and they're all desperate to see you in the flesh. We've got a dinner coming up in a couple of weeks. Why don't you come down and say a few words?'

She scrunched up her face a bit, making an effort to change her expression to something approaching humility. 'Listen, Holly, I admit I wasn't sure about it at first. I wasn't sure of *you*, to be honest. But this was a great idea of yours. The polls are amazing, and we're even getting a whole *new* bunch of donors coming forward with money.'

•

When it came to the fifth rally at a place called Opheim, Montana, Holly went along herself. The crossing was in the middle of empty prairie, but a recently built electric highway crossed the frontier there, and there was a large plaza straddling the border, with US and Canadian customs posts facing each other in the middle of it. There were no big towns nearby, but – and Holly had checked this – there were several big federally run trailer parks within a couple of hours' drive which were the home of many thousands of weather refugees, mainly from the southwest.

Holly flew over there with Slaymaker in his private drig, and when she'd overseen the preparations, she took her place in the large and growing crowd. Parked buses and cars clogged the highway for several miles to the south of the border as what turned out to be more than five thousand people crammed themselves into the America side of the plaza. Just across the frontier, a few hundred Canadians had come to listen too, and there were about fifty Mounties in front of them, lined up along the border and looking tense and grim. As in Oroville, there was no river or any natural feature to mark the frontier. The Medicine Line was made visible on the plaza itself by a red and white striped plastic pole, held up by a row of plastic trestles, in order to stop cars from simply driving round the customs posts where the computers would check and record their details. One of the poles had been broken at some point and repaired with a crude bandage of silver duct tape. Out on the prairie the border was completely invisible.

Slaymaker stood on a small platform just to one side of the US customs post. Holly had arranged to have big maps projected on to twenty-foot-high screens: Mercator projections, as ever, with America in a dull desert red and a huge sprawling Canada in a lush, verdant green.

Slaymaker was fierce and powerful, very different from the courteous, attentive and almost humble persona he presented when you met him one-on-one. He was charming, funny, out-rageous, warm, folksy, and yet at the same time somehow very dangerous in rather a thrilling way. She could sense the tough wise-cracking trailer-park kid right there, the kid who'd figured out he was smarter and more determined than any of the others, ready to beat the shit out of anyone who messed with him. And he employed to perfection his well-practiced technique of appearing not well-practiced at all: that regular-guy trick that allowed him to give out all kinds of signals that his followers would be able to pick up, but which he could take back later if need be, apologizing for the roughness and clumsiness of his untutored tongue.

Everything went just the way she had planned when she put the speech together with Quentin and Jed.

'I'm a man of peace, friends. I'm a God-fearing man and a man of peace. I do *not* seek conflict with anyone. But there is a problem that now faces us on this continent, a problem we're going to have to face sooner or later. And unlike others, I refuse to be silent on it. If I put things in a bit of a rough-and-ready way, well, I'm sorry. I didn't go to Yale or Princeton, as you know. Truth is, I dropped out of school at sixteen, and wasn't in school all that much before then either. I'm a truck man, first and foremost.

'But I keep my eyes open. I notice what's going on around me, and I see what all of you can see. Things have changed these last thirty years. Things have gotten a little tougher. We have land that used to be under the plow that's now nothing but desert sand. We have whole towns abandoned because there's no practical way of giving them water. We have big coastal cities that are staggering under the punches that the storms keep dealing out. And on top of that, we have northern cities that are struggling to cope with all the folk coming in from other parts. So what we've got here is *one* bunch of decent hard-working folk who've lost their livelihoods, and are struggling to make their way, and *another* bunch of decent hard-working folk who'd like to help but are kind of up against it themselves. And *all* of us, wherever we live in America, have got worries about where we're going to be and how we're going to make a living, ten or twenty years down the track.

'And now here's where I get to the bit that upsets some folks. Here's where I get people yelling at me. But all I'm doing is pointing out something that anyone can see who chooses to look for one moment at a map of this great continent of ours. It's just that most people are too polite to speak about it.

'And here it is. We're kind of crowded here in the United States. I know the good people in the northern states of America will do their bit, like they always have done, paying out taxes to help their fellow Americans to move up and join them, and helping us build new cities and towns. But our northern people can't do everything, no matter how much they might like to. They have the goodwill, they have the generosity, but they just don't have the slack. So what are we going to do? Well, I can't help noticing that just to the north of us, four or five yards from where I'm standing, there's a huge country, bigger than America itself, much of it damn near empty. Just its three Arctic territories – there they are, look, people, lighting up right now – make up a land area that's one-third the size of the entire United States. But all three of them together have a combined population that's less – can you believe this? – *less* than the population of Little Rock, Arkansas. And those three almost empty territories are just beginning to come out, all fresh and shiny and new, from under the ice right now, while our western states are losing good land every day to dust and sand, and our eastern states are being battered every summer by storms.

'We all know the name of that country just over those barriers, but maybe I'd better not say it out loud, because each time I do, it seems to get me in trouble.'

Slaymaker paused here, and five thousand people laughed and began to chant the name that he was pretending to be too cautious to say, while the Mounties watched stony-faced from the far side of the frontier.

'What's that? *Canada*? Really? Well, okay, but remember you said it first not me. You people are going to have to take the blame!'

A big happy cheer of assent went up on the American side. Holly had figured that people would enjoy this little conceit of them being the ones who'd stuck their necks out. People liked to be told they're brave and tough and individualistic. They just didn't like *being* those things so much.

'Don't you worry, Mr Slaymaker,' some guy yelled out, 'we've got your back.'

Slaymaker pointed at him, grinned, gave him a thumbs-up. 'Much obliged, *compañero*, much obliged. But seriously, folks, I bear the Canadian people no enmity. They're English-speaking North Americans, the same as most of us. The only real difference between them and us is the fact that they live north of an invisible line that someone drew with a ruler across a map, and we live south of it. Oh yeah, and the fact that they took a little longer than we did to say goodbye to English kings and queens.'

This got a big cheer too and Holly suddenly felt tears rising behind her eyes. There was a feeling of elation and release welling up in that crowd that was very moving. These were people who'd felt humiliated and powerless, and finally they were being given some hope and something to be proud of.

'And maybe,' said Slaymaker, 'the fact that some of them say "hooss" when they mean "house" and "aboot" when they mean "about".'

More cheers and laughter. Holly nodded and smiled. She'd road-tested every one of his little jokelets in focus groups.

'Seriously, folks, I bear the Canadian people no ill will. I don't want to take their homes from them, or their farms, or their businesses, let alone their beautiful country. But I do say to them they've got to *let – us – in*.'

There was loud applause. Good. The gear-shift from jokey to serious had worked perfectly.

'And I mean they've got to *really* let us in, not one at a time, with temporary visas, and not a lousy twenty thousand a year, which might sound a lot, people, but really is nothing at all compared with our population of half a billion or even theirs of fifty million. No, they've got to open their borders and let us in as fellow citizens and equal partners. That's the new frontier now, up there in the Yukon, and the North-Western Territory, and…uh…Nun… Nunny Vat…'

Good, that got a laugh. He could of course pronounce the name of Canada's sole Inuit-majority territory perfectly well (although it had to be said he hadn't heard of it until Jed told him about it). But Holly had learnt from her surveys that most Americans didn't even recognize the name, let alone know how to pronounce it, and she wanted them to think of him as one of them.

'Nanny Pat, Nonny Vit...whatever the heck it's called...' clowned Slaymaker, as they'd agreed he would do if he got a decent laugh the first time round. 'Let's just hope my old geography teacher isn't watching this, or he'll have my ass.'

There was more loud laughter and applause.

'But seriously, people, look at the map. Look at that empty space. Look at those big islands up there. We've got people here in America who *need* that land. We'll build the towns up there, we'll create the jobs, and we won't ask the Canadians to spend a single cent of their hard-earnt money, but our people do need some of that land that they aren't using. It can't be allowed just to stand there empty.'

Once again, the gear-shift had worked perfectly. Holly had to admit that, for all his faults, for all his slowness at grasping hold of the latest twist in the story, Quentin was great at pacing. The smiles had faded but the applause was as loud as ever.

'Like I said, I tell it how I see it. But did you hear me say anything bad about Canada? No you did not.'

More cheers.

'Did you hear me speak of wanting to harm those good people over there in any way, or take away their livelihoods or their homes?'

Still more cheers, and shouts of, 'No we did not!' The warm-up people from the buses were in the crowd to help get these responses going, but Holly was pretty sure they hadn't been necessary.

'Did you hear me say anything,' Slaymaker called out, 'that would justify the government of Canada in whining, as it did after my speech last week in New York State, about "a gross violation of national sovereignty"?'

'No we did not!'

'Quite right, my friends. I'm not telling Canadians how to run their country. They do that very well for themselves. All I'm saying is: let our people in, let them build new towns and cities, let them do for your country what Americans have always done best – create wealth, create opportunities, get things moving.'

He paused for a few seconds to let people chant out his name and then raised his hands for quiet. 'America doesn't stop at frontiers,' he said. 'Never has done. That's not what America's about. We *open up* frontiers, and then we roll up our sleeves and we make things happen. *That's* America. We make things happen! We make things happen for everyone. And woe betide anyone who tries to stop us.'

Loud excited clapping and shouting. And then a new thing happened, something that Holly hadn't planned for at all. People started to push against those plastic barriers, yelling at the Canadian cops to get out of their way. And to their amazement, delight and scorn, the cops did just that.

The news hubs loved it, and so did the whisperstream. Later, as the Americans who'd crossed the border were finally persuaded back by the humiliated Mounties, or wandered back of their own accord, Holly sat beside Slaymaker in his personal drig and flipped through instant reaction interviews on the drig's broadscreen. Poll data was invaluable, but individual responses gave a feel that aggregated data just couldn't deliver.

'I was going with Montello,' said a man from Olympia, Washington, 'but I'm starting to change my mind. I don't go along with everything Slaymaker says, but he sure as hell is standing up for America.'

'You know what I noticed?' said a woman from New Jersey, after been shown footage of the Opheim rally. 'It was all that empty space, stretching away, like...I don't know...like an ocean almost, with no houses or nothing, just grass.' She didn't seem to have noticed that the prairie extended on both sides of the border. 'I think the senator's right. We gotta to be allowed access to that space. That's where he scores over all the others, because the one thing we need is space.'

'Thing that gets me,' said a plump young man from Detroit, 'is that the Canucks were on the British side when we fought for independence. So how come they still get to control all that land, and say who can come in there and who can't? Why did we ever let them get away with that?'

'Because they pretended to be our friends,' said his equally plump girlfriend who'd been sitting next to him, leaning in now so as to be sure she could be seen.

'Yeah,' said the young man. 'They made fools out of us, really, I guess. But I reckon Slaymaker—'

'*President* Slaymaker.'

'Yeah. I reckon President Slaymaker will put a stop to that.'

Slaymaker laughed, turning to Holly and offering her his bottle of cola to clink against her can of gin and tonic.

'*We'll* put a stop to that,' he said, 'President Stephen Slaymaker and Whisperstream Wizard Holly Peacock.'

CHAPTER 32

Rosine Dubois

'd never been on any sort of demonstration before, nor had
Herb, and nor had Pete or Tracey or any of the people I knew
in the camp. We'd never really bothered with politics at all. But
the Slaymaker people were laying on free beer, free food, and even
free childcare for our kids after school, and we thought, *Well, why
not?* It'd be fun. It'd be a day out. Best of all, it'd be a break from
those lines of metal trailers, and the sound of kids crying, and tired
mums and dads yelling at them to shut up.

Yes, and Senator Slaymaker had stood up for people like us
when no one else seemed to care. I reckoned we owed him a bit of
support. Tracey felt the same. She'd told me that Pete and her had
always voted for the Christian Party. 'But we're backing Slaymaker
this time if he gets the nomination,' she said. 'We both agree about
that. He might not be in the Christian Party, but he's a Christian
man, and he tries to behave like one too.'

We had a lovely time on the bus. We had this great courier
called Sandra, a big loud merry woman from Chicago who got us
all laughing with jokes about Canada – some of them a bit strong
for my taste, but never mind – and had us practicing some stuff we
could all chant out together when we got up to the border there:

'*Slay – Slay – Slaymaker! Slay – Slay – Slaymaker!*'

We hollered it out together like a bunch of excited kids, and even poor sad old Pete laughed till the tears ran down his face. I sat next to Tracey with a couple of other women, and we just talked and joked non-stop the whole way. Pete and Herb weren't quite so close as me and Tracey had become – in fairness to Herb, poor old Pete wasn't exactly a fun kind of guy – but after a couple of beers, they seemed to get on pretty well too. By the time we piled off the bus at a service station about half a mile from the crossing – other buses unloading all around us, and more pulling in behind us all the time – we felt like we were going to a party. Everyone was shouting and singing and waving the placards and flags that the Slaymaker people had provided for us. Some people had dressed up as Uncle Sam or George Washington. There was even an American eagle with a big beer belly.

But when we got up to that big plaza where the border posts were and saw those Canadian cops lined up on the other side with their shields and visors, it felt a bit different, a bit more serious, specially when Mr Slaymaker showed us those maps, and that huge green country up there, way way bigger than the whole of America, and all of it pretty much empty, so he said, except for just a little narrow strip, just on the other side of the border, where they all lived. The Bible says we should turn the other cheek, I know, but I don't mind admitting that it made me feel kind of mad. Herb had shown me pictures of some of that land which he'd found on the stream: beautiful green fields and empty houses. What were they keeping it *for*? What *use* was it to them?

After the senator had finished speaking, we chanted out '*Slay – Slay – Slaymaker!*' just like we'd practiced on the bus. 'You'll be on the broadscreen tonight,' Sandra had told us. 'All the top news hubs are going to be there! So make sure you holler as loud as ever you can. I don't want to hear any voices that aren't hoarse when you get on the bus to go home.' We sure did our best not to disappoint her.

When Mr Slaymaker had finished talking, Herb had an idea. 'Look at those piss-ass cops through there,' he yelled to me and Pete and Tracey over all the noise. 'Do they really think they could stop us?'

Pete didn't even bother to answer. He just took Tracey's arm and led her forward, with me and Herb following after, and he put his hand on the plastic barrier, and turned round and winked at us all. You've got to bear in mind that he'd never been in any demonstration or nothing in his life before. And you've got to remember what a poor miserable guy he was most of the time, and how he cried like a kid when those kids trashed his little vegetable garden. But right now he had a big grin all over his face.

'Well, what's the worst that can happen?' he said, or bellowed it more like, because everyone was yelling and hollering all around us.

'The worst that can happen is they shoot us,' Tracey hollered back, 'and then we'd never have to go back to that goddam trailer park.'

Other people were watching him, giving him the thumbs-up as they waited for his lead, while the crowd kept yelling, 'Slay – Slay – Slaymaker!' And then Pete just gave a little nod and shoved that plastic barrier over. We all stepped across it, a whole bunch of us, and then there we were in Canada.

Of course there wasn't really anywhere over there to go, but we had a bit of fun teasing the Mounties, who just drove up and down in the road in their trucks, stopping by groups of Americans and pretty much begging us to go back.

'Hope you've got a note from your mom for this!' Herb called out to one young guy, who looked like he hadn't even started to shave. But after an hour or so we got bored and walked back into America by ourselves.

'I'll tell you something,' I said, as we climbed back onto our bus. 'I'll never forget the expression on those cops' faces when we busted through.'

Herb laughed, his face shining and happy like I hadn't seen it since before Superstorm Simon. 'They didn't even try and stop us,' he said. 'That's what gets me. They just stood aside to let us pass.'

I put my arm through his and rested my cheek on his shoulder. He put his arm round me and kissed me on top of my head. Which was something else that hadn't happened for a long time.

'Well, me and Tracey always said we'd like to travel abroad,' said Pete. 'Looks like we finally got our wish. An afternoon in Canada, and it didn't cost us a dime.'

It was lovely to see him joking about like that. Tracey gave him a kiss, and we all cheered.

CHAPTER 33

When Richard got back from a drama class the following afternoon, he found that Holly had returned and was upstairs working in her study. He strode straight up.

'Are you and Daddy Slaymaker trying to start *a war*?'

She'd been working on ripostes to questions about the rally, so her answer was well rehearsed. 'No, of course not. Read his speech. He made it completely clear that he's not challenging Canadian sovereignty over any part of its territory.'

'And yet that's exactly what the crowd there did.'

She'd been looking at her cristal, but now she pushed it to one side.

'They were angry people, Rick. You can't blame Steve for that. I was there, don't forget. A large part of that crowd were people who've lost everything. Steve's not responsible for the fact that people like that feel angry. All he's trying to do is find a way forward that we can all live with.'

'It would have been nice if he'd thought about that thirty years ago, when he was still paying millions to professionals like you to rubbish the science that said this was where we were heading.'

'So he's not perfect. But before you judge him, can I ask you yet one more time what exactly *you're* doing about these problems he's trying to fix? This is a man who starts work at half past six every day and works solidly through to eight or nine at night, not moving around words on a screen, or playing make-believe in a drama studio, but making real stuff happen.'

Richard bowed his head, letting the defensive anger subside before he answered. 'Slaymaker's energy is immense, Holly, I've never disputed that. But, God damn it, that doesn't make him *right*!'

'No one really knows what's right, Rick, no one. But there are two kinds of people in the world. The ones who get on with stuff and the ones like my dad who just sit and criticize.'

'So which kind was Attila the Hun?'

'Oh, for Christ's *sake*!'

She went out after that. She wanted to watch the hub news without his disapproving presence beside her, so she took herself down to the bar in the village. Richard watched the broadscreen on his own.

President Williams was the first item. She was in a difficult position. International good manners required that she dissociate herself from the inflammatory behaviour of Senator Slaymaker. But to go too far in that direction would have been electoral suicide, because Slaymaker's demands on Canada had been hugely popular: all through the day, large crowds had been taking part in pro-Slaymaker demonstrations in most large US cities. So she criticized the senator's 'intemperate language, lack of clarity and lack of sensitivity to the feelings of our friends in Canada' but, at the same time, complained about the incompetent policing of the event by the Canadian authorities. And she spoke of the importance of her forthcoming talks in Ottawa, and the need to move very quickly there on adjusting Canadian immigration quotas to take account of 'changing realities'.

Suzanne Ryan, the Canadian prime minister, had been so close to Jenny Williams on so many issues that the North American media had dubbed them 'the Gray Sisters', but now Ryan's own support base demanded a strong and angry response to what had happened at the Opheim crossing.

'It's all very well for the United States government to try to dissociate itself from the inflammatory language of Senator Slaymaker,' she bellowed in the House of Commons in Ottawa, 'but actions speak louder than words. When more than five thousand Americans gathered at a single frontier crossing, where were the American police? Why was it left to the Canadian security services to attempt to stem the tide, and what right did the American government then have to complain about the way it was handled? Have we ever denied the right of the United States, now or in the past, to rigorously protect its southern border against illegal migration from Mexico? Is anyone seriously arguing that our police, who did not cause a single injury, were in some way inferior to the US Border Patrol which shoots dead roughly ten – that's right, *ten* – Mexicans a month?

'Yes, and why, when the Canadian, Norwegian, Danish and Icelandic governments are all now asking the Council of Nations to urgently consider a resolution confirming the right of Arctic countries to determine their own immigration policy, did the United States choose to turn away from these four old allies and stand alongside Greater China in indicating its intention of vetoing any such move? It seems that the United States prefers to associate itself with China's land-grabbing activities along its northern border, than to stand by its old friends!'

And then Montello and Frinton came on, both of them saying that of course Canada should do more, and they'd always believed that, but Slaymaker wasn't handling it in the right way.

Richard turned off the screen. In the silence he found himself suddenly stranded, almost unable to move, as if he'd switched off his motivation along with the screen.

Meaning depended on there being a future, he thought. People could bear the thought of their own individual annihilation, but they needed to feel that when they were gone, they'd be leaving something behind them, whether it was children, or a farm, or people who remember them, or something they'd made, like his books. Okay, they were fooling themselves in most cases – most people vanished without a trace – but there needed to be a future for us to even be able to kid ourselves.

He had an impulse to call Alice. They could discuss the rehearsal, and no doubt get onto the news. And Alice always made him feel better about himself. Her obvious interest in him always reassured him that there was something here that merited interest. But then he noticed that Holly had gone out without her jacket. The sky was clear outside and the night was growing cold, so he thought he'd take it down to the bar for her.

The dark ridge lowered above the village. Thousands of stars blazed down. The tiny figure of Richard made its way along the empty, dimly lit street, past houses with drawn curtains, and here and there the flickering light of a broadscreen.

Holly was sitting by herself at the window of the bar, frowning with concentration as she muttered silently to her jeenee, her hands shaping punctuation marks. She looked very tired and, for some reason, very young.

He tapped on the window, holding up her jacket. She started, but as soon as she saw it was him, her face broke into a smile that instantly melted him.

He went inside. The rocket music was playing as usual. Space rocket sounds whooshed softly around the bar, while a female voice lamented a beautiful starship captain, who'd flown away to far, far Centaurus.

'I thought you'd get cold.'

'That's nice of you, dearest. I'm just about done with this. Shall we walk back together? I can finish off in the morning.'

She slipped her arm through his as they headed home.

'I don't think you're like my dad in the slightest. You know that, don't you?'

'I'm relieved to hear it.'

They stopped and kissed. Her lips were soft and warm.

'Dad would never have thought of bringing me my coat.'

They passed the white church, the little park, the vehicle charging station. They didn't talk about Slaymaker. They didn't use the time to talk about their future together, just about small ordinary things.

It is hard to believe that things are really going to change, when they are still there right in front of you, the same as ever.

Holly couldn't sleep, though. She crept back downstairs – how different their living room felt in the middle of the night with only her there – and flipped on her cristal, telling the jeenee to pull up the day's haul from her scoopers, and sort them into semantic bundles.

Show me a Canuck and I'll show you a traitor. That, with many variations, was the last twenty-four hours' most frequent catch, with over a million iterations already on the whisperstream, increasingly accompanied, as time went on, by either a hangman's noose or a revolutionary-era tricorn hat. The message seemed to be of human origin, and certainly wasn't generated by any of Slaymaker's feeders, though they had enthusiastically recycled it, and they had, on Holly's instructions, been reminding the whisperstream for several days that the Canadian colonies had taken the British side in the War of Independence.

The AIs that controlled feeders routinely generated their own small polls to check the impact of new messages. These revealed that the 'Canuck traitor' message had been most popular among low-to-medium skilled voters in the eighteen to thirty-five age group. North and south of the country, the approval rating among that particular demographic group was over 80 percent for men and 70 percent for women. For both genders, the addition of the noose image increased the popularity rating by two points. The tricorn hat was popular, too, even though less than 40 percent of this same demographic group recognized the reference to the American Revolution, and over 20 percent believed that Canada's treachery had been to side with America's enemies during the various global wars of the twentieth and twenty-first centuries. Even though the opposite was actually true, Holly's more down-market feeders had duly recycled messages to this effect, for their brief was to amplify any message, any message at all that would chip away at the idea of American–Canadian solidarity. *Canada helped the Japanese attack Pearl Harbor* and *Canada helped the Arabs attack New*

York had both proved popular, with something like ten thousand iterations each. Even the more exotic *Canada helped the Arabs attack Pearl Harbor* had proved to have its fans.

Factual accuracy meant very little to the whisperstream, flowing along its countless separate parallel channels like the buried *id* of human society, hidden away, often denied or decried by its own creators, yet far more powerful than anything that lay above. Factual accuracy – factual accuracy even as an *aspiration* – was for the broadscreen-based news hubs, and only a minority of the population ever looked at those. Down in the stream, as in art, it wasn't the literal truth of a thing that counted, but whether it felt true in your gut.

The only good Canuck is a dead one: that was pretty popular too (and again apparently human in origin and not generated by any of Slaymaker's feeders) and so were images of burning or bloodstained maple leaf flags. Among the higher-skilled/lower-professional demographic a popular message that day had been: *The Canucks caused this mess and now they damn well need to help us clear it up.* This was human-generated as well, although it seemed to draw on some work Holly had done with her feeders a few days previously in which she'd pointed out that Canada had been a major oil producer at one time, and therefore a major contributor to the world's current weather problems. (America had produced much more oil than Canada, but of course that was entirely irrelevant for these present purposes.)

Holly laid her cristal down on the table. She looked round the room, she and Richard's little familiar living room, with that smart cream-colored sofa they'd bought at the Seafront Warehouse in Seattle, the broadscreen with the loose wires at the back, the old-fashioned side lamp that had belonged to Richard's grandmother, the bold, bright semi-abstract painting of a Cascades mountainside in the fall that was their wedding present from Ruby. In the daylight, or in the evening when other people were there, that room was full of familiar meanings and associations, but now in the middle of the night, all of that was gone. It was just a box filled with random lumps of inanimate matter.

'A message from Ruby,' her jeenee whispered through the implant in her ear.

Holly tensed. 'Okay, read it to me.'

'Hi Holly,' the jeenee said. 'Can't sleep. Very upset by what's happening on the border. Everyone here's very scared, and me and Ossia have been getting abuse just for being American. Can we talk sometime?'

'Put her through,' Holly told the jeenee, and almost at once there was her friend's kind face on her cristal screen.

'I couldn't sleep either,' Holly said.

Ruby was tense, talking quickly as if she'd had to rehearse what she was going to say in advance and was now gabbling it out like a script. 'I really don't want to think badly of you, Holly, I really don't, but I know you're part of this and I just don't get it. I had a woman in a store yesterday tell me to fuck off back to the States. Ossia is convinced that she lost a big role the other day just because she's American. Why are you doing this? What has Canada done to deserve it? What have Americans in Canada done to deserve it?'

'Listen, let's meet. Let's have a meal together, and I'll explain.'

CHAPTER 34

Holly wished she hadn't suggested this idea almost as soon as she had spoken it, but Ruby ran with it, booking a restaurant five miles from the border on the American side. She also invited Ossia, along with Sergio and Mariana, which wasn't what Holly had in mind at all. They met among tropical plants, with a pianist and a flautist playing soft liquid geometry music with an AI music machine that gathered their notes and built them into a wonderfully intricate tower of sound that constantly changed but never lost its architectural symmetry. Beautiful dishes were laid in front of them. Everyone was angry with Holly.

'*Jesucristo*, Holly, I just can't believe you are carrying on with these rallies after Opheim,' Sergio rumbled almost as soon as they'd ordered.

'Exactly,' said Ossia, coldly furious. 'What kind of politician encourages people to cross the border of another country?'

'A very reckless and immature one,' said Mariana.

'A realist,' Holly said.

'Oh, come on!' exclaimed Ossia.

'A realist,' Holly repeated, 'and, by the way, Ossia, I thought you were against borders of any kind?'

'Oh *please*, Holly!' snorted Sergio. 'That wasn't just people crossing a border. That was an act of aggression.'

'We're asking a great deal of northern voters,' Holly said. 'They have problems of their own, but we're asking them to voluntarily shoulder a burden. The only way we've been able to get them to agree to it is by saying that at least part of the load will be shared by others even further north.'

'You can't just use—' began Sergio but, to Holly's surprise, Richard interrupted him.

'Seems to me,' he said slowly, 'that people like us – delicados if we really must call ourselves that – people like us have never quite got politics. We think of it as something you debate round a dinner table like this, or in the whisperstream at best, and maybe sign the odd petition once in a while, or go on a march. We see political discourse as a way of demonstrating our moral credentials, and we act as if we believe that, for our views to prevail, all that's needed is for us to prove irrefutably the moral superiority of our ideas.'

Sergio was trying to break in, but Richard held up his hand to stop him. 'But, as you know, I'm a historian, and history tells me that what we call politics is barely politics at all. Our politics is a game, a ritual of purification, a way of washing away the sin of our privilege. But real politics is about *deals*. It's about building coalitions. It's about the implicit contracts between leaders and followers. During the twentieth century, the rough equivalent of what we call delicados were called liberals, and for a time back then prosperous liberals did have a kind of contract with the poor – *if you guys vote for us and our weird modern ideas, we'll look after you and fight your corner* – but in the end liberals took that contract too much for granted, and it failed. Poor people turned to more con-genial leaders who didn't lecture them about their prejudices, and we ended up with the Tyranny. We should learn from that. No one is going to listen to people like us lecturing them about what they should think or who they should care about. If you want people's votes you have to make them feel that you know what matters to *them*, that you care about what *they* care about, and that you're going to stand by them in some way. And I think that's what Slaymaker has managed to achieve with Holly's help. This restaurant isn't America. Life isn't easy for most people. Whether fairly or not, Slaymaker's managed to persuade a whole lot of those people that he's got their back.'

Holly was startled. He had never said anything quite like this to her. Even now, she could tell, he was going against his own instincts to say it, but he was articulating something that had always seemed obvious to her. The other four were like children. They liked to think of themselves as being on the side of the good guys, but they made no serious effort to change anything. But she *had* changed things. Out of all the half billion people who lived in America, she was perhaps the one individual who had actually changed the outcome of the coming election, because she alone had found a way of drawing support away from Montello and Frinton, a way of winning support from northerners and barreduras both.

'But what about Canada?' said Ossia. 'Doesn't Canada have some rights here?'

'You're in favor of open borders, Ossia,' Holly said wearily.

'Borders open to people who really need somewhere to go.'

'Okay, well, you and Ruby are the Canadians here – why don't you let in some Mexicans, or Bangladeshis, or South Americans? Why don't the two of you organize a campaign to make that happen?'

She looked into her friends' faces. They *were* like children. And just for a moment, they were all daunted into silence by her adult voice.

'Oh and by the way,' Holly went on, 'it's true that more Americans are going to move to Canada as a result of this, but they won't come in huge numbers. Slaymaker of all people does *not* want America's population leaching away into Canada. America is his moral universe. Last thing he wants is for Canada to grow and America to shrink. His primary objective is to build new towns and cities in the northern states of the USA.'

'So we should just stop crying and put up with it? Is that what you're saying?'

Holly looked straight into Ossia's eyes. 'Yeah, actually, it is. I'm sorry it's a bit uncomfortable just now, I really am. But it'll pass, and I suspect that even now it's a lot less uncomfortable up in Canada than it is in our displaced persons camps here in America, let alone in the rest of the world.'

CHAPTER 35

Next morning, when Holly had headed off to the campaign HQ in Seattle, Richard sat down to work on a chapter and realized that he wasn't going to get anywhere. There was something going on in his head, some inner struggle, which made it impossible to concentrate. Holly had gone by train, so he put on his running things, took the car and headed out into the forest. Those dead trees held a gloomy fascination for him. Those miles of bare bone-like trunks, where the dominant life form was the lichen that dangled from the dead white branches in long gray strands, had a certain perverse appeal, like some vast graveyard, or the ruins of a forgotten civilization. But he was actually heading for a more hopeful place a couple of miles off the road, where the Federal Adaptation Agency had cleared away the dead wood and planted a few hundred acres of new trees from northern California. Species that were dying off down there in their original habitat were now well suited to the new weather conditions up here, and the FAA had brought up flowering plants to go with them, and birds and insects. The hope was that in due course this entire ecosystem would move out into the dead forest and bring it back to life.

Richard jogged along the path of a little stream as it wound through the dead white trunks in the open sunshine, and suddenly there were green leaves around him, the bright, bright green of spring, with birds singing and the stream winding in and out of sunlight and green shade. It wasn't exactly like the old days – few of the trees were taller than he was – but it was life, all the same.

There was a spot some way into that patch of green wood, a flat outcrop of rock surrounded by trees, where he liked to sit and think. He'd solved many writing problems right there, and ironed out niggles from his life. But as he approached it, he heard voices ahead of him, and smelled cooked meat. It turned out an encampment had sprung up there. A couple of old trucks were parked up, and there were half a dozen roughly built tepees constructed from branches, old tarpaulins and plastic sheeting. A skinned deer was roasting over a fire with men and woman sitting round it, and children were playing in the stream. All the people were black and, when they spoke, he could tell straight away they came from way down south: Alabama, Mississippi, somewhere like that, deep down in the Storm Country. They were living in the forest like Indians, and they really didn't want him around.

'What's your business here?' demanded a burly guy with a shotgun.

'Just having a run, *compañero*, just having a run. Didn't expect to find you guys here, to tell the truth.'

The man wasn't actually pointing the gun at Richard, but he had his finger resting on the trigger. Not far behind him, another big man was standing, unsmiling, with a machete.

'You just keep on running, then. We don't need no company.'

'Okay. Well, this is kind of where I was headed, so I guess I'll just turn round and go back.'

'You do that. And find some other place to run from now on, you hear me?'

As Richard made his way back through the green wood, he noticed something that he hadn't spotted before. A few of the new trees from California were dying, attacked perhaps by the same fungus that had killed the trees in the forest beyond. They were only saplings, but one or two of them already had dead branches, with gray beards of lichen. He felt a stab of grief, so strong that it was almost like a physical wound.

There was a deep contradiction inside him. On the one hand he loved history. He loved to think about it and write about it. He loved the drama and the sweep of it, the huge unstoppable forces, as elemental as glaciers or tides. On the other hand he didn't like change. He wanted life to be steady. He wanted the world around him to remain exactly as it was. He might write books about history, but he was afraid to even think about the history that was happening right now, though his own wife was riding the wave.

He would go to the next border rally himself, he decided. He would make himself go and watch.

It was at Peace Arch, Blaine, right next to the border crossing that he and Holly had used when they went north to visit Ruby and Ossia. The arch itself stood on the frontier itself between the north- and southbound lanes of the coastal highway. It commemorated the peace treaty that ended the War of 1812 between the USA and the British colonies that were to become Canada. A few years back, he and Holly had stopped to look at it. On the US side of the arch, an inscription read, 'Children of a common mother' and on the Canadian side were the words, 'Brethren dwelling together in unity'. A symbolic iron gate inside the arch was permanently open, with the words 'May these gates never be closed' inscribed above it. And the park in which it stood, half in the US and half in Canada, had no border post of any kind, so a visitor entering the park from either end could wander freely back and forth across the international frontier, while on either side of them, traffic flowed north and south on the electric highway.

Now the park was filled with many thousands of angry Americans, Slaymaker addressing them from a platform erected beside the arch itself. With Holly's help, Quentin Fox had crafted a more flowery speech than usual for the occasion, in keeping with the rhetoric of the arch itself.

'Don't turn us away, Canada! Honor the pledge inscribed inside this arch! Don't close these gates of friendship! Let us in, not just in ones or twos, but in our tens and hundreds of thousands, to establish new towns for ourselves in those northern lands of yours, where we can be prosperous and useful, contributing to the wealth of your country as well as our own.'

Richard was standing on the western edge of the park next to the southbound carriageway, at more or less the meeting point of the park's Canadian and American halves. The Canadians had established a line across the park about ten yards behind the arch and across roads on either side of it, defended by several hundred riot police with shields and body armor and helmets that hid their faces. On the American side of the frontier, there were a few dozen Washington State police on both the northbound and southbound roads. None of them had riot shields or helmets, they stood at ease, and there were no water cannons or armored cars waiting behind them, as there were on the Canadian side. If the Canadians had wanted to portray themselves as the heartless dogs in the manger depicted in the American whisperstream, they could hardly have done better.

As Slaymaker's speech progressed, Richard watched bouts of cheering and chanting morphing, more and more frequently, into abuse directed at the Canadians. The odd stone was thrown, and once an opened can of red paint. As far as he could tell from the coverage of previous rallies, the mood here was darker and angrier than it had ever been before.

'Let us in, you Canuck bastards!' shouted a very fat woman a few yards away from Richard. 'Or are you just going to stand there and watch us starve?'

At the end of his speech, Slaymaker asked if there was anyone from the audience who wanted to say anything. Holly had organized a parabolic microphone that could be focused on any part of the crowd, along with a camera that would zoom in and show the speaker on the same giant screens that had been displaying the usual Mercator maps of North America.

'This arch is supposed to celebrate peace with the British,' said an elderly woman, 'but we shouldn't never have made peace with them in the first place, if you want my opinion.'

The whole crowd cheered.

'I just hope for their sake that those Canucks never find themselves without a home like what's happened to me,' said a gnarled and suntanned farmer, 'because, boy oh boy, we're going to *laugh* in their faces.'

More big cheers. These speakers, with the license of being ordinary people, were expressing the vitriol that Slaymaker himself had been scrupulously careful to avoid. Richard wondered for a moment what that last speaker's response would have been, back in the good years, if some destitute refugee from Mexico or Nicaragua has asked him for some of *his* land? But he knew that was a pointless exercise. People weren't consistent. All of humanity possessed the same basic toolkit of principles but everyone selected only the ones that suited their present purposes.

'Those Canucks could sure learn a lesson from you, Senator,' said a large black woman from the South. 'You coulda sat in your ranch in the mountains, enjoying the nice cool air. But here you are fighting for people like us. God bless you, Senator. If you want my opinion, you're worth more than the whole damn nation of—'

Suddenly a shot rang out. Richard didn't see who fired it. Like everyone else, he instantly ducked, his heart pounding. But it was very near to him, and, in the stunned silence that followed, he saw a Canadian police officer, one of the many on the southbound carriageway just to his left, wince as the bullet hit him. The Mountie's colleagues pushed forward and surrounded him, but they knew that they themselves were in the line of fire. Many pulled out their own guns, pointing them warningly in the direction of the American crowd.

The crowd moaned and murmured and began to surge this way and that, like turbulent water along a rocky shore. And meanwhile, on the American part of the road, a strange new thing was happening, never seen before. The American police had drawn their guns and were pointing them, not at the crowd, but at their Canadian counterparts.

'Keep this calm, people,' Slaymaker bellowed from the platform, where secret service officers had moved swiftly to surround him. 'Keep this calm. We don't know what's happened over there. I need you to be patient and show some American dignity. Wait till your way out becomes clear, and then leave the—'

One of the Canadian officers interrupted him with a loud hailer.

'Any more shots in our direction and we open fire.'

'You open fire, *we* open fire,' shouted out an American cop. There was a loud cheer from the crowd and someone lobbed a stone into the Canadian ranks.

'Thanks for that,' Richard muttered bitterly. 'That's *really* going to help.'

'I want no more shots fired,' boomed Slaymaker. 'I ask our American police officers over there to put away their guns. And I ask our Canadian friends to do the same.'

The American police did as he asked, but people in the crowd kept on yelling abuse and throwing things at the Canadians, in spite of voices around them calling out to them to stop, and the Mounties kept hold of their weapons. Richard sensed very clearly what was about to happen. So did everyone else in his section of the crowd, which, like some sort of heavy viscous fluid, was slowly pushing its way out of the park onto the part of the southbound carriageway that was safely behind the line of American police. It was impossible to move quickly at first, but more space opened up as people reached the asphalt and many broke into a run. Meanwhile behind them, their more reckless compatriots continued to taunt the Mounties, in spite of Slaymaker's amplified voice continuing to call for forbearance.

Richard opted to walk not run. He had never before been in a situation where bullets had been fired and more seemed likely. He felt oddly unafraid, even a little elated. This was history, he was thinking. This was what history was like.

As he reached the American frontier posts, he heard a burst of gunfire behind him, followed by screams and wails. No one nearby knew what had happened. It was only later that he learnt that three

American demonstrators had been shot dead. But in his mind he saw corpses like broken dolls, and still-living people bleeding to death in a no man's land where no one could reach them.

CHAPTER 36

Slaymaker had come pretty well out of Peace Arch, that was Holly's first reaction, sitting in the campaign offices in Seattle and flipping back and forth across the stuff that was appearing, second by second, in the stream and across the hubs. Lots of American flags were flying, tear-stained declarations of solidarity were pouring out toward the families of the three dead Americans from every corner of the country, and, above all, only a very small minority seemed inclined to blame Slaymaker. She'd have to wait a few hours for detailed polls, of course, but there was plenty of footage of the senator appealing for calm and trying to control the crowd, and the entire video of his speech showed him talking in a measured, statesmanlike way about the historic friendship between the two countries. Crucially, too, all the deaths were on the American side. The only shot that had actually come *out* of the crowd had merely injured a Canadian policeman, and not very badly, at that. At one point, the US cops had taken out their own guns, but they'd ended up helping the wounded rather than shooting back.

Holly called Slaymaker and he got back to her as soon as he was safely away from the Peace Arch.

'Hey, Holly! I guess you heard what happened?'

She hadn't been conscious up to that point of feeling anxious, but she could tell now that she must have been very agitated, because of the calmness that instantly came over her on hearing his voice. It was as if she could only now allow herself to recognize the sense of darkness and dread that had been building inside her. But she felt fine now, level-headed and in control. She listened to herself as she began to set out her thoughts on how to play this new situation, and realized that what been half-formed ideas up to that point were already crystallizing into a coherent strategy simply as a result of speaking to him.

She was still talking with Slaymaker when Richard sent her a message to say he was okay. To her own shock she realized that it hadn't yet occurred to her to call him.

'Give me a minute to call Rick,' she told the senator. 'He was at the rally himself. I'll call you straight back.'

Rick was furious when he got home late that evening.

'I could easily have been one of the ones who died, Holly. Do you realize that? No, I guess not. Because you haven't even bothered to ask me. You knew I was at a demo where a fatal shooting occurred, but you didn't think to call me until I messaged you, and even then, you didn't ask me where I was in the crowd or what happened. But I'll tell you anyway. I was very near the Mounties who started shooting. If I'd hung around for two more minutes, I'd have been straight in the line of fire.'

'I'm sorry I was slow to call you. I feel really badly about that. I don't know why, but somehow I just knew you were okay. But I should have called you anyway and I'm sorry.'

'The shooting was your fault in some part, Holly. Have you thought about that? Your fault for helping your pal Slaymaker stoke up hostility.'

'Oh, come on. I can show you the speech if you like. At no point did Steve advocate violence. Some random guy in the crowd fired a shot and the Mounties lost their heads. It could have happened in any crowd situation.'

'Damn it, Holly, I was *there*! Don't tell *me* what happened! The guy fired the shot only a few yards away from me. I felt the tension in the crowd beforehand, and I saw the fear on the Canadian side afterwards. Canada might look big on the map, Holly, but in terms of population it's a small country, and you and Slaymaker are intimidating them. And yeah, okay, your—'

'All we're doing is asking them to take some responsibility for fellow North Americans who are victims of—'

'Don't spin me the fucking party line, Holly. I'm your husband, remember! I'm the guy you say you love! I was there, alright? I was an eyewitness to the provocation. Yeah, your precious Steve doesn't call for violence. Yeah, he remains his normal affable self. But don't tell me you haven't noticed the rage beneath that amiable surface? The burning rage. I mean, for Christ's sake, how could anyone have had a childhood like his and not be full of rage? He's just very very good at managing it.'

This was a genuinely new thought to Holly. She remembered the quality that had exhilarated her when she had watched Slaymaker at Opheim. She'd called it dangerousness, but she could see now that rage was another name for it: controlled and very concentrated rage. How odd that she hadn't spotted it before, like a fish not noticing the existence of water. And how odd that she hadn't thought of calling Richard as soon as she heard about the shooting. She had no explanation that was convincing even to her. The thing about having somehow known that Richard was okay was just a way of saying that it hadn't even occurred to her to worry about him.

'This was never going to be painless,' she said. 'This was never going to happen without conflict and anger. But if we left things as they were that would have been worse. Look what's happening over in Africa, look at Central America. Do we want our own Memetic Hordes?'

She felt a real passion rising up inside her as she was speaking. The deaths at Peace Arch, and her own odd indifference to Richard's safety, had made it necessary for her to believe even more deeply in Slaymaker's project, if she was to preserve her sense of herself as a decent person. And she was drawing on all of her professional skills to talk herself into doing just that, choosing her words and her arguments as she did for her clients when she rummaged on their behalf in the dressing-up box of human values – those fallen fragments from the third dimension – for the clothes that would show them in the best possible light.

Jenny Williams flew to Ottawa for her meeting with Prime Minister Suzanne Ryan. At their initial joint press conference, the president made clear that she wouldn't accept any sort of excuse for the indiscriminate killing of unarmed US citizens by Canadian police officers, and demanded reassurances that the officers concerned would be identified and brought to justice, but she also said that she couldn't condone the inflammatory rhetoric of Senator Stephen Slaymaker.

'I ask our Canadian friends to remember that the United States, like your own country, is a democracy. However much we might regret the language used by certain figures in both of our countries, they are entitled to say what they wish. And when it comes to Senator Slaymaker, it's important that we recognize that many Americans share his concerns, even if they disapprove of his methods. I ask the Canadian people to understand that anyone standing for election in America, myself included, *must* be able to convince ordinary American voters that something is being done to settle the displaced people from the southern and southwestern parts of the country that won't put an unrealistic amount of pressure on our northern states. The US is spending more than any other country on the planet on reversing the carbon dioxide glut that's at the heart of the problem, but – and I'm going to speak bluntly here – unless I can go home with a generous deal on the immigration issue, Canada may find itself having to deal with President Slaymaker not President Williams.'

In her reply, the Canadian prime minister was noticeably careful not to dismiss out of hand what the president had to say about immigration, and she proposed an urgent summit conference of all the governments concerned, 'to look creatively at the whole issue of migration to the North American Arctic, right the way from Alaska to Greenland'.

'You see!' crowed Holly, as she watched the news on the broadscreen with Richard. 'You see! Some movement! No way would Williams have achieved that without Steve behind her playing the bad cop.'

She noticed how Prime Minister Ryan was choosing to draw Greenland into the equation, softening the sting for her electorate by mentioning yet another sparsely populated Arctic land that could share the load. Someone on Ryan's team had borrowed her idea!

'And this was you?' said Richard. 'It really was you that made this happen?'

He had studied the Anglo-Saxon invasion of England, the decolonization of Africa, the American Revolution. He knew just how brutal the process of change was in the human world, and how ruthless the leaders of change had to be, whether history ended up labeling them as good guys or bad. But he had never expected to see it this close to him.

CHAPTER 37

Slaymaker had returned to DC for the dinner with his donors, and Holly flew down to join him. 'They're all *so* keen to meet you, Holly!' Sue kept telling her. 'We all keep telling them how smart you are!'

Inside the drig, she opened her cristal and began to work on ideas for the next move.

Obviously the first thing she had to think about was the issue of the shootings. All her polls so far had shown they'd done Slaymaker no harm at all. On the contrary, by increasing the general anti-Canuck mood, they'd bumped up Slaymaker's already soaring ratings by several points. But you could never take these things for granted. New stories could turn these trends around in a matter of hours. Before setting out, she'd commissioned specialist research AIs to find out everything possible about the American victims and their families, and to identify family members, friends and neighbors who'd be willing to speak to her. It was awful those people had died, obviously, but there was no denying that it was a public relations *gift*, so much of a gift, in fact, that she found it hard to make herself wait for the bios before she began to write imaginary scripts in her head:

These were regular ordinary hard-working Americans, not prone to complaining, not prone to political activity of any kind...

Jill was sixty-two and had never been on a demonstration before in her life...

Ted, fifty-seven, was a pillar of his local community. 'Didn't matter who you were, Ted always had time for you', as one former neighbor recalls...

But of course, this was silly. She needed to wait for the real names and bios and, even once those were available, the first priority would have to be to look after the survivors. Slaymaker had a reputation for warmth, and that needed to be maintained.

Meanwhile, there were other things to think about. There was the injured Canadian cop, for one thing. The fact that that cop hadn't died made her job much easier, but she still needed to find a way of batting away the inevitable claims that the whole ugly incident was the direct result of Slaymaker's deliberate provocation. That was job number one.

And then there was the question of what next? Peace Arch was obviously going to have to be the last border rally, so what else could be done to keep up the momentum? Holly wondered briefly about Greenland, that huge island, which Prime Minister Ryan had raised. Perhaps Slaymaker should make something of that. Greenland was very big and very empty, and yet its southwestern corner, so her jeenee now told her, had cattle ranches, sheep farms and even some summer crops. There would perhaps be some benefits, she thought, in not just picking on Canada. And Greenland, with its minute population and its small, distant and not-very-interested mother country, was *such* an easy target.

'It's essentially an Indian Reservation,' she muttered experimentally, watching her words scroll out on her cristal screen and testing their weight. 'It's an Indian Reservation maintained in North America, for historical reasons, by a small European country. Less than seventy thousand people live in that Reservation – the population of a small city – but it's bigger than *the whole of Mexico*. Come on! There's a crisis going on! Let's get real here!'

But again she was getting ahead of herself. Sometimes this happened with her. Ideas tumbled out over each other, the next one coming before the previous one had even been fully formed. It usually happened when there was something underneath that she was trying not to think about. And the truth was she was very nervous about the donors' dinner and the speech she'd agreed to make. Holly was confident about many things – she could call anyone at all and talk to them without the slightest worry – but public speaking wasn't one of them. Richard would have been much more at home with it.

She'd already been carefully over the guest list but now she went over it again, memorizing the names and faces, and trying to ensure that she knew, for each individual guest, not only where they came from and how they'd made their money, but at least one personal fact. Lucy Vandemon-Rock, for instance, was a big donor who'd only just recently come on board. She came from Vermont, and her family's immense wealth came primarily from the building materials industry – in fact, VR Cement and Aggregates, in which she personally owned a 51 percent stake, was America's largest producer and wholesaler of cement, sand, concrete mixers and building cranes – but Holly guessed that what she'd most like to talk about was that her dog 'Sparky' had won first prize in his category in last year's AKC show.

•

She was above Washington, and the drig's engines were beginning to roar as it forced itself downwards, when the news began to break about the arrest of the man who'd fired that first shot at Peace Arch. It could hardly have been better! His name was Pierre Artois and he was French Canadian from Quebec, with a history of mental illness, violence and involvement in the darker fringes of Quebecois nationalism. He'd apparently told neighbors that war between 'the two Anglo nations' would be the best thing that ever happened to Quebec.

Holly started sketching out a press statement at once.

'A Canadian national, standing in Canadian territory, shoots a Canadian policeman,' she began, 'and this becomes the pretext for the deaths of three unarmed American citizens.'

But was that really needed? Did she need to make it a blaming thing? Wouldn't Slaymaker come over better if he were magnanimous? She tried again.

'It was neither America nor Canada that broke the pledge of Peace Arch. It was a crazed individual who hated both countries equally, and wanted to stir up hate where there should be understanding.'

Yes, that was much better. Best to leave the nasty stuff to the feeders.

Sue Cortez and Ann Sellick met her in the Diamantina Hotel, said to be the most expensive in DC. Coffee and cakes were set out in an exquisite meeting room, with a view of the hotel's famously tranquil Japanese garden. Slaymaker and Jed were still on their way.

Sue was all over Holly, reaching over the table and taking both of Holly's hands in hers. Whether she really *liked* Holly any better than before was impossible to tell, but she could certainly see that Holly was serving her interests. It now seemed very likely that Sue was going to be the campaign director of a historic election victory, and she knew that it was Holly's border rallies that had made that possible.

Ann was more guarded, her own role and status more directly challenged by Holly's privileged position and success. Holly needed to make the first move. 'Outing Cynical Sam as an AI was just genius,' Holly told her. 'Still smile whenever I think about it.' Winning Ann round by flattery had never been possible in the past, but it was a sign of how different things were that the thin, spider-like woman now almost audibly purred with pleasure.

'A classic AI mistake,' Ann said, pursing her tiny mouth. 'You learn to spot them. It had been told to mock folk who asked for government money when they lost their homes. It didn't have the instinct to know that the rules were different if those folk came from the north.'

Then Slaymaker and Jed arrived with breaking news of a new deal struck between the Gray Sisters, and everyone turned on their cristals. Canada was to increase its annual quota of red passes for Americans to 250,000, a more than tenfold increase.

They all turned to Holly but she just smiled. 'Sorry, Jenny,' she said, 'but it's too little, too late.'

The others hooted and cheered.

'Too right,' said Slaymaker, reaching over the table to squeeze her hand. 'Too damn right, Holly. You've run rings round the old gray lady.'

'You surely have,' said Sue. 'Jenny's so dizzy trying to follow your lead, she hardly knows which way she's facing.'

CHAPTER 38

Richard met some of his friends from the school for a drink: Dave, Sanjay and Alice. Dave was a big blond guy from Colorado who taught physics. His husband, Sanjay, was a lean, sharp-tongued AI consultant.

'No Holly?' Sanjay asked.

The bar was a softly lit brick-lined basement on the eastern edge of Seattle. There was jangle music playing softly in the background, those long skeins of ascending arpeggios piling one over the other.

'No. She's down in DC.'

'With Slaymaker? Dave keeps telling me this stuff and I can't quite believe it.'

'Yeah, really. She's with him most of the time. Maybe I should write to one of those relationship advice sites. *My wife spends all her time with the next president of the United States. I know he's strong on family values, but should I be worried?*'

'*PS He seems to want to move us all to Canada,*' Dave added. '*Does that make a difference?*'

'Does she *agree* with his politics?' Sanjay wanted to know.

'No, but she thinks he's right about his move-everyone-north program. And that's the part that she deals with.'

'Well, I agree with him about Canada too,' Sanjay said. 'I mean, look at all that empty space, those green meadows. It's kind of an indulgence, wouldn't you say, with the world as it is, for one country to insist on keeping all that to itself.'

'These rallies are stupid and provocative,' Dave said. 'People throw up their hands about that shooting but, really, what did they expect? But aside from that, yeah, I agree, we need to be able to move some people north.'

'But it shouldn't just be Americans,' Alice said. 'There are people south of the Mexican border that need the space a whole *lot* more than we do. Why not open up all borders everywhere and let people move wherever they want? Why do we need borders at all?'

'So Holly feels *really* strongly about it, does she?' Sanjay asked. 'Dave tells me she's given up most of her life to it.'

'I never heard her say anything about it,' Richard said, 'until she met Slaymaker. She was never very interested in politics. Now she works on it sixteen hours a day.'

'Mmm. I thought you were kidding just now, but maybe you really *do* think there's something going on between her and him?'

'No I don't actually. Not sex, anyway. But she's pretty obsessed with the guy. His wife thinks she's Slaymaker's daughter substitute.'

'His *wife*? You discuss these things with Slaymaker's *wife*?'

'I met her once.'

'Well, come on, Rick, *tell*! What's she like?'

'Quite quiet, a little sad, but maybe kind of playing on that sadness, so as to seem brave, if you know what I mean, and to seem interesting. You know like some people do? She's an actor, after all. Seriously, though, do you guys *really* think Slaymaker is right to demand access to Canadian land?'

'Sure,' Dave said. 'Like I say, I didn't like that rabble-rousing stuff along the border, but, yes, basically I agree that we have to find ways of redistributing the population of the world. It'll buy us some time.'

'Just buy time?'

'Of course. We've set so many feedback loops in motion now that the atmosphere is going to carry on heating up for some time. Whether the Venus scenario is our ultimate destination, I don't know.'

'The Venus scenario being...?'

'That the oceans boil.'

'Ah yes, *that*.'

'Obviously what we really need to do is reverse what human civilization has done to the atmosphere,' Dave said. 'That's the part that Williams has got right. It may be too late. But it's our best option. Even if we do, though, and even if it works, it'll take decades, and things will get a whole lot worse before they get better.'

They all allowed themselves to take this thought in, while the jangle music continued to unfold its interlocking rhythms, like silver wheels spinning round inside each other, some going one way, some the other, and the alcohol seeped into their bloodstreams.

'It's odd how rarely we talk about this stuff,' Alice said. 'We know it, but we hardly ever go there.'

'I don't think it's odd at all,' Sanjay retorted. 'It's like your own personal death. You know it's going to happen. You know it's not going to be pleasant. But why spoil the rest of your life thinking about it? In fact, come to think of it, why even spoil an evening? Let's talk about something else. Why did we come to this shitty bar, anyway? I hate jangle music.'

'No you don't,' Dave said. 'You've got a large collection of the stuff.'

Richard found himself oddly detached suddenly, as far away from them as Holly was from him, watching this little corner of the world, and seeing just a tiny part of a giant clockwork toy that was slowly unwinding to the intricate but emotionless rhythms of jangle music.

We are children, he thought. *We're children pretending to be grown-ups. The world is arranged for us by others, and, like teenagers do, we sneer and talk scornfully as if we knew better.*

'I found a diary of my great-grandmother's the other day,' Alice said. 'She kept it for about a year when she was in her twenties, before she had my grandpa.'

'What was in it?' Dave asked.

'Oh, you know, quaint twenty-first-century stuff. Cellphones. Airplanes. She comes over as a smart, interested, well-informed woman. She was a politics teacher and she often talks about what's happening in the world, not just her own life. A revolution in Egypt. A big banking crisis they'd had. That kind of stuff. She talks about these things, she has views about them, and a couple of time she even *does* something: you know, write to her congressman maybe, or go on a demo. But weirdly there's only two lines in the whole thing about the way things were going with the weather.'

'Which were?' asked Dave.

'*Heading for Thailand. Second Asian trip this year. How great is that? Should feel guilty, I suppose – global warming and all that.*'

'And that's it?'

'*Si.* That's it.'

'How did that make you feel?' Richard asked, pulling himself back into the world.

'Well, I wasn't born then – my grandfather wasn't even born – so, in fairness to her, she didn't know me as a person, but when I read it there, it felt for a moment like...'

She hesitated.

'Like your great-grandma didn't give a shit about you?' he said.

'*Si*. That. Exactly that.'

She considered this for a moment. '*Exactly* that,' she repeated, 'though in fact she was a kind and sweet grandmother to my mum and her sisters, from what I've heard, and they loved her dearly.'

'There were plenty of things they *could* have done back then,' Dave said. 'Plenty of things.'

'It makes me think of Faustus,' Richard said to Alice. 'You know what I mean? Mephistophilis is quite clear with Faustus that his soul will go to hell in twenty-four years – he lays it right out there in so many words – but Faustus just laughs and says there's no such thing as hell, even though Mephistophilis' very presence is proof to the contrary, and even though the whole deal depends on hell being powerful and real.'

Alice smiled and nodded. '*Come, I think hell's a fable*,' she quoted, instantly assuming the persona of the medieval scholar.

'*Ay, think so still, till experience change thy mind*,' Richard answered in the soft, smooth voice of Mephistophilis.

'*Why, think'st thou, then, that Faustus shall be damn'd?*'

'*Ay, of necessity, for here's the scroll / Wherein thou hast given thy soul to Lucifer.*'

'*Ay, and body too: but what of that? / Think'st thou that Faustus is so fond to imagine / That after this life, there is any pain? / Tush, these are trifles and mere old wives' tales.*'

The other two gave them a round of applause, and they all moved on to other things, Richard glancing at his cristal for a moment to make sure he hadn't somehow missed a message from

Holly. But no. Nothing to say she'd arrived in DC, nothing at all. He was disappointed, and yet there was also a part of him that felt released. He switched off his cristal.

Dave and Sanjay went home fairly early, leaving Alice and Richard well on the way to being quite seriously drunk.

'I wonder what it would be like if we knew for certain the world was really about to end?' he said, as they moved closer together to fill the space that the other two had vacated.

'No one would bother to write books, or teach school,' Alice said. 'That's for sure.'

'There'd be no right or wrong in the usual sense,' he said. 'There'd be no point. Whatever you did, the end result would always be the same.'

She looked straight into his eyes. 'All that would matter would be the present moment,' she said. 'Not the record of the moment, not its consequences, not its wider significance, but only the moment itself.'

CHAPTER 39

Sue had given Holly a $10,000 budget for a dress to meet the donors, but Holly didn't actually get to choose the shimmery white thing she ended up wearing, because that was the job of Dirk, the full-time fashion adviser to the Slaymaker campaign, whose main task was to pick out the dresses Eve wore for public appearances, and help Senator Slaymaker maintain the regular down-to-earth look which, or so Dirk maintained, was the hardest part of all.

He checked Holly over before she stepped out onto the stage. 'You are looking *fantastic*, Holly! Like something out of a fairy tale!'

And then she was out there, facing a hundred of America's wealthiest people, who were all watching her and clapping and smiling from their beautifully set dinner tables. Stephen and Eve Slaymaker had just been addressing them, Eve looking lovely in an amazing green dress that had probably cost ten times as much as Holly's. Now the two of them welcomed her to the stage.

'Listen carefully to this smart smart woman, people,' Slaymaker told his audience. 'I certainly do, and it works for me every time. She is just *so* good at figuring out how to make things happen.'

'And isn't she *beautiful*?' exclaimed Eve.

While the people clapped Holly again, she walked to the podium and looked out, giving herself a few seconds to match the faces to the names and bios she'd studied and memorized. There was Randy Lancaster, for instance, over there on the right with his fourth wife Lana. His family's power base was in Seattle, and it was said that, over the last five years, 25 percent of all the new homes built in America had been built with Lancaster money. Here in front of her was Donny Bonito from Oregon who, among other things, was America's biggest producer of construction-grade steel. At the back and toward the right, with her husband and daughters, was Rhianna Morgan, from Michigan. Her family's core business was in heavy machinery – bulldozers, diggers and trucks – but they'd diversified over the years, via road building and the construction of motels and service stations, into pretty much every part of the US economy. At the table next to her was Fox Lamont, the Juneau-based businessman whose family had for three generations been building and acquiring office blocks at prime city locations, the richest man in America's fastest growing state.

Many of them had stood up to applaud, but now they settled back down into their seats, a room full of very rich people, watching Holly with shining, hungry eyes.

'America has been slowly tearing itself apart,' she began, 'and the senator's rivals seem quite happy to accelerate that process. The great thing about Stephen Slaymaker, the unique thing, is that he wants to strengthen America's foundations so our nation can stay whole and strong. It's going to mean sacrifices, but sometimes sacrifices are necessary. This country wouldn't even exist if people hadn't been willing to make sacrifices.'

That got a big cheer. Sacrifice was always a moving and uplifting idea, and particularly so if you were not the ones who were going to have to make it.

'The key to asking people to make a sacrifice is to ensure they know that others too are being asked to play their part. That's why we've been working so hard on the Canada angle. It's only part of the picture. As you know, all the senator's most ambitious plans are for our own northern states, but we need to show the long-suffering people of those states that they're not going to have to shoulder the burden, all by themselves, of welcoming in these millions of new-comers. My job is about getting that message over, and I'm pleased to say we've succeeded beyond our expectations. It's almost as if we gave voice to something that people were thinking, but didn't quite know how to say.

'Tragically, utterly tragically, three Americans have had to die for this. It's awful beyond words. But I guess the important thing now is to make sure they didn't die for nothing...'

Afterwards the Slaymaker team joined their guests, while waiters passed invisibly among them. Billionaires and trillionaires selected drinks and canapes from the trays that appeared in front of them as if from empty air, while their eyes searched the room hungrily for their grateful hosts. Holly wandered among them in her shimmery dress, and they welcomed her eagerly, occasionally asking her questions, but more often instructing her. They were used to being respectfully listened to by those on whom they bestowed their wealth.

Holly was lectured on the constitution, and on free enterprise, and on the appalling decadence of the continent where she'd been born. She was reminded of the need to encourage wealth creators.

She was informed that what made America great was that its people stood up for themselves. A twenty-one-year-old billionaire, whose family's wealth dated back to the cotton fields of the antebellum South, lectured her about the importance of self-reliance. A timber trillionaire called Tracey Patel told her that most Americans had it too easy. The owner of three million low-cost housing units warned her to watch out for kindness. 'It's Senator Slaymaker's one weakness,' she informed Holly, raising an admonitory finger adorned by an enormous ruby ring. 'He's too generous. And I'm afraid it's America's weakness too.' And she made Holly promise her – actually promise her out loud, as if she was a child – to always remember that, and to steer her boss away from the temptation to be too nice. Her own enormous wealth, Patel pointed out, watching Holly's eyes all the while to ensure she was being listened to with sufficient attention, was evidence she knew what she was talking about.

All their lives, these people had been courted by the ambitious, sought out by the beautiful, flattered by those who depended on them, and reassured by the entire political class that their own entirely selfish pursuit of luxury and power was in fact uniquely virtuous and a boon to everyone. Holly loathed them all, but she had to be nice to them. 'Hey, Holly,' Slaymaker would call out to her. 'Come on over! These great people are dying to meet you!' 'Holly dear,' Eve would murmur, 'can I borrow you for moment to introduce you to my lovely friend here! I've just been telling her how much Steve relies on you.' And there would be another one of them, watching her with greedy shining eyes, like a pampered child waiting to rip the wrapper from yet another expensive present. Holly had several job offers and three sexual propositions, which she had to deploy all her skills to decline without bruising egos or causing offense. By the end of the evening she was completely drained, as if vampires had been sucking her blood.

She went out by herself to walk in that Japanese garden. She watched the fish under the lilies, the water trickling down over the rocks. It was a beautiful place at night, with its stony outcrops and little trees subtly lit by lamps hidden among the rocks and under the water. Concealed vents silently pumped out warm air around every bench, and a structure of giant transparent petals, fifty feet above her head, had closed over the whole garden to keep out the evening chill. Some of the rooms in the hotel cost $20,000 a night, and for prices like that, guests expected even nature itself to be reimagined from scratch and delivered up for their pleasure. She sat on a stone bench and tried to call Richard but his cristal was turned off, and she remembered he'd said something about going for a drink with some friends. She felt very far away from anything that felt like home.

And in that odd, lonely, disconnected state, she thought of the people who'd died at Peace Arch and for the first time really did grasp, for a few moments at least, that, right now, somewhere out there beyond the fantasy world of this hotel and garden, there were real people consumed by grief because of what had happened. Right at this very moment they were beating on the impenetrable wall of loss. It would dominate their lives, that cold wall, for months and years, and perhaps even forever. And those people wouldn't have died if it wasn't for—

'Hey, Holly! Are you okay?' Slaymaker had come out to find her. 'We were all looking for you! I wanted to tell you how well you did! They all just loved you. And we did too!'

'That's good.'

He sat down beside her, the large, warm, male presence that

Holly usually found so reassuring. But now she wondered who he really was, and whether the Slaymaker she thought she knew was simply a shell, a performance, a screen onto which she'd projected her own needs, her own fantasies. He wasn't quite the same as the others in there – he was rich, but he wasn't born to riches, and he didn't have their sense of entitlement – but maybe he was their dupe all the same, or even their puppet? Being president was an awful lot of work, after all, and work was something you left to your minions.

'You don't seem too pleased about it,' he observed.

'I'm fine. Just tired. It's hard work playing a part like that, don't you think?'

He leant forward, resting his elbows on his knees so he could peer up into her face. 'I don't think you *are* fine, Holly.'

She hesitated. 'Yeah, okay. Well, if you want the truth, I didn't like any of those people. I really didn't like them at all.'

Slaymaker watched her, but didn't speak, waiting to see what else she had to say. Behind him, a little black duck paddled slowly by over the glowing water of the stream, wandering around the gentle little waterways of its tiny, perfect world.

Reluctantly Holly made herself look him in the eyes. 'I mean, do *you* like them, Steve?'

He laughed. 'Those people? *God* no! I can't stand them! Horrible people. Snakes, every one of them.'

He was his old self again suddenly. Holly laughed and, seeing her relax, Slaymaker relaxed too, sitting back again, folding his arms over his chest as he laughed with her, but still watching her closely. 'None of them know what it's like to struggle in this world,' he said. 'They like to think they deserve what they have, but the truth is they haven't earnt a penny of it.'

'But we still have to suck up to them.'

'Afraid so, Holly. We need a *lot* of dollars, and I'm pretty rich, but I'm not *that* rich. I mean, even if we just look at the work you're doing with those feeders, and your broadscreen ads, and your rallies, it's cost us maybe twenty billion already, and that's only *part* of the campaign.'

'I guess I've always thought of your philosophy as being that people should stand up for themselves, figure out life's problems their own way and not expect others to do it for them.'

'Yup. That's exactly what I believe in, Holly. I figure the really good things in life are the things we've won for ourselves.'

'But none of those people have had to win anything for themselves.'

'*Exactamente.* They were born with so much money, most of them, that they would've had to have been complete idiots not to be able to get even richer.'

'And your policies are going to let them get richer still by building your cities for you. You're going to get tax money from everyone and then give it all to this little handful of...well, your word, snakes. I mean, *Jesucristo*, Steve, no wonder they want to fund your campaign! And you do it all in the name of free enterprise and of hard-working Americans being able to get on and get ahead in their own way, when in reality it's all about this handful of billionaires, who've never had to work hard in their lives, sucking the blood out of the rest of us.'

He regarded her face for a while, his arms still crossed over his chest. She never saw Slaymaker cringe, she never saw him lash out. He had an exceptional ability not to become defensive, or at least not to let defensiveness show.

'I guess you always get snakes,' he finally said. 'I wish you didn't, but I guess you always do. I suppose your ma and pa would probably say you're bound to get snakes in a country like ours, but, well, I don't know a lot about history, but you got some pretty nasty folk in their system too, didn't you? Some pretty serious snakes. In fact, I'm pretty sure no one's ever come up with a snake-free system. Maybe it just can't happen. I don't read the Bible much, but wasn't there a snake there right at the beginning? Maybe that tells us something.'

He stretched back, long and lean in his immaculately and very expensively ordinary jacket and white shirt.

'There are no snakes on my actual team, though,' he said. 'Sue, Ann, Phyllis: those are all people who've had to work to get where they are. Jed is kind of an exception – his family have been rich for a hundred years – but the thing about him is that he's a snake that knows he's a snake. Know what I mean? He's an honest snake! I tell him as much and he admits it's true.'

He glanced quizzically into her face. 'You *are* right, Holly. Those people are going to get even richer on our building plans. They're going to get a whole lot richer, and, yeah, that's why they're helping us, and paying for your good work and everyone else's. But I'm not doing this for them. I'm doing it so we don't have to go on seeing those miserable trails of trucks and cars on our roads, and those beggars on the streets who used to own their own farms. That's not how America ought to be.'

One of those little ducks was back right in front of them, a pretty little shadow, framed by clumps of bamboo, floating on the very softly glowing water. It called softly. It was as if Holly and Slaymaker were looking from the real world into a kind of heaven where nothing ever happened at all.

'Well, I guess I always knew the snakes were there,' Holly said. 'I just didn't have to meet them before.'

Slaymaker nodded. 'Maybe it was a mistake asking you to come to this thing. God knows, you do enough for us already. Let's make a deal that I let you carry on with what you do best, getting over the Reconfiguring America message, and we don't involve you in anything else unless you ask. How about that?' He reached out and squeezed her hand. 'I'd hate to lose you, Holly, and not just because your smart idea has probably won me this election. I just like having you around, you know? Your British accent. Your sharp tongue. The way you ride a horse with no fear at all. I'd hate to lose all that.'

She smiled and briefly put her own hand over his to show him her moment of alienation was over. She loved the times she was alone with him. She loved his *presence*. She'd never really thought before about the way people used that word 'presence' in the sense of authority or charisma, but it struck her now that it meant exactly what it said. When Slaymaker was with you it felt like he was really *here*. Rick knew he ought to be, but there was always something distracting him. Her parents had always maintained a fastidious distance from everything. Her friends flickered restlessly in and out of being present, distracted every few minutes by their jeenees, or by their own preoccupations. But Slaymaker was just *here*.

The duck called softly, a sound that came from only a few yards away, and yet was somehow in another world.

'I like working with you, Steve,' she said. 'I like the way you let me be me. I said I'd help you with this election and I will.'

'I know that, Holly, but I meant afterwards. When I'm in the White House. I want you to carry on working with me then.'

'In the White House?' Holly repeated dumbly, and a strange emotion came over her which she couldn't even have named. Like being hemmed in and being released, both at the same time.

CHAPTER 40

He was alone with Alice in her apartment late at night, and that was a big step. But then he was inside her and that was another thing entirely. Only a small thing, one might say, when you actually considered what was entailed, a marginal overlap of two bodies that had previously only existed side by side, and a small, familiar, quite ordinary sensation. But a step had been taken that couldn't be reversed or talked into non-existence.

He was inside her, and he couldn't change that now, so he persevered. He and Alice ground and grunted away for a short time and then some part of him outside of his conscious control decided to pull the plug on the whole unpleasant thing and he came. Cold clarity returned at once: sex, after all, is basically a delivery system, and it shuts down as soon as it's done its job. The world was *not* about to end, or not for a while at least, and actions did still have consequences. He longed to be alone. Alice pressed her face into his shoulder, hiding herself against his skin. He made a quick calculation to see if there was still time to catch the last train back out to Schofield, but there definitely wasn't.

They rolled apart.

'Sorry,' he muttered, 'that was kind of inept.'

'It's never easy the first time, I don't think. Except in movies, and movies *always* lie about sex.'

'I guess.'

'And...well, there's Holly, isn't there? You're still with her. We should have waited.'

'She's far away in DC with Slaymaker. Meeting a bunch of trillionaires.'

'But she still exists.'

Richard reminded himself that he'd always liked Alice, that he'd always found her attractive, and that, in terms of interests, he had much more in common with her than with Holly. But right then, he couldn't summon up any liking at all. The one aspect of her that dominated his perception of her was a certain naivety born of privilege – 'Why do we have to have borders at all?' – that he had occasionally been irritated by in the past. It was as if, he thought, the cosseted nest she'd grown up in was so far from the machinery of the world that she didn't even know it existed.

He wished he could be in his own bed, by himself, without this entire evening having happened, and he sensed that she felt pretty much the same. But, rather than face their discomfort, the two of them began to kiss again, and biology reinstated its incentive scheme. This second time worked better in a physical sense. If he tried hard, narrowing his consciousness right down to a kind of tunnel vision, he could even describe what he was experiencing as pleasure. They came together and then tried to sleep, though both knew that in their agitation they would wake at some point and fuck yet again, and that each time they'd get a little better at it, a little more used to it.

Alice did sleep, or, if not, she gave a very good imitation of it, but Richard couldn't. He lay awake, listening to the wind blowing through the trees outside. Soughing, that was the word for it, he thought, but it was really just white noise, like a waterfall or waves on a beach. Sometimes the wind blew up and it suddenly became louder, as molecules of air – nitrogen, oxygen, carbon dioxide, water – rushed toward an area of lower pressure. Sometimes it faded to almost nothing. The material world out there was doing its own thing, as it always had done, and would do still when no one remembered Alice or Holly or him.

PART 3

CHAPTER 41

In the summer of the third year of Slaymaker's presidency, Holly had taken three days out for a long-planned break in Vancouver with her old friend Ruby. Tomorrow, Ruby was going to take her to some art shows. Today, their first day, they'd been out watching seals on an island in the strait, and soon they were going to eat in what Ruby thought was the city's most interesting Sino–Canadian restaurant. Holly felt as if she was twenty years old again, right back in her first few months in America, during the wonderfully happy early days of her friendship with Ruby. She'd come to New York without any clear plan, other than putting an ocean between herself and England. She didn't know anyone there, and she felt no affinity with the people in the place where she worked, so she was very much alone. The city, with all its millions of people, felt hidden away from her behind its brick and concrete walls, leaving her with only the streets. And they were just conduits people passed through. She'd been sitting by herself in a bar on Greenwich Street, drinking gin and mint, and feeling very small and alone, when Ruby had come up to talk to her. Ruby was twenty-five then, and had been living in New York for five years. She'd heard Holly's foreign accent and seen she was alone. They got on straight away. Ruby introduced Holly to all her friends and showed her round the city. New York was no longer behind a wall. Holly was inside.

'You were lovely, Ruby,' Holly said, as they sat with drinks in front of them in the warm light of early evening, watching the cars streaming over the Lions Gate Bridge. 'It was like suddenly discovering I had this cool big sister – cool *and* incredibly kind: what a killer combination – who'd look after me and watch over me until I found my way. I just totally *loved* you.'

She was very aware as she spoke of the harsh things she'd said in the past to Richard about Ruby – that Ruby was a spoiled child, engaging in play while others ran the world – and she felt ashamed. The reason why Ruby had helped her so much in New York was precisely that Ruby *wasn't* a child, even back then. She was a kind and thoughtful adult who didn't just think about herself. And Holly wondered why she'd she been so harsh on Ruby for having limits to her capacity to engage and empathize, when she'd admired Slaymaker so much for the very same thing.

Ruby leant over and kissed her on the cheek. 'Well, I loved you too. You were so alive, so open to everything, so full of energy, battering away at America until it let you in. I won't say you weren't afraid of anything, because I know that's not true, but I loved the way you simply refused to let fear be a factor in any choice you made. I always knew you'd go far, right from the beginning.' She chuckled. Her deep warm chuckle was one of the most endearing things about her. 'I can't say I guessed you'd end up in the White House, but now that it's actually happened, I have to say it kind of figures.'

They talked about New York in the past, but New York right now was on its knees. A series of huge storms had been hitting the east coast of America that summer, and one of them had struck land in the city, a whirling power saw that tore down trees, ripped off roofs, sucked out windows and sent torrents of water running down the streets. It had coincided with a particularly severe drought that was gripping inland states way up into the Midwest. As the two of them sat outside on that balmy evening in Vancouver, long queues of heavily laden trucks and cars were trailing northwards and westwards across the USA.

'What's your feeling,' began Holly, a little hesitantly, not wanting to complicate or put at risk this happy reprise of their old friendship, 'what's your feeling these days about the US settlements in Canada?'

There were three new cities in Canada, one in each of the country's Arctic territories: Lincoln City in Yukon, Jefferson in the Northwest Territories, and America City in Nunavut, the largest of the three. The cities had deliberately been established far away from any major population center, and although they were less than three years old, they were already home to several hundred thousand people.

As Holly had feared she would, Ruby tensed. 'Uh, I'm sort of okay about them, I guess. I know the locals up there aren't happy, especially in Nunavut, and I feel badly for them, because their culture has been under threat for so long. But, well, I guess it's not turned out as bad as many people thought, and I understand – I *think* I understand, anyway – your point that Canada needed to share a little bit of the pain of this exodus that you've been organizing. Canada couldn't expect to be preserved as a kind of museum, I suppose, with all the rest of the world crumbling.'

She glanced uneasily at Holly, then looked away. 'I don't like all this stuff you see in the US whisperstream, though. Mean Canucks, brave American settlers. I know there are always some idiots, but that is *ugly*. And it's completely unfair, too.'

Holly swallowed. She couldn't disclose that she was behind a lot of this stuff – she'd even chosen the name of America City herself because of the role she wanted it to play in her narrative – but Ruby would surely know she had some part in it.

'I guess you could look at it as a way of letting off steam,' Holly ventured, 'while America goes through this traumatic change.'

Ruby watched the cars on the bridge, rather than turning round and looking at her. And before she answered, she downed the remainder of her drink in a single gulp.

'Well,' she said, 'I suppose it doesn't really hurt anyone.' She finally glanced at Holly, managing a wry smile. 'I couldn't do your job, Holly. Playing chess with real people.'

'I guess it is in a way.' A sharp sadness was growing inside her. It was coming home to her that the two of them could never really recover the friendship they'd had in New York. They'd shared everything about themselves back then, and that could never happen again. 'But we storytellers are part of how politics works. Suzanne Ryan will have people just like me advising her. Jenny Williams used to. Making things happen in politics is all about stories. They're what allow people to let go of one reality and embrace another.'

'I think I'll stick to light and color. It's more—' Ruby broke off, hearing voices raised inside the bar, and looking round to see what was going on. 'Hey, there's something on the broadscreen.'

Before Ruby had finished speaking, Holly's jeenee had already told her what the something was. A bomb had exploded, blowing the entire façade off the still-uncompleted city hall of America City, Nunavut. People had been killed – twenty-seven as it was to turn out, with more than a hundred injured – and a group calling itself the North Canadian Army had claimed responsibility. The Slaymaker administration had been nagging Canada for some time to do more to curb this alliance of Salvationists and Inuit activists which had repeatedly threatened to attack America's 'illegal colonies'.

'Steve wants a meeting with you and Jed,' Holly's jeenee told her through the implant in her ear, 'to discuss how to manage this. The air force can send a drig with a sleeping cabin. Can you get down to DC for a morning meeting? He'll probably be flying up to America City tomorrow night.'

'I'm so sorry, Ruby,' she said, full of grief, knowing that this might be the last time that she and Ruby met like this, 'this has been so lovely, but we've got a crisis here, and I've got to go.'

CHAPTER 42

When Holly joined Jed and the president in the Oval Office next morning, the two of them had obviously been there some time, sitting face to face on the pair of large red sofas where Slaymaker liked to work and talk, with the table in front of them strewn with papers. Slaymaker had his own relationship with Jed. There was something about Jed's aristocratic scorn for everything that the president found fascinating, whatever he said to Holly about Jed's rattlesnake morals. They'd clearly been deep into something when she arrived.

'Great you could come down, Holly.'

A big broadscreen on the wall behind him was scrolling through images of the damage. America City was growing very quickly and already had nearly 200,000 residents but, squatting there between two bare lakes in a flat treeless waste, it still looked more like a trailer park surrounded by a building site than a real city. The half-finished city hall, built in a classical style with a portico and columns, had been its most distinctive and city-like building, but now columns and portico lay in fragments over the plaza in front of it.

'So what are your thoughts about how we handle this?' Slaymaker asked.

She shrugged. 'This is awful for the people involved, but from a public relations point of view, it isn't a problem. The truth is that pretty much all news from Canada these days is helpful to our overall strategy. If our people up there achieve something, that's an instant injection of national pride right there. If our people come up against problems, we use them to keep up the pressure on Canada. Obviously, Steve, you'll need to publicly accuse the Canadian government of not doing enough to crack down on the NCA, and naturally you'll hint that, unless they *do* crack down, we're bound to wonder if they really mean what they say at all, or whether they secretly want the NCA to succeed. Maybe take the position that you'd *like* to believe that the NCA and the Canadian government are two different things, but you need to be convinced.'

Canada was, as she understood it, a sideshow. Altogether, about 400,000 Americans had been settled in those three cities in Canada's Arctic territories, but more than ten times that number had moved into the new settlements in Alaska, Washington, Idaho and Montana. Slaymaker had made it very clear that he wanted to move people *within* America, as far as possible. But, by keeping the public's attention on what was happening up there in Canada, Holly was providing an outlet for resentments that otherwise would have set Americans against one another. So, small as the Canadian settlements were within the Reconfigure program as a whole, she spent half of her budget on publicizing the triumphs and travails of those three outposts at Lincoln, Jefferson and America City, turning them into a kind of perpetual soap opera about plucky Americans in their small and incredibly isolated cities, surrounded on every side by devious Canucks. Americans as underdogs was a powerful story with immense appeal, made almost perfect by the fact that it coexisted in every American's mind with the awareness of America's overwhelming might. It was like being a child again, listening to an exciting adventure while all the while safe in your bed. And meanwhile, under the cover of that vivid and engaging story, the new cities in America's northern states could quietly continue to grow.

'And while you put out that message,' Holly said, 'I'll keep using my feeders to suggest links between the NCA and the Canadian government.'

'That shouldn't be hard,' Jed said. 'The NCA are an offshoot of a political party that has seats in all three of the—'

'Of the territorial legislatures. Yes, I know that, Jed, thank you very much, and I've ensured that a good 40 percent of the American public knows it too. I'll be able to bring that close to 100 percent now that the NCA are actually killing Americans. It was all a little abstract before.'

Slaymaker laughed. 'Poor Canada. They don't stand a chance against you.'

'There's other stuff we can use too,' Holly said. 'I've been building up this story about the NCA leader being a former colonel in the Canadian army. There's no hard evidence for this, but our scoopers found the rumor on some third-rate Canadian news hub in Saskatchewan.'

'It's like I was saying earlier, Steve,' Jed said, 'Given that Canada's job is to be our symbolic enemy, the NCA are making it a *whole* bunch easier.'

For a second or two they all watched the bleak images of America City flipping by on the screen.

'Of course, I know you'll be very generous and supportive to the survivors, Steve,' Holly said, 'and I'll make sure that everyone gets to hear what's happened to them and the help you're giving.

Pretty much everyone in America will be able to get behind that. And we'll work on the back stories, too. There'll be some inspiring narratives for sure.'

'There sure are,' Slaymaker said. 'Jed brought me in some print-outs, as a matter of fact. We were looking at them earlier.'

'And we need to push ahead with settlement,' Jed added. 'Keep moving more people in. The terrorists mustn't be allowed to win, yada yada yada. And if there's any obstruction from Canada with visas and so on, well, it's the same response. We ask them whose side they're on, ours or the NCA.' He laughed. 'Christ, this is all so easy, isn't it? This Canada thing just runs and runs. Pure genius on your part, Holly! Pure genius.'

Slaymaker flipped off the screen. 'The way you two guys talk,' he growled, 'you might think this was all about the story and not about real people at all.'

Jed composed his face and made it serious. He didn't believe that anyone really cared, but the *belief* that they cared was, he knew, important to many.

'This is my job,' Holly said, 'and it's the job you gave me.'

'*Por cierto*, Holly, *por cierto*.' Slaymaker was instantly humble. 'I'm sorry. I know we need to do this stuff.'

She stood up. '*Bueno*. I'll go and get on, if that's okay? There's a lot to do.'

'Oh, wait a minute,' Slaymaker said. 'You may as well take this stuff on the people who died.'

Slaymaker was very old-fashioned in some respects, and he liked things printed out for meetings. He picked a bunch of loose papers up from the table between them and handed it to her, look-ing into her eyes as she took them, and momentarily cupping his spare hand over hers. He had a way of locking his gaze with people, so as to establish a channel of contact that felt real, even if it only lasted for a second. He and Holly didn't see so much of each other now he was president. They'd talked about going riding again sometime, either up on his ranch or down in Camp David, but there never seemed to be time.

'We must fit that ride in sometime, Holly. I'm going to set my diary secretary onto it as soon as I'm done with Jed.'

As communications director for the Reconfigure America Federal Agency, Holly had her own offices along Pennsylvania Avenue, a quarter mile from the White House, and her own handpicked team of staff: communications professionals like herself, rather than Freedom Party hacks. But she had a room in the White House set aside for her use when she was there and she went there now. There were a few people here she needed to speak to, and she meant to try to catch them face to face while she was in the building. But, before she did anything else, she couldn't resist having a quick look at the papers Slaymaker had given her.

They were basically a summary, one page on each, of what was known so far about each of the twenty-seven people killed by the NCA bomb: age, place of origin, marital status, whether they had children, and whatever was known about their journey from their original home state to America City, Nunavut:

>...originally from New Orleans. Home destroyed in flood after
>Superstorm Zelda...

>...moved to America City from Nevada, via an Illinois camp.
>Used to run a general store, but town couldn't supply water any
>more.

...single mother, raising three kids after death of husband:
suicide following bankruptcy...

Twenty-seven pages down, Holly discovered that Slaymaker had given her another document, or part of one, presumably by mistake. It was just a single page, handwritten, apparently by Jed, and headed 'The Texas Option'.

CHAPTER 43

After he'd slept with Alice, Richard had decided that he and Holly were going to break up. He didn't know if that was what he wanted. It just seemed to be what was happening. And, when she came back from DC and told him that she'd accepted a job in Slaymaker's upcoming administration that seemed to confirm it. She seemed to have made her own choice. He actually felt a little relieved to discover that it wasn't going to be all about Alice. Perhaps this wasn't going to be so hard, after all.

'Well, maybe it's time for you and I to call it a day,' he suggested. They were sitting at their small kitchen table with all their familiar things around them, and even as he spoke he realized how naïve he was being.

'*What?*' Holly's whole face changed in a single moment, becoming angry and scared and wild.

'I'm just saying that you clearly want to move to DC. I don't. Even if I *did* move down there, I know I'd hardly ever see you, just as I've hardly ever seen you these past months.'

'So you're saying – what? – that people who do demanding jobs have no right to an understanding partner? *Jesucristo*, Rick, we're supposed to *support* one another!' She was really angry, really hurt, her eyes welling with tears. 'God damn it, I've been thinking of this as my home and my refuge, and now I find you're calmly planning to get rid of me!'

And she doesn't even know about Alice, Richard was thinking. 'I thought...' he began. 'I guess I thought you'd more or less gotten rid of *me*. You spend so much more time with Slaymaker, and you're clearly much more interested in him than you are in me.'

'Oh, for Christ's sake. I've been helping him fight an election and it's taken a lot of time. You know what I'm like. I need projects, I need to be busy, I need do stuff, or I start thinking too much and get miserable. You always said you liked my energy.'

'I do. And that's what you like about Slaymaker, isn't it? I write books, he does things that make people want to write books about *him*. These days, a new one comes out every week. But you know it's not much fun living with a woman who keeps telling me how useless and pointless I am, compared with another guy.'

She studied his face for a few moments.

'I'm sorry if I made you feel that way, Rick,' she finally said, 'but you've got it completely wrong. I love it that you're a thinker and a daydreamer. I always have done. I love it that you're different than me. For Christ's sake, that's what drew me to you in the first place. You were this quiet, dark, handsome, incredibly smart man, who could speak Anglo-Saxon and Latin, and knew *Beowulf* by heart, and lived his life halfway between this world and places that most people never even think about. I loved that. I *still* love that. Jesus, when I introduced you to Steve, and you recited that stuff to him I was *so* proud of you. Couldn't you tell? You were showing him and Eve something that they'd probably never come across in their whole lives! A whole world they'd never even glimpsed. He still sometimes speaks about it.'

Richard was taken aback by this. 'But…But the fact remains that whenever I—'

'Whenever you criticize, I immediately tell you how much more Steve has done with his life than you have. I know. I can see now that was horrible of me. But believe me, Rick, I don't want you to be like Steve, I really don't. I don't want you to be like me, either. All I'm really asking of you is that you let *me* be me.'

Her eyes were bright and shining in that way they had when she was fighting for something. She was really pleading with him, and this shifted the balance between them in a way that he hadn't expected. He felt wanted, and he remembered how the two of them had once been: him and this smart, fierce, restless Englishwoman. He remembered a time right back at the beginning when she put her arms round him under his jacket, walking out of a bar in New York: 'You know what, Rick? I can't believe just how much more *interesting* you are than anyone else I've ever met.'

Holly was still talking. '…and I'll ask for a vacation soon after the election,' she was saying. 'We can get to know each other again. And then, well, you wouldn't need to move to DC, you know. I'm going to earn a whole pile of money. I can rent a decent-sized apartment down there with room for both of us, and we can keep this place as well. I'll come up here regularly, and you can come down and spend time there whenever you feel like it. I know it's going to be hard, but please let's give it a go. Don't make me choose between you and the most amazing career opportunity I'll ever have in my life.'

She came over to him, she took his hand, she reached up to kiss him.

Around him in the room were the familiar objects that framed their lives together: the reading lamp, the glass door out onto the yard, the broadscreen with the loose wire, the cream-colored sofa...All these things were sitting there as if this was just another ordinary moment in Richard and Holly's home, and time was still rolling peacefully forward. They were there to tell their usual story, the same as every other day.

I slept with Alice, was all he had to say, and all of this would end.

Two whole worlds lay before him, one a continuation of the world he knew, the other tantalizingly new, only to be reached through an inferno of rage and disintegration. Four words, two seconds, that was all it would take to move from one to the other, to step into the fire.

But he found he couldn't say them.

'Okay,' he told her, 'it sounds hard, but let's try to make it work.'

CHAPTER 44

Johnson Fleet

Senator Slaymaker called me personally after they shot Karla at Peace Arch. He asked me all about her. He wanted to know about Jade and how she was doing. And he asked me why we'd chosen to come to Peace Arch. I told him about the flood, and about how I couldn't get the money to rebuild my business. He promised me that when those new towns started being built, the ones in the US and the ones up in Canada, I would have top priority for a home there, and there'd be government money to help me to get established.

He stuck to his word, too. First priority for those places normally went to homeless folk from the trailer parks, but there was a special exception made for me and Jade. I opted for Canada because it was a completely new start. We needed something like that to get us through. And, when the new cities started to take shape, it turned out that car mechanics were badly needed in America City.

So we relocated to America City. Jade started high school there. I set up a new garage with that government money. New robots, new diagnostics, everything.

AC wasn't much of a place back then, just mud, and cranes, and scaffolding, and sad little saplings stuck into the ground here and there, but it was a new beginning, and all of us who lived there knew we were going to build it up into something, I guess like when the first settlers came to America. Outside of the town they were planting out trees for forestry, and there was a cattle ranch, and hundreds of greenhouses. Inside the town, the government had put in that big deep-drill thermal power plant, street after street of pre-built houses were being laid out, and a couple of factories had moved in, attracted by federal grant money: one making lithium batteries for cars, another making parts for cristals. Not bad for a city that hadn't existed a year and a half ago!

There was one thing about AC I didn't like, though. We were all Americans there, and that was good – we used American dollars, we flew the American flag – but as far as the law was concerned we were in Canada. The city was a free-trade zone, but we had to pay income tax to the Canadian federal government and to the territory government up in Iqaluit, which, as far as I could tell, gave us back diddly squat in return. Man, those Inuit people up there had made such a fuss about us coming to live in *their* land, and all the Canuck politicians in the territories were yelling and screaming that the federal government mustn't let us Yanks have Canadian citizenship, mustn't let us vote, mustn't let us do *shit*. But they sure as hell didn't mind taking our money.

Not that I wanted their damn citizenship anyway. I hated the Canucks – nobody in AC liked them, but I had more reason than most – so why would I want to be one of them?

And what *really* stuck in my craw was the police. We couldn't have our own American police. We had to have Mounties. They were pretty much the only Canucks in town, but they were still the ones who enforced the law. So I was an American, in an American town, and yet I had to see those people every day strutting round the streets, coming in and out of their station near the city hall, in the very same uniform as the bastards that murdered my wife.

A bunch of people in all three cities set up an outfit called the Pioneers' Union to give a voice to us American settlers, and one of my customers told me I should go along to one of their meetings, seeing as I felt so strongly. I guess there were about fifty people there when I first went and they were all sorts: men, women, older folk, young people, Mexican Americans from way down along the southern border, storm people from Delaware. Everyone had their own story about how they ended up here in America City. But what hit me was that we were all Americans. It took being on our own there in the middle of Canada for us to be able to see it. We were Americans, up here in our little towns, and we needed to stick together now we had great big Canada all around us.

The guy who invited me was called Pete Suarez and I guess he and his wife Tracey were kind of an example of what I'm saying. I guess if I'd met them back in Idaho, I'd have just dismissed them in my mind as a couple of dusties from the trailer parks. They'd been farmers in Southern California. Twenty-five years ago, they'd managed to get a mortgage to buy their own farm, the first ones in their family to achieve that. They could only afford it because of falling land prices, and I guess that might have given them a clue, but they decided they'd make a go of it somehow. They did alright at first, too, but then the rain stopped coming when it should, and in the end they'd just had to walk away. And now they'd swapped sunny California for Nunavut wilderness, borrowed government money just like I did, and spent it on greenhouses and lights. They were growing peppers and tomatoes, right up in the north of Canada.

Tracey had made me sit at the front, and when the meeting started, she stood up and introduced me as the new guy, suggesting I share a few things about myself and how I got to be in America City. *Jesucristo*, that was *not* an easy thing to do. I couldn't tell my story without mentioning Peace Arch and when I got to that bit, I just couldn't hold it in any more.

Well, they all stood up, every single one of them, and the woman who'd been sitting next to me came right up and hugged me. She came from Delaware, a friend of Tracey's whose name was Rosine, and I guess a lot of people would have called her storm trash. I would have myself back in Dickensville.

'Well, you're not on your own any more, you hear me?' she said. 'You've got yourself a whole big bunch of friends right here.'

Not everyone there had lost a wife, of course, and I kind of stood out because I was the only one whose wife had been killed by the Canuck cops. But every single person there had lost *something*: a home, maybe, or a business, or a marriage that fell apart under the strain. At least three women had had husbands who'd killed themselves when they couldn't see any way forward. We'd all suffered, and we were struggling still as we built this city up. We were in no mood to let a bunch of Canucks stand in our way. Like Pete Suarez said, this place was a wasteland before America City. We were the ones who'd made it into something. And that made it damn well ours.

We'd been there nine months when the bomb went off. My garage was up and running by then, with robots and diagnostics paid for with government grants and low-interest loans. Jade was making new friends at school. I'd just started to date a lovely woman from

New Mexico called Coral: her husband had committed suicide when his business went bust. And, in the middle of all that, the so-called North Canadian Army blew the front off the city hall.

And these were the facts about the NCA. First off, they were one and the same thing as the North Canadian Front, a completely legal party in Canada that was part of the government in all three of the Arctic territories. Second, it was an open secret that the guy in charge of the NCA had been a colonel in the Canadian army. Seriously! The Canucks tried to deny it, but it was a plain fact, straight from a Canuck news hub.

So I wasn't having any of that shit about the NCA being a tiny minority, and the vast majority of the Canadian people being totally opposed to violence, blah-blah-blah-fucking-blah.

No. Crap. Utter horseshit. The murderers in the NCA and the murderers in the Mounties were all in it together. And yet we were expected to believe that the Mounties were going to get to the bottom of this and bring those killers to justice!

Well, we talked in the AC Pioneers' Union, and we talked with the PU people in Lincoln and Jefferson, the other two cities, and we agreed two things. One: we had to have our own American police force. Two: we had to have full representation for Americans in the territory legislatures. No taxation without representation. Isn't that the principle America was built on? We were just three little towns surrounded by a great big country, but we were not going to be pushed around by Canucks.

We printed banners and we got ourselves organized. We got tens of thousands out in the streets, day after day, surrounding the Mountie police stations, and the offices of the Commissioners from Ottawa, demanding they fuck off out of our towns.

And I was right up there in the front. I was full of rage, and rage turned out to be pretty powerful stuff. Those damn Mounties could shoot me if they wanted, like they shot Karla, but I wasn't about to back away. There were thousands of us and only a few of them, and they knew if they tried anything, we'd string them all up. We just needed to hold together.

People sensed something in me. I felt my PU friends around me watching me, waiting for me to take a lead.

CHAPTER 45

The single handwritten page was obviously just notes that Jed had jotted down for his own use. Under the title at the top of the page was a list headed 'Spending Options':

Pioneers' Union: Key. Essential continue to give all support poss. Not technically a political grouping at all, just a mouthpiece for settlers, so US gov may give freely/openly, particularly as it is v popular with US voters. But obvs v political, in fact. Funds and advice will fully professionalize this group, encourage emergence of leaders, develop policy.

Our Canada Party: *Very* valuable to us as a divisive force. Can be relied on NOT to offer deals. *Well* worth stepping up funding through third parties for final days of election.

North Can. Front/NCA: Obvs any investment by US gov would be very risky, and require *super*-careful management through many intermediaries, but potentially *huge* benefits, because NCA prevents compromise, encourages settler separatism, and promotes anti-Can feeling in US.

And that was the end of the page, though it was clearly the first of more than one. Holly read it through a second time, checking that it really said what she thought it said, then went back to the Oval Office. Werner, the president's business manager, stopped her outside the door.

'Sorry, Holly, but he's onto the next thing.'

'Okay, but I think he'll want to see me anyway. Just go in, will you, and tell him I've got something that won't wait.'

Slaymaker was by his desk. He'd just put on a tie and was straightening the knot. She'd caught him at a moment when he hadn't expected to see her, and his face seemed different, unfamiliar, as if he'd laid down the mask he wore in her presence and put on another one in its place.

She held up Jed's notes. 'What in hell is the Texas Option?'

'Holly, I'm going to be heading off to meet the prime minister of Denmark in about five minutes. Straight after that, I'm going to fly up to America City, but then—'

'Are you going to tell them up there that you're thinking of giving money to the people who've just killed twenty-seven of their neighbors?'

He reached out for the paper she was holding, took it from her, and laid it on his desk. Slaymaker never showed his anxiety, but Holly could tell he was going to get that piece of paper shredded as soon as she left the room.

'I'm not going to tell them that because it's not going to happen,' he said. 'It was just one of Jed's rattlesnake ideas. In fact, I think he was probably kidding, though he was a damn fool to write it down.' He touched her hand. 'Listen, Holly, I really do want to talk to you about this. After I've been up to AC, I'm planning to spend the weekend in the Cascades with Eve. Why don't you come over there and we can have that ride we've been promising ourselves?'

Werner came in again. 'We need to go, Mr President. The drig's about to land.'

Jed had gone to work at home. She'd never been to his place before. It turned out to be quite a modest little brownstone house across the river. Everything was very neat and contained: a couple of rather nice paintings, a ceramic piece here and there, all very taste- ful but rather cold and sterile. She wasn't sure what she'd expected but it wasn't this. It made him seem more fragile somehow.

He was a kind of delicado himself, she thought, a dark delicado, his nihilism the product of a kind of squeamish fastidiousness. This was a new insight, and with it came a whole chain of others, appearing more or less instantaneously in her head, as if they'd been taking shape for a while in some obscure workshop in her brain. Like Holly, Jed had learnt at some point in his life to be suspicious of claims people made about caring. (Perhaps his par- ents paid for his expensive schooling, bought him everything he needed, told him they loved him, but yet he felt no love?) He'd come to understand people's claims to care about things as a pretence, a performance, a made-up story. But he'd gone way beyond Holly's idea of a third dimension that was out of reach. He'd decided he didn't believe in caring at all. Or that was the story he'd chosen to tell himself. Shockingly, perversely, as it seemed to her now, he'd chosen to confine himself *completely* to two dimensions, a decision that, weirdly, was both difficult and cowardly.

It was a warm day, and Jed had been working in his tiny back- yard. There was a table and a couple of chairs out there on the pink concrete patio that constituted the entire yard, along with a dozen or so shrubs in glazed pots. Jed's cristal lay on the table. She sat down on the spare chair, brushing aside his offer of coffee.

'I saw some notes you wrote. The Texas Option. What in hell does that mean?'

Jed winced slightly but summoned a half-hearted version of his trademark wolfish grin. 'Ah, well, you grew up in England, so I guess maybe you don't know that much American history? You see, Texas—'

'And what the fuck were you thinking about, suggesting we give money to the NCA?'

He sighed. It was just *such* a waste of time, his sigh said, having to attend all the time to the silly foibles that other people thought of as their principles.

'Well, that was basically an extension of your own original idea, Holly. You pointed out we needed an enemy, someone external to ourselves to be angry with, and, *Jesus*, were you ever proved right! That Canada idea of yours was quite literally the most amazingly successful political move I've ever seen. But we'd have still more leverage if Canada got even easier to hate. The NCA have already massively helped us with that by letting off this bomb, so I figured maybe we could build up the NCA even *more*, while simultaneously identifying it with—' He broke off. 'But, wait, I don't need to tell you all this, do I? You know it already! Every damn day, you're putting those rumors out there about the NCA being in cahoots with the Canadian government. You must know that the nastier the NCA becomes, the better it is for us.'

'So you were proposing to fund a group that has already blown up a bunch of people, simply because you thought we could turn that to our advantage?'

'People are going to get killed in this process, *however* we handle it. After all, you've already drawn blood yourself at Peace Arch.'

She winced. There was no doubt that those three people who died at Peace Arch would still be alive if she hadn't organized that rally.

'But it was just a suggestion,' Jed told her. 'Nothing more. It's a move that's been played many times in history, but I really didn't expect Steve to go for it, even though, like I say, it would really just be an—'

'An extension of my idea? No it damn well wouldn't be! I said we should make *demands* of Canada. That's all. Demands. I said we should make Canada take some of the pressure.'

'Okay, but how about the Canuck jokes, eh? What about the time you told Slaymaker to rile the Canadians as much as he could? How about the lies about Canada – let's call them what they are for once! – you have your feeders pump out every day? Trillions of dollars' worth of lies. And you've even got feeders that pretend to be Canadian, haven't you, whipping up the Canucks as well. Well, it's only one step from that to—'

'We play pretty dirty, I'll admit that. I don't like it, but everyone else does and we have to do it to keep in the game. But it's more than one step from that to giving money to people who want to kill us.'

Jed shrugged and made a rather elaborate show of politely stifling a yawn. People pretended to care when they really didn't, Holly knew that, but it seemed that *not* caring was also a performance. 'Well, whatever,' he said. 'It's academic anyway because, as you might expect, Slaymaker wasn't having it. He agreed with you. He thought my idea was just "plain wrong".'

He said this in much the same way that you might speak about some silly religious fad of an otherwise sensible friend. 'And to be honest, it *would* have been pretty risky. I mean, if we did it and it got out, that would be grounds for impeachment right there.'

'So you left a note about it lying on the president's coffee table.'

'Oops. And I'd been so careful not to leave a digital trace!'

'So, okay, I won't ask about the Our Canada Party, though they're a pretty nasty lot too, but—'

'We've been building them up for some time. He's fine about that. I was just suggesting a bit of extra support now that—'

'Tell me what you mean by the Texas Option.'

'Texas was originally part of Mexico. A lot of Americans settled there, and eventually they broke away from Mexico, and briefly became an independent country, before joining the US as a state. Something similar happened in California. Hawaii, too, in a way. It's a way of taking territory from another country without actually directly invading it.'

'So…What are you saying…? We're actually planning to *annex* those three cities to the US?'

'Not just the cities. They're not viable as enclaves. The whole of those three northern territories.'

'*Jesucristo*, that's half of Canada!'

'It's going to happen, Holly. We may as well get it over with. We just need to create a political context where compromise is impossible, hence my—'

'Listen, Jed, Canada was *my* idea. No one was talking about it until I suggested it. It was a completely new thing. No one knew what I even meant, remember? Not even you.'

'You opened something up, Holly. You can't have been the first person to see all that spare land up there, or to figure out that one day it was going to be the best real estate in North America. But no one had ever articulated it. It had literally been unthinkable. Canada was a friendly country, as the Canucks keep pointing out ad nauseam. They traded with us. They were part of the same military alliance. They subscribed to the same kinds of values. And, whatever the misinformation your feeders have been so helpfully putting out, they did actually stand staunchly beside us in one way or another in almost all of our many wars. So, even though powerful countries all around the world were muscling into their neighbors' lands – the Chinese and the Russian Far East, the Japanese and Sakhalin Island, et cetera, et cetera – none of us, not even a rattlesnake like me, had ever thought of doing something similar to Canada. You opened up a chink, Holly. That was your genius. You opened up a little chink, like a tiny crack in a dam, you made it bigger with all your feeder campaigns and your rallies, and now history is taking over.'

He stood up, picked up a watering can, filled it from a tap. 'It's like sex, I guess,' he said. 'Once you start, things kind of build their own momentum. Going a little way in and then stopping – it's never been a popular option.'

'But we *can* still stop. All we really needed Canada for was to make our people feel that someone else was sharing the load. We've achieved that. It worked. Slaymaker got elected, and those new cities of his are going up in the northern states. Okay, we've got some problems to resolve with the settlers in Canada, but—'

'Just a few. As you may have noticed, right now they're rioting in the streets.'

'There are problems to resolve,' she repeated, 'but there have got to be ways round them!'

Jed was about to water a purple azalea. He paused and looked round at her. 'We really *can't* stop, you know, Holly. Politics doesn't work like that. Every action creates new facts that then have to be dealt with in their own right.'

He turned back to his shrub. The pot overflowed as he watered it, and a little stream ran out over the pink concrete of the patio. 'I mean, for one thing we've brought into being a multi-trillion-dollar industry. There is literally no precedent in our history for this current construction boom. It employs tens of millions of Americans, whose votes we rely on. It's created untold wealth for people whose money we need to stay in power.'

'Nothing's stopping us from carrying on building cities.'

He trickled water over a miniature lavender bush. 'Another new fact is the settlers up there. They've become a hugely powerful force because of the key role you've assigned them in the story that holds all this together. A couple of years ago those people were just a ragtag collection of barreduras who no one liked and no one wanted, but these days there's not a single woman or man in Congress who'd dare to suggest that a demand that came from our brave pioneers was unreasonable or excessive, however outrageous it actually was. They'd be too scared of being seen as unpatriotic, or siding with the Canucks, or giving succour to the NCA. In fact, most of our politicians are absolutely falling *over* one another to prove just how much they support our darlings. For instance, I guess you've seen there's a new proposal to give the settlers full representation in Congress, as if they were citizens of a US state. It's completely unprecedented – even DC doesn't have that kind of representation – and it's actually quite bizarre, given that we're also loudly demanding that those same people should have full voting rights in the Canadian legislatures. But name me one congressman who's dared to point that out!'

'That's got nothing to do with annexing territory. It's just supposed to ensure that settlers aren't forgotten down here in DC.'

Jed attended to a miniature rose, the breeze catching a lock of his rich brown hair and flipping it about. 'That's the stated intention, yes, but does anyone seriously believe there's any danger whatever of us forgetting them? Stated intentions are only ever the surface. Come on, Holly, you know that! You know that better than anyone! Beneath them there are unstated intentions. And then of course there are unconscious drives, the intentions even *we* ourselves aren't aware of.'

He stopped and turned toward her. 'And if you go right down to the bottom of it all, of course, there are the forces of nature, which are actually the most fundamental driver here. *Si*, *si*, we're building all those cities in the northern states, but in twenty years' time, the dustbowl will reach right up to North Dakota, and the superstorms will be ravaging New York City not just once in a while but every summer. There really won't be any niceties at that stage, believe me. *Everyone* will be able to see that the Arctic land is the good shit, and anyone with the ability to grab some of it will do so. Believe me, Holly, one way or another, we're going to end up taking that land, just as the first settlers in America were always going to end up taking the land from the Indians. We may as well get on with it.'

Holly didn't answer him straight away. 'I wouldn't have had you down as a gardener,' she said.

'Oh, I like plants. They're alive, but they have the decency not to have feelings. *Far* preferable to human beings.'

'I remember you pointing out that in the long run even the Arctic will be no use.'

'Oh, *por cierto*, but that's the day after tomorrow. Nobody *ever* thinks about that.'

Jed put down the watering can. The overspill from the azalea pot was crossing the patio, a little stream that bulged above the surface, held together by surface tension. As Holly watched it, it reached a groove between two sections of the pink concrete paving and there, instead of continuing forward, it spread out sideways, creating a kind of front along the groove. Since more water was still flowing into this front from behind, the surface tension was bulging more and more, and it was obvious that it would eventually break somewhere or other, after which the water would continue across the patio, but it was impossible to say exactly where that break would occur.

'It's like it's struggling to decide,' Holly said.

He followed her gaze. 'What? The water?'

'*Si*. It's full of tension. In fact, it's quivering with tension, like a living thing feeling pulled in different directions and trying to make up its mind.'

He watched it with her for a second or two. 'Is that even an analogy?' he said. 'Isn't this essentially what a decision *is*? We feel a pressure building up, we sense how close to breaking out it is, but we can't tell in advance exactly where that will happen. Isn't it that combination of pressure and uncertainty as to the outcome that we experience as choosing? But of course we're mistaken. Each of us is just the meeting point of a bunch of different forces. Where's this *get of jail free* card that releases us from the laws of nature?'

'Well, I'm seeing some different sides of you today. The would-be funder of terrorists. The patio gardener. And now the homespun philosopher.'

He glanced at her. 'Ah well, Holly, that's me, you see. Jed Bulinski, renaissance man.'

To her annoyance she found herself smiling, and turned quickly away. Somehow the two of them were sliding away from the reason she'd crossed the city to see him.

'Our scoopers have been picking up a lot of new stuff lately,' she said, 'stuff which I guess is pretty much on the lines of your Texas Option. *If those Canucks give our pioneers any more shit, they should just declare independence...What are we waiting for? Why don't we send in the Marines?* That kind of thing. It's of human origin, as far as I can tell, and not from any organized source.' She glanced across at him, eyes narrowed. 'That's unless you know better, of course?'

'No, I don't.' He saw the skepticism in her face and laughed. 'Really! Cross my heart! I don't get involved with feeders and all of that, it's not my bag, and I don't have a budget for it.'

'Perhaps it's Ann. She sometimes strays outside her brief.'

'God damn it, Holly. Take some responsibility! Don't try to pin this on other people. This whole phenomenon is your creation. The separatist messages, the riots in America City, they're just the logical extension of what you've been pumping out ever since your first border rally. Yes, and I bet your feeders are recycling this separatist stuff even as we speak!'

'I recycle anything that focuses on Canada. It's mood music. It encourages debate, it concentrates people's mind on a topic that up to now they didn't think about. That doesn't mean I agree with it all, or expect it to be implemented as government policy.'

Jed snorted. 'Sure. It encourages debate. Listen, Holly, the world used to fight over oil, and more recently it's fought over copper and lithium and water, but in the days ahead of us the real must-have strategic asset is going to be Arctic territory. You still talk as if the Canada thing was just a sideshow – a sort of PR stunt and nothing more – and the city-building in the northern states was the real deal. But actually, leaving aside Alaska, the true situation is precisely the opposite. Those Canadian territories are the main attraction, and it's our northern states that'll turn out to be the sideshow.'

'But I keep saying it was me that raised Canada, and I—'

Jed shrugged. 'Sometimes we know more at an unconscious level than our conscious minds will allow.'

The trickle of water had broken out from its groove in the concrete, Holly noticed, about two centimeters to the left of where it came in.

'I could use a drink,' she said.

'Sure. Why not? You like gin, yeah?'

He went into the house. She leant forward and watched the water. She felt immensely weary. She had thrown so much energy into the agency these last three years. It had made her feel enormously powerful. But that had been an illusion. A foolish soap bubble. *No one* was in control. Just as Jed had said, every human being in the world was simply a node, a meeting point in a network of inhuman forces.

CHAPTER 46

Margot Jeffries

I was no fan of Slaymaker's Canada project. I hated his gratuitous bullying of our harmless neighbor. The outrage after the shootings at Peace Arch reminded me of a bunch of kids who'd cornered a terrified animal and deliberately goaded it, and were now screaming because it had finally lashed out and bitten them.

And more than anything, I hated the double standard. Down in Arizona I'd let that border, just fifty miles south of me, dam up all that desperation and misery beyond the horizon, and got on with my life as if it wasn't there. And it wasn't just me that let that happen. All of America was the same. And it seemed to me that, if our principle was that each country should deal with its own misery, however the weather might change, then surely we should stick to that principle even when it didn't work in our favor? If you just take the principles that happen to suit you, and then put them back in the box again when they work against you, they aren't really principles at all, are they? They're just self-serving stories.

But what changed my thinking was that encounter with the woman in the drugstore back in Illinois. It made me see that these people I lived with on the trailer park just weren't welcome in America any more. Prosperous, comfortable America saw them as outsiders, pretty much as they saw Mexicans and other foreigners. Of course in my case, as the drugstore woman had kindly explained to me, I didn't have to be one of them. I could have moved to a city and eventually resumed an ordinary middle-class existence. But I found I just didn't feel like playing my middle-class Anglo card. I felt like staying with the people I'd met in the camp.

And so, after Slaymaker became president, when those new cities started going up, and people I knew on the trailer park started heading off to one or other of them, I decided to take that option too. Professional folk were in short supply in all of those new cities, whether the ones in America or the ones in Canada – I guess that was precisely *because* it was easy for professional people to move to and re-establish themselves in existing communities – and all of them badly needed teachers. I could have moved to one of the new towns being built in the north of the USA and ended within fifty miles of Chicago, or Seattle, or Anchorage, but I thought to myself, *What the hell, let's go the whole hog, let's make this as much of an adventure as it can possibly be.* And so I opted to go to Nunavut, Canada, and live in a half-built city that was nowhere near anyplace at all.

That's not to say I'd suddenly come round to Slaymaker's way of thinking. Not at all. I still didn't trust the man, and I still didn't like what he'd done. But Canada is like America in that it's full of immigrants from all over the place, who got there in all kinds of different ways. I figured we were only another wave. In due course, one way or another, we'd become part of Canada, the same as the Scots, and the French, and the Irish did, and the Chinese, and the American loyalists, and the runaway slaves from the Underground Railway, and the Ukrainians and all of the others who'd come before us.

I moved to America City and taught school. I taught thirty-five fifth-grade kids in AC North Elementary, about half of them from the desert states like me, and most of the rest from the Storm Coast states between southern Texas and New York. How difficult this strange new place was for all of them! So cold, so gray, so little to do. But I guessed their parents told them, as I did myself, that this was just the beginning. America City was scheduled to double in size year on year, and at some point we'd end up with buildings that didn't look like shipping containers, and parks that didn't look like war zones.

Maybe one day America City would even be big enough to support a shop selling handmade pottery, and I could give up teaching again and go back to making beautiful things, which was my real vocation, I guess, if the word means anything at all. I'd already bought myself a new kiln and was making pots in my spare time, including some I was pretty pleased with.

And oddly enough, in this cold, ugly, mosquito-ridden building site, surrounded by hundreds of miles of bare granite and cold water and yellow tussocky grass, I felt quite happy. I'd go as far as to say that I felt glad that I'd been forced to leave Arizona behind me. I could quite easily and comfortably have spent my whole life down there, *por cierto* I could, but I'd have been doing essentially the same things over and over, and now I was part of something completely new. And in Nunavut, of all places! Nunavut! To be honest, I'd barely even heard of it before.

Even though there weren't any Inuit settlements near us, I began studying Inuit art, which is actually very beautiful, with the idea of incorporating some of it into my work. I planned to take a tour round the territory on my next summer vacation – or some of it, anyway: it's three times the size of Texas! – and I took a course in

Inuktitut, the indigenous language. Of course, I knew we weren't really any more welcome in Nunavut than we had been in Illinois but I thought I'd make an effort, all the same.

I was pretty unusual in that way, though. Take Melanie, my next-door neighbor, for instance: she didn't even know who the Inuit were until I told her, and she wasn't at all interested when I did. Her attitude was, so what? So what that, somewhere in this vast territory – three times the size of Texas, as we kept being told – there were a small number of indigenous people?

'There was a bunch of Indians down the road from where we used to live in Alabama,' she said. 'Well, they called themselves Indians. They didn't look much different from you or me. They had a little amusement park called Creek World. My pa took me there once. It was okay, I guess, but there weren't that many rides.'

And we never really met the people who'd lived in Nunavut before we arrived. The locals were hundreds of miles away. America City's site had been specifically chosen to ensure that we didn't run up against one another. Neither the US nor Canada wanted that kind of trouble.

But we got trouble anyway, as it turned out. The bomb went off outside the city hall. Everyone in AC knew of someone who'd been injured, or killed, or been nearby. Our head teacher was badly cut by flying glass. Another teacher had her eardrums burst by the blast.

The bomb had been planted by the North Canadian Army, a largely Inuit group that was a militant offshoot of a political party that operated in all three Canadian territories. It saw itself as defending the local way of life against a flood of immigrants that threatened to sweep it away. And actually I could kind of understand how they felt. Come to think of it, from a purely logical perspective, you'd think that *any* American ought to be able to understand how they felt, given that fears of being flooded by migrants from the south had been one of the main elements of America's political conversation since long before I was born.

But of course we were us and they were them and different rules applied. In fact, now that they'd been defined as our enemies, any attempt to understand the NCA's motives was more-or-less treason as far as most people were concerned. They were murderers and that was that. There was nothing to understand.

We'd barely begun to process the city hall bomb and its aftermath when the Pioneers' Union began making demands. They insisted we had to have full voting rights in the territorial legislatures, and our own separate police force. Big crowds came out onto the half-built streets of America City (and, so we saw on the hubs, the streets of Lincoln and Jefferson, and in cities all across the USA itself), people shouting and marching in support of the Pioneers' Union demands, people roaring through megaphones, people waving American flags and burning Canadian ones. 'Enough is enough!' I heard people saying to one another over and over in AC. 'We bent over backwards to fit in with what the Canucks wanted, and this is how they repay us!' It was everywhere, the same words almost, repeated again and again. It made me think of those dances that bees do, so the whole hive knows which way to go.

Eventually the trouble got so bad that they shut down the school until further notice, because barely any kids were coming in. I drove out to a little lake I'd found about ten miles to the south of the city, sat on a flat rock, and watched the ripples on the water and the gray clouds blowing by above me. Back in the city, they were screaming abuse at terrified Mounties. I couldn't stop that, any more than I could stop an ocean tide, but I really didn't feel like being part of it.

CHAPTER 47

Alice had found a new job as soon as Richard told her he was staying with Holly. He'd heard she was with some jangle musician in Seattle. Richard tried to make the two-home arrangement work, giving up his own job at the school and dividing his time between Schofield, Washington and Washington, DC, but the traveling was irksome and, as time went on, his visits to DC and hers to Schofield had become less and less frequent.

When Holly came up after the bomb in America City, it was the first time she'd been there for four weeks, and she seemed to him changed. She was oddly distant and agitated. She resisted any questions about what was going on for her but, when she'd had several drinks in quick succession, she began to speak as if she was in some dangerous place, and was relying on him to keep her safe. 'You're my anchor, Rick, you know that?' she said several times. 'You're my anchor. You're my link to reality. Don't let go of me.'

The story that had grown up between them over the years had been the opposite of that, that part-joking, part-irritated, part-affectionate story of the kind that couples tell each other about their relationship: *Richard* was the one in danger of drifting away from reality – into the Dark Ages, or Elizabethan England, or whatever he happened to be writing about at the time – and she was the one who stood on solid ground.

In the morning, she drank a pint of coffee and readied herself to go to see Slaymaker at his ranch, where he was staying after his much-publicized visit to America City. He'd gone to comfort the bereaved and injured, but he'd ended up negotiating the departure of the Mounties.

As the car reversed itself out of their little drive, she was already giving instructions to her jeenee.

He watched the news on the broadscreen. Big demonstrations were taking place in all three of those grim artificial cities that Slaymaker had built in Canada. An angry crowd had gathered outside the Canadian embassy in DC. The Canadian government had just offered to carve the American cities away from the territories they were in. Each sat in the middle of its own fifty-mile-square concession, and Prime Minister Ryan offered each of these three squares a self-governing entity in its own right. But the Pioneers' Union was insisting it be allowed to participate in the government of the territories as a whole, which, given that settlers were already more numerous than the local population in all three territories, would mean putting American settlers in charge of most of northern Canada. Neither the locals nor the Canadian authorities were prepared to accept this. Effigies of President Slaymaker had been burnt in Whitehorse, Yukon, while in northern Nunavut, Inuit activists spread out a huge banner, a hundred meters long, which simply read, 'THIS IS *OUR* LAND'.

'It *is* your land,' Prime Minister Ryan assured them, on a flying visit to the territories. 'And it's Canadian land. The Canadian government will stand beside you as we search for a way of integrating American settlers without undermining your own proud traditions. We will not be deflected from that search by the extremists and wreckers on either side.'

Ryan was fighting for survival, though. She was in the final days of an election campaign, she was widely seen as having given way to Slaymaker too easily, and the fiercely anti-American Our Canada Party had overtaken her in the polls, having suddenly emerged from the margins of Canadian politics into the mainstream, with a powerful organization and a formidable war-chest. Our Canada's leader, Gwendoline Thomas, was drawing huge crowds to her flame-lit rallies in Canada's Anglo heartlands.

Holly returned quite late, just when he was thinking about giving up waiting for her. She still seemed agitated, pouring herself a large whiskey and downing it in a few gulps, though she insisted that she and Slaymaker had sorted out all the issues that had been bothering her.

'I think maybe I should go up to my office and do a bit of work,' she said. 'I said I'd go for a ride with Steve tomorrow, but on Monday morning I'll have a bit of time before I fly back to DC, so we'll be able to have a nice leisurely breakfast together, if you're not rushing anywhere yourself.'

CHAPTER 48

Rosine Dubois

What was so unfair about that bomb is that we chose to come up to Canada so as to not be in anybody's way. Back in Montana, when the Reconfigure America scheme came in, I'd made Herb sit down with me in front of the broadscreen and look at the different places we could move to. I wasn't having any more of his talk about how it was 'up to you, Rosine. You're the one who wanted to leave in the first place'. I'd worked out a little system where we wrote down a score out of ten for each one and we both separately ended up giving the highest score to those three places up in Canada. We figured the reason for that was that there was no one else near them. We were sick of being made to feel like we weren't welcome and so we picked a place where no one lived at all.

There was *nothing* here when we first arrived. And I *mean* nothing. Back then, America City looked pretty much like the trailer park we'd come from down in Montana, but with no town nearby and no farms, just dirt and cold water. There was just one single road coming up to it from the south (which America had paid for anyway), and a whole lot of lakes, and nothing else. You'd have to travel for hundreds of miles to get to anything that looked like a town and, from what we'd heard, that was more of a village really, with no roads going out of it, and only a little airstrip to connect it to the rest of the world.

Looking back at the time before we moved up here, I think Herb had been in shock, ever since Superstorm Simon. He'd driven me nuts back in that trailer park, sitting there in front of the broadscreen doing nothing at all, hour after hour after hour, but I can see now he just didn't have it in him back then to do anything else. He picked up a bit when the border rallies were going on, but it was only when we starting reading more about America City that he really began to get interested again. There was something exciting about starting over like that.

'And one thing's for sure,' Herb said with a chuckle. 'If there's any place on Earth those superstorms are never going to reach, it's up there. *Way* way up north, and pretty much as far from the ocean as you can get.'

I hadn't seen him so lively since we went up to Opheim. Thinking about it now, I guess that had been a first glimpse of what it might be like to be with a whole bunch of people in the same situation, all working together to make things better.

But life wasn't easy when we first came here. There was no city hall then, there were none of these big buildings that sprang up over the next few years: the biggest building back then was that giant thermal power plant steaming away. And even though it was April, the weather was cold and gray. We were used to warmth, and we were used to color too, specially the color green, that lovely green of the trees, swaying in the warm breeze. And, okay, there were little flowers in Nunavut, among the bare gray stones, and they were kind of pretty but they were no substitute for what we'd left behind. We had to wear coats all the time, and the mosquitoes were worse than any we'd known before.

But there was a decent house waiting for us, made in a factory in Illinois, which we could afford to rent and had the option of buying later, and it was warm, however cold the weather outside. And there was work for both of us, too, in the offices of two of the big construction companies who were building the city from scratch. I have to say, it was all *way* better than we could have hoped for when we set out from Delaware. In fact, in money terms we were actually better off, and we wrote our folks back down south that they should kiss goodbye to superstorms, and come up and join us. Most important of all, we were surrounded by people who'd arrived from outside like us, not folk who thought they owned the place and resented our being there. AC people are pleased when more people arrive and new houses are built between us and the bare country outside.

One guy we knew called Johnson Fleet – he lost his wife at Peace Arch, and became the secretary of the Pioneers' Union in America City – used to talk about how, up here in America City, we were all just Americans together. It wasn't *quite* that simple. Herb figured that Johnson couldn't quite believe he was hanging out with dusties and storm trash and had to keep reminding himself it was okay. There were still tensions in America City, between black people and white people, people from the east and people from the west, and so on and so on. But, that's human nature, isn't it? And at least if someone called us storm trash, we could just call them dust trash right back. Because storm trash and dust trash: there weren't many there who weren't one or the other, apart from a few like Johnson who'd had their troubles in the north. We were all pretty much in the same situation, and we knew it was up to all of us to make something of this place. That kind of brought us together.

And then that bomb went off. I was only a few blocks away, shopping with Copeland, so near that we felt the blast of it, and could hear the screams of the people from the plaza. Lord, what a sound! Like hearing the souls in hell. I couldn't stop thinking about it. I felt so angry with the people who did that, it almost made me sick. What harm had we done them, way out here, with none of their towns anywhere near? Sweet Jesus, there had to be *somewhere* for people like us to live! There had to be somewhere other than that storm-wrecked country where a dead woman hung like a flag.

CHAPTER 49

When Holly reached Slaymaker's ranch, everything was ready for her. She was about to make small talk with Eve, but Eve just laughed and shoved her straight out of the door into the stable yard, where the president was saddling up two horses, with food and drink already packed.

They rode quickly up the same path they'd followed before, a couple of secret service men riding a respectful distance behind them, and a drone circling overhead, but they went at a much faster pace without Richard or Eve to hold them back. (Those secret servicemen had clearly passed some kind of advanced riding test to get their jobs.) Holly loved this, directing this powerful animal many times her own weight, while at the same time trusting the creature to find his own way over the uneven ground. She had to be entirely focused so as to move with the horse, rather than bracing against him, as he skirted rocks, crossed scree, dipped down into gullies and climbed out again, constantly shifting the angle of his body in relation to the slope. It was a strange hybrid of surrender and control in which both Holly and Slaymaker were entirely absorbed. If they spoke at all, it was only about the ride and the horses.

'He's never liked this bit.'

'Hey, we pretty well *flew* down there, didn't we?'

At the top of the ridge, they looked down into a smaller side valley, much of it wooded. A stream flowed along the bottom of the valley, sometimes dividing around little rocky islands. Many small side streams flowed down into it from the slopes on each side. The horses splashed through the ones that crossed their path. And now they picked up speed, the big beasts breaking into a canter along the straight stretches and only slowing down briefly to negotiate stony twists and turns. Eagles, riding the currents high above the horses and their humans, cocked their heads briefly to check them out and then continued their search for pikas and marmots.

At the bottom, Slaymaker pulled up in a grassy spot beside the stream, and they jumped down and released their horses to graze. The secret service men did the same, hanging back thirty yards so that the president and his adviser could talk without being overheard. There was a stone fireplace with a pile of wood ready and some slabs of rock to sit on, overlooking the stream just at the point where two channels of it came together again after dividing round an island. The churning water gave out a constant blast of white noise. Holly and the president lit a fire, put on a pot of coffee and a couple of steaks.

'So...' Slaymaker said, 'the Texas Option.'

'Tell me first of all if you ever gave, or even considered giving, any money to the NCA.'

'Of course not, Holly. They've just killed our people. Of course I wouldn't give them money. But don't be too hard on Jed. Remember I pay him to think the unthinkable. That's his job!'

'But you *are* giving money to other parties in Canada.'

'Oh, *por cierto*. The same as they give money to US parties.

Jenny Williams had half a billion from the Canadian government, you know. And who can blame them? They knew she'd be easier to deal with than me, and they did what they could to tip the balance in her favor! If I'd been them, I'd have done the same.'

He glanced at her. 'But that's not where your problem lies, is it, Holly? What's troubling you is us taking their land.'

'I can't believe it's not troubling you.'

'We need those three territories to the east of Alaska. Canada's a friendly country, I know, but that's a lot of space to be left almost empty, and we need it a whole lot more than they do.'

'Just those three territories?'

He studied her face. Slaymaker was always very careful never to flinch or look away. 'Sure. If any other part of Canada wants to join us, that'd be great, but it's those three that I reckon we need most. And of course I'm working with the Danes on a deal about Greenland, too. Between them, those three northern territories plus Greenland will give America plenty of elbow room for when things get *really* tough weather-wise. Plenty of space, and plenty of options.'

'For a generation. A lot of the science says it's only a matter of decades before the heat gets to be a problem even up there.'

Slaymaker's eyes glazed very slightly. These matters just didn't engage his imagination in the same way as the question of land. 'Sure. Well, maybe we need to revisit those Christmas trees, or the sulfur aerosols or whatever. But that's not going to turn things around for some time, and we need the land right now.'

'So how does this work? Right now the Pioneers' Union is demanding control of the whole of the territories. When Canada says no, they declare independence and we recognize the three territories as an independent country? Is that it? And then we invite that so-called independent country up there to join the USA?'

He turned the steaks, then took the coffee off the heat and set the pot on a warm stone beside the fire.

'That's the way I'm starting to think. Jed's going to be over here this evening, and I thought maybe the three of us could sit down together and sketch out some plans. We need to think about the timing of all this, with my second term campaign coming up.'

She looked away from him for a moment, toward the two streams of water as they smashed together. A small bird waited on a stone by the water's edge, tipping its head this way and that, and from time to time suddenly jabbing down with its beak to pluck some titbit from the current.

'But it's a big thing,' she said, 'taking Canada's land.'

'It *is* a big thing. But I was never easy, as you know, with the idea of too many of our people moving north and becoming Canadians. That would mean Canada ending up being the big country in the end, and America a kind of Mexico.'

'I found an interview the other day with a Canadian cop who was there at Opheim. Nice guy, about your age, looks and talks a bit like you. He says he's always had very friendly feelings for Americans. And he also says he's always liked *you*. In fact, he told his wife, only a couple of months previously, that he wished they had someone like you in Canada. And then he looks up at the interviewer and he's really distressed. "But then suddenly the guy turned on us!" he says. "I just can't figure out what we did to deserve it." I'm wondering how you would answer that guy.'

Slaymaker's eyes were fixed on her face, attentive as ever and yet at the same time completely closed off.

'When I went into the trucking business,' he said, 'we still had manually driven trucks. Cars were self-driving, but trucks were only semi-robotized and still had to have a driver, just in case. Then the law changed and fully driverless trucks came in. They were way cheaper to run than trucks with drivers – *way* way cheaper – and we had no choice but to go over to them, or our competitors would have put us out of business in a year. So I had to lay off all our drivers. There was no way this was going to feel fair to them, or make sense, but I had to do it. And it's the same now with this Mountie guy, and people like him. It won't feel fair to them, of course not, but that doesn't mean we can get out of doing it.'

'Why can't we?'

'It's like that stream there. I could dam it up, I could build the dam higher and higher, but sooner or later, it's going to break through. All we can hope is that in the end we find some new configuration that works, and then we can be friends again with good people like this Mountie guy of yours.'

The little bird poked and pecked by the water's edge.

'Something else I thought about,' Holly said. 'Nunavut is the last territory of any size in the whole of North America where indigenous people are still the majority. That's quite something, don't you think? A last refuge. Even the name of the territory means "our land". Doesn't it bother you that we're going to snuff that out?'

'Yeah, but whatever we do someone's going to be unhappy. A guy showed me some figures a couple of days ago: the number of farmers from the southwest who've gone bust and committed suicide. It ran into thousands. And this guy pointed out to me that for all the people who actually kill themselves there are going to be – what? – ten, twenty, fifty times more whose lives are ruined too, but just can't quite bring themselves to take that final step. A bit like my mom. She just about kept going, but life didn't give her anything in the way of happiness.'

He laid down his cup, glancing round a moment to see what the horses were doing. 'Listen, Holly, I've not had much education and like to say I think with my guts, but I do try to get the facts. There are about forty thousand people in Nunavut, and, sure, that's a lot of people. If they really want to live apart from the rest of us, we can give them a reservation but with the world like it is, they just can't expect to keep a territory all to themselves that's three times the size of Texas!'

He fetched the steaks and they ate them between slabs of bread, washed down with thick muddy coffee.

'I hope they *don't* want a reservation, though,' Slaymaker said. 'I guess you know my great-grandmother – my mother's mother's mother – was a full-blood Cherokee. I'm very proud of that. It's a great thing to know that some of my people have been living in this beautiful country for thousands of years. But I'll tell you another thing I'm proud of my great-grandmother for. I'm proud that she left the reservation, got out of that little backwater, stopped holding onto a past that was finished, and jumped into the great big scary river of America. It didn't work out so well for her. She had a lot of problems, and so did my grandma and my ma – liquor, violent men, all of that – but, the way I figure it, these things take generations. If she hadn't done that, she wouldn't have been the great-grandmother of a US president.'

'So you really are going for the Texas Option then, *si*? It's not just another rattlesnake idea?'

'America needs that land. And in any case, those settlers aren't coming back, and they aren't going to turn into Canadians. If I don't take that land, America will find itself another president who will.'

CHAPTER 50

Richard was asleep before Holly got in, and he woke before her in the morning. There she was beside him, lying on her side, her mouth slightly open. Remembering what she'd said about being in no rush, he slipped downstairs, put on some coffee and made waffles, flipping on his cristal for news. The top story was that the Canadians were offering an extraordinarily generous new compromise.

Excited by this news, he took the breakfast upstairs on a tray. Holly stirred sleepily. 'Oh waffles, great. Thanks, Rick, just what I felt like.'

'Good day yesterday?'

'Yeah, sure. We had a nice ride and we sorted some things out.' She reached up to him, pulled him close so she could kiss him.

'Did you see the Canadians have come up with a new proposal?'

'Yeah?'

'Yeah, they're offering to—'

'Oh come on, let's not talk about that now!'

They kissed some more. They had sex for the first time in several months, and then they drank coffee and ate cold waffles side by side in bed.

'This Canadian offer,' Richard said afterwards, picking up his cristal. 'It really is incredibly generous. They're prepared to carve away a great big piece of land for American settlement that connects up all three of those new cities of yours. They're saying that Americans can settle anywhere in that whole area, as many as we like, and they'll be entitled to full Canadian citizenship after a few years.'

'Interesting,' Holly said.

'I thought you'd be a bit more pleased than *that*!'

'It's certainly something, but we need access to the far north.'

'Well, once our people have Canadian citizenship, they'll have the same right to move north as anyone else in Canada!'

'I guess so.'

'And, if you think about it—'

Richard broke off. 'Oh wait,' he said bitterly. 'You already knew about this offer, don't you? Of course you did. And I guess you know how Slaymaker's going to respond to it as well? In fact, you probably wrote his answer!'

'No, I didn't know. Last I heard, their best offer was autonomy for America City and the other two cities in their fifty-mile squares.'

Her hand was shaking, just as it had been on the evening she arrived. She felt herself being torn in two.

Her father had died a few months previously and she and Richard had been over to England together. She'd dreaded it in several different ways, but one of the things she'd particularly dreaded was meeting her parents' friends. All these obscure old British political dissidents, soldiering on there, and her working for the other side.

She'd expected hostility, arch comments, sniggers, sarcasm. But actually, and much more painfully, she'd encountered kindness. It was her father's funeral, and no one seemed to think her political choices were relevant just then. Even her mother's therapist friend, Antonia, stubbornly refused to live up to the negative caricature that Holly had painted of her in her mind.

'I wasn't very close to Dad,' Holly told her gruffly, when she offered conventional condolences.

'I know,' Antonia said, 'but sometimes those kinds of losses can be the hardest to get over.'

'Why would that be?'

'I think it's often to do with finally having to give up on the hope that maybe things could be different.'

And Holly had to admit to herself that she didn't feel Antonia was trying to control her, or be superior to her, or any of those things. Antonia was a strong person, it was true. She knew what she wanted in life, she stood up for her own way of seeing things. But Holly admired those qualities in Slaymaker so why not in her? There was no doubt that Antonia had been a support for her mother. And all she was doing now was offering Holly an insight from her own experience that might possibly be helpful.

They weren't monsters, these people, that was what she couldn't help noticing, however much she'd made them so in her imagination. They were cautious people, it was true, and determinedly provincial people, who'd led pretty timid and unadventurous lives. But that wasn't a crime, and, actually, it wasn't even the whole picture. They'd stuck to their political commitments in a Britain where people like them were regarded with deep suspicion and often outright hostility. Pretty well all of them had experienced some degree of harassment from the political police. And at least one reason that they all had such dull-sounding careers was that their views precluded them from advancement. No one who openly sympathized with foreigners in Britain in those days was going to be able to rise to any level of seniority in a public service post, and nor was anyone who suggested that Britain itself must share the blame for the weather problems that had led to so many millions round the world having to flee their homes. But these people did still publicly express such views in spite of the hostility. They still went on their demos, they still handed out leaflets. And, futile or not, that took courage.

Holly could see all that, as she and Richard mingled with the guests, nibbling at the vegetarian snacks and drinking too much of the organic wine. And yet these were the people who she'd needed so badly to distance herself from that she'd crossed the Atlantic and joined the staff of a Freedom Party politician who thought that foreigners had to look after themselves.

She'd trembled then, too, standing there in the back garden of her parents' small suburban semi, a chilly wind ruffling the leaves on the trees, a drig's engines roaring far above as it began its descent toward Heathrow, and a water feature gurgling a few yards away in the next garden but one. Then, too, she'd felt herself at the intersection of two contradictory forces.

CHAPTER 51

Relieved to escape from Richard's questions, she set off back to DC, calling Slaymaker on the way to the airport.

'This is an incredible new offer from Ryan.'

There was a pause before the president answered. 'We're going to refuse it, Holly. It's come too late and we need to stick to what we've been asking for: settlers to have full voting rights in the territories.'

'But Ryan can't deliver that. She knows if she does the settlers will secede.'

'We don't need anyone to deliver anything, remember!' His tone was kind but firm. He deferred to Holly about stories and presentation, but not when it came to outwitting adversaries. 'What we need is a reason to take that land. If Ryan fails, Gwen Thomas gets in on election day, and she won't be willing to do a deal at all. Which is exactly what we need.'

It was useless to tell Slaymaker that Ryan's offer would make the land available to Americans too, just so long as they became Canadians. That wasn't enough for him. Above everything, he needed Team America to come out on top. And so, she knew, did his voters. People expected their leaders to stand up, not for the whole world, but for them. Wasn't that Richard's point about that king from *Beowulf* who raided his neighbors to provide for his own people?

Holly sat trembling in the drig, pulled in different ways, unable to move forward one way or the other.

The horse was bolting, she told herself, casting around for a story that would allow her to carry on. You could ride it, try to steer it a little, gradually calm it down, or you could let it fling you off. The one thing you *couldn't* do was make it stop in its tracks.

But for more than an hour, she couldn't even bring herself to open her cristal.

'What can I do for you?' her jeenee asked when she finally did, a little cartoon figure bowing on her screen.

'What's happening out in the stream about this Canada business? Grouped semantically, what are the leading messages?'

But before the jeenee could answer, she changed her mind. She couldn't bear to face the roar of anti-Canuck rage that would be echoing and re-echoing round that dark cave of bats.

'Cancel that,' she said. 'Tell me what names people are proposing for this new country that's going to break away. What names, what flags, what songs?'

She couldn't face the game of chess, but she could at least work on branding. That would be soothing, like coloring in.

'New America,' the jeenee answered her, 'the United Territories of America, the Arctic Union, Northland...'

'We'll go with Northland,' she said, as various ugly and complicated flag designs paraded across her cristal.

'They're awful,' she said. 'Let's draw a better one. Make the top half blue. It can be the Arctic sky. That's good. And put three stars up there. That's it, but further up, right along the upper edge, one in each corner, one in the middle. Yes, that's great. Now make the bottom half three equal-sized stripes, red, white, red. No, that's *too* like the American flag. Try reversing them, though. Make them white, red, white. Yes, that's much better. Blue at the top. White, red, white at the bottom. It can represent…I don't know… the unbreakable bond between the three territories, forged from blood and flame across a land of ice.'

Now it was just a matter of having a few thousand feeders put the name and flag out there in various ways, and they'd soon be a fait accompli. She absorbed herself quite happily in that task for the rest of the journey.

It was only when the drig had actually touched down at Reagan airport that she realized that yet again she hadn't thought about Richard for the whole flight. She'd told him he was her anchor but she forgot him completely when he wasn't present.

That scared her. And yet when she'd climbed into a taxi and given the AI her instructions – an obvious moment for calling him, or at least sending him a friendly 'arrived safely' message – she just couldn't help herself from having one more quick look at the flag she'd designed for Northland.

Blood, flame, stars. What was it about words like that? They acted like seed crystals in a chemical solution. A feeling stirred inside her when she looked at the flag and remembered the symbolism she'd arbitrarily assigned to it. It was an imaginary flag for a non-existent country, but she really was quite close to tears.

'I must send a message to Rick,' she said to herself. But somehow she needed first to tell her jeenee to commission a song about her flag, set to a suitably patriotic tune. There were plenty of AIs out there that could whip up a thing like that.

And then, when she'd set that up, news started coming through about a second bomb, this time in the new city of Lincoln in the Yukon, and so she turned all her attention to that.

CHAPTER 52

Margot Jeffries

I wondered sometimes who was really pulling the strings. It all unfolded so quickly, and all the significant actors on either side seemed to work together toward the same eventual outcome, as if this was all some kind of dance, however much they claimed to hate each other.

It started with the bomb in America City, followed by the days of angry demonstrations that eventually drove out the Mounties completely, leaving a vacuum which the Pioneers' Union militia stepped in to fill, under their newly elected leader, Johnson Fleet, the chisel-jawed widower of Peace Arch.

Next there was the amazing offer from Prime Minister Ryan – her swan song, as it turned out. Americans like us were being offered the opportunity to come into Canada in whatever numbers we liked and gradually become part of the life of this stable, prosperous nation. You'd think we'd be delighted with a deal like that. But when I spoke to my neighbors, or friends from the school, I couldn't find anyone who had anything good to say about it. For one thing, I was told, it came from a Canuck and Canucks couldn't be trusted. Had I forgotten that these were the people who'd just killed twenty-seven innocent Americans? For another thing, it was obviously a trap. It might sound generous, but the Canucks' real objective was to cut us off, not only from our home country but also from the northern parts of the territories which we'd need to access in the future. This was typical of Canucks, I was told. They had repeatedly betrayed America throughout history, from the American Revolution, when they sided with the Brits, to 1812 when they burnt down the White House, to the Fourth Copper War only a few years ago when they didn't send ground troops, though they'd been perfectly happy to send their extraction companies in afterwards when our soldiers had secured access to the mines. And in any case, it wasn't going to happen because old Suzanne was finished and Gwen Thomas of the Our Canada Party was going to be the new prime minister.

With her flaming red hair and her fiery eyes, like some kind of Canadian Boadicea, Thomas made a much more convincing enemy than sensible, reasonable Ryan, and many exciting stories were being told about her. It was apparently an open secret, for instance, that she planned to drive all us Americans out of Canada. Some said she'd kill us all.

I wanted to ask people how they would have felt in the past if America had done the equivalent of what Ryan was doing and offered Mexico a whole new US state to settle as many of their people in as they wanted? (Imagine the howls of outrage!) But I knew from experience that there was no point. People just refuse to hear these parallels. There's always some reason why the two cases are not the same.

And then, as if to confirm the doubts about the trustworthiness of Canadians, the NCA set off another bomb over in Lincoln,

Yukon, and followed it up two days later with a rocket attack on Jefferson in the Northwest Territories. I have no idea what they hoped to achieve by these attacks. It seemed obvious to me that they were playing straight into the hands of the American settlers' movement.

Sure enough, the PU militia transformed itself from an amateur police force into a ragtag army. They got hold of a couple of small drigs and some trucks and began carrying out 'military exercises' and patrols across the granite fields and lakes outside the city. A splinter group from the PU called the American Freedom Fighters carried out a revenge bomb attack on the Nunavut capital of Iqaluit on Baffin Island, killing a bunch of people who were presumably no less innocent than the ones who'd died at America City and Lincoln. But again this wasn't a parallel that anyone wanted to hear. Those walrus-munchers had it coming was the general feeling in AC.

Those three-star flags started appearing everywhere, and some anonymous person wrote a maddeningly catchy patriotic song called 'The Bond of Flame' about brave little American stars in the Arctic night. Guys and young women rode through the streets of AC on the backs of trucks, with machine guns slung on their backs: elaborately nonchalant, chewing gum or wearing mirror shades, intoxicated by their coolness and power. That feeling would disappear pretty fast, I couldn't help thinking, if the NCA ambushed them. Difficult to feel cool and powerful if a shell has turned your legs to mincemeat or your lower jaw has been blown away.

But you couldn't say things like that. There was a whole lot of stuff you couldn't say. I guess it was the same in 1775. A critical mass is reached, and after that either you go along with the newly formed nation or you're a traitor. Three women in Lincoln who'd been foolish enough to go out with Mounties were paraded through the streets with shaven heads.

Meanwhile, the Canadian army sent troops into the principal Canadian towns in the three territories: places with names like Yellowknife, Whitehorse, Hay River and Rankin Inlet. The US government condemned this as 'provocation' and lined up its own troops on the Alaska border.

I hated all of it, but I guess that's like saying you hate bad weather.

CHAPTER 53

The declaration of independence happened just two days after the Canadian election. Holly was with Steve and Eve Slaymaker at the White House, watching the big broadscreen in the Executive Residence, along with Jed, Ann Sellick, who was now press secretary, and Sue Cortez, who was now the White House chief of staff.

The Pioneers' Union had declared a new United Republic of Northland with jurisdiction over the entirety of all three territories. America City was to be the nation's capital, and one of the leaders of the Pioneers' Union was appointed interim president until formal elections could be held. Holly watched a ragged honor guard from the new nation's 'army', as they raised a giant version of her three-star flag in front of the half-ruined city hall. The new young president awkwardly saluted the flag, in a cheap suit that was a little too tight for him. Holly glanced round at Slaymaker and was surprised to see his eyes filled with tears.

A servant brought in bottles of champagne that had been chilled in readiness, and the team toasted the United Republic of Northland and its future, with as much feeling as if they genuinely didn't know that it was their own creation and that within a few months it would cease to exist.

Sue Cortez, to Holly's amazement, actually gave her a hug. 'Who'd have thought it, eh, Holly? Who'd have thought, when you pointed out Canada on that map in Steve's ranch, that in less than four years we'd have come to this?'

On the screen, excited crowds were waving three-star flags in all three of the American cities in Canada and right across America itself. And then the story flipped over to Canada and the new prime minister, Gwendoline Thomas, who'd just told parliament that she'd send her air force and army to suppress the American rebellion. Everything was going to plan.

Slaymaker came over, placing one hand on Holly's shoulder and one on Sue's. 'If it wasn't for Holly's idea,' he said to Sue, 'it would have been Frinton or Montello here in the White House, and our country would be tearing itself in two. I mean, when's the last time you heard even a peep about state frontiers?'

Soon after that, the party ended. Slaymaker needed to call his fellow president up there in America City, and offer his congratulations, and then he was going to talk to the generals.

As Holly climbed into her car and told it to take her back to her apartment, she took out her cristal and found that Richard had tried to call her seventeen times.

She could easily have called him back on the thirty-minute journey to her DC apartment, but she put it off, riding across the city in a strange dazed state of dread. She let the car drop her off and take itself off to park, stepped into the lift, and rode up to her front door on the eleventh floor. She took off her coat and shoes, poured herself a glass of wine, flipped on the broadscreen and had her jeenee reach down for her into the whisperstream, where American pride and anti-Canuck rage were roaring like Niagara Falls. She told her jeenee to make a few notes about things to work on in the morning. But all the time, the dread inside her was growing. She knew she needed to call him.

Rick answered at once, like a lynx leaping on its prey.

'So now I know, Holly! I finally know why you didn't want to discuss Ryan's peace offer, and I know what you and Daddy Slaymaker were talking about on his damned ranch! I can't get over the cynicism of it. The callousness. But above all your *duplicity*. All lovey-dovey with me, when all the time you knew you were brewing this. I can't believe you could even think of it. You had an offer from Ryan, you had an amazing offer, but instead—'

'Rick, it's not as simple as—'

'I hope you're ready, Holly. I just hope you're ready for the blood that's now going to flow.'

'Richard, please, I need you to—'

'*Oh Richard, you're my anchor!*' Rick cried, mimicking her British accent. 'No, Holly, no, no, no! I am *not* your anchor. An anchor's a thing that holds you back. And you made quite sure, didn't you, that holding you back was the one thing I was *not* going to be able to do.'

'It's more complicated than you think, Rick. If we hadn't—'

'I've got CNN on the broadscreen right now. I guess you know that Prime Minister Thomas announced a shoot-on-sight policy about two hours ago for any Americans found outside the fifty-mile squares? I guess you know the Canadian air force has already attacked some of the militia units up there? I'm seeing more Canadian drones taking off right now, one after another, from a base in northern Ontario, each one with four air-to-ground missiles. Think about that, Holly. Some of those Americans you sent up there are riding around right now in their silly pick-up trucks, playing at being soldiers, and they're going to be dead before the morning. Yeah, and *then* what's going to happen, eh, Holly? Have you and Slaymaker thought about that?'

'Of course we have, but you've—'

'We're through now, Holly. That's it. I've waited four years for you to let me back into your life, and that's long enough. And if this is the life you want to lead, I don't want to be part of it anyway.'

Her mind felt numb, but her body knew this was a calamity. She was already shaking violently now, when suddenly she realized she was about to throw up. She ran to the toilet to retch out the White House champagne in three sour convulsive gouts.

She tried to call Richard again. He didn't get it, she was going to tell him. The only way they'd got any concessions at all out of Suzanne Ryan was by piling on the pressure, and by the time she gave way, events had moved on, new forces were in play and it was already way too late. But his jeenee wouldn't accept her calls.

She sampled the whisperstream again. There was no way anyone could stop that Niagara now. A hundred thousand top-grade feeders calling out for peace would have been drowned out completely by that mighty roar. Just in the last hour, her jeenee told her, there had been over thirty million iterations of calls for a nuclear attack: *What are we waiting for? Nuke those Canuck bastards. Turn Toronto into a sheet of glass...*

CHAPTER 54

Rosine Dubois

I've never seen Herb so proud and so happy as he was when he joined the Pioneers' militia. You wouldn't have thought that was such a great way to spend your time, bouncing and banging along in the back of a pick-up with nothing to look at but empty lakes and bare rock and yellowy tussocks of grass. But he just loved it. I guess all his life he'd thought of himself as a guy who played it safe, worked in an office doing a job that anyone could do, never made much money, never did anything that marked him out as different or special in any way. But now he'd come home from the office as Herb Dubois, Assistant Data Supervisor, who'd spent his day muttering to jeenees, and he'd put on his uniform, and straight away he'd become a whole different person, standing up straighter and pulling in his belly as he went out again as Sergeant Dubois, United Northland Army, heading off into the cold and dark to protect America City.

Me and the guys did this, me and the guys did that. He was always talking about it. In fact, I've got to admit, it got on my nerves. He liked to think he was a soldier, but it wasn't as if the militia ever actually had to fight anyone. They hardly met anyone at all out there, and it counted as a pretty exciting day when Herb and the others stopped a truck of Inuit caribou hunters one time, and sent them back the way they came. The way he told it, you'd think he'd done something really brave.

Still, Herb felt he was someone, and that was good.

Once or twice, a thought came into my head about those Delaware state troopers and how they treated us when we were trying to get away from the storm, and I wondered if those Inuit people felt a bit like we'd done, like they were suddenly foreigners in their own country. But I put that thought firmly out of my mind. This wasn't *like* Delaware. Delaware had farms and fields and houses and churches and roads, but no one had done a thing with this country until we came here. It was empty for miles and miles. Nearest place to America City of any size, or so I'd been told, was a nickel mine more than a hundred and fifty miles away, with maybe two hundred yellow-coat miners living in dorms. And even that was owned by an American company.

I figured those Canucks lost any right to our sympathy when that bomb went off in front of our city hall.

Then we had the Declaration of Independence, and suddenly we were living in Northland. We all waved flags in the street and sang that new song about the three lonely stars and the bond of flame.

Over in Ottawa, the new prime minister, Gwen Thomas, stood in front of a giant maple leaf flag and warned us she was sending the Canadian army into the territories, and we'd better stay inside our fifty miles. But our new Northland president, in all his wisdom, announced that the Northland army would fight back. Of course, Herb insisted on going out in his truck that same night, 'to show those Canucks we don't scare easy'.

'Don't do it, Herb,' I said. 'Sit this one out. We're not talking about a few Inuits now, we're talking about a real army. We're talking about professional soldiers who've been properly trained, with drones and drigs and lord knows what else. You guys won't have a chance. And you won't achieve anything either. You need to sit this out, and wait for the US army.'

'No way, Rosine,' he said. 'That would be desertion. Our job is to defend Northland, whether it's dangerous to us or not. You heard our president. You heard him say that—'

'Oh come on, Herb. Our *president*? That was Johnson Fleet, for Christ's sake! Remember how you used to laugh at him for being so proud of himself for getting along with storm trash? What does he know about fighting wars?'

Herb laughed angrily. 'What are you saying, Rosine? Because we have the honor of being a friend of our president, that means we don't have to listen to him when he calls for our help?'

'Listen to yourself, Herb! Just listen to yourself! This isn't real. Can't you see that? *President, country, army, honor...*None of it is real. This is like...I don't know...It's like some little kids' game except that you're playing it with real guns against people who could really hurt you.'

'Well, I sure am sorry it's not real to you, Rosine, but it's real to me. More real than anything that's ever happened to me. And now, if you'll excuse me, I've got a patrol to lead.'

I yelled after him as he walked away, really yelled, with tears running down my face: 'Herb, don't *go*!'

Carl was crying too, but Copeland took his dad's part. '*Jesucristo*, Mum, what are you doing? Dad's just going out on patrol.'

Herb was too angry to turn around and look at us as he climbed into his car. He just told it where to take him and then bent over his cristal as it drove off.

We never saw him again. Not even his dead body. The Canucks fired down a rocket from the sky and it blew Herb and the other three into little pieces.

CHAPTER 55

Within an hour of the news that Canada had attacked and killed members of the so-called Northland Army, President Slaymaker had ordered cruise missile strikes on half a dozen Canadian air force bases, and declared the airspace of the Northland Republic to be a no-fly zone. What had begun with cartoon dogs and jokes about three Canucks in a bar had become thousands of tons of metal on the move, thousands of gallons of rocket fuel igniting, megatons of high explosives blasting through concrete and steel.

Gwen Thomas announced that *all* Canadian airspace was a no-fly zone for the USAF, and a Canadian drone attacked a troop transport heading for Jefferson, with 653 men and 327 women on board. The drig was unarmored and it cracked open like an egg. A news hub drone that was accompanying it shot a piece of footage that was to appear that night on all of the hubs, and ricochet back and forth across the whisperstream. It was of a young woman with blonde hair falling through the sky, her eyes apparently wide open, her arms and legs flung outwards as she slowly cartwheeled toward her death.

·

Holly was to watch that clip many thousands of times. The young woman was an army engineer called Specialist Susan Wright and was almost exactly the same age as Holly herself. Holly searched for everything that was known about her: her school years, her hikes in the Cascades, her little brother Craig, her policeman fiancé Damian, her fondness for speed-jangle music, her mother who was a nurse, her aptitude for maths, her childhood bedroom with the teen pictures still up on the walls.

It would have provided excellent material, but Holly didn't use any of this information to make stories for her feeders to put out into the stream. She told no one about it. She didn't recycle it in any way. No one knew of her obsession. A war with Canada might have happened anyway without her – things like it were happening all over the world – but Holly knew that it wouldn't have happened in exactly this way. Perhaps it would have been worse – how could anyone know? – but there was no doubt that it was Holly who'd set in train the particular sequence of events that led to the death of Specialist Wright, when she pointed out Canada on that old map on Slaymaker's wall.

And though she spent many hours learning about Susan Wright, what Holly came back to most of all was that little fragment of footage. She would play the clip on repeat, pausing sometimes, zooming in, trying to knock the reality of it into her head. This had been a real person, as real as she was, alive and out there in the world. This real person had been sucked, fully conscious, out of an exploding drig and, as long as she remained conscious, she'd had no choice but to fall, to feel herself falling with nothing to grab hold of, knowing that in just a few minutes she would be dead and broken, somewhere on the ground below.

CHAPTER 56

Slaymaker sent tanks over the Alaska border and bombed the Ministry of Defense in Ottawa, reducing it to rubble. All across America the Stars and Stripes flew side by side with the three-star flag of plucky little Northland, allowing Americans simultaneously to revel in their country's military might and bask in the righteousness of the underdog.

The tanks rolled across the Yukon. The Navy sent aircraft carriers to menace Canada's coasts.

After a two-day lull in fighting, a US drone in the vicinity of Lincoln shot down a Canadian army drig with two hundred soldiers on board. Gwen Thomas ordered a retaliatory missile strike across the border against a USAF control center. One of the missiles went wide, and blew up in an elementary school in a Detroit suburb. America responded with another series of devastating cruise attacks on Canadian air force bases.

There was another pause in the fighting. As battered, bloody Canada slumped in its corner and America swaggered about in the ring, the premier of Quebec, Michel Morin, declared that this was a family quarrel between two Anglo nations and French Canada wanted no part in it. With immediate effect, Quebec was an independent state. America recognized the new Quebec republic at once. Gwen Thomas accused Morin of treason and ordered his arrest – 'You are gonna hang, Michel, you are gonna hang so high!'– but her authority was dwindling. No one acted on her words and the following day, the premiers of Alberta and British Columbia also dissociated themselves from the Canadian federal government.

What was left of the Canadian armed forces wasn't willing to be wiped out with Thomas in some kind of heroic *Götterdämmerung*. Thrilled, eroticized almost, by the scandalous destruction their country had wrought, rapt Americans watched on their cristals and broadscreens as Canadian officers climbed from limousines outside the prime minister's chateau-like residence above the Ottawa river, to place Gwen Thomas under arrest.

Suzanne Ryan came back as the head of a 'provisional government of national unity'. But by now there *was* no national unity. As she hastily arranged a ceasefire with America, Canada lay in pieces all around her.

Holly came up to Schofield to collect her things. She insisted to Richard that the destruction of Canada had never been the plan. Not her plan, and not even really Slaymaker's. 'It's not what it looks like,' was actually the phrase she used. And she spoke rather wildly about forces outside of Slaymaker's control, and overflowing dams, and difficult choices, and unstoppable momentum.

The two of them had a huge row then, quite unlike any they'd ever had before: savage, bitter, full of the rage and hate that both of them had been swallowing for years. He told her she was utterly ruthless, that she was without loyalty or principle, that she was willing to sacrifice everything to her own ambition. She told him he was a nobody and always would be, a creature of the shadows, afraid of the light of the sun.

He'd been working on a chapter about St Gildas, who'd watched the destruction of Britain, and seen its cities, churches and literature, its history, its Celtic language, its Christian and Roman culture, all swept away by the pagan invaders from Angeln, Saxony and Jutland, who eventually became the English.

CHAPTER 57

When the ceasefire was agreed, Slaymaker called Jed and Holly to the Oval Office to discuss his next moves. The overall plan was pretty clear. Northland needed to be supported and built up prior to annexation, and the independence of Quebec needed to be entrenched. As the three of them talked, a new assumption seemed to emerge that Canada's western provinces would be persuaded to accede to the United States, thus uniting Alaska and Northland with the other forty-eight states in a single vast bloc encompassing most of the continent. Somehow it just seemed inevitable but, all the same, Holly did find it strange hearing her own voice calmly sketching out ways of driving the wedge still deeper between the virtuous westerners, who were almost American already, and the *real* Canucks in Ontario.

'You okay, Holly?'

Slaymaker was looking at her with concern. It was unusual for her to lose her focus.

'Sorry. I was distracted for a bit there. Been sleeping rather badly lately.'

'Sorry to hear that. I thought you looked tired when you came in.'

'I am tired, I must say, but I'm okay. What are we talking about?'

'I was just observing,' said Jed, 'that in fifty or a hundred years' time, the most valuable of the territorial assets we've just acquired won't even be the mainland part of Northland. It'll be those big islands way up there to the north. Baffin Island, Ellesmere Island, Greenland. One day those will be the most populous states in the USA.'

Slaymaker's eyes were positively shining at this prospect. 'So maybe we need to make a start on settlements right up there, *si*?' he said. 'Cold and icy as they are, shouldn't we start laying the foundations?'

'Or maybe we need to look at the Christmas trees again,' Holly snapped, 'and the sulfur aerosols and so on. Because, as Jed has pointed out many times, after we're done with those islands, there's nowhere left to go and your precious America will finally be completely fucked, along with the rest of the world.'

Jed laughed at her outburst. He didn't believe in those kinds of fixes, he didn't think the political will could be summoned up to implement them, and he wasn't that bothered in any case – or so he'd decided to tell himself – by the prospect of the world's end. But Slaymaker composed his face into a concerned expression so that Holly would know he really was taking her seriously. 'I think you're quite right, Holly,' he said. 'We need to get back to that, now we've secured the land.'

He thought he meant it too, Holly didn't doubt that. He could certainly understand the logic of it, and would probably make some small steps in that direction in the months ahead. But she knew this stuff didn't grab his imagination like the idea of all that new land, and all those new cities and states. When you grew up on a trailer park, she supposed, you didn't think about long-term plans.

CHAPTER 58

Rosine Dubois

When President Slaymaker came up to sign the Treaty of Accession, it was early May. Over on the east coast the weather was already getting hot and those huge giants of air were coming together out in the ocean, to smash into the land once more. But up here in America City the air was still cold and sharp, with snow on the ground, ice on the lakes, and an icy blue sky above us.

All the way from the airport to the Freedom Plaza, people were standing by the roadside waving US flags and the three-star flag of Northland. I told the boys that, if we couldn't feel happy, we could at least feel proud. We and these other people all around us had built a new city, a new community, out of pretty much nothing at all.

And there was something special for us to be proud of too, because we were going to receive a medal on behalf of Herb. The next day, there was going to be a ceremony where Herb and the other guys who died in that truck were going to be awarded the Medal of Honor. We talked about how proud Herb would have been of that, and we kind of laughed through our tears. Herb carried twenty, thirty pounds more than he should, he liked a beer and he liked to spend plenty of time in front of the broadscreen. He really wasn't the hero type, and he knew it, but now the president was going to give him a medal for courage.

The city hall was being repaired, but it still wasn't safe to go inside of it, so the ceremony was held in the big conference room of the Hilton Hotel that faced it across the plaza. There were maybe three or four hundred invited guests in there. They were what you'd call prominent people, I guess: city councillors, business leaders, officers from the Northland militia, some from America City, some come over from Lincoln and Jefferson. We all settled down and waited for a while, and then someone called out, 'Ladies and gentlemen, please stand for the president of Northland and the president of the USA!'

And there was President Slaymaker, tall and strong, with those bright eyes of his darting about, taking everything in, pointing and waving at folk here and there across the room. His beautiful wife Eve was beside him – she always looked kind of sad to me, like she was the mother of America, worrying about us all – and next to them were Johnson Fleet and his new wife Coral.

I guess it was like it says in the Bible about a prophet in his own country but I'd never quite gotten used to thinking of Johnson as President Fleet. I couldn't help remembering that confused, angry guy who showed up to our Pioneers' Union meeting, and broke down in tears. Yeah, and then I thought of what Herb had said: 'That guy can't quite believe he's actually talking to storm trash,' and I couldn't stop myself from smiling. Coral looked pretty tough. She looked like she was going to grab every bit of this new fame she possibly could, and all the money that came with it.

We sat at the front, me and my boys, all stiff and awkward in their new suits and ties, along with the relations of the three young guys who'd died with Herb: Vince, Luigi and Jon. For Vince just his mom had come and his little sister. For Luigi it was his mom and dad. For Jon it was a girlfriend who looked about seventeen, along with her dad. I had my friend Tracey Suarez with me, who'd been my neighbor in that trailer park back in Montana. She was over seventy now, but still working away with Pete just outside the city in their glasshouse farm.

Johnson came to the front and made a speech. It was quite a pretty speech, I suppose – he must have had people to write it for him – about how Herb and the others had gone out on an ordinary pick-up truck to defend the people of America City, though they knew they were up against a ruthless professional army with tanks and rockets and fighter drones.

So why did you tell them to go, you fool? I thought. *Why couldn't we have just waited for the US army?* And for a moment there I was so mad I felt like grabbing both boys and walking out. I mean, it wasn't even as if Johnson didn't know what it felt like to lose someone you loved!

But I told myself that, however dumb Johnson had been, that didn't take away from the fact that Herb had been brave to go. And I guess you had to allow for the fact that Johnson wasn't exactly used to this president business.

'They were real Americans,' Johnson said. 'They stood up against the Canuck bullies, just like our forebears stood up against the Canucks' old friends, the Brits. Let us not forget, people, that there'd be no America if it wasn't for guys just like Herb and Vince and Luigi and Jon.'

Then Slaymaker himself came forward, and we were called up one at a time to collect the medals. Me and the boys were first. Carl was still a kid, Copeland was a big lanky awkward man-sized teenager, both of them proud, upset, happy and embarrassed all at once, but they were keeping it together really well.

'I am so sorry for your loss, Mrs Dubois,' said Slaymaker as he shook my hand, and gave me the medal in a beautiful little presentation box. 'And you boys too,' he said. 'My, you're fine lads. Your mom must be very proud of you.'

'We met you once before, Mr President,' I told him. 'Our house was all smashed up by Superstorm Simon. We were on the interstate. You came down in your drig to see what was going on, and really and truly, yours was pretty much the first friendly face we'd seen since we'd left home.'

He'd leant forward as I was speaking so as to be sure to catch what I said, and now he studied my face for a second or two with those famous blue eyes. 'Do you know what, Mrs Dubois, I do believe I remember that. You had a big old blue pick-up truck, didn't you? I remember saying hi to these two boys in back. They've sure grown a lot since then!'

When the medals were all given out, we stood at the front of the stage with the presidents and first ladies, while a band played the 'Star-Spangled Banner' and 'The Bond of Flame' and then it was time for them to go outside and meet the people waiting outside in the plaza, the Slaymakers going up the aisle first and then the Fleets.

Us families of medal-winners waited up there on the stage, knowing that when the two presidents were outside, we'd be asked to go and join them and be introduced to the huge crowd that was waiting out there. You couldn't hear them, but you could kind of sense them somehow: all those thousands of people.

I whispered to Copeland and Carl how proud I'd been of them. Copeland was amazed that Slaymaker had remembered us out of all the people he must have met. 'But our truck *was* blue, wasn't it, Mom? He couldn't have guessed that!'

A hubbub of voices rose up in the room, as everyone began to talk to the people around them. And then suddenly there was a faint crackling sound from outside, like firecrackers, which you could only just hear under all those voices.

CHAPTER 59

Margot Jeffries

After the war ended, a lot of people came up to America City, some to stay, but many just to see the place. A lot of trashy tourist stores sprang up. That three-star flag was printed on paperweights and tea towels and cristal covers and Christ knows what else. You could buy plastic polar bears and walruses, maps of Northland that lit up and played the 'Bond of Flame', snow spheres you could shake with 'Greetings from America City' round the base, and tricorn hats printed with the date of Northland's Declaration of Independence.

I thought to myself, *If that rubbish is selling, there's sure to be a market for something a bit better.* I'd built up quite a stock of my own pottery by then, and I sourced some more from other craftspeople I'd met in AC, and old friends back down in the US. So I gave up my job at the school and rented a store. It went better than I'd dared to hope. There were *plenty* of tourists coming up who wanted nice things to take home, and lots of locals came in too, people who were doing alright, and were seeking to make their homes more beautiful as they put down roots.

I had a new idea then. I decided to try to source some stuff from real local artists. I got a plane up to a place called Baker Lake, an Inuit village several hundred miles to the north of us. I met an amazing sculptor up there called Emily Saviktaaq who carved beautiful compact little scenes out of soapstone, and I persuaded her to bring some of them down to America City.

That was a *bad* idea. Poor Emily was spat at in the streets, and jostled by people who called her 'terrorist scum'. You'd have thought that, seeing as we'd taken over their land, the least we could do was embrace the people who lived in it. Especially when most of us had experienced what it was like to be made to feel like unwelcome strangers in your own country. But folk didn't see it that way in America City, not even my neighbor Rosine Dubois who was always kind to everyone.

'I don't want them anywhere near me,' she said about Inuit people. 'I don't trust them. Not after the bomb, and not after what happened to Herb.'

I would have thought the chances that the Canadian air force men who killed her husband were Inuit was extremely small, but that kind of logic went nowhere, and in the end I gave up trying to argue. The kindest thing she could come up with as far as Inuit people were concerned was that perhaps they could be given one of those islands up north as a reservation, and leave the rest of us alone.

But anyway I'd made the contact with Emily, and, through her, with other artists she knew further north. There are different ways of looking at this, but I guess I provided them with a market for their work which they wouldn't have had before. I was learning from them too, of course, and I thought maybe we could build bridges for the long run by learning from each other. But maybe that was just me assuaging my guilt.

I guess it's always been that way. The hard men take the land by force. We soft types move in and make it nice again, like the stolen land was nothing to do with us. A kind of good cop/bad cop routine.

I'd made up my mind to stay away from the Accession celebrations, just as I'd stayed away from the demonstrations after the bomb, as a kind of one-woman protest against the dishonest narrative that made Canada into the big bully and Americans somehow the victims.

But then I had one of my changes of heart. I lived in America City, didn't I? I was making use of the land that American threats had obtained, just as, when I was in Arizona, I was taking advantage of that cruel wall, fifty miles away, which kept poverty away from my pretty town. Was I going to spend the rest of my life benefiting from the tough unfair things that other people did, while pretending their actions had nothing to do with me?

Rosine was going to receive a posthumous medal on behalf of her husband for that brave but completely futile thing he did in what was now grandly called our War of Independence. A whole bunch of my neighbors were planning to go along to Freedom Plaza to cheer her when she came out after the ceremony. And I went along with them. I wasn't sure how comfortable I was going to be there, but in the end I cheered with the rest of them outside the Hilton Hotel, and even waved a three-star flag that someone put in my hand.

I actually quite enjoyed it. I didn't manage to push *all* my doubts out of my mind, but I swallowed enough of them to be able to share the general feeling of optimism with these neighbors of mine who'd been through so much to get here. Whatever you might say about flags and patriotic songs and all of that, they sure are good at bringing people together.

There was a big screen put up outside the hotel so we could see the ceremony inside, and when Rosine and her boys collected their medal from Slaymaker, we all made ourselves hoarse with yelling and hollering. That felt really lovely, not because Herb was really an American war hero, but because this was Rosine – good, warm, tough Rosine, who'd been through so much – and I had no reason whatever for not wishing the very best for her. We sang the 'Star-Spangled Banner' and then we positively bellowed out 'The Bond of Flame':

> The bond of flame, the bond of blood,
> Across the Arctic snow:
> We'll keep it strong for ever,
> Against every threat and foe.
>
> Three little stars, three lonely stars,
> Shining in an Arctic sky:
> Our light will never falter,
> Our light will never die.

Would you believe, it actually brought tears to my eyes?

Slaymaker and his wife came out first, to a huge roar of delight, followed by Johnson Fleet and his wife, and for a few minutes all four of them just waved and smiled while we cheered and swiped the air with our flags and threw out rolls of tickertape in red and white and blue.

Soon, we knew, Rosine and her boys would come out too. We were about halfway back in the crowd, but we were absolutely determined that she and the boys would be able to sense our presence, and so every single one of us was clutching a whistle or a horn or a rattle or some other noisy thing that we'd been saving for this moment. I had a tambourine. I was all set to bang it when a strange sound came from the front like a series of firecrackers.

The president – the real president, I mean, not the make-believe president of Northland – looked kind of startled, but we still had no idea what had happened when the secret servicemen rushed across the stage and surrounded him.

Then a low moan swept out through the crowd like the shock wave of an explosion.

CHAPTER 60

They were called smart bullets: tiny guided missiles fired by a gun. You could select their target using the screen of an ordinary cristal and, after that, as long as you pointed the gun in the right general direction, the bullets would do the rest: perfect for a time like this, when there'd be no opportunity for a second shot.

There were three of them. They left the gun at quarter-second intervals and, as they crossed the Freedom Plaza, minuscule computers inside them monitored the target, noting his movements, calculating and recalculating his likely position at the moment of impact. Tiny gyros adjusted their direction of travel accordingly.

Slaymaker had invited Holly to go up to Northland with him.

'This is your achievement as much as mine, Holly,' he'd said, but she'd declined.

He studied her face for a moment. She felt that she had no defenses against his powerful gaze, that he could see perfectly well she was planning to leave his service. But if so, he said nothing about it.

'Okay, Holly, if you're sure. I look forward to seeing you when we get back.'

At his arraignment, the assassin's eyes were bruised and swollen and he could hardly walk across the room. The untrained vigilantes who called themselves the Northland police had clearly beaten him, though he'd never denied what he'd done.

His name was Tobin Coyne. He was twenty-five years old. His father was an Irish-Canadian nickel miner, a violent and abusive drunk who'd left when Tobin was seven. But Tobin identified himself entirely with his Inuit mother and the Inuit culture that had survived for so many centuries in an environment where few would even think of trying to make a living: hunting whales from kayaks, fishing through holes in the ice, building shelters with skin and bones and driftwood.

Just to surrender would be to concede that power was all that counted. That was how Tobin saw it. However futile it might be to resist, he could remain himself only if he tried.

It had been much the same when he was four years old and his father was beating his mother. Tobin had screamed at him to leave her alone, pulled at his clothes, kicked him on the legs. And though the old man barely even seemed to notice, he kept doing it anyway. It was better than doing nothing at all.

Three bullets, one after the other, at quarter-second intervals, crossed the clear still air of Freedom Plaza. The first one missed Slaymaker, but the second pierced his lung, and the third went through his heart.

AFTERWORD

olly enters the warmth and brightness of the terminal. There are stores and restaurants, information points and check-ins. Foreign workers in yellow jumpsuits sweep the marble floors.

She walks over to the viewing window and searches the sky for the drig. She can just make out a little speck, a fleck of mica glinting in the sun. But very quickly it becomes a distinct image, a toy, a scale model, and finally a real machine, an enormous powerful machine, laboring toward her through the layers of freezing air. She can almost feel the expenditure of power involved, the straining of metal muscles, as it forces itself down to the solid earth.

A small tornado of powdered snow swirls up. Up here it does still sometimes snow in June.

The drig's engines swivel forward and it begins to trundle toward the passenger bridges on its massive tires. Four bridges lock into place along its hull.

Holly makes her way to the arrivals area and finds herself a place at the railing. People start to emerge from the gate. First a young black guy in a business suit who doesn't expect anyone to meet him, glancing at his cristal as he heads for the car hire offices. Then a white couple pulling two giant suitcases. Then a young Inuit girl who is greeted with hoots and yells by eight or nine members of her extended family. Holly notices how they've learnt to ignore the hostile, suspicious eyes of the people around them by making a kind of bubble around themselves.

Passengers are soon emerging in a steady stream. But after ten minutes or so the stream thins to a trickle and she's one of only a handful still waiting. She asks her jeenee if she's missed a message, but it says no. She wonders if she's somehow got the arrival time wrong, or if he's changed his mind.

'Just check the passenger list, would you?' she tells her jeenee. But she's barely finished speaking when there he is, all by himself in the area between the gate and the railing. He is grayer than he used to be, and not quite as thin, but still unmistakably Richard. It's been eleven years since they saw each other.

'Rick!' she yells. 'Over here!'

A guarded, cautious smile as he heads toward her. They hug rather formally.

As they pull apart, she can see him registering the giant portrait of Stephen Slaymaker that beams down benignly at the arrival gates.

And the image comes into her mind, as it does most days, of a blonde young woman, tumbling and spinning down the deep, deep well of the sky. To escape from the vertigo, she grabs Richard's hands much more vehemently than she'd intended. 'Welcome!' she tells him, as she feels him tensing uncomfortably. 'Welcome to America City!'

She tells the car to take a scenic route. They go right into town, through the tall towers of the business district, past the Fleet Mall, where you can shop without a coat even in January, and into the plaza in front of city hall where the Freedom Monument, carved from Nunavut granite, honors the heroes of the War of Independence. Then they swing out over to Lakeside Park, with its clumps of half-grown pine trees, its pathways lightly dusted with snow.

Richard wants to stretch his legs, so they button up their coats, and walk down to the lake. The dome and portico of the new State Capitol stands right in front of them across the water.

'Funny how we still build them in the classical style,' Richard observes, 'after all these centuries, and in a continent that Rome had never even heard of.'

In front of the Capitol, three giant flag poles stand side by side, the flags flapping and flicking restlessly. On the left is the state flag of Nunavut. In the middle is the American flag, with its thirteen stripes and its sixty stars. (Or thereabouts anyway: states are being added at quite a rate these days, and the flags don't always keep up.) On the right is the three-star flag of the nation of Northland.

'They still fly that Northland flag, I see,' says Richard, as they begin to walk along the lakeside path.

'Yup. It's very popular up here, even though Northland only lasted a few months, and even though most of the current population arrived after the annexation.'

They walk along the lake for ten minutes then turn back across the park toward the car.

'So remind me,' says Richard, 'these days you're working on…?'

'I've got my fingers in several pies. It's the same kind of thing as before – PR, campaigning – but I'm trying to challenge myself a bit more.'

'What? More than winning a presidential election? More than annexing a country?'

She doesn't answer this – or doesn't appear to, anyway.

'I actually designed that Northland flag,' she says after a few minutes.

'*You* did? You're kidding me? It used to be *everywhere*! It used to—'

'I also chose the name of Northland and the name of America City. But that's all trivia really, isn't it? If it hadn't been that flag or those names, there would have been others. America was always going to annex the territories at some point, whatever we did, just like China was going to take over eastern Russian and Japan was going to take over…what's its name?…that Russian island.'

Richard considers this claim in silence.

'So what does a *real* challenge consist of?' he asks after a while.

'Making things happen that weren't going to happen anyway. For instance, persuading people to spend money taking carbon out of the air. That's hard. Even now when absolutely fucking *everyone* can see just what that stuff has done. Even now when we're having to move the USA to the goddam Arctic!'

She turns to look at him as they continue to walk beside the lake. The water is very clear, very empty.

'And you're writing a book about Slaymaker?'

'I thought I'd give it a go. It'd be a new thing for me, writing about someone who lived in my lifetime. There are already a million books about him, obviously, but I was kind of hoping you'd have a few insights that would give me an edge.'

They drive to her house at the city's northern edge. The June snowfall passes, and the sky clears. Holly shows him round her home. It's a beautiful building, but curiously empty and austere.

Monastic, Richard thinks, penitential even. On the dresser in her bedroom he's surprised to see a small print of that famous image of the woman soldier falling, a tiny cartwheeling shape with nothing around her but sky. And right next to it, a tiny nativity carved in Inuit style from a piece of soapstone.

They're into a second bottle of wine when they finally come back to Slaymaker.

'He wasn't a bad man,' Holly says. 'I mean, you tell me one president in the history of America who didn't get involved in a war? It's just something they have to do. Like that king of yours, remember? The one in *Beowulf*.'

'King Scyld.'

'That's the one. Slaymaker came from a place where life was hard and there wasn't much love. He didn't try to make himself care about things about things he didn't care about, and he didn't try to stop himself from caring about the things he did. I know we should, of course. We should let reason moderate our feelings. But there was something refreshingly…I don't know…I guess *natural*…about the way he just went with what he was.'

'The foundling who became a king,' says Richard, standing up and walking over to the triple-glazed picture window that forms one entire side of Holly's dining room.

'I can't get over how light it is. It looks like mid-afternoon.'

Holly comes over to join him, and they stand side by side, a couple of feet apart, looking at the bare rock, the black earth, the empty water.

'We were going to have kids once, remember?' Richard says.

'I remember them,' she says. 'Their names were Penny and Saul.'

ACKNOWLEDGEMENTS

My thanks to my former colleagues Eve Slaymaker and Hollie Peacock, and to Eve's husband Nigel Stephen Slaymaker, for the loan of their fine names. Just to be clear, the characters named after them do not resemble them in any other way, except perhaps in respect of a shared fondness for dogs.

Many thanks to my always perceptive editor Sara O'Keeffe, and, as ever, to my agent John Jarrold for his support.

Special thanks to Nick Brooks and to my son Dom for conversations about climate change that persuaded me I should write this book in the first place. I am solely responsible, however, for any flaws in my portrayal of the effects of global warming.